The L   d of Nuorg

Mystic thought he was still alive, although he was not sure why. How long had he been in here? However, he assumed that since he was more interested in surviving, time was not a major concern right now. How long he would stay in here, where he was being taken and where he was, were all out of his control. Eventually, he hoped, he would stop sinking, if that was actually what was happening. He was awkwardly confused by the water that was surrounding him, for it seemed to be moving, as a whole, right along with him. The water did not rush by him like a raging river. He was not tossed and thrown about with reckless abandonment. The water did not allow him to rise to the surface as the water in the Black Pond had done on occasion. Undoubtedly, it was not the same kind of water that living things drowned in, for he had never felt any urgency to paddle to the shallows, which was good, because there were no shallows available.

Copyright © 2009 Chris McCollum

Hardcover ISBN: 978-1-60145-994-7
Paperback ISBN: 978-1-60145-995-4

All rights reserved. No part of this publication may be reproduced, stored in a retrieval system, or transmitted in any form or by any means, electronic, mechanical, recording or otherwise, without the prior written permission of the author.

Printed in the United States of America.

Any similarity to real persons, living or dead, is coincidental and not intended by the author.

MessyHouse Publishing
Franklin, TN
2009

The Land of Nuorg

Chris McCollum

*This book is in memory of
my Father*

*and in honor of
my Mother*

*who allowed me the freedom
to be creative*

1

One ordinary day under an ordinary sky in an extraordinary Great Forest, Mystic, a wise and rather large gray Wolf, was playfully digging a hole to bury a small skeleton. The skeleton was that of a poor Seagull which, at some point in the past, had reached the end of his life. Why he decided to bury these remains on this particular day is a question that may never be answered. Let it be said, had everything not happened just as it did; the outcome of this day and the many others that followed would have drastically changed not only this story, but history as it is known today.

After digging a short time with his large paws, the hole was deep enough. It was, after all, just a small bit of bones. He sat on his back legs and rested, as all Wolves do, and curiously studied the new hole. He wondered why he had dug a hole in this area of the forest at all. He had never dug a hole here to bury a bone or to bury anything. This was the South Quarter of the Great Forest where he was not exactly permitted to go. Secondly, it was too far from his sleeping quarters for, normally, he liked to nap in his own dwelling during the day unless, of course, he was on an adventure. This was certainly no adventure, at least not yet. He usually never traveled this far from home for no reason. The significance of this moment escaped him.

Mystic let out a very deliberate and cautious breath, "Humph." He looked away from the hole for a moment of further contemplation and was ceremoniously distracted by the glorious magnificence of the Great Forest. Mystic turned his big, intelligent eyes to the hole and gave it one last thoughtful glance.

After this short rest, Mystic stood. He walked to the Seagull's remains, retrieved the bones from where they had rested, quite unaware of what was going on around them, and very reverently, placed them into the shallow hole.

"There", he said to himself, "What was so difficult about that?"

Something about that hole fascinated Mystic. He stood almost motionless eying this creation as if it was alive and breathing. Call it instinct or extraordinary canine perception, but Mystic did not trust it. For reasons unknown to him, his whiskers were beginning to tingle. The tingling crept down each whisker. Soon, one by one, his whiskers began to twitch. Individually, they twitched slowly at first. Then each began to twitch quite frantically until they warned Mystic trouble was most definitely close at hand.

In this situation most gray Wolves would have asked for advice, but not Mystic. He was alone in this. The lesser Wolves left Mystic to run alone. He was, after all, their leader and was charged with the responsibility to come back and warn them should anything out of the ordinary take place. They never really tried to keep up with him or the odd friends he ran with. Did they really care where he went or whom he went with as long as he protected them against whatever harm might come their way? The answer, of course, was definitely, no!

As he stood in place, Mystic was becoming increasingly uneasy. Something about this moment did not feel right. This, he thought, was not the usual way of things in the Great Forest and could quite possibly mean some kind of danger. But what kind?

***

Danger was approaching. Not the kind that would hit you in the nose, but a distant danger that could pop up overnight like weeds in a garden or lie dormant for unknown periods of time. If so inclined, this danger, left unattended, could destroy every living and good thing in the entire world. The danger also could draw the pleasantness and frivolity right out of a perfectly serene and fun-seeking land, if given the least opportunity.

This was a danger for which no one could prepare. This danger could turn Mystic's world inside out. The seldom talked about "Terrible Years" began this way. If they were to have a resurgence, they would, like a cancer returning to a host, return stronger and more prepared to wreak havoc on whatever crossed their path in a next life. This danger was so woven into the daily routine that it would not be immediately or positively identified by Mystic or any other land walker.

That kind of danger was possibly in this hole Mystic had dug. He slowly and very carefully began to inch his way back from this mysterious thing, this…this hole in the ground. But why was this hole so different? He had dug thousands of holes in his lifetime. He began to ask himself why he had decided to bury those bones.

***

Mystic waited, strangely hypnotized by the unknown. He could not take his eyes off the hole. Suddenly to his wary eyes, the shallow bottom of the hole dropped away to nowhere with a deafening whooshing sound. He jumped to full alert then froze. The sound, Mystic instantly realized, had originated deep from within the hole. The only comparable thought that came to his mind was that of an immense giant creature, living under ground, inhaling a very deep and violent gasp of breath.

The bones Mystic had placed in the hole disappeared. Poof! Like an old magic trick, they were gone. Mystic remained absolutely still for the instant as the long gray hair on his shoulders stood straight up and the tips of his ears remained stationed at full attention. His large Wolf eyes were opened as wide as they possibly could as he watched in complete bewilderment. His whiskers were now dancing up and down his snout. Sensitive Wolf ears were next to warn him of the now clearly present danger that was boiling directly under his feet.

"It's here!" his ears told him. "Move! Move back. Move to the side. Run. Do something Mystic. You can't just stand here. Run," his ears cried again. But as much as he would have liked to, he couldn't move.

Mystic remained frozen where he stood. He did manage to brace himself as he settled slightly back on his haunches, spreading his massive paws much farther apart than normal. He bowed his head and concentrated on trying to scan in all directions at once. His eyes were bouncing left to right, up to down, down to up and diagonally. (This last feat is extremely hard to accomplish and can very easily make one awkwardly dizzy.)

Fortunately, Mystic had four sturdy legs on which to balance. He let out a very low and unpleasant growl. His, higher-than-normal, intelligence usually brought words to his mouth, but at this time, in this place, nothing but this growl could escape from his clenched teeth. The ground began to tremble terribly and fear began inching its way up Mystic's tense spine like a spider scurrying across its web to capture and eat a helpless fly snared in a beautiful silken trap. It is said to this day, in that forest, that every living animal with two legs or more felt what Mystic felt at that very instant and that those creatures much, much older told unpleasant stories of a certain terrible tremble many years before.

Everything was shaking or was it just Mystic? He did not know and, at the time, he was far too busy trying to stay on his feet. He did not have time to worry about what else was trembling. He was absolutely positive that this disturbance was felt by everyone and everything, near or far in the Great Forest. He was, for the most part correct. The trees were swaying, the ground was heaving and small pebbles were bouncing back and forth beneath the large boulders that sat quivering about.

The poor old Seagull's bones had vanished right in front of Mystic's eyes along with the dirt, the sand, the rocks and everything else that had existed within the small area of that hole. Mystic noticed, as he watched the hole, that it was gradually getting bigger. Piece by piece, small and large chunks of ground on which he was standing disappeared to wherever the rest of the hole had gone. The whooshing sound was growing faint, but nerve-wracking amounts of dirt were crumbling and falling away directly beneath him.

"Oh, mercy, when will that stop?" Mystic thought to himself.

He was terrified. He could not force his muscles into moving his body anywhere, even while the edge of hole was steadily creeping towards him. When would this trembling stop and, if it did, would the hole stop growing? Fear had now traveled a path all the way up Mystic's spine and was now beating on a drum between his still alert ears.

Completely out of ideas, Mystic concluded he had no other option. Instinctively he called out for help. At least, he tried. Like the rest of his body, Mystic's mouth was paralyzed by fear of the unknown

"Vincen, Vincen, can you hear me?" Louder Mystic! "Vincen, please, can you hear me? Vincen, Vincen help me!"

It was all he could do. He hoped that some noise had gotten beyond his wavy canine lips and that the sound, no matter how weak, had miraculously made its way to Vincen's ears. Vincen was his best friend and wisest teacher. He was also the most majestic Eagle in a long line of glorious Eagles in the Great Forest. He was far wiser than his 150 or so years would indicate. Vincen was among the only true natives of the Great Forest. Even the Hawks and Falcons of the nearby meadows, mountains and valleys came seeking his advice. Mystic had cried out just as he had done several years before when he first felt fear tugging hard on his life. But that was another story for another time. This time he could only hope that Vincen was close enough to hear his desperate cry for help and come to his rescue once again.

***

As he did day after day, Vincen was resting on his favorite perch, high in the top of the tallest and oldest oak tree in the forest. This perch had been handed down in Vincen's family for generations. No sky traveler could even remember the name of the first Eagle to wrap talons around this coveted branch. It had been handed down to Vincen many, many years ago. Legend says this particular perch also became one of the first lookout posts overlooking the meadow back in the days of the Terrible Years.

So far, this too, had been an ordinary day for Vincen, just as it had started as an ordinary day for Mystic. It was good to get old, the Eagle thought. There were the usual occurrences of too many feathers falling out when he groomed himself and an occasional ache or pain. But after all of his years high above the land walkers, he was doing quite well, thank you. All of the worries and distractions of being young and foolhardy no longer affected his disposition and time was something he seemed to have plenty of. No more did he race the young Eaglets. No more did he chase Wolf pups and young Badgers for fun. Those times were gone now.

All Vincen seemed to concern himself with now was watching the peaceful day-rounds turn in to peaceful moon-times from high atop this world of his. He had so many fond memories of growing up, learning the Eagles' many ways and studying their folklore. That, lately, seemed like some other Eagle's lifetime. Now, even the smallest of life's pleasantries were things he enjoyed daily and to the fullest. Yes, Vincen was content in thinking the young of this day would never have to live in desperate times. Those Terrible Years of old were now read about in the history manuscripts. Those that studied them could only imagine what life could have been like living day to day and hideout to hideout, never knowing who would come home and who would not. Yes, life now was so perfect, almost too perfect. Every now and then Vincen's thoughts would wander off to the stories he'd heard of that earlier day and time. He could only imagine how he might have reacted to the adventures his ancestors had learned to deal with on a daily basis.

Vincen's family was "The Family" to be descended from if you were an Eagle. Sky-travelers told stories of the Vincen Eagles that amazed even the most callous listener. Reverent to a fault whenever Vincen passed their way, it was if they worshipped the very sky in which he flew. Vincen was far too humble to pay the tribute much mind, but he was respectful of the well wishes. His family included brave warriors, wisened intellectuals and every day heroes. Too young during the battles to witness first hand any of courageous displays of bravery, Vincen had, so far, lived a long, peaceful and productive life thanks to those who sacrificed before him . For that he was very grateful.

The Terrible Years and the clean-up afterward had taken his family away from him. Everyone but his twin sister, Mustanghia, had either been killed or lost in some of the most vicious battles and marches of that day. His Father was the direct heir to the Great Forest. Vincen's great Grandfather's Father had come to this forest seeking refuge for his family during the Terrible Years. He relocated the entire family to this area because, at the time, the Great Forest was off the beaten path.

Vincen and his sister were born in the Great Forest. They were born in the same aerie that Vincen has made his bed in every night since. His family returned to the land of the battles of the Terrible Years frequently to fly scouting missions and, one by one, they never came back. Vincen and his sister were too young to really miss them as they each failed to return. The Hawks and Falcons of the Great Forest raised the twins as their own. They taught them to hunt, eat and survive while the Owls of the area nurtured the young Eaglets' minds and never let them forget their heritage, especially, the importance of being a "Vincen Eagle." There would never be, in Vincen's mind, living creatures as wise as the Owls.

While no exact story has been told of their parents' demise, all rest assured that their end befitted a royal pair. Vincen's sister had flown away several years before on a personal mission. She was determined to find out what peril had awaited their parents. She left Vincen to oversee the Great Forest alone. Vincen's sister had received the adventurous side of the "Vincen Eagle" personality and so, was aptly named, Mustanghia, meaning "swift adventurer." Vincen's side of the family provided him with leadership and sensibility far beyond that normally allocated to Eagles.

Vincen and Mustanghia were a perfectly matched set and, although Vincen had yearned for the adventures his Sister told him about, they both knew that his path in life was to lead and protect the living creatures of the Great Forest. This was, after all, their Great Forest. Mustanghia occasionally sent Vincen messages by Falcon and once or twice a year she would come back to her home aerie. Then she would tell her beloved brother about facts she had discovered and stories she had heard. Vincen looked forward to those visits with his sister. He hoped that one day she would bring news of their parents' survival. However, no news of the latter had been discovered, leaving Vincen to constantly urge Mustanghia to stay with him in the Great Forest. Earlier in his life, Vincen often wished that she would bring back with her a She eagle, especially one that might be looking for a mate. Unfortunately, Mustanghia never brought any visitors back with her and, come to think of it, his sister hadn't been back in quite some time. It might have been several years now.

Vincen didn't like to dwell on bad happenings and, probably, blocked out the amount of time that had passed since Mustanghia was last in for a visit. Oh well, he wished her the best and looked forward to the next time she would come and share new stories with him. Vincen could not broach the subject of any harm touching her. There was, furthermore, no denying it: Vincen was growing lonely.

He had often wondered about raising his own Eaglets, but that seemed to be out of the realm of possibility this late in his life. In a manner of speaking, he did have two children. Vincen's brood started out, and ended, with a pair of ragtag orphans. During different times in the past, he had either rescued or nursed back to health these "children" of his. They gave him some pleasure, as a Father, and at times he could easily have run each of them off for good. He guessed every Father felt that way once in a while. Yes, this duo had surprised him. Each had been a runt and both had experienced different disasters in their younger day-rounds. As fate would have it, they both turned out remarkably well. Each one had developed strong individual talents and worked together quite harmoniously. They graciously gave all the credit for their successes to their adopted Father, Vincen.

Sitting on his perch, Vincen had been observing the young four-leggers playing carefree along the edge of the meadow where the Quiet River ran into the Old Pond. How he longed for those early years. Those times had been so enjoyable, frolicking with his brothers and sisters, occasionally swooping down to give a friendly ride to a terrified Badger or Wolf pup. Given a slight urging, he would race with his Father up to the family aerie built into the cliff that faced the meadow from the south, just to experience the view. He once chased a ruthless band of poachers away from the Great Forest, through the Great Plains, across the Little River and away for good. This had brought him quite a bit of adulation from the land walkers.

He fondly remembered the many, many years of classes taken at the foot of the very wise Owls in their small forest of trees on the meadow's north side. The Eagles were the warriors and the leaders. But the Owls, if it weren't for the Owls and the Eagles' willingness to learn, who knows what might have become of this world he now surveyed from this most honorable perch to the east on the west side of the Great Forest.

Vincen felt a slight shudder in the old tree, but gave it only a passing thought. It was only when he heard a bombastic whisper of frantic yelping on the wind that he became anxious. Yelping? It was coming from inside the Great Forest. The location, however, did not seem that familiar to Vincen. Where exactly was it coming from? Vincen turned his head from side to side and clicked his neck up and down until he located the exact spot where the plea originated. The voice sure sounded familiar to Vincen, but why would Mystic be over in the South Quarter of the Great Forest. He hadn't been there in years. Vincen had given him a good talking to the last time he came scampering in from there. What was even more interesting to Vincen was the yelping. Adult gray Wolves usually don't yelp, especially when they are as intelligent and powerful as this gray Wolf. The yelps had initially sounded like a scared little puppy in a fight for his life. That was exactly the situation several years ago when Vincen had, once before, come to Mystic's rescue.

Fortunately for Mystic, Vincen was very close in Eagle terms. Eagles, Vincen had once told Mystic, see great distances and see far beyond other creatures. For that reason, Eagles measure distances in shorter lengths than other creatures. Where a land walker may describe a distance as "one hundred tall oaks," an Eagle would use "ten pursuit beats." The Eagle logic simply stated thusly, one large Eagle, in hunting pursuit, can travel as far as 10 ancient oak trees are tall with one full beat of his wings. (Of course, the extending and closing of the wings is understood to be one beat of the wings. There is no half beat of the wings and there is no one-quarter beat. There is only a pursuit beat, leisure beat and training beat.) Mystic was living lucky. Vincen definitely heard something and quickly calculated the distance to 27 pursuit beats.

Vincen, sensing a terrible calamity shot skyward from his perch. With one swift cycle of his immense, powerful wings he was propelled into the sky high enough to pinpoint Mystic's exact whereabouts. He circled, only briefly, and spotted Mystic outside of the thick canopy of first-growth branches. With his sharp eyes focused on the Wolf's dire position, Vincen shot down to Mystic's side faster than one of the shooting stars that can be spotted every night from his high perch. He swooped down with every intention of getting to Mystic's side before whatever trouble that was coming arrived and he succeeded.

"Mystic, my son what is it?" Vincen hastily asked his young friend upon landing.

Vincen's eyes were so totally focused on Mystic that he made no notice of the growing hole in front of the Wolf that was, even now, inching closer to the both of them.

"What could you have discovered, or gotten yourself into, that you should make such a horrendous, ear-shattering noise? What terrible incident brings me down from my watch?

Vincen abruptly noticed the hole and paused to stare into it before continuing. "Mystic, why have you dug such a large hole in the South Quarter? Why are you even in the South Quarter? You know very well this place is not known for any good or decent thing." Vincen hurriedly asked these questions as he surveyed the Wolf's statue-like body position.

Mystic was still frozen. No muscle in his body was ready to move as yet, and fear was really beating on that drum in his head now. His eyes rolled in Vincen's general direction and, if he had had no fur, Vincen would have noticed that his skin was as white as new snow and covered with ridge after ridge of goose bumps.

"Come on, my boy, say something", demanded Vincen. "What is it?"

Mystic failed to move. It was not from a lack of trying. He was desperately trying. He couldn't move, or coax into moving, any bone or muscle in his body. His poor head was ready to explode. BOOM, BOOM, BOOM. Fear was continuing to pound that dreadful drum in his head and the hole, after settling on a good pace, was continuing to get bigger.

"Mystic, speak to me. I demand to know what is going on and I mean now! Why did you call so loudly?" demanded Vincen, in the sternest voice he could muster.

BOOM, BOOM, BOOM! Would fear ever release Mystic long enough to allow him speech again? He was only able to process thoughts now, not speech and, right now, those thoughts were concerned with that hole. Would that hole ever stop expanding?

Vincen hopped up on Mystic's strong neck, leaned over those large gray Wolf ears and demanded one more time, "Speak to me!"

Vincen clamped down hard on Mystic's neck with one of his magnificent claws and, this time, got Mystic's full attention. Fearing a swat by Mystic's snout, Vincen quickly hopped to Mystic's shoulder for safety. He knew this spot well. He often perched on this shoulder during long travels through the Great Forest. If the trees got too thick, Mystic would often invite him down for a ride to keep from having to yell up at the Eagle to carry on conversations. Vincen would gladly oblige for fear of falling out of the sky from flying too slowly. These land walkers traveled very, very slowly as far as Eagles were concerned.

BOOM, BOOM, BOOM continued the drum.

"Ouuuuch!" growled Mystic as he aggressively swung his head in Vincen's general direction.

The hole continued growing. It was, at Mystic's last recollection, about as wide as he was long, excluding his tail of course.

"Finally", overstated a very exasperated Vincen.

After what seemed to Vincen like days, Mystic feebly replied, "My dear Vincen, please look for yourself."

Mystic's eyes slowly rolled from where Vincen perched on his shoulder, then back to the hole, as if he was pointing to it and then slowly back to Vincen. Mystic was still struggling for balance and under no circumstances was he going to even attempt to point with either of his paws at the mysterious opening for fear of falling into it and going who knows where?

"I, I cannot explain what is happening, Vincen. Look at this hole!" he exclaimed.

Mystic cautiously rolled his eyes back to the hole again, still refusing to lift one paw off of the ground. "Is it still growing? Oh, I hope not."

Mystic's eyes rolled back to Vincen. "I called out so suddenly because an ominous fear has a hold of me. It is making such a confounding racket in my head that I cannot think clearly. Furthermore, I cannot explain this hole in this spot or, for that reason, why I dug it in the South Quarter in the first place. I can't explain why I am even in the South Quarter. For those reasons and more I have called for help my dear friend. As you can see Sir, if you feel the need to do so, peer over the edge. This is not a normal hole and its actions, up to this moment, are strange and highly out of the ordinary. I was hoping that, of all my friends, surely you would hear my cry. Maybe you would know what I have just discovered. I did not realize that I called loudly, I thought I was barely able to utter a sound past my clenched jaw."

"And, if I may continue, my other friends are comfortably out of hearing range and would think I was attempting some kind of trick. I assure you Vincen, I am not. I believe this thing, is attempting a trick on me, and, at the moment, is succeeding Sir. With, all of my favorite hole-digging spots to choose from, I was drawn to this exact spot on this very day, obviously, for reasons beyond my control. Vincen, please enlighten me as to what this could possibly be so that I may cease this uncontrollable shaking."

"Grab hold of your senses Mystic. I can't talk to you unless you become more rational," stated Vincen.

Slowly, after hearing those words in Vincen's soothing tone fear eased up on Mystic a little while the beating of the drum faded away somewhat. His dear and trusted friend was with him now. Vincen's calming voice seemed to shoo the drumbeat out of Mystic's head and that, to Mystic, was quite a relief. He felt his mind returning to him and was very relieved to find that his body was again able to move under his own control. Also, and this should not be discounted, the hole had finally stopped growing.

Vincen lifted his wings and, with them, tapped the air enabling him to rise from Mystic's shoulder. He landed gracefully on the ground beside Mystic leaving no particle of dust unsettled. He lightly staggered over to the edge of the hole with his head and neck clicking new angles from which his keen eyes studied his surroundings. He scratched at the hole's edge with his talons until he found a stable spot to stand. His intense eyes continued to study every speck of dirt and every blade of grass within two training beats. Once satisfied he was on stable ground, Vincen firmly gripped a solid spot of earth at the edge of the hole and peered down. He peered way down into the hole with his Eagle eyes and seemed to study the hole for quite some time shaking his head in amazement or, as Mystic had studied it, in total and complete bewilderment.

Vincen was not satisfied with anything concerning this hole. He hid his true uneasiness from Mystic and feared what he could not comprehend. Mystic had been deathly frightened. This was no time to make light of that fact. At one point, Vincen found himself peering so deeply into the hole that he almost toppled in. Instead, he collected his balance, lightly flapped his wings and steadied himself. Finally, he loosened his grip on the ground, stepped back, and looked at Mystic.

"Well?" Mystic hesitantly inquired.

Vincen shook his head, tightened his brow and relaxed. When he did, all of the feathers on his head slightly rose and fell back in place. He said, "My boy, I have no idea what that is, I have no idea where it goes and I have no idea how it and you came to be together right here, right now. Let me study on it for a while. Please Mystic, step clear away from the opening so that I may stop worrying about you and begin thinking about that opening, hole or whatever it is."

Mystic was relieved and very willing to oblige Vincen's request.

Vincen was puzzled. He paced around and around and around the hole. The feathers on his wings were swept back in such a way as to give the casual observer the notion that he might have his hands clasped behind his back. Of course, this would be the wrong thought since Eagles have no hands. Vincen continued to pace. Suddenly he exclaimed "Ah no, sorry, that's not it," and he kept pacing. He then asked, "Mystic, what were you doing exactly? Tell me everything."

Mystic obliged and told the story to the Eagle from its start, early that morning, to now. He did not omit a detail and kept the narration void of any misgiving wanderings. If he had not been eternally thankful for Vincen's presence, Mystic would have become slightly annoyed with the Eagle's continuous strutting as he circled around and around and around the hole, again and again and again as the story unfolded. Mystic was getting a bit queasy watching the Great Eagle. When he had finished with the last detail, he lay down on the now still ground, closed his eyes and waited for the forthcoming answer. When the answer would come he had no idea, but he felt sure it was coming. Vincen was an older bird and patience was needed when dealing with him in a matter such as this. One couldn't imagine all of the knowledge, experiences and handed-down wisdom the old Eagle's mind was sorting through at this very instant.

Vincen had been pacing in circles for some time now. Mystic feared the Eagle might get dizzy, tumble into the hole himself and that he, the rescuee, would have to become the rescuer. It wasn't long before Mystic put that ridiculous notion out of his mind. Still, Mystic, though now resting, opened one eye and kept it glued to Vincen, just in case.

"Let me see. Several years ago my Father mentioned something about the South Quarter and its significance during the Terrible Years, yet this hole does not obviously remind me of any one event," Vincen quietly muttered to no one in particular, continuing to circle 'round the thought-provoking spot.

"Please, Sir", Mystic begged as he rolled onto his back, stretched his long legs and twisted a kink out of his neck. "Is there anything I might add to help you in your research?"

"No thank you, son, I haven't room for your knowledge, my knowledge and my own questions in my small head. Perhaps, if my head was as large as yours, then maybe. But my head has room only for my thoughts at the present. You have provided me with plenty of information. It is now left for me to sort through. The complicated order of events is, without a doubt, curious. I must urge my thinking in the direction of a solution. If you will permit me, I'll get back to my task," argued Vincen.

Vincen may have sounded a bit put out by Mystic's questioning, but truthfully, he wasn't. Vincen was more disturbed by the fact that Mystic had even entered the South Quarter. The Owls had warned Vincen about the South Quarter since he learned to fly and he had repeatedly passed these warnings on to Mystic. The reason for Mystic's being here was another riddle for a different day.

Mystic wasn't sure how he should take those tart remarks, yet he decided to stay silent and watch Vincen pace. Now, he had the top of his nose laid flat on the ground as he watched, upside down, as Vincen paced.

"Now it was Vincen's turn to be annoyed. Vincen had been watching Mystic out of the corner of his eye and had about enough of this increasingly juvenile behavior. "For all my ancestors' sake would you please turn over, be still and act like a grown Wolf?" Vincen said quite harshly. "Why are you watching me upside down?

"I'm sorry sir, I had to stretch," replied Mystic as he reluctantly rolled onto his belly, stood up and shook the dirt off his back. Mystic was feeling better now. The rest, although a short one, had revived him.

"Now where was I?" asked Vincen.

"You had just reprimanded me for watching you upside down."

"Oh yes, I remember."

"Oh well", go on", Mystic replied.

"What? What did you say Mystic, Quick son, what did you just say?" Vincen asked excitedly.

Mystic blankly replied, "I said oh well, sir."

"Well, well, well, why did that spark my memory? How were you watching me briefly ago? Tell me, Mystic. How were you watching me?" Vincen was on a roll. Thoughts were rapidly progressing in that old head of his.

"I was upside down sir, that's all. I was scratching my back" Mystic said sheepishly. "Why? Is that important?"

"Yes, it certainly is. I believe it's coming back to me now. Yes, I am remembering bits and pieces. I think I'll have it shortly."

Vincen was really strutting now. His wings were rising and falling with his every breath. Mystic felt a tiny gust of wind every time those excited wings closed back onto Vincen's sleek body. He was an old Eagle, but there was no denying the power and speed he possessed. Suddenly, Vincen stopped.

Mystic, who had been following the parade so intently that his eyes continued to proceed half way around the circle even though Vincen did not, was surprised by the abrupt halt. Vincen's stop startled Mystic. His eyes quickly backtracked and refocused on Vincen who was now standing at full height and the Eagle had his wings stretched above his head in a victory position. Mystic was not sure, but he thought the Eagle was smiling. His eyes were as bright as the midday sun. The wise old Eagle had figured something out. That much was definite. Just maybe, all of the pieces to this puzzle had come together at last.

Vincen was ecstatic and shouted so loudly that Mystic knew every land walker in the Great Forest must have heard it. Mystic was surprised by the Eagle's complete lack of restraint.

"My son, you have stumbled on 'The Well of the Ground Below.' I should have come to this conclusion sooner. You gave it away the minute you said, "well." My grandfather told me stories of an ancient well filled with purple and green water. This well had appeared at various times over the past thousands of years, although, there is no modern record of its appearance in recent history."

"My Grandfather, though he had never seen it, promised me it had existed. I went on expeditions when I was very young to find it and never did. As I got older, the old story lost some of its charm and I never pursued it again. You, my boy, have discovered an enchanted, forgotten part of the Great Forest's history! Now, we must do whatever we can to fill up the hole and tell no one what we have seen today. If I told you the rest of the story, you would be more frightened than you were not knowing what it was. This must be that well. It must be!"

Mystic was confused. He sat back down rather lazily and exhaled a heavy sigh. His head hung like a dead weight resting on his chest. He closed his eyes then raised one paw and brushed it deliberately across his brow in a disgusted fashion. He couldn't help thinking that Vincen may have finally reached senility.

Everyone knows that wells have water; if not, they are called holes, and holes normally have bottoms. This hole had no water, so it wasn't a well and it had no bottom to keep the water from flowing straight through it, and into wherever it led. So, it wasn't a hole either, yet, Vincen, undeniably, called it a well. He did not say dry well. He said well. As in a deep hole with water in it. In his now dazed mind he could see water running into the hole, but he could not reason how it could ever rise to level ground with no bottom from where to start. How would the water ever know where to stop so that the well would begin to fill up? Mystic was skeptical of this proclamation. He raised his head, closed his eyes again and stretched his neck in a wide arc.

He collected himself and boldly stated, "Sir, there is no water in this hole. It cannot be the well you speak of."

"Oh", replied Vincen rather disappointedly, "That must have slipped my mind."

Just as those words passed over Mystic's sensitive ears he heard, or thought he heard, a gurgling sound emanating from deep inside the hole. His ears perked up to full alert mode and his eyes opened wide in search of the sound. "Obviously," Mystic thought to himself, "If that is water I hear, then this well needs no bottom from which to spring."

Vincen noticed Mystic's demeanor change and quickly picked up on it.

"Mystic, what is it? You look frightened again".

"Not necessarily frightened, but Sir, I may have underestimated your wisdom and I apologize. We need to step closer to this hole. I think I hear a faint noise coming from deep inside it. The noise reminds me of gurgling water," Mystic stated calmly.

Vincen perked his head up also and started clicking his head around in an attempt to pick up the sound. It was no use. An Eagle can certainly see better than a Wolf, but he could not hear nearly as well and his beak was not picking up any strange vibrations. "I will join you at the edge of the hole, Mystic," he said as he carefully picked his way over to the rim.

Mystic's canine curiosity was beginning to overwhelm his common sense. He would have to be very selective now in any action that he took from here on out. He surprised himself by rushing over to the hole's edge. He had almost forgotten the fear that consumed him the last time he was this close. If curiosity had, indeed, killed the cat, then Mystic had better hope that the same saying did not pertain to members of the canine family. He was acting very cavalier in the face of this unknown malady.

"Please Vincen, step into the hole and see if your eyes can spy what I hear," he said matter-of-factly.

Vincen was peering into the hole and, upon hearing that request, immediately jerked his head so he could look directly into Mystic's eyes. He pulled himself up to his full height, clasped his wings to his sides and adamantly asked, "Step into the hole? Mystic, have you gone absolutely mad?"

Mystic did not even turn to see the look in Vincen's eyes. A peaceful serenity began claiming him. He was feeling quite calm, not at all like before. The hole had cast him into a mysterious trance. He never took his eyes out of the hole. He casually droned to Vincen, "Looks like nothing to be concerned about to me."

That was it. Vincen could take no more of this attitude and viscously snipped at Mystic's front left leg with his vice-like beak and actually drew blood. "Mystic, look at me!" he demanded.

Mystic let out a loud yelp as Vincen's sharp beak cut past his fur and into his skin. He jumped back in pain and immediately began to shake uncontrollably. His eyes glazed over and Vincen could clearly see that fear had throttled him once again.

"What happened, Father? Why have you wounded me?" Mystic asked as a child would.

"Did you not hear me speaking to you as you looked into the hole?" he asked.

"No sir, I did not. All I was thinking about or hearing was the water. I thought I saw it rising up to greet me. Excuse me, what did you say?" Mystic questioned meekly as he began to lick the blood off his leg.

"I asked you if you had gone mad and, by all my reckoning, I believe you did, at least, for the short time that you stared into the hole," Vincen explained.

The water began to bubble up. It bubbled and gurgled and slowly began to fill the hole that just minutes before had no bottom. Mystic and Vincen gazed silently, stone still, as if they were both hypnotized at the water as it slowly rose to the edge of the opening. "Where was this water coming from?" they thought in unison. The water was not rushing up to the top. It was rather merrily making its way up to the edge with a slow circular motion, which was directly reversed from the direction in which Vincen had been pacing. Could it have been coincidence? Perhaps. They glanced at each other then back at the water with tremendous wonder in their eyes.

The two watched the water rise for about five clicks of an Eagle's eye. This was the way of telling how long a day-round lasts in the Great Forest and was widely accepted by the four-leggers in the surrounding lands as the day keeping standard. This method of day keeping had been explained to Vincen by the Owls. As far as Vincen knew, they probably originated it. The Owls explained that with the Eagles keen sight, it is only reasonable to think their eyes are the most sensitive to light and, in being so, have been observed actually clicking with each movement of the sun. One complete keeping of the day-round lasts exactly 365 Eagle eye clicks. The keeping starts and stops when the sun is first and last seen over the mountain's head. The Owls often debated whether the number of day-rounds in the entire day keeping record should remain at 365 also. The two legged land walkers had explained to the Talkers, who in turn, explained to the Owls that their year was the same as the Owls entire day keeping record except that the Owls were missing all of the 366th day, of which the two-leggers only used one quarter of anyway. The Owls decided to omit that 366th day altogether for reasons that were never fully understood. The Owls day round included sun time and moon time and a method was devised for partitioning the two, but it never got much attention since the defining line was always moving. The Talkers used their own partitioning table for farming and other odd reasons, but the Owls saw no reason in that practice either. Suffice it to say, the two methods of day keeping were close enough in form and function that several words and descriptions found their ways into both methods of day keeping, or as the two-legged land walkers say, time.

Just as the water rose as high as it could, it calmly and politely stopped. Mystic took a step back, twisted his head at Vincen, tilted it to the right side and asked, "Does that water look suspicious to you Father?"

Vincen, glaring at the water, answered, "It's been said that once you take water from this well you are never seen again. Please be careful, Mystic."

Vincen, sensing that Mystic was a little frightened because he usually never spoke to him with such revered respect, continued: "Well maybe, no, it truly can't be the 'Well of the Land Below'." Look at the water. It is too clear. It looks more pure than the water we drink every day from the well by the Little River. As a matter of fact, that may be the clearest water I have ever seen. I can also see it is deep. I believe you could sink for several training beats and fail to reach bottom."

Mystic felt a little more at ease. He stopped shaking again and his fear waned. He carefully moved closer to the water's edge. Vincen turned his head slightly to catch a sudden breeze and noticed that an object of some kind had started to glow near a small grouping of trees at the edge of the clearing. He had no idea what was glowing or why and dismissed it along with the sudden breeze.

Vincen told Mystic, again, "Be very careful. Don't get too close to the edge, my dear boy. We are not sure that we know everything about what is happening. Let us be cautious and patient as we struggle to figure out this strange phenomenon."

Mystic, ever the curious one, could not stand the waiting. Every time he looked at the water he was struck with an odd yearning to get closer. With Vincen's attention turning to the breeze, Mystic couldn't help himself and silently dipped his left, wounded paw into the water. Immediately the pain in the paw was gone. Was it possible? In order not to distract Vincen's attention from the breeze that had come out of nowhere, he silently picked his paw out of the water and to his disbelief the wound had healed and all traces of the cut had been washed away. He looked into the water and saw no trace of blood or dirt. This was odd. He placed his paw back in the water and decided to let Vincen know what was going on.

In a very trance-like calm, Mystic said, "Look Sir, My paw is in the water and nothing has happened. See there is nothing to be afraid of. Nothing is wrong here."

"What!" Vincen exclaimed and began flapping his wings and bouncing up and down out of anger. Vincen had quite a temper and Mystic had just unleashed a good dose of it. "Mystic," he screamed, "what have you done and why, Son? I told you to be patient. We know nothing of this water." Vincen turned and angrily paced away from this ridiculous turn of events.

Mystic began to act strangely once again. The beating of his heart increased at an accelerated pace. But, even as he sat at the side of the well in fear or wonderment, outwardly, he looked quite relaxed, almost too much so. He was, obviously under some other power besides his own. Keeping with his outward appearance, he rather casually replied, in a quiet, hypnotized manner of speaking, "Vincen, this water is very cool. It is not cold like water of mountain lakes. It is just so perfectly cool. I wonder if it may taste as wonderfully pleasant as it appears."

Without asking for permission, Mystic silently dipped the second front paw into the calm silent water. He was very careful not to disturb the surface more than necessary and began to lap up some of the tempting crystal clear water with his tongue. Suddenly, the instant his rough textured tongue nicked the water's surface, Mystic was overwhelmed. His existence in the Great Forest was shrunk and placed into, what seemed to his canine brain, a light, airy bubble whisked away on top of a river as it plummets down a tremendously violent waterfall.

He was helpless. His memories, his rank in the line of leaders of the Great Forest, his strong, well-defined muscles, all of his senses, his complete life in the Great Forest, everything he ever knew or would know was sucked within this tiny fraction of time. He felt an uncontrollable something reach out and grab him from the other side of the water. Whatever it was, it was very strong and very determined to have this Wolf. This sudden, undeniable force was heaving the large Wolf under. No strength Mystic could muster could stop this unrelenting tug.

The water encircling his paws gently started to swirl again. At the same time, the swirls began to bring slight changes to the water. The water was changing color. It was no longer crystal clear. It was now turning a beautiful purple and green just like Vincen had described earlier. The water, though still purple and green, had the clear, see-through look of the colored gemstones that were common up in the mountains. He struggled desperately to pull his head away from the water. It was just too little, too late. As Mystic was being forcibly drawn into the well, the water was no longer swirling. The water was crashing and banging into itself, beating its colors against one another. Wave after wave emerged and died tragically into its next increasingly larger, more thunderous companion. Mystic began screaming for Vincen. It was a valiant effort. His cry for help was muffled by the surging water.

Once Mystic's tongue had touched the water, the oddly calm surface of the peaceful water was broken. It immediately transformed into a living, tenacious creature. The fraction of time was so instantaneous that the great Wolf had no time to brace himself or plan another strategy. One final, helpless yelp did escape his gritted teeth as he vanished into the water and beyond. As Vincen turned to admonish Mystic again for unbecoming behavior, he caught the last of the commotion. At the last possible instant he turned, missing it all. He watched shivering and helpless, his beak frozen agape with an unintelligible word falling clumsily to the ground as his dear friend plummeted beneath the surface. Horror shone brightly in his large, keen and astonished Eagle eyes as the last hair on Mystic's tail glided beneath the water's surface.

In an instant Vincen was at the edge of the well. He stared straight into the water and could see Mystic sinking. Farther and farther down he went. He could also see that Mystic was not struggling to get out of the water. Mystic looked to be eerily calm and peaceful. The Wolf was not putting up any fight. This was very odd. Vincen watched as Mystic sank deeper and deeper into the well, he was now calling it a well because it had become a hole filled with water and that constituted a well in his book. He watched Mystic until he was out of Eagle's sight. A land walker would have lost him long ago, but Vincen's remarkable eyesight had given him extra time to study what was happening. Finally, Mystic was gone.

Without a moment to spare, Vincen extended his wings and clapped them together with a thunderous roar. He propelled himself as high as he possibly could with one beat of his wings. (This was approximately as high as three pursuit beats are long.) What should he do? What could he do? He was in dire need of ideas and, at the moment, none were to be had. He shot up and out of the South Quarter and immediately made his way over the Great Forest. He was making excellent time, even for an old Eagle, and the rush of wind that accompanied each of his pursuit beats left trees, land walkers and tall grass quivering in his wake. Where were Mystic's friends? He was certainly going to need their help and then some.

2

Bubba, a spirited young Cheetah and his helper, a slightly older fellow, Lightning, the irregular Badger, were over in the far north side of the Great Forest building a fort. From here, Bubba reckoned, he and his friends would have the best chance to protect the Great Forest from any future invasion, should any invasion ever take place.

Lightning enjoyed assisting Bubba with the construction of the fort, although he could not bring himself to tell the young Cheetah that there had been no evil invaders for over 50 and 10 complete day keeping records, or 510 years and he doubted that any would come again during his lifetime. A jolly fellow, Lightning happily went along with the youngster's imagination often wondering what toils he could have gotten into had he not lived such a normal and quiet Great Forest cub-hood. This pair of land walkers got along wonderfully well given their difference in age and were quite inseparable. Though Lightning was reaching young adulthood and developing interests in concerns more in line with his age, he could always find time to spend with his adopted little brother.

Bubba, entering his middle early years. was always ready for an adventure. If he could not find an adventure, his imagination would often create one second to none. He was constantly begging Lightning to practice great warrior tactics he had heard so much about during his young life. He often persuaded Lightning to practice under the moon when the larger four-legger would rather be resting, but Lightning also heard it was the best way to sharpen one's senses and reflexes, so he happily, but begrudgingly, entertained his young friend. Bubba was quickly becoming a very powerful and muscular Cheetah. Easily the fastest land walker in the Great Forest, he was the only land-walker who could keep pace with the Eagles flying at pursuit beat. Not only could he keep pace for short periods of time, he could tail them for long, extended periods of time and, more often than not, move far ahead much to the Eagles' dismay.

Lightning envied Bubba's speed and endurance, but if judging by brute strength alone, Lightning would win any contest with no questions asked. Even though he had lived nearly his entire life in the Great Forest, many times the curious still asked Lightning why he was called "the irregular Badger" and no one particularly knew why. It had been said that his mother gave him the additional moniker when he was a very young Badger barely able to take one or two steps without falling completely over himself. She told him one day, or so it is said, "Lightning, I am so proud of you. Now that you are learning to walk, you are well on your way to becoming a regular Badger just like me, your Father, your Brothers and your Sisters".

Lightning could not have known that his simple reply would have such a direct bearing on the rest of his life. "Mother, oh mercy, there must be more out there to see and visit. I don't want to be a regular badger. I want to see what I hear stories about. I want to see the world beyond the Great Forest and meadow. I want to cross the Little River. I want to see the other side of the mountain. I want to go on adventures. I want to be irregular!"

"So", his Mother replied, "who has told you so much about what lies outside of our land? It was once a dangerous world beyond the Meadow. Badgers just don't need to go looking for trouble. We aren't really the adventurous type."

Lighting did not want to believe this. He could not believe this.

"But Mother, Father told me about the old stories. He said that maybe one day I could venture out if I was careful. He told me to eat all of my meals, do all of my chores and listen to my elders. If I did, I would grow up to be like his Father's Father and be a warrior. Please Mother, say I can be irregular."

"Okay little one", she said softly. "You can be my little irregular Badger if you would like. You can also tell your Father, as will I, he will never have to worry about your eating. You are growing splendidly well. You are growing as fast as lightning races across the sky and nearly as big as a mountain itself!"

His Mother didn't bother to tell him that his Father's Father's Father was a worrier and not a warrior. He had lived at the end of the Terrible Years and had seen too much destruction. He had been wounded protecting his young family and worried about their safety for the rest of his life. He never let them out of his sight again.

And there it was, from that day on this curious little cub would be known as "Lightning, the irregular Badger." As the years passed he grew into quite an irregular Badger. He was the smartest, bravest and strongest Badger in the area. His heart was the kindest in the land. He was always rescuing smaller land walkers and on occasion placed birdlets back into their nests in the high trees at great risk to his own safety, for Badgers don't climb trees that well, but for some reason, this was one skill he developed quite nicely. He became so respected that nearly every day some creature would ask him about the old ways of the Great Forest or about what he thought waited in the day-rounds to come and he could never figure out why they were asking him in the first place although, if no one was asking him, then he would certainly be the one asking. As his Father instructed he continued to eat his meals and anyone else's who couldn't find the time or stomach for such. Eating was one habit that he never, ever, ever missed and he had grown! He had certainly grown! One day to come, his Mother was sure, he would be called "Lightning, the Irregular Badger" Duke or King of something, but, of course, you know how mothers are.

***

"Oh mercy", said Lightning, "Its 30 clicks past middle day time. We have been working so hard that we have forgotten to eat. Let us take a short rest and have some nourishment, shall we?"

"Sure", said Bubba eagerly, "What did you bring?"

While Bubba and Lightning were discussing food, Vincen circled up from the South Quarter and flew westward over the Dwelling Places. "Where could those two be today?" He couldn't blame them for wandering off. It was, after all, a beautiful day for an adventure. How would he break the news to these two, if he ever found them, about Mystic's horrible accident? Would there be any way to rescue him or would this be another terrible loss that they would live every day to get over and never do so? They had already experienced so many tragedies in their young lives. Life could always play so unfairly. The Owls had always told him that there were no promises outside of hope. Right now, hope was all he had and he was betting Mystic's life on it.

Vincen circled the Dwelling Places and tipped his wings to several land walkers as he dipped low among the small trees and dens that rushed by. Everyone below wondered what could have possibly made Vincen so excited. He found no indication to think that the two creatures he was looking for were anywhere around this area. He gracefully regained his pursuit altitude and turned north at the far west side of the Great Forest and picked up considerable speed as he caught a tail wind blowing with him, coming in from the west.

"Where could they be?" he asked himself.

***

Lightning sat down at the edge of the fort and opened his pack. He began to lay out his lunch by pulling out berry muffins and fruits and nuts, lots of nuts, and bark kakes and dried roots and clutches of poke salad leaves. The amount of food Lightning was able to carry constantly amazed Bubba. He had enough food on the ground to feed a complete family, including a Mother, Father, several pups or cubs and a few extra friends.

All of the food looked delicious to Bubba and he was hoping that he might be able to share a bit of it. In his rush to begin this morning he had forgotten to prepare everything he would need for a complete day-round adventure. Well, usually, he forgets lots of things. He was still, and would always be, the youngest of the friends. He had much to learn, especially when it came to being prepared. Always excitedly thinking ahead, he normally left his dwelling with nothing but his rapier.

"Do you plan on eating all of that food at this one sitting?" Bubba asked as he stared at the massive mounds of food. Drool had begun to drip out of his mouth at the sight of those berry muffins.

"Why yes, of course," replied Lightning as he began with the nuts, crunching and chewing them whole, like they were supposed to be eaten that way. "I'm sure you brought enough food of your own, didn't you. Where is your bag?" He was now eating whole, small fruits about the size of large onions commonly referred to as droopers.

Bubba had not sat down yet. After all, he had brought nothing to eat anyway, so why bother. He slowly walked around the fort as if he was looking for something misplaced while Lightning watched him and kept eating the fruits. "Bubba", Lightning asked with a little chuckle, "Did you misplace your bag once again?"

Bubba, knowing full well that Lighting knew he had brought no such bag, looked away from the fort and bashed himself over the head with his long tail. "Why, why, why?" he muttered to himself. "Why can't you remember to bring something to eat!"

He was frustrated with this lack of discipline and crept over to the nearest bit of shade and plopped down on the ground, turned his head around and flicked his long tail into his mouth and chomped down on it. He bit it absent-mindedly and paid a dear price for doing so. After a torturous moment of intense pain he swung his head over to look at Lightning who was now eating the bark kakes. Feeling very humbled, he replied, "As you well know, I forgot my bag again. I will just lie here and watch you eat, if you don't mind."

With that he curled himself into a half circle and bashed himself over the head with his tail again. This time, however, he had the misfortune of forgetting that he had just bitten that same tail and he had just reminded himself, in a rather brutal way, that it was still hurting very badly. He wasn't about to let Lightning know this, so he closed his eyes, wrinkled his forehead, gritted his teeth and swallowed the grand amount of pain.

***

Vincen was now heading to the far north side of the Great Forest. "They must be over here," he thought to himself. This is the area of the Great Forest where the two had grown up. They used this area as the staging point for many of their wonderful adventures. They often tired of staying around the Dwelling Places and, ever since they could find their way home, Vincen had let them wander up to the North side. Just below Vincen, now, was the Black pond. Most two-leggers rationally think it is so named because it borders the edge of some of the richest and most fertile soil in the lands called the "Black". The two-legger land walkers can grow any plant food imagined in this soil. The Talkers have told tales of immensely large fruits and vegetables that grow here. The four-legger land walkers tend to stay away from the Black because of legends regarding past incidents there, so they haven't witnessed these amazing tales with their own eyes. The land and the streams about it drain directly into the pond and for that reason the water is always muddy black. However, the young birdlets and land walkers have for years told scary tales about the pond's name. But even during the Terrible Years, it was called the Black Pond because of the color of the water and that was all.

Now, if you ask Mystic, which no one could right now, he would tell you another story about the Black Pond.

3

In the period preceding the Terrible Years, Mystic's family pack of gray Wolves had the run of the north side of the Great Forest. The area, which they ruled, stretched from the far border of the Black, across the Meadow, completely around and through the Great Forest and over the mountain to the middle of the Valley. There a small river runs, which separates the gray wolves' area from that of the timber Wolves. Mystic was told this history by Vincen who had learned it from the Owls. After the Terrible Years the two-legged and four-legged land walkers went their separate ways and the two-legged land walkers became quick to blame any misdeeds on the four-legged land walkers. Only the Talkers could mediate between the two and Talkers had almost disappeared completely from the lands surrounding the Great Forest. It was a quick and incorrect reaction to one of these misdeeds that was responsible for the first major disaster in Mystic's life.

The story was told to Vincen, by the owls, that several of the two-leggers farmed huge tracts of land on the outskirts of the Black lands. Each tract measured many, many square leisure beats wide and long. Each farmer, in turn, rented part of this land to four-leggers who, in payment, would give the farmers milk, wool, eggs and occasionally the whole body of a suddenly dead four-legger. This last payment was never totally understood by the four-leggers. There was a growing tendency for this method of payment to occur more and more frequently. It seemed that, as the farmer's numbers increased, the amount of full body payments increased. There was fear running through the four-leggers of a deadly sickness that was taking their kind at ever-increasing numbers. It was a similar situation, or lingerings thereof, that caused the demise of Mystic's family.

The rumor had been spreading among the farmers that Sheep and young Cows were being mysteriously killed. A few of the farmers who had no Talkers in their immediate families began to suspect that the gray Wolves were killing their renters. This did not bode well for the gray Wolves. If the Talkers had been around, they would have told the farmers that the Wolves would not kill a fellow four-legger for any reason. A myth was spreading that the Wolves were also eating the bodies of the dead Sheep and Cows.

This myth was preposterous. There had been a pact made in the early day-rounds among the four-legged land walkers of the Great Forest that forbid the consuming of one another for food. Even during the Terrible Years, when food was so hard to come by, no four-legged land walker sank so low as to eat a fellow land walker. Even the Great Birds of Prey, which included the Eagles, Hawks, Falcons and Owls refrained from eating land walkers. Now, water-residers were a different story. No water-resider had ever partaken of any pact and no Talker had ever been able to communicate with them. For this reason and many others, they were still a very reliable food source. The farmers, out of ignorance concerning the pact, set out on a quest to hunt down and kill every Wolf in the land. This was a terrible mistake. But as a result the Wolves were hunted relentlessly and killed off in vast numbers.

Mystic's family set out on their fateful journey in search of a Talker. They had heard from a trusted Hawk that a Talker would be at the bridge over the stream that runs alongside the town where the farmers gathered each morning to do their trading. He would be waiting to have a meeting with the Wolves. The meeting was to benefit all involved. The Talker desperately wanted to hear the Wolves' side of the story in order to state their case with the townspeople. The Talker figured once the townspeople heard the other side of the argument they would understand the Wolves were not to blame for the loss of four-leggers. This town, however, was quite a distance away. Mystic's Father had been told by the Hawk that the town lay at least one thousand pursuit beats away. That was easily a two day-round trip one way.

Knowing the trip would be long, Mystic's Father had selected the strongest Wolves to travel the full distance and meet with the Talker who, in turn, would explain the Wolves' side of the story to the two-leggers. He allowed the Mothers and young pups to travel half the distance, settle in for the night and await their return the following day. Mystic, the youngest and smallest of his family was too tiny to make even the half trip. His brothers and sisters always called him the runt. This was especially cruel since Mystic did not have anything to do with the fact that he was so much smaller that the others. Mystic's siblings all had Wolven names like his parents. His three brothers were named after the three rivers that ran powerfully down from the mountain. They were Rushing, Blue Rock and Rapid. His five sisters were named after his parents' sisters. Their names were Protector, Keeper, Hunter, Gatherer and Swift. Mystic's name was never given much thought, mainly because his Father did not want to waste a name on a Wolf pup that would surely die before 30-day-rounds passed. His Father later regretted that mistake after Mystic proved to be the wisest, although the smallest, of his family pack. Mystic was named by an Eagle. The Eagle noticed very early on the wisdom and intelligence this Wolf runt possessed. The Eagle had named the runt Mystic after his own Eagle Grandfather.

Mystic's mother decided before the trip was made that Mystic would be hidden among the tall grass in an old log near the edge of the Great Forest. She made him a bed for the nights and left him plenty of food. Looking out for his safety, she arranged for a dear family friend to check on him periodically until their return.

Mystic's Father, as the story goes, made a dreadful mistake of trusting the Hawk. Loyalty and trust were two of his greatest traits and he pursued them unerringly. He did not know, nor did he ask about the peril the Hawk was in or the punishment the Hawk's family would receive if the Wolves did not come to meet the Talker. How could he have known? He trusted the lives of his pack to the honesty and integrity of Hawks in general, of which this Hawk was most definitely a member.

The pack started out early on their journey with Mystic's Father, a huge mountain of a Wolf, properly named Giant, leading the way. He was followed in succession by his brothers and the fastest she-Wolves of the pack, who weren't yet mothers. In total, there were about 22 Wolves in the first group followed by the remaining 53 mothers, yearlings, ancients and pups. Seventy-five Wolves in all, the entire pack, with the exception of number 76, Mystic, who was resting and playing innocently back at the log at the edge of the Great Forest.

The trip to the halfway spot was uneventful. Giant and his immediate secret sharers were glad it had been so. Secret sharers were a very close-knit group of any particular type of land walker. They usually included the smartest, wisest and fastest of the particular walker's group. The Wolves had theirs, as did the Badgers, Foxes and etc. It was a dangerous business trekking into town, especially for a large pack of falsely accused Wolves in this very unsettled time. Giant decided to have one of his secret sharers stay with the second group as a watcher. Should there be any trouble the watcher would alert the whole second group and send the warning signals ahead by a howling code. This was a primitive form of communication for the Wolves, but it worked well in times of need. Not that many land walkers understood howling, so, it worked very well when the Wolves were trying not to alarm any of the other land walkers. The Wolves ruled the Lands in and around the Great Forest and they took the protection of the less skilled and weaker land walkers seriously. Giant decided to leave his youngest brother, Ears. Ears had the keenest sense of hearing of any wolf in the pack. He would be the perfect watcher.

Once the pack arrived at the halfway point, Giant gave instructions for the bedding down of the pack to Ears and then set up the howling code. Three short howls followed by a long howl was the signal for "all's well." Any variation of that set of howls, any variation at all, was a signal for danger. If the first group got into trouble they would howl to the second group and visa versa. Whichever group heard the howling deviate from the "all's well" set would immediately, split into pre-arranged groups and run along different pre-selected paths back to the forest. Giant's group would head directly for the second group's bedding spot to protect them at all costs. All small groupings that successfully returned to the Great Forest were instructed to regroup at the spot where Mystic camped in his log.

Giant and the lead group had a brief rest and a bite of food after the planning session, then returned to their journey. Again, nothing out of the ordinary happened. It was a beautiful day and the sun and wind were smiling on them. The group made quick time of the remaining 500 pursuit beats and arrived on the outskirts of the town halfway through moon time. It was dark as the group came in silently. Upon their arrival, Giant sent his middle brother, Shine, in to scout for the Talker. Giant told him where the Talker would be and asked him to stay quietly away from the stream. Giant assumed that one training beat would be close enough to scout the stream and far enough back to remain concealed until sun time began. If the Talker showed up as planned, he would come back and join the group and the secret sharers would then meet with the Talker. If he sensed trouble of any kind he would howl for danger and make a hasty retreat to rejoin the group as they broke off and headed back to the Great Forest.

Shine was honored to be chosen the watcher. He proceeded with his part of the plan exactly as his brother had requested. The stream's water was running. With his excellent Wolf ears, Shine followed the sound and found the stream quickly. He lay down in the grass on a small hill over looking the wooden arched bridge where the meeting was to take place with the Talker. As he scoped the area Shine was a little surprised at how open the space was. He had imagined a very hidden, out-of-the-way spot for a meeting such as this. Though uneasy at first, he put that thought to rest and concentrated on staying awake until sun time began.

"The Talker should arrive as soon as the sun appears over land's edge," the Hawk had explained to Giant. And so, Shine waited patiently and listened alertly. Just as restlessness began to sneak down his spine, the sun did break over the land's edge. Soon thereafter, a two-legged land walker appeared in the clearing. Cautiously, the two-legger walked over to the bridge and stood there waiting, glancing about attentively for any activity. Wolves are not really interested in what the two-leggers wear so Shine made no note of it. Instead, he silently hurried back to the first group. He reported to Giant that a two-legger had indeed appeared as it had been said. There was a very good possibility that he may be the Talker the Hawk told them about. Giant arched his head back, turned it a little and searched to find a small bit of relief. The leader of the Wolves was so hoping that this sojourn had not been in vain.

The group of secret-sharers assembled in proper order, of course, and followed the Brothers back to the bridge. The two-legger was there just as Shine had said and, more importantly, just as the Hawk had described. The group quietly assembled at the base of the very hill that Shine had waited and watched from. Giant decided to walk up to the two-legger first. If there was no problem, he would then call in the rest of the group. He did not want the Talker to feel threatened in any way. Threatened two-leggers seemed to be one of the major problems in this muddle anyway. Giant walked majestically up to the two-legger and, at the same time, the two-legger turned to see an enormously large gray Wolf coming his way. Well, what would happen now? They intensely studied each other for a short while. Giant, comfortably feeling like he needed to initiate the conversation, asked, "Are you the Talker of which the Hawk spoke?"

"That would be me," said the two-legger. "My name is Frederick Mounte, descendent of the Hewitt-Mountes and the Hawk is my beloved friend, Rust. I have been sent to meet with you, I presume, and you are?"

"As was no doubt stated to you, I am Giant, Leader of the Gray Wolves of the Great Forest," replied the gray Wolf. "First, there are many with me as you can see on the hillside. May I introduce you to the rest of my party?"

"Certainly", replied the Talker. "By all means, please do".

With that, Giant called for the group to join him. Two by two, the six secret-sharers led the formation. The six gathered at Giant's flanks standing alertly strong. Each secret-sharer took his place at Giant's side alternating left to right as they approached. The remaining sentinel group fanned out forming a barrier between Giant, the secret-sharers and uncertainty. "These are my friends and my family," he proudly proclaimed to the Talker. Of what shall we speak?"

"You have quite a handsome following Giant. Your size is immense and so those of your pack." Frederick Mounte addressed Giant sincerely. "We shall speak of these oddly misguided times. The farmers' losses of renter animals are quite disturbing although I can absolutely see no reason to blame your kind. There are other troubling issues I wish we had more time to discuss, but I must deal with those issues later," the Talker answered.

"I speak with few words, Frederick. Please do not confuse my short plea with arrogance or ignorance, for I am neither. You must tell the farmers the gray Wolves are not killing the four-legged land walkers or renter animals as you say. Our ancestors made a pact long ago not to kill or eat any fellow "animals." We have existed on a new choice of food for ages now. We eat only fruits, vegetables and plants. We do, now and again, eat the water-livvers should we get the urge to get wet. They are quite hard to catch, so we don't partake of them often. When our little ones are sick we do trap a few and use them as healer food. They have ingredients that fight sickness quite well," Giant explained. "Please let the farmers know, so that we, once again, may co-exist peacefully.

"I have no reason to doubt you Giant, my new friend. I will carry your truths to the farmers. I hope they may listen with a patient ear. For your protection, please make hastily away. Once the farmers arrive for trading, they won't react lightly to seeing a pack of Wolves on their doorstep," Frederick warned as he reached for Giant's paw.

"Frederick, take my paw as a promise of good faith. The Wolves are not the problem here," Giant repeated as he laid his massive paw into Frederick's outstretched hand.

"Then the conversation is sealed Great Gray Wolf," replied the Talker as he grasped Giant's sinewy paw and released it.

"Frederick, you are welcome in the lands of the Great Forest whenever you may pass our way. Thank you and please do your best to convince the farmers that we are not the evil here," said the mighty gray Wolf.

With that, Giant turned to his group and with a nod of his head dismissed them. He bowed his shoulders to Frederick then led the secret-sharers away, up and over the hill. The rest of the group remained on alert until Giant was safely out of sight. They peeled off one at a time as Frederick watched the highly intelligent creatures disperse.

"Well Frederick," came a whiney voice creeping out from under the bridge, "That is not exactly the way this meeting was supposed to develop now, was it? What did that useless Wolf say to you anyway? Might I add, why didn't they kill you? It would have saved me some trouble."

Frederick replied, "The Wolves are not the problem with your livestock. They have no interest in killing or eating other animals."

"Poppycock," came the reply from under the bridge. "They are Wolves and, by the size of them, I can tell they have eaten plenty of our livestock."

"Don't say our livestock! You don't even own one head of livestock. You are nothing but a hired helper, a miserable one at that. You have worked every farm in this town until you overstayed your welcome. You then proceed to the next farm where the next kindhearted farmer takes you in. After a fill of your whining stories, the cycle repeats itself. Now you have turned every farmer in this town against you. You are maniacally searching for any reason to make yourself a hero so these trusting people will allow you to stay in this town. I have known you were the root of the problem all along. I came to this town to do a good deed and was paid with blood money. I am afraid to ask where you got it, but I am sure it has something to do with all of those dead or missing animals. I am a Talker and am blessed to be so. I have done an injustice to those magnificent Wolves and will do whatever I can to stop what I see developing into a merciless slaughter," Frederick answered.

The tail of the last Wolf was disappearing over the hill. Frederick suddenly felt heaping waves of anguish pummeling his body. He immediately acted on the feelings of regret that were churning explosively inside his stomach making him nauseous. He did not trust this man. What had he been thinking? Why had he let it come this far? There was something terribly wrong with this man's motives. Frederick knew he had to act quickly. He frantically turned in the direction of the Wolves, then yelling as loudly and boldly as humanly possible to the exiting group. He cried "Run, Friends, run! Run away quickly! You have been betray..."

The whiney voice, from under the bridge, manifested itself into a small, cowardly, slightly overweight, pale shadow of a man. This man was definitely, no farmer. He had no intention of ever letting those Wolves leave this town alive. In an instant, he stepped behind the Talker, pulled a hefty club from under his coat and brought it crashing down on Frederick's back nearly breaking him in two. Frederick slammed to the ground in a heap. The farmer's helper looked down at the helpless, broken pile of the Talker, laughed through several rotten teeth, then commented in a very sniveling and rude tone, "I, my stupid friend, think you have just done enough."

This poor excuse for a two-legger immediately headed for the wide hard clay street at the town's edge ripping his clothes as he went. Town's people were there as usual on a bright clear morning, milling about, setting up carts and outdoor shops of all kinds and shapes. Several groups had already gathered. Trading was soon to start. This vulgar individual summoned enough strength to break into a tragically awkward run toward those gathered. As he ran, he screamed and flailed his arms in a cruelly convincing fashion. "Help me, protect me! They are coming! The Wolves are coming!" He tumbled to the ground for effect and continued, "They have killed the Talker. I just escaped with my life! Those treacherous creatures almost had me." He began sobbing hysterically, "Please! We must kill every one of the evil creatures!"

Frederick was not dead, though soon he might wish to be. After the wicked little man had run off, Frederick came to and, though the pain in his back was mind boggling, crawled his way under the bridge. He carefully pulled his body under the bridge where it was dark and cool. He did his best to get comfortable before he passed out from the pain. He reached out for a lump of grass on which to rest his head. Pulling it to him, he noticed it was not grass at all. The lump was the lifeless, warm body of a large red Hawk. He feebly crawled, gently cradling the Hawk's body to the darkest recess he could find in case his attacker came back to finish the job. Frederick tightly closed his eyes, set his chin and folded his body as tightly as possible, given the pain he was experiencing. He tenderly brought the Hawk's still body to his chest, held it tightly and wept. He bent his quivering head down to where his face, drenched with tears, was now buried in the Hawk's splendid plumage. Through the tears streaming down his ashen face, he whispered to the Hawk's unhearing ears, "I am sorry Rust, my dear old friend. I am terribly sorry." The pain became unbearable and, for Frederick, light faded to pitch black.

Meanwhile, the vile little man was taking advantage of the townsfolk's attention. The ranting, raving and all of those fake tears concerning the killing of the Talker were stirring the townsfolk into a scared and furious vigilante group. "How could we have been so blind?" he cried.

Whatever he said worked. The little fellow's only true talent was crafting words and theatrics into deception and lies. Every farmer he had encountered so far had fallen for his clever ruse at one time or another. This atrocious man wove lies and deceit together as well as the farmers' wives wove wool into coats. He performed a splendid job of inciting these gentle people into a revenge-fueled, bloodthirsty mob.

"We can't have these Wolves running wild. They will kill all of your children," he continued, choking back laughs and turning them into wails of despair. "We must attack them now…and kill every one of the vicious creatures…before they escape! We must chase them down and be done with them once and for all!"

He could see it coming. He was going to be the hero in this senseless battle yet. He was already counting the ways to profit from it. He would be famous and adored in this town, one way or another. So what if a hundred or so Wolves got slaughtered in the process.

The farmers and regular townsfolk couldn't believe what they were hearing. Why would the Talker be harmed by the Wolves? What would he have told them to make them so angry? The pathetic human managed to climb back on his feet as every man, young and old, hastily grabbed any tool or utensil that could be used for killing. Then they assembled back at this coward's side. He fell once for show, shakily regained his feet and pretended to struggle as he led a large throng of weapon-carrying two-leggers down the clay street to the bridge. He was quite relieved and pleasantly surprised when he stepped off of the road, peered under the bridge and could find no Talker. Now, his talents would revel in their horrendous duties. He could now truly incite a riot. "See, the Wolves have taken this poor man's body away. There is no doubt they will surely eat him tonight as a sad moon watches from above. Poor, poor Frederick. We must avenge his murder. We can wait no longer! Please, we must hurry. The Wolves will escape. Townspeople, it could be your family next," he lamented.

That was enough. His last statement sent the crowd into a wild frenzy. Even the two-leggers who hadn't known what to believe were now giving the crazed little man the benefit of the doubt. The next hideous sound heard was that of horses' hooves as they came thundering over the arched wooden bridge carrying the most affluent farmers and their sons. These privileged few could afford animals to ride as well as animals to work the farms. The affluent, not at all prone to this kind of violence, charged after the Wolves with a budding, but bewildered hatred. Hundreds of two-leggers were after the Wolves. Blood boiled in their eyes and various kinds of killing tools were gripped tightly in their hands. The bright morning sun quickly fell behind ominous black clouds that were racing in, rolling across the sky like a thick acrid smoke. The darkness blotted out the beautiful blue morning canvas. The overhead of remarkable landscape frowned with a dark, deathly cold. A sinister, chilled wind began to howl through the trees. It burst past the thin line of trees, over the small hill and down on the black loamy soil. Death was in this foul wind. This was madness!

From deep under the bridge came a feint whisper falling away, "Run Giant, Run. I'm so sorry." Then the whisper was heard no more.

***

Giant's exceptional hearing let him witness from afar the two-leggers brief argument as it developed. The last Wolf to come over the hill met nose-to-nose with Giant as he sped back to observe for himself what the commotion was all about. He glanced at the bridge and witnessed the small little man standing over the crumpled body of Fredrick with his club raised high into the air. He stood watch as the Talker helplessly crawled underneath the bridge. With his wolven ears he heard the pitiful moans of the Talker and heard the mindless cries of a small little man as he ran crazed in the streets. Giant's large ears heard the wind before it started to blow and his wise whiskers prickled as the clouds began to roll. There was nothing to do now but escape. How did this happen? He had no time to doubt himself. There was only time to run and not enough of that. Who would survive? No one knew for sure. Giant knew all too well that the time to flee was disappearing behind those hideously black clouds. It was obvious to the wise Wolf that Frederick Mounte had known nothing of the betrayal. Danger was not coming; it was here. They must spilt up and run. Run as fast as they could toward the Great Forest.

The betrayed Wolf gave one long and mournful howl and rushed straight for the sentinel group he barked, "Run." As he passed the dazed secret-sharers he told them, "We have been betrayed. Some of us will make it safely back to the Great Forest and some of us will not. There is nothing to do now but run. Each of you knows your route, so take it. Take it now. Go," he demanded. He turned to Shine, looked him in the eyes and said, "I love you Brother, protect our family and if we see each other again, I will celebrate the occasion. We came in trust and that trust has been dashed violently away. Go Shine, may we meet again." He stepped close to his brother and nuzzled his strong neck and licked his snout. "Now go, Brother, go! Don't come back for me, or let the cold wind of this coming death catch you!" He howled longingly again.

Just as Shine ran off to join his small group, the first horse and rider came over and down the hill. The rider was stunned by the size of the huge gray Wolf that stood in his path. The Wolf had nowhere to go. He had waited too long. He had no idea how to fend off a two-legger on a Horse. Could he speak to the Horse? Could he tell it to stop? Suddenly, it did not matter anymore. He froze rock solid as pain and futility swept through his veins like boiling blood. This mistake could have been avoided. All that came to his mind was that whatever tragedy followed, it was his fault. The Wolf shivered as an extremely cold wind cut through his fur like a knife. The two-legger raised a huge ax with a glistening edge high in the air and brought it swiftly and unwaveringly down. It came down hard. The blade, well used from tree cutting, was expertly sharpened and begrudgingly wielded. The heavy tool fell on and through Giant's massive head. Giant was the first and greatest Wolf to die in this heartless, confusing and senseless killing spree.

The killing had now started and spread across the black land with a vengeance. The Wolves were losing at an alarming rate. Badly outnumbered, one after another they were cut down by dazed and eventually remorseful farmers and town folk. Why? Why? Where was that worthless instigator, the one that started it all? It was obvious to most and soon to all that he was nowhere near the bloody, pitiful and tear-littered battle zone.

These Wolves were not used to protecting themselves from crazed hunters. The older, skilled Wolves had heads that were easily larger than their attackers. One swift bite from their powerful jaws would drive their canine teeth deep into soft human flesh and bones. A single bite to the neck would have easily and quickly dispatched any of the attackers. So many of the Wolves could have easily killed back, but that was not their way. The large ones were killed protecting the small ones and the small ones were killed protecting the tiny ones. It was a one-sided slaughter. This bloodletting spree went on and on as each Wolf was chased to exhaustion and killed. The second group fared no better. All of the Mother Wolves fought valiantly to protect their little ones. But, it was to no avail. The little ones were either trampled by out-of-control Horses or hit by errant clubs or mallets.

The Horses' eyes ablaze with the horror, frothy, steaming foam dropping in huge clumps from their mouths and nostrils, were horrified. They had never, before this day, been used in such a destructive, insanely murderous manner. The poor, unwilling draft four-leggers did their best to retreat from the killing. The riding steeds that rebelled were, in turn, kicked, whipped or beaten, if necessary, to force them on. These Horses never were the same trusting animals around the two-leggers, and many of them simply ran away in shame after the slaughter, never to be seen by the two-leggers again. A few of them made their way to the Great Forest and lived the remainder of their day-rounds in shame and retribution.

Mystic's Mother, Sky, never made it back to Mystic's side. She was lost when the second group tried to fight back, as were all of the Wolves in the second group. She had seen Shine when he first came running in with Ears and begged him to rush back and rescue Mystic. "Please, go save Mystic," she cried. "He will be so alone."

Shine dashed around the second group, dodging in and under stampeding Horses' hooves and swinging blades, frantically trying, in vain, to rescue any Wolf possible. It was no use. At last, after feeling the cold wind Giant talked about rushing through the fur on his tail, he heeded his brother's command. He spotted Sky as she fought to save a smaller Wolf and again raced to her side. He pleaded with her to return with him to the Great Forest, to not only save her life, but to rescue Mystic. This plea from Shine stopped when his eyes froze on Sky's massive, fatal wounds. Sky was being swept away by the cold wind. They both realized she would never make it back. Ears overheard the conversation and demanded to stay by Sky's side and, furthermore, demanded that Shine do everything in his power to save the last remaining gray Wolf of the Great Forest.

Ears yelled at Shine, "It is your duty Brother. You must ensure Mystic's survival. I will stay with our brother's mate. I will nurse her wounds if any good will come of it."

Shine ducked as a pummeling blow from a large mallet glanced off his thick neck then, regretfully, made an escape for the Great Forest. Sky fought hard and bravely. She would quickly succumb to her wounds as the deathly chill rippled her fur. Ears was soon shamelessly destroyed while he valiantly took up Sky's battle to protect the last of the Wolf pups. This horrendous battle decimated the Wolves. It now was up to Shine to save the one last Wolf of the Great Forest.

***

The great Eagle landed on top of the log, clicked his Eagle eyes into the hollowed out middle and checked on the small furry pup as he lay sleeping soundly. To himself the Eagle thought, "This little fellow is fine. I only hope his pack is faring as well." He reached in with his sharp beak to delicately cover the pup with the straw that his mother had thoughtfully left in the log with his food. The Eagle hopped up the log, turned toward the little pup and whispered, "I will be back, little one. I must be off to check on the progress of your Parents' journey. Too, I must meet up with the red Hawk."

The Eagle flew high in the sky. The Hawk had told him the town was one thousand pursuit beats away. Even an Eagle would take the better part of a sun time to go that distance. Instead, he circled high above the Black and waited for a sign or message from some other passing sky-traveler. None came and the Eagle had a very bad feeling developing in the pit of his heart. He circled for more than 150 clicks before he grudgingly found a resting perch. During his rest the feeling in his heart grew steadily more depressing. Up again, into the sky. He must find out some news, be it good or bad. He was now expecting more bad than good. He had circled for 40 clicks when he saw movement far away in the field below. The sun glimmered brilliantly off of whatever it was. He circled lower and, as the movement came closer, realized that it was a Wolf. The brilliant coat glistened brighter than the strongest sun's reflection off of clear water and that meant only one thing, it was Giant's brother, Shine. He had been named for the way his coat absorbed light, twisted it just a little and reflected it radiantly back to the world. He picked up his pace and headed directly for the young Wolf.

Shine was easily the most athletic Wolf of the pack and had been for most of his life. Now he was nearing exhaustion. However, he was stubbornly determined to carry out his brother's wish that he had long ago given up any idea of self-preservation. He would do whatever it took to carry out his older brother's urgent plea or summon death trying. He would find Mystic, now one of the last two surviving gray Wolves of the Great Forest. He would see to it that his nephew was protected and, when he was older and possibly able to understand, he would tell him of the great killing that had, so soon ago, taken place. Yet, even in Shine's weary state, he was well aware that no four-legger, Wolf or not, would ever make sense of the killing. He had raced for home at a full run since leaving Ears and Sky behind. Nothing could stop him now. The cries of his mortally wounded packsters were still ringing mournfully in his ears, haunting his every determined stride. He raised his tired head and victoriously caught a glimpse of the dark line that represented the first growth tree line at the edge of the Great Forest as it rose invincible just at the edge of the Black, tightly outlining the horizon.

"You're almost there," he thought to himself. "You must make it. A bit more and you will be home."

He was having trouble running now, yet he pushed forward with only adrenaline and a deep longing to be home to fuel him. His tongue was hanging like a dry, withered leaf from his mouth and he had far earlier stopped perspiring. Every extra ounce of moisture in his body had been drained from him, but still he would not let his rapidly dehydrating muscles rest. The pads on his paws were worn raw and blood oozed between the cracks in the caked-on clumps of dirt. His ears lay flat on his head, as if dead, and he had no energy left for hearing. He was running blindly now. His mission was not over. He continued at a deathly pace. "Almost there," he whispered to himself over and over. "Almost there, almost there..."

***

The Eagle had seen enough. He knew Shine was in dire straits. The Wolf's determination was admirable and also life threatening. How could the Eagle help? He made straight for the Black Pond. He knew there were large lily pads growing near the edge. These would be an excellent water source for a Wolf in very desperate need. "By now, his exhausted body must be screaming for water," surmised the Eagle. He gracefully swooped down to the water's calm skin and, with his expertly guided talons, fiercely pulled the largest lily pad he could find out of the pond, roots and all. He proceeded at full pursuit speed to intercept Shine. He did. Shine never broke stride and was unaware of the Eagle's presence. The Eagle slowed his beating wings to match the heroic Wolf's pace. He gently placed the water laden lily pad on the Wolf's shriveled, muscular neck and sped directly back to the Black Pond for another.

Shine could not believe what had happened. The weight of the fully soaked lily pad crumpled him to the ground. With the soothing water now soaking his moisture-depleted body, his mind struggled with decision making. Could he not enjoy this refreshing feeling for just another moment? No, he could not. Some attacker might still be on his trail. He struggled to regain his footing. Putting all four feet under him again, he clumsily began to get his stride back. Not much later, he saw no clouds, but he felt rain. He was sure his mind was playing tricks on him. First the drenching lily pad and now rain? He knew it was his destiny to make it to Mystic's side now. He increased his pace, forcing his will on his weakened body, pushing it far too hard regardless of the moisture or rain or whatever. He could now plainly see the Great Forest's outer ring, a first growth tree line magnificently shielding the forest beyond from all comers. He could feel welcome coolness radiating out, drawing him closer and closer to home, as he moved steadily onward. The water from the lily pad had momentarily refreshed him, although it was only a small drop compared to what his body was calling for. His dry fur soaked up every drop of water the lily pad had to offer. The Wolf never broke his stride.

Again, the Eagle came diving in with a third lily pad after squeezing a second one almost dry with his talons as he floated over the brave Wolf. He placed this lily pad directly on Shine's head. Again with a forlorn look in his brilliant eyes, the magnificent Eagle headed back to the Black Pond for yet another and another and another.

Shine, breathing deeply, but not deep enough to satisfy his oxygen-starved lungs, looked up with staggering dizziness, read his bearing and located the specific tree under which laid the old hollow log. He adjusted his direction and made a morbid, direct assault on the log. He was home at last. "Where is the pup," he asked himself. "Oh, please, where is the pup and let him be alive!"

Shine, revived by a blood bond and slim hope, sniffed up, then back down the log. He stuck his sun blistered, dry nose into a pile of straw that filled the hollow of the log. Frantically searching through the straw, he heard the most wonderful sound he had heard in the last two-day-rounds. The pup whimpered as it awoke from a deep, peaceful sleep. "You are alive," Shine breathlessly whispered, "You are alive." The pup looked at the large Wolf and playfully swatted Shine's dry, weathered snout.

The Eagle returned from the Black Pond with another lily pad and dropped in onto Shine's back. Shine raised his head, his sad, sunken eyes told the Eagle more than he wanted to know.

Shine softly whispered, "Vincen," and collapsed in a large furry pile at the side of the old hollow log. His dirt-caked chest was heaving as it desperately tried to inhale a complete breath of air. The Wolf was exhausted, nearer to death than he had been in the heat of the dreadful battle.

Vincen could only admire his courage and did not look forward to hearing the details, if he ever did. Vincen, holding back all emotion, quietly replied, "Rest Shine, if you should wake up you can tell me everything." Vincen pulled the lily pad up to the Wolf's mouth so the water could spill into the parched, gaping mouth, constantly gasping for air as the Wolf's body resiliently clung to life. Vincen flew off to the Black Pond several times over the next 30 clicks and brought back nearly 20 lily pads. He placed them all over Shine's body and several were placed where they would drain into his mouth. Vincen looked at

Mystic, who had no idea of what the big fuss was all about, and told him, "Mystic, your uncle is sleeping. Let us let him sleep and when he awakes, we will discover the facts of why, he alone has come back to us." Vincen was not sure Shine would ever wake again.

The vigil started. Vincen's main objective was to keep Mystic from bothering his deep-sleeping uncle and, at the same time, defer questions about Mystic's parents until later when he could get the full story from Shine. Vincen took Mystic on walks to collect food in case Shine did wake up. Vincen also flew to the Dwelling Places and borrowed a water container from one of the Dwellers. He brought it back to the Black Pond and filled it to the brim with water. Vincen had it waiting at Shine's side should he need it. The Wolf had now been collapsed for 150 clicks. He was breathing a bit easier. Vincen's hopes for Shine's survival were increasing. Shine had arrived back at the Great Forest at early sun time of the third day-round since their disastrous journey had begun. This was not entirely unusual, but it was much earlier than Sky had told him they would return. The horrible thoughts that Vincen was having revolved around the fact that Shine was the only Wolf to return and he had done so at such a high price to his well being. Sun time was fading and the Great Forest was getting cooler as moon time approached.

Vincen continued to check on Shine, all the while keeping Mystic quite occupied with hunting food for his uncle. Fortunately, Mystic was old enough to hunt for food and young enough not to ask too many questions concerning his uncle's solo return. Mystic was now napping in the old hollow log. Vincen took great advantage of this quiet time. He flew to a perch high atop the nearest tree and searched the land's edge for signs of the returning Wolf pack. There were no signs to be found. Something had gone horribly wrong. He had not seen any sign of the red Hawk either. Both of these strange happenings were, again, beginning to bother the great Eagle.

"Vincen, Vincen, are you still here," a voice barely audible asked from ground level.

Vincen was immediately at Shine's side to comfort the ailing Wolf. "I am here, friend. You must lie still until you regain some strength," Vincen answered softly.

"I am all that is left of the pack Vincen. I am all that is left. Ears and Sky demanded that I return to Mystic's side. I came to protect the Prince of the Great Forest. I tried Vincen. I tried. He and I, alone, are all that is left of the Gray Wolves of the Great Forest." Shine's voice faded.

"Shine, I have food for you. Mystic and I have collected all that we could find. We have enough for three or four Wolves. Please, do you have the strength to eat?" Vincen asked.

"Yes, I can eat. I cannot guarantee how much information I can give you on the demise of the pack, but I shall try. Vincen, it was a slaughter," Shine continued, "Too many two-leggers with too many killing tools on too many horses."

"Please eat," urged Vincen. "Start with some droopers."

Shine nibbled at the droopers slowly and mouthed some plant roots. He then drank water from the basin before continuing with the fruit. Vincen carefully studied Shine's breathing and body movements, looking for some sign that the Wolf's health was improving. He did not find any. Shine's breathing was becoming more labored as he ate. Vincen was worried. "Shine, can you tell me anymore about what happened."

"Yes Vincen, I will tell you what I know. We made it to the meeting place in good measure. Giant set a camp halfway for the youngsters, ancients and Mothers. The secret sharers and the remainder of the pack went on to the predetermined spot. I was sent to scout the area and watch for the Talker. He arrived exactly when you told us he would and exactly where." Shine then drank another helping of water and ate another drooper.

"Take your time," added Vincen. "Do you know the Talker's name?'

"Yes Vincen, the Talker introduced himself as Frederick Mounte, descendent of the Hewitt-Mountes. He was a very orderly two-legger and had no idea of the impending doom. My dear brother stated our plea as Frederick obligingly listened. He believed him. He asked for his paw to tender the conversation. Giant offered his paw and the promise to intercede for us was sealed. We turned to collect ourselves for the return here, to our home." Shine broke down and could not speak anymore. He began to cough and he turned his head away from Vincen and threw up most of the food he had just eaten. Vincen moved directly in front of Shine's eyes. The Great Eagle gently said, "Steady, son. Slow down. You are not well. You must save your energy."

"Vincen, I can no longer deceive myself. I have noticed how you are overly concerned for me. You see what I feel. I will not make it through the moon time. I will likely join my brothers very soon. I can't speak too quickly. I fear I will run out of life. Vincen, we were all hunted down and slaughtered. The pups were killed. The ancients were killed. The Mothers fought fearlessly. They left their marks on more than a few two-leggers. Vincen, the two-leggers did not seem to know or understand why they were attacking us. I could not hear everything for the roar of horses yelling warnings to us and the mad ravings of the two-leggers. I am sure that the two-leggers did not know the exact reasons for the massacre." Shine was breathing heavily and struggled to get the words out of his mouth.

"The Horses were yelling at us to run, Vincen! The Horses demanded that we attack our attackers, but we couldn't. Although we were once born to be ferocious warriors, our ways have changed. I suggest, as Mystic grows, you teach him to be the warrior we were born to be for his own sake. My brother was such a good-hearted leader. He never saw evil in any living thing. I tell you, Vincen, as a witness, evil is out there. It may be hiding far away, but it is out there. Mystic must be prepared for it. The Horses were crying for us Vincen as the two-leggers beat them into running through us. Several Horses threw their two-leggers and I saw them running swiftly away from the blood. They are not to blame. I haven't much left now Vincen. Sky demanded that I protect her runt son. We knew he was special as do you. As my last request Vincen, I ask that you raise him as Giant and Sky would have seen fit. They loved you, Vincen, as they showed when they requested you to watch over him in their absence. They trusted him to your protection as do I. My errand is finished. May I see him?"

Vincen pulled himself to full height then strutted over to where Mystic was sleeping. He nudged him awake and got him to his feet. "Come Mystic. Your Uncle would like a word with you."

"Is he going to be well again?" Mystic asked.

"Come with me," Vincen replied.

Mystic stepped up close to his Uncle's beaten face and sat down in front of him.

Mystic asked, "Yes, Uncle?"

Shine raised his head and, with fresh tears running down his long snout he replied, "Mystic, my young Wolf, you are the last of the Gray Wolves of the Great Forest. I have come many beats to tell you that your Mother, Father and the rest of your pack wishes you well. They will not be returning to you. I will soon be leaving you as well. Vincen, the Great Eagle of the Great Forest and wise and dear friend, of both your Mother and Father, will lead your pack from this day on. I have one last thing to tell you, young one. From this day-round on you will no longer be Mystic the runt. I proclaim, with Vincen, of the Great Vincen Eagles as a witness, that you Mystic, youngest son of Giant, the Ruler of the Great Forest and his forever mate, Sky, you, Mystic, are now The Prince of The Great Forest. You will abide by the Gray Wolf code and will diligently serve your lands under the wing of Vincen until he sees fit to release you and further proclaim you Ruler of the Great Forest. I love you, nephew."

Mystic stood at attention with tears flowing freely from his wide eyes. He stepped up to Shine's ears and replied. "I will forever love you, Uncle, as I will forever love my Mother and Father. I ask that you tell them so when you see them. Tell them further that I accept this honor and I will one day see them again." Mystic stepped even closer to Shine, laid down at his neck, gently nuzzling him.

Shine looked at Vincen. He noticed that the Eagle had bowed with outstretched wings to the new Prince of the Great Forest. Shine tried to smile and nuzzled Mystic back. His eyes were clear and his coat was once again "shining" under the moon's light. He laid his large head next to Mystic's small body. He then closed his large, caring eyes for the last time.

Vincen turned, flapped his wings and rose quickly into the cold moon time sky. He flew higher and higher. Mystic, still weeping softly snuggled into his uncle's neck. Sometime during the night, he heard a loud and piercing cry of an Eagle's pain and anguish released somewhere high over the Great Forest as a very cold wind swept through, chaffing the Black.

4

"Oh mercy, here," urged Lightning, the irregular Badger. "I have not left you out, little brother. Of course I have brought food for you. Don't I always take care of you, little friend? Well, usually either Mystic will or I will. Please come and eat some real food so you can quit taking bites out of your own tail."

This lighthearted ribbing embarrassed Bubba. For sure enough, either Mystic or Lightning had always brought food for the Cheetah as long as his young mind could remember. He couldn't recollect being anywhere without them or their food. Only today, and odd it was, Mystic had decided to pursue adventuring alone. This surprised Bubba. Mystic was not one to go off on his own. It was not out of fear, but Mystic just always loved company. Why Mystic had not told Lightning where he was heading or what he would be doing at the start of this sun time was odd, very odd indeed.

"Well," prodded Lightning, "Do you want some food or not?"

"Yes, yes, of course I do," replied Bubba eagerly. "Lightning, another thing, do you have any idea why Mystic took off so early on his own today? Why wouldn't he want us with him? What if he needed us for protection?" Bubba always assumed Mystic was helpless without the Cheetah nearby.

"Would you come and eat some food and quit asking so many questions. I *am* trying to eat here. If you don't hurry, I could very well end up eating the food I have so graciously set aside for you," Lightning said, quite annoyed. It was clear to see that his willingness to share was diminishing quickly. "I have no idea what was on Mystic's mind this day-round. He started out very early and, really, it was none of my business. He is the Prince of the Great Forest. He will go wherever and whenever he chooses, with or without my permission. Should he ask us, we will accompany him to the ends of our lands or to the ends of our lives. Here, young Cheetah. Eat this drooper before I do."

"As you wish," answered Bubba. Bubba sat up. The Cheetah was careful not to step on his sore tail. He quickly scampered over to where Lightning had spread out the food. Bubba stood eyeing the choices. Finally he chose the fruit that he disliked least. Bubba preferred waterlivvers, if he had his choice. He was not that crazy about fruit. Lightning told him years ago that he would come to enjoy the food of the Great Forest if he would just give it a chance. Well, Bubba had given this selection of food a chance and had not yet learned to enjoy it. He was, after all, a Cheetah. "You know Lightning," Bubba continued as he ate a small drooper. "I am getting restless. Building this fort is fun, but I think it is time for another adventure, a real adventure!"

"Bubba, every time we leave the Dwelling Places it is an adventure," Lightning said. "One knows not whether you will bring food, get lost, hurt yourself or just confound us with your questions. Up until now, you have fulfilled three of those four measures. That is enough of an adventure for me," he answered as he began to eat a dessert of poke salad.

"Thanks for thinking so highly of me, oh great huge one," Bubba snickered and, losing his bearings for an instant, sat down hard. He saw Lightning chuckling while motioning with a large clutch of poke salad leaves at something on the ground directly below where he was about to sit. "Fine, oh great round one!" Bubba said as he sat down hard on the ground.

"Owwwww!" A loud cry came roaring out of the Cheetah's jaws as soon as he completed his abrupt landing, then popped back up immediately. He had paid absolutely no attention to where Lightning was pointing and had absentmindedly failed to move his poor tail out of the way of his haunches. Lightning's stomach began to heave violently. He was no longer chuckling. He was laughing very loud gut-busting, rolling laughs. He was spitting poke salad all over the place and was trying to retain his balance. He rolled onto his back and continued laughing at the unfortunate young Cheetah. "Oh mercy, young one," he laughed while looking straight up into the towering trees, tears pouring around his big round jowls, "What am I to do with you?" He laughed a deep wonderful laugh for a long, long while.

Meanwhile Bubba stubbornly gritted his teeth and shed some tiny tears of his own, although they were not laughing tears.

***

The Land of Nuorg

"There they are," Vincen thought out loud. "Whatever are they doing?" Vincen dropped from the sky like a stone into the middle of the eating break, startling one out of a laughing stupor and the other out of a private pity party. "I have some tragic news of the most desperate kind," he said urgently to the two surprised friends.

Bubba and Lightning scrambled to their feet, immediately standing at attention. The laughing and crying stopped at once. "Why Vincen? What has happened for you to burst in here so recklessly?" queried Lightning.

"My dear young friend, we have a desperate situation. A horrible dilemma is developing if it has not completely done so by now. I have scoured the Great Forest in search of for you too long. I have several dreadful feelings encompassing my rational thought at this moment."

Bubba was clueless. He usually lost the battle of understanding when Vincen talked in the olde style as he was doing now.

"It pains me so to converse with you so tersely when short, urgent planning and quickness of actions is of the utmost pressing importance. Do my bidding at my request and ask not several questions of me. I shan't excuse you to do such. Mystic is at a loss for our current situation, being such, that our dear wolven friend is no longer of this land. We must assemble our needs quickly and, armaments at the side, spring into this dreadfully dire situational crisis that he finds himself surrounded from outside to within."

Bubba's ears relaxed, he slouched slightly and with a glazed uncomprehending look in his eyes, turned his head to Lightning for an interpretation. Vincen was upset, more upset than he had ever been since Bubba had known him. Bubba glared directly at Lightning, furrowed his brow, squinted, tilted his head at a sideways angle and asked, "Is Mystic in trouble?"

Lightning sternly gazed back at the Cheetah, as the remaining poke salad leaves fell crumbled from his tightly clasped paws. He explained, "My not so excellently witted young friend, Mystic is in terrible danger. He has been swallowed completely by something." He allowed his enormous head to swivel back to Vincen and asked respectfully, "Where must we go and what are we to do?"

"To the dwelling edge of the South Quarter, my friendlies. Hasten not. Brought with your sibling and to the place of my ceased direction shall you and your necessaries follow," Vincen answered.

"Oh mercy Vincen, please speak so I can understand. My mind is working too fast to understand the olde speak. It will take several clicks to comprehend what you just told us. I beg you to speak in a manner we can recognize. Without a doubt, we need to know," Lightning pleaded.

Vincen stomped around in no specific pattern. Eventually he gathered himself ever so slightly and deliberately stated, "You two, go to the Dwelling Places and get whatever food you can quickly pack. Bring it hurriedly to the dwelling edge of the northwest side of the South Quarter. We must hurry! Too many clicks have passed since Mystic left me. Bring your weapons!"

Vincen was well into the sky and gone before a dazed Cheetah or confounded Badger could ask another question.

Now this last bit of information got Bubba's attention. Vincen never approved of weapons in any fashion. He had always, up until now, been agitated by their presence among the trio, but now the Great Eagle was requiring them for this travel.

"Well?" said Bubba.

"Oh mercy," replied Lightning. "We have certainly got us an adventure now. Follow me. No, wait. Bubba, you are the fastest. Go to the Dwelling Places and get my ax- pike. You know where it is. Next, go to Mystic's dwelling and retrieve his wand/staff. I will collect the food as I go. I will take the direct route through the middle of the Great Forest, which should be shorter, and meet you and Vincen at the northwest side of the South Quarter. Bubba, we are depending on you not to forget anything. Please hurry. I have never seen Vincen that excited. Now go."

"Yes Lightning, I will not forget anything and I will meet you just where Vincen has requested." Bubba was off, instantly running faster than Lightning had ever seen him run.

"Please don't forget the wand/staff," Lightning yelled loudly as the Cheetah disappeared from sight.

Lightning made off through the Great Forest opening his pack every time he came upon something that seemed remotely edible. If there was a fruit, he picked it. If there was a nut, he gathered it. If it was a plant worth eating, he pulled it. He would not be able to prepare any bark kakes or poke salad properly, and those were his favorite foods in all the lands.

The Badger reasoned with himself as he hurried through the Great Forest trying to answer the question that would not leave his mind. What had happened to Mystic? What was Vincen trying to say? Vincen's behavior was highly unusual. What complicated the situation further was the way Mystic had also acted highly earlier this day-round when he had spoken with him, only briefly, as they were both headed out of the Dwelling Places but in different directions.

***

"Good to see you as always," Lightning greeted Mystic as he passed the Wolf on his way to Bubba's dwelling place. "Are you not coming with us on this fine day-round?" the Badger asked. "After all, it was your idea that we work on Bubba's fortress today."

"I apologize. Lightning, I remember nothing of what you say. I must not have been thinking too clearly if I did schedule the work. I must be off on my own today. I feel there is something else calling to me. It began late during the last day-round. I must give it an ample amount of my attention. You and Bubba must continue working on that fort of his without me. Should I finish my mission soon enough, I will meet you both on the north side. I can't explain to you why I need to go alone. I can't explain to you where I am going either, because I don't know where I am going! I am following a gut feeling that has burrowed its way into my head. There is no real reasoning to explain. I left those lazy timber Wolves with a few tasks to do 'til I return. I doubt they lift a paw toward accomplishing any of them. When I get back, should it be early, I will, more than likely, be completing those tasks for them. Timber Wolves are so lazy and temperamental. I have no idea why we took them in. I suppose I am the Wolf leader and I guess it was my destiny," rambled on a very peculiar-acting Mystic.

"Very well Mystic, you know where we will be," replied a very suspicious Badger. Wait a click. Where is your wand/staff? Shouldn't you have it with you? It's your weapon of choice isn't it?" Lightning was having a difficult time comprehending these lapses in Mystic's judgment. "Pardon me, but I can't understand this Mystic. Your only weapon you leave behind on an adventure that takes you to who knows where for a reason that you cannot figure out?"

"Please, Lightning, I don't understand your unending questioning. My wand/staff? Really! Where is your ax-pike? Don't you think you need that as well?" said a very agitated Mystic. "What good would my wand/staff do for me.? I know not where I go or for what, so why would I need a weapon? Do you suppose you know something that I don't?"

"Well, no," answered Lightning. "As for my ax-pike, it's too heavy to lug around for no reason. As for your wand/staff, I would just assume that one who travels for unknown reasons to unknown places would take every precaution available to him. Excuse me for suggesting such a thing. I will be on my way!" The Badger abruptly turned his overly large-sized body and walked away in a huff.

"So be it," retorted Mystic. "I'll be on mine as well!" Mystic shook his head, took one inquisitive look back at the miffed Badger and continued on his way.

***

Thinking back on their meeting, nothing about their conversation made sense to Lightning. Now he was genuinely worried about Mystic's behavior. Mystic had never missed an opportunity to work on the fort with them, nor had he ever left those slow-thinking timber Wolves to do anything alone. It had been Mystic's idea, not so long ago, to construct the fort to keep Bubba's mind from wandering. That youngster always wanted to go adventuring. No small adventure ever seemed to satisfy that one. He had his mind set on a great adventure full of danger and mystery. Now, it seemed to Lightning, that Mystic's mind was doing the wandering and, too he thought, Bubba might actually get his great adventure after all. Well, whatever the reason for Mystic's strange actions earlier, it wasn't turning in to anything good.

***

On his trek across the Dwelling Places, Lightning made a detour from his path that early day-round to check on Mystic's dwelling. In case something was amiss, he could summon Bubba and have him chase down the obstinate Wolf. Lightning cautiously stopped in front of Mystic's rather large, royal dwelling. It had been a home of awesome, simple splendor back in the days of Giant and Sky. Lately it had been in need of some loving care and Mystic just didn't have the help he needed to put the place back in good repair.

The Badger studied the Dwelling for a click or two. In due course, he decided everything was as it should be, everything except the wand/staff that is. There it was on the large front stoop of the immense dwelling. Why had Mystic left it there? He would never intentionally leave it out in the open. They had both wondered about the origin of the wand/staff. They protected it from overly curious eyes, lest it should disappear. They had imagined that it had once been a tool of great power. They spun story after story about what it might have been ever since they had been old enough to do so. But still, there it stood.

Lightning glanced around curiously, plus he noticed the sun was rising fast. He decided everything was pretty much normal, outside of the wand/staff's location. Making one last scan of the stoop, he thought his eye caught a glow about the wand/staff. "That's odd. Why would it be glowing?" He surmised it must be the bright sun playing tricks on his eyes. He hurriedly continued on his way in search of the young Cheetah.

***

The Badger was making good time through the forest. He should meet up with Vincen and Bubba in somewhere around 10 or more clicks. For a Badger of his proportions, he was moving extremely fast. He had collected enough food to last several more day-rounds, as long as no one ate too much. He filled his pack until it could absolutely hold no more. Water was the problem. Wherever they were heading, he certainly hoped they would find water...and Mystic.

Bubba raced to the Dwelling Places, finding the ax-pike right where he knew it would be. He collected it as it lay on the floor beside Lightning's, enormously large, well-worn, often-used table. The ax-pike was a giant tool. Maybe he should have thought more about how he would carry such a hefty piece of gear. It was too late to worry about that now. He quickly scavenged the den for straps to secure the ax-pike to his back or side or wherever he could fit it. Some lengths of rope and a torn floor mat were laying on the back stoop, so he fashioned an unlikely looking scabbard using these scraps and, more than anything else, a significant dose of imagination. With his ever-present rapier snuggly on his back, he fastened the scabbard like a harness around his barreled chest, stuffing small, soft pieces of bedding between his fur and the roughly textured ropes. The head of the ax-pike ended up in front of Bubba's shoulders, between his legs, acting as an odd sort of battering ram. Once the substantial tool was secure, he swiftly made his way to Mystic's dwelling on the far side of the Dwelling Places.

The young Cheetah frantically searched for the wand/staff. "Where could it be?" he asked himself. He could not find it anywhere! It was neither inside nor outside the dwelling place of the Prince of the Great Forest. Feeling his actions becoming futile, he curtailed the search. He must meet up with Vincen and Lightning as he was told. That meeting was to take place without incident. He vigilantly circled the dwelling once again and raced off. With his incredible speed, he arrived well before the Badger, but the Eagle had beaten him to the rendezvous point.

"Oh where is that Badger," Vincen asked Bubba. "If he wasn't so enormous, I should have flown him here.

"I'd like to see that," Bubba answered lightheartedly. "There is no way you could have picked that Badger up and flown him anywhere!

"Yes, yes, I know, I know, I know" Vincen answered as his pacing became increasingly agitated. Eagles are never late. Vincen's patience wore thin when dealing with tardiness. "Where is that Badger?" he demanded.

No other words were said. The wait was spent in silent paces. Each individual's mind was exploring thought after thought on the facts, as they were, to this point. Vincen's thoughts dealt more with trying to answer the questions posed to this point, while Bubba's were of the mounting dangers the three of them might face after this point. Further, Bubba explored how they might be able to combat each and everyone they might face. Not too many more clicks had passed before Lightning showed up, but for the original two, the time spent waiting could have very well been an eternity. The Badger could not have shown up soon enough.

Lightning came rushing up to the others. Though nearly exhausted, he was ready and willing to initiate any plan that Vincen's wise mind had devised.

"Got the food!" announced the weary Badger. "What do we do now?"

Vincen was first to speak as he circled Bubba. "Well, I see that the young one has brought the weaponry. Good my young Cheetah, you have your ever-present rapier I see. You have, as well, Lightning's ax pike." Turning his elegant head to Lightning he continued, "One day Lightning, you must tell me where, or how, you ever came to possess that thing? However, we shall talk about that later, if we are allowed to

The Land of Nuorg

do so. Turning back to his inspection of the Cheetah, he asked, "Where is Mystic's wand/staff?"

Lightning angrily burst in, rather un-politely, "Bubba, I begged you not to forget anything. You only had two items to retrieve. How could you have possibly forgotten the wand/staff?"

"But Lightning, I didn't forget the wand/staff! I made the trip to Mystic's dwelling just as you asked. I searched and searched in vain for the wand/staff. Please believe me, it was nowhere to be found. I looked inside. I looked outside. It was not there! I tried. I really tried. I was running late, but I looked everywhere at least three times. You must believe me. It was not there!" Bubba pleaded dejectedly. "It was not there."

"I know for a fact that it was there. I saw it earlier when I went by to make sure everything at Mystic's dwelling place was normal, for he, most certainly, was not. I saw the wand/staff as plain as I see your spots young Cheetah. It was standing on the stoop just at the front door, leaning precariously on the door box," Lightning declared quite adamantly.

"But I am telling you both again, it was not there!" Bubba felt hurt because Lightning obviously did not believe him.

Lightning's stare never wavered from Bubba. "Vincen, it was there. In my haste, I even thought I saw it glowing. The oddest of the odd things I have seen with my own eyes. The sun must have caught it just right, because, as I stand here before you, I thought it was glowing," said the Badger.

Bubba shook his head defiantly, "No! I'm telling you, it was nowhere to be found!"

Vincen did not want to see this type of interaction between the two friends. Time was getting away from them. "There, there now you two, stop this bickering. It is doing Mystic no good. I assure you," Vincen calmly stated as he stepped between the quarrelers. He looked up at the Badger, "I don't believe Lightning, that this young one would tell us a false story. He well knows what is at stake." The Eagle was speaking normally again, much to Bubba's satisfaction.

Lightning reluctantly backed away from the confrontation with the Cheetah. He placed his paws on the top of his head and began to pace. "Vincen, there still lingers something here that disturbs me." The Badger stopped and addressed the Eagle directly, "If I saw it, and I did," Lightning said. Taking a paw from his head, he non-maliciously jerked it at Bubba then continued, "And if he didn't, then where is the wand/staff and, if it is missing, who has it?" Lightning's pointing paw came down to join the other now wrapped around his colossal back. He looked with bewilderment at Vincen hoping for a good answer.

"I don't know," answered Vincen with a shrug. "We can't be concerned about that now. We must enter the South Quarter, locate the clearing where I last saw our departed friend, exhaust all means known to us and find him. We must find him. The Great Forest's legacy depends on it! I will lead. You two shall follow. Stay with my pace and do not wander off my lead. I will lead you down the most manageable path to the clearing. The trouble I see immediately is this: we know enough to stay out of the South Quarter and not nearly enough to go stomping directly through it."

With that Vincen gave the pair a determined stare, flapped his wings and was off. The four-leggers desperately struggled to match the Eagle's pace. They miraculously managed to stay on Vincen's tail as he carefully searched out, then, flew over, the clearest path the land walkers could possibly travel. Nothing was said. The land walkers were intensely studying the Eagle's flight path and had no time to talk for fear of losing the trail. Vincen knew exactly where he was going, although he was having trouble following an indirect path that avoided the dense underbrush that, otherwise, would have slowed their progress. "How I wish they could fly!" he mentioned to himself more than a few times.

What seemed like ages passed agonizingly by as the trio traveled within the unfamiliar confines of the South Quarter. The land walkers never wavered from the path blazed by Vincen. When they did encounter some seemingly impassable obstacle on the trail, Lightning dropped down on all four of his massive legs and powered his way over or through to the other side. Size had its advantages and Lightning, the irregular Badger, had plenty of size to spare.

Suddenly, Vincen made a sharp descent into a small clearing. How Mystic had stumbled upon this clearing this day-round was just one of the many mysteries Vincen's brilliant mind had yet to figure out.

Lightning and the young Cheetah arrived soon thereafter, huffing and puffing, looking quite the worse for wear. They had barely managed to crawl out from beneath the last and most impenetrable thicket of underbrush that, in most cases, certainly would not have been passable. Thanks to badgered determination, Lightning's

The Land of Nuorg

strength, in addition to his ax-pike still strapped to Bubba's chest, they burrowed, clawed and finally forced their way through the dense blockade. At last, clear of the intimidating vegetation, they managed to stand up once again.

The land walkers were filthy. They each had mud, thistles, thorns, sand and heavy coatings of dust all over their bodies. They would never be welcomed at any self-respecting Dwelling Place in this dreadful state. They took a click to stretch some very cramped muscles. Taking turns, they beat the dust off each other. Needless to say, Lightning nearly knocked Bubba down repeatedly as he playfully swatted his much smaller friend.

The last obstacle had been the most difficult challenge of the trek. So far, so good. Once stretched and relatively dust-free, Lightning and Bubba had a moment, at last, to take in their surroundings. They ogled in amazement at this secret clearing. Looking at each other, each wondered silently to himself the same thing Vincen had been thinking. "How did Mystic find this place?"

Vincen proudly looked them over, shaking his head as he studied their slovenly appearance. One more thing, the Cheetah's tail was beginning to ache again. With all of the past excitement Bubba had forgotten how he'd taken his frustrations out on his innocent tail. He was now remembering that incident vividly. The tail hurt. It hurt a lot.

"Here we are," Vincen, pronounced matter of factly. "Now we must find that Wolf!"

5

After several complete day keeping records of normal life in the Great Forest, the four close friends, minus the Wolf, were finally, going on a real adventure. It was their collective wish that Mystic, already traveling on this adventure, was faring well. Since none of the four had ever experienced a real adventure, they were a little hesitant of the unknown, but eager to get started. The group further desired for this to be a successfully safe adventure. As well, all hoped they would return with their beloved friend and leader, and, in the back of their minds, secretly wondered if any of them would ever return at all.

Bubba was nervously searching the clearing for the hole that he had imagined Mystic falling into. He was confused with its absence, although confusion was not that uncommon to the young Cheetah. As he was backtracking from the clearing, he stepped in a shallow, drying puddle. "Oops, I'm glad that wasn't much bigger," he thought.

Vincen alertly noticed Bubba's reaction. At the top of his voice he shouted, "Watch where you are stepping, Cheetah. I believe that is the location of the very hole that swallowed our friend!"

"This one?" Bubba gasped, somewhat surprised, as he instinctively withdrew his paw from the remaining water in the puddle. He carefully backed away, never taking his eyes off what he had thought was a completely non-threatening puddle.

"Yes, I believe it is. That is the very hole!" Vincen said again, hastening to Bubba's aid, as the Cheetah continued his retreat ever so cautiously.

Lightning arrived at the location shortly thereafter. He was sure that Vincen was joking. "Sir, there is no way a large gray Wolf could submerse his front paw into that hole, much less be swallowed by it entirely! Why, it's barely a puddle," he added. "I would certainly never fit through it."

The Land of Nuorg

With a chuckle to break the tension, Bubba casually stated, "That is an understatement, your great hugeness." He turned to Vincen and continued, "That hole, most certainly, has a bottom so there is absolutely no way to fall through it. It is hardly deep enough for me to step into. I hardly noticed when I did."

"Contrary, friends, to what you must think of this puddle, you must continue to trust me," Vincen said. "This is precisely the place where I last saw our dear friend Mystic. It is the very place we must enter to find him, wherever he went. There must be a legitimate explanation for its considerable shrinkage," Vincen said puzzled. He lightly ambled away from the puddle muttering, "At the very least, I hope there is an explanation."

The hole was drying up. It continued to shrink as the trio warily studied at it. Just watching the hole shrink was mesmerizing. Suddenly, out of everywhere, a mysteriously strong breeze rushed in. This breeze was not unlike that which had distracted Vincen's attention much earlier. Vincen froze. "Don't anyone move. Stay as you are, where you are," he commanded. His head began clicking around. His eyes darted about determined to find the cause of this uneasy disturbance.

Bubba and Lightning froze like statues. They didn't even breathe. The only parts of their bodies that did move were their eyes. Bulging eyes were now protruding out of their sockets, straining to catch a glimpse of whatever had caused the breeze. Without much more warning, from behind a small clump of trees an oblong object came charging across the clearing. It was not a large object, but would obviously do some damage if it were to crash against one of them. It was traveling as if it were being pulled by a rope behind a very fast pair of Horses at full gallop. Not one of the three saw it as they were still gazing above the trees, searching for the breeze's origin. The object sped across the ground. It passed too close to Vincen, too quickly. The air movement in the object's wake very nearly upended the flabbergasted Eagle. He had not seen it coming and that disturbed him. The object veered off near Vincen's feet and bounced directly behind the Cheetah.

"Yeeowwww!" cried Bubba as the object bounced down on and off the very spot on his tail that had been hurting so badly. "Catch it, Lightning, quick!" Bubba shouted.

Lightning was not overly fast for a long distance, but he was strong and quite fast for a short period of time. He used every bit of his quickness and strength to throw himself fast enough at the object to capture it as it was about to enter the remainder of the hole. He could not have timed his perfect lunge any better. Whatever the object was, it was now under one enormous Badger. Still moving toward the hole, the unidentified object was dragging the astonished Badger with it. Vincen cried out to Lightning, "Please grab hold of whatever that thing is, Lightning!

The hole began to gurgle and gasp. "Look at the hole!" shouted Bubba. "It seems to want whatever Lightning is lying on quite badly."

To Vincen's astonishment Bubba was right. "Lightning, whatever is under you belongs in that hole. Do not let it go or we will never see Mystic again!" he demanded.

A flurry of activity involving the three friends and the object made for quite a comical scene. All present would have thought the ordeal hilariously funny had it not been happening at such an ill-advised time.

"Sir", Lightning uttered through a fiercely set chin, "I am trying. A little help would not hurt at this moment. Bubba, get between me and the hole in case I can't hold whatever this is." Lightning visibly struggled to secure in his strong paws the object that was eluding his grasp so willfully.

Lightning struggled valiantly to get a grip on this determinedly pesky object as it unremittingly squirmed, though finally slowed, trapped under his tremendous body weight. He slowly struggled to a sitting position holding the thing trapped under one tree trunk-sized leg. His paws had the object pinned from each side. He slowly and very carefully lifted his leg just enough to wrap one of his paws around the still jostling object. "This thing has a mind of its own," he said to no one in particular.

Vincen and Bubba watched intently as the Badger, at last, got a grip on the lively object. Bubba had cautiously moved between the Badger and the hole being very careful, this time, to keep his tail out of the way. "I got your back!" he told Lightning Badger reassuringly.

Vincen looked at the young Cheetah and admired his bravery. "I hope you do young one, I hope you do."

"There, I think I've got it," announced Lightning. "I will pull it out on three. Please be ready to assist me should this thing be hungry," he said as he cautiously looked over at the two wide-eyed, amazed onlookers.

"Sh, sh, sure, Luh, Luh, Lightning, wha, wha, whatever," Bubba stammered. He had suddenly felt fear snatch his whole body out from under him. This pang of fear hit the Cheetah unexpectedly hard. In a flash, long suppressed memories roared back to the present. He was instantly reminded, far too graphically, of the earlier tragedy in his life.

6

P oachers. They were truly, the nastiest, the cruelest, the most notorious enemy of the four-legged land walkers of the Great Plains beyond the Rushing River to the east of the Great Mountain. Where they came from was unclear, but come they did, slowly at first, but in vast numbers as time passed. The poachers oozed out of the black moon-time like death-starved banshees. They had no goal in life except the destruction of any valuable living creature, be it land walker or sky-traveler. Where there was a life there could just as well be a death. The poachers definitely cared more for the latter. The more deaths incurred by select four-legged land walkers, the more gold and silver lined a poacher's swelling pockets. They were fond of referring to their innocent victims as "profits." Certain dead four-legged land walkers brought a good amount in trade with stores, for provisions, for cash. Greedy, filthy wealth could be had if one poached correctly, tirelessly and without conscience. Greed-ridden wealth was bought by killing lots and lots of "profits."

The poacher's chosen "profits" had been running for day-rounds on end. Running and hiding. Hiding and running. One by one the numbers of the "profits" were dwindling. No self-serving poacher would leave a territory unless the territory's "profits" were numbered at or below zero. Every "profit" was worth the effort, but one particular kind was extra valuable. These "profits" were fast four-legged land walkers who made the hunt most interesting and the kill even more satisfying. Only a poacher who knew his business well could successfully hunt these creatures. These "profits" were Cheetahs, the fastest land walker ever to live, the most valuable profit when properly taken and the fastest land walker yet to disappear.

Shuko was not royalty. His name meant "Safe Keeper." His family had never ruled any area of land just as they had never been ruled by any land. The land where they now roamed was unfamiliar as was every land through which they traveled. They were always displaced, but they were still free to roam, even in the face of danger. Shuko and his family had grown used to roaming under an always looming threat of danger. Poachers were as much a part of their lives as the sun. Family numbers were dwindling and each day they were questioned whether they would all see each other again. This was a miserable life for any creature to be subjected to. Shuko's kind had lived with the risks while always hoping for a better way of life.

Shuko had heard many stories of the Great Forest from several sky-travelers. The sky-travelers would fly in once and again on their way to and from the Great Sea when the high invisible currents would wind them in the same path as the wandering Cheetahs. They told tales about the abundance of peace that had come to the Great Forest after the Terrible Years. They shared that all four-legged land walkers were welcome within the trees of the Great Forest. The gray Wolves had once ruled the Great Forest and now the lone surviving Prince was regaining a strong leadership role there, thanks to the Great Eagle. The two-leggers were not especially welcome anymore after the "killing" of the Wolves. Two-leggers stayed far away from the Great Forest out of a fear of deathly revenge. Every now and again, a Talker would travel through the Great Forest on horseback repenting for the misguided two-leggers that were deceived into that awful display of bloodletting.

The Cheetahs, Shuko made clear to the sky-travelers, had no tolerance for two-leggers of any kind. In Shuko's mind all two-leggers were capable of taking "profits" and he had no desire to associate with any of them. He made this distrust blatantly obvious to every member of his family. He was determined to get his family safely to the Great Forest. He often thought, though a bit morbidly, that it would be the last thing he would ever do.

"Shuko, they are coming again. We must be moving," a magnificently breath-taking Cheetah was whispering in his ear. It was half moon time. It was as dark as this day-round would become. The beautiful mother of Shuko's many litters of cubs was the most amazing Cheetah ever to walk the land or race the wind. She was not an unusually large Cheetah, but her markings were striking and her eyes betrayed a wisdom privileged to few creatures. She had known Shuko since they were both tiny cubs searching for cover among the high grasses of the Great Plains. The pride was larger then, but, of course, the poachers had been fewer.

Their latest, surviving offspring was a bit too much like his father. This medium-sized cub had an attitude that was not all that polite. His snout was constantly on the receiving end of swats by his Mother's stern, yet gentle disciplinary procedures. His attitude and wisecracks betrayed an extraordinary sense of direction, his mother's intelligence and an unquenchable thirst for adventure. But far too often he would open his mouth instead of his mind. He was called "Bubanche" which meant, "Quick Witted." He was quite a titanic storm of energy in what was still a small package.

"Yes Kotay, I have heard their rumblings, the noisy fools. Now is the time. We must move on. Where is the cub? Did you retrieve him from his cover?" Shuko asked.

"Here I am, Father," came the energetic cub. "I'm ready, can we go? I know the way. I've been scouting it since Mother woke me. Please, may I lead the way, please?" the cub begged.

"Sure son, lead the way." Shuko saw much of his own personality in this little fellow and thought better of suppressing the energy that seemed boundless in his son. "There is no one I would rather have at the head of the trail. But, please son, try to hold the speed down to a run. You have grown into the fastest Cheetah that your mother and I have ever known. We are not as fast. Please temper your stride with ours."

"Thank you father, thank you," came the excited reply and they were off.

"Shuko, do you think it wise to let the cub lead the way?" asked Kotay.

"My dear mate," Shuko answered seriously, "have you noticed how few of us are left? I will tell you. The three of us are all that is left. We were hidden too well to be found. That cub of ours has an uncanny knack for covering where no living creature would think to look and that is usually right under their snouts. Just before moon time the poachers arrived and took the others. I did not tell you or Bubanche. The news was too devastating. We may not make the full day-round Kotay. I have let the cub lead in case we have to divert the poacher's direction should they come from behind us. If anything happens to us, he must run and not stop. I have warned him against using the intelligence your blood has been so kind to pass down to him. He must not use that keen sense of his until he absolutely trusts those around him. When he deems that time to be right, then all around him will be pleasantly

The Land of Nuorg

surprised, I'm sure. Now, his only chance to make the safety of the Great Forest is his unfailing speed. He must rely on it alone if we are no longer around to safeguard him. There is no adult Cheetah who has ever lived that can match Bubanche's speed when he is running at half his normal gait. There is no poacher who can either. When he runs, he will be safe. He has no idea how fast he truly is."

"I fear for us Shuko," Kotay responded somberly, gently moving to his side. "I have a very uneasy feeling in my bones that I have never felt so strongly before. It is almost like I know when we will be taken. The time for that, I feel, is coming shortly. My nerves are ill at ease."

"I know, Kotay, I feel the same as you. We must be strong and sacrifice ourselves if necessary for our son. He is our future. Surely the Prince of the Great Forest will see his unique gifts, as have we, should he arrive there," Shuko said proudly.

"As you say, Shuko he is an amazing cub. He is so much like his father," Kotay humbly agreed.

"Do not forget, he gets his appearance, no less than his intelligence, from his beautiful mother!" Shuko mentioned as he tried to lighten the now somber mood they shared.

The night of traveling went without incident. The next sun time arrived while the Cheetahs covered themselves the best they could. The tall grass was now giving way to more rocks and barren land. They were nearing the foot of the Great Mountain. Should the poachers decide to follow them here, the Cheetahs would have nowhere to hide. It was a chance they had to take to gain freedom from fear of capture and the strain of being on the run. The closer they got to their destination, the more they began to long for the protection of the Great Forest. That moon-time, before Bubanche went to sleep, his mother and father came to him with grim expressions on their faces. They carefully explained to their young cub the developing situation. They explained they were running out of the cover they had trusted for so many years to keep them safe. Shuko told his son over and over again that to be free he must run, run faster than the wind. The cub assured his parents that should anything happen to them, he would run for the Great Forest. He would grow into a son that would make them proud. He knew they would be watching from somewhere. Kotay gently walked to her son's side and affectionately nuzzled him as she covered him for sleep. "Rest well my son," she whispered.

Death was not something that alarmed the Cheetahs. Poachers and the death they inflicted stalked them every day from birth. Cheetahs would be taken, a tear would be shed and life as they knew it would continue. Never would a Cheetah talk long of death. They would simply state that one of their own had been taken. Whether by a poacher or fatal accident, the Cheetahs believed that being taken also had its advantages. If a Cheetah were taken, the race for life would be over and the enjoyment and peace of whatever lay ahead would then begin. It was hard for them to imagine that running for their lives was all there was in store for them. They felt confident there was something more.

Bubanche would, more than likely, understand should his parents be taken. He would miss them. He would shed some tears, but they had taught him well and they had prepared him for the worst. He would survive. He always knew, as Cheetahs are taught, that nothing in his life was to be regretted and every day lived was one more day to celebrate.

The poachers successfully tracked the Cheetahs to the foot of the mountain. They would rest until morning and take their "profits" as soon as light revealed the Cheetahs hiding place. There was one Cheetah that would bring an exorbitant amount of trade in this bunch. It was a female and would be worth the effort of tracking the two adults and one cub all the way to the mountain. Her fur would make some fortunate two-legger a very handsome, expensive coat. That brand of thinking is what drove the poachers on.

They had to take the "profits" before they made an escape over the mountain. Even the poachers knew of the danger and certain death that lay on the other side of the mountain. No poacher, no matter how brave, would ever go over the mountain for a "profit." It would be suicide and poachers were a cowardly bunch. The horror stories that had been told to them of the Wolves and Hawks that lived on the mountain down to the other side made their despicable skin crawl. No poacher would ever cross that barrier.

The Wolves, they were told, would eat two-leggers alive. Sometimes the Wolves would eat just enough of a two-legger to make him unable to move. A horrid, slow death would follow. The red Hawks of the mountain would circle the dying two-legger, swooping down for a tasty bite if they got the notion. The Hawks also stood watch over the dying two-leggers to alert the Wolves of any potential rescuers. The rescuers would be dealt with severely as well. Death by one of these Wolves would wait and wait until the two-legger lay begging to die. The Wolf would come sit by the two-legger and howl for hours on end taking a savage bite out of the two-legger whenever the pain would make him numb. The Wolf would stay with a dying two-legger for as many days as it took until the two-legger finally, mercifully died a slow, disgusting death. The Wolf would then drag what was left of the two-legger's body to the foot of the mountain for all to see. A bloodcurdling howl from the Wolf warned all two-leggers of the danger that trespassing on the mountain would bring. The howl also told the Vultures it was time for their meal. The Talkers had told of these horrors every time they visited around the two-leggers. The Talkers of the Hewitt Mountes were especially graphic in their renditions of the story. It is told among the two-leggers that those Talkers had experienced the worst of the Wolves.

Moon time did not arrive too quickly for this family of Cheetahs. The poachers were near. Kotay could smell their foul odor in the air. She knew Bubanche soon would be traveling over the mountain alone. Shuko very quietly woke his son and gave him the last directions he would ever receive from his father. "Son, now is the time. They have found us. They are now searching us out. You have but one thing to do. Do you know what that one thing is, Bubanche?"

"Yes Father, I know," replied a heartbroken, yet determined Cheetah cub.

Kotay arrived silently. The look in her eyes told the two males that it was definitely time for Bubanche to be off. "Bubanche, my little wonder, use your speed and make the Great Forest. There is a Hawk above. He has been circling since the Poachers arrived. I am sure he will be the one to lead you over the Mountain. Our time has come. Your Father and I will head in different directions as you make your escape. Do not come for us. Now, go son, run. Run as fast as you can." Kotay took one look at Bubanche then Shuko. She nodded to Shuko and licked the top of Bubanche's head with her tongue. "Never forget my love for you, son," she said and she was gone.

Shuko gently nudged his Son on his way. "My love for you is truly great, young Cheetah. Be gone, Son!" With that he snarled a vicious roar and was off. He sped away in the opposite direction from that Kotay had just taken.

The poachers heard that roar and immediately made their way to the source of the sound. Bubanche had heard everything his parents had told him, but he could not leave them. He began running directly for his Mother. "Mother," he cried.

Not too far off Kotay heard the cry and stopped. She roared back at him, "Run away to the mountain, Bubanche. The other way"!

Her warning to her beloved son was all that was needed for the poachers to trap her. The badly worn net fell over her the instant she hesitated. "That was such a nice thing of her do, wasn't it?" one gruff voiced poacher said to another standing close by. "I didn't think catching her would be that easy. Not with the little one close and all. It's too bad these "profits" have so little smarts. If they were only half as wise as we are, taking them would be so much more interesting."

"Funny you mention that little one. Take a look at the treasure I have in my net," came another raspy voice walking up to the first two carrying a net slung over his shoulder.

Kotay looked at the third voice and screamed, "Noooooo!"

The third poacher, a small, slightly overweight little two-legger, laid the net on the ground slinging his leg over it to settle the frisky cub long enough to club him. "Wait a minute," he said, "This little fellow's hide is prettier than his mother's. I think I'll keep him for my own coat." With that he reached down and carefully peeled the net off of the struggling cub. "Watch that, you little rascal," he said as the cub extended his claws, raking them across the poacher's arm sending thin lines of blood trickling down the arm. He reached down, grabbed the cub by the scruff of the neck and tried vainly to hoist him into the air. The cub fought with great tenacity. He squirmed so much that he knocked the poacher's thin sword out of its scabbard on the side belt of the grotesque two-leggers middle section. It fell to the ground as the cub was eventually lifted high into the air. The cub and his mother made eye contact one last time as the thin blade of the sword lay shimmering under the moonlight. The cub would never again take his eyes off of that small sword.

"Noooooo!" Kotay screamed again.

Out of a barely noticeable clump of rocks, the other adult Cheetah sprang onto the back of the poacher holding the cub high. The menacing Cheetah sank his razor sharp teeth into the shoulder of the poacher right where the base of his filthy neck connected with his sweaty back. A paw with extended claws ripped flesh from the

The Land of Nuorg

poacher's face as the Cheetah's teeth gripped the sinewy muscles that held the two-legger's back together. The poacher immediately dropped the cub. The cub hastily picked up the sword in his mouth and scampered off at a very high rate of speed. The male Cheetah was relentless in his attack on the two-legger and clawed savagely at any part of the poacher's body that moved. The Cheetah released his hold on the two-legger's neck just long enough to rip another chunk of the shoulder off of the poacher's body as his claws continued their rampage on the flesh that remained intact. The poacher was now on the ground twisting and writhing in pain. The first poacher was still holding on to his "profit" as the battle between Cheetah and two-legger continued.

"Kill this monster!" he managed to scream to the second poacher before his voice was silenced by the Cheetah's claws.

With that, the second poacher raised his club. He began violently swinging at the crazed Cheetah. With each arc of his club he made solid contact with the determined Cheetah's body. Blow after blow of bone-shattering strikes rained down on the Cheetah, but he would not release the mortally wounded two-legger. The Cheetah shook the defeated poacher's heavy body as every ounce of energy drained from them both. Finally, the Cheetah relented. The final crushing blow came to the base of the Cheetah's skull. This blow ended the Cheetah's attack once and for all.

The first poacher turned on his "profit" in rage. He struck her while she was still trapped in the net. He stabbed her once in the side with his spear making sure not to damage her magnificent hide. One puncture wound, expertly placed, successfully took her life. The poacher yelled for his lone surviving accomplice, "Go find that cub. I want a matching set! Do not come back without him, or I will kill you as well!" he continued. The first poacher looked at the dead two-legger in disgust. "Fool," he muttered. He then joined in the pursuit of the cub.

The raptor had been circling and witnessed the whole bloody rampage of the courageous Cheetah and the mindless slaying of the female. The Hawk flew lower, much lower, and increased his speed. He had a target to hit and it must be perfect. One mistake and he would fail. He couldn't miss this opportunity. Down he flew. He leveled off just above ground level, blowing right past the second poacher who was in full stride chasing their common target. The sky-traveler aimed his honed talons at the scruff of his target's fleeing neck. "My," he thought to himself as he struggled to catch up, "this is one very fast four-legger." The Hawk was undaunted by the Cheetah's speed and picked up his pace significantly. "This should just about do it," he told himself. With a perfectly timed capture the sky-traveler pulled up the front of his body, extended his accurately aimed talons and plucked the Cheetah cub right off of the ground.

The second poacher was witness to the incident. He cursed the wind and whatever else was within hearing range with a hatred-laced, loud voice, his clenched fists flailing harmlessly in the air. How would he explain this to the first poacher? The poacher's valuable "profit" had instantly turned into the Hawk's next meal. He, with good reason, dreaded going back to camp.

The sky-traveler arched his head skyward, flapped his mighty wings and carried his prize proudly to an altitude suitable for flying safely over the Great Mountain. He majestically left the foot of the mountain in his wake. The cub was in no danger of falling out of the sky-traveler's strong grip and relaxed. He could not help but think that he had escaped out of the fire and into the pot. The two of them flew for some time without ever trying to say a word to each other. Eventually, the Cheetah--after all, he did have that attitude his parents had talked so frequently about--said to the Eagle, "Suh, suh, Sir Ha, Hah, Hawk, are you ga, ga, gawin, going to ea, ea, eat me?

"Certainly not, little Cheetah cub, whatever gave you that idea?" answered the sky-traveler gently. "And I am not a Hawk. I am an Eagle!"

7

"Steady, Lightning. Make sure you have it," Vincen warned.

"I'm ready, one, two," counted the Badger.

"Wuh, wait just a click," ordered Bubba, regaining his senses. "Are you sure you have it?"

"Yes, I am sure. Now, if you don't mind, I'll be on with the count. Remember, on three. One...two...three!" Lightning pulled the object out from under his enormous leg and held it high with both of his strong forearms so, whatever it was, it would not have a chance to attack any of them. "There," he said looking straight at Vincen, "What is it?"

The Badger had fought with this object that was now towering over Bubba's and Vincen's heads, but had yet to look at it. Vincen saw what it was and so did Bubba. Vincen's whole body slumped as his eyes rolled to the top of their sockets to view what Lightning was holding. Bubba had to push the bottom of his mouth back up with his front paw and hold it there for fear of it falling completely off of his head.

Vincen marveled at the object as it wavered gently side to side under its own power. He clicked his head up and to the side so he could catch a better view of the object the Badger was holding so high off of the ground. He had never known that this object possessed any kind of power. But, contrary to all common knowledge, there it was, acting very much in possession of some power. It was certainly giving every indication that it held some kind of secret that no living thing in the Great Forest had ever known existed. A faint light continued to glow from inside. "I find this hard to believe. Now our mystery, by a culmination of strangeness, complicates itself," Vincen stated deliberately.

Mystic's wand/staff was glowing. Obviously Vincen and the Badger had not been tricked by reflections of the sun earlier in the day-round. Vincen had, most definitely, seen a glow behind the trees. After this latest revelation, he understood the glow had come from the wand/staff. Lightning had not imagined the wand/staff glowing either, when he saw it standing next to the door on Mystic's stoop. It had absolutely been glowing. But why? Vincen suddenly became more determined than ever to find out.

These friends were now on an adventure with twists and turns that were beginning to overwhelm even Vincen's wise, experienced mind. Bubba was dumbfounded as he continued to hold his lower jaw in place. Lightning was now holding the wand/staff with both of his strong, massive arms. He was too concerned with not losing his grip on the wand/staff to bother with any explanations of why things were happening as they were.

The wand/staff began to slowly circle above Lightning's head as Vincen and Bubba watched. The Badger was noticing, as well, that with each circle the wand/staff became heavier. It had begun to pulsate with an intermittent rhythm. The glowing and pulsating were becoming increasingly stronger. Lightning was struggling to hold the wand/staff steady. He was afraid of what would happen if he lost his grip. Would this thing be able to seek out and kill each of them? It certainly had acted as if it easily could have when it was barreling toward the gurgling hole. He made up his mind that he was not going to relinquish his hold on this object no matter what it did. If it got out of control, then so would he. This adventure was becoming serious now. Only those who were strong and strong willed would survive. Lightning, the irregular Badger was sure of that.

Bubba let go of his jaw and, much to his relief, it stayed in place. "Vih, Vih, Vincen, wha, what hah, has ca, caused tha, that to ah, ah, act so stra, stra, strangely?" The young Cheetah was terrified. He began to feel, again, the same way he had on the day his parents were taken. His ultimate fear at the moment was of becoming a Hawk's next meal.

It was the Cheetah's good fortune or destiny that Vincen had been out scouting on that fateful day. Vincen had been doing a favor for the son of an old friend and had accidentally come upon the poacher's murder of the two adult Cheetahs. He had witnessed everything that happened that morning. He was not going to let, under any circumstances within his control, that terror-stricken Cheetah cub to be chased down and killed. He had seen enough death on that day. He had not hesitated as he heroically swooped down making the daring rescue much to the disdain of the surviving poachers. Vincen was surprised, if not impressed, by the Cheetah's great speed in addition to being mesmerized by his incredible coat. Vincen had never seen a four-legger with such a handsome coat since the day Shine had died from a broken heart at Mystic's side.

"Son, I have no idea why the wand/staff is acting like it is'" answered the Eagle trying to calm the Cheetah. "I believe this mystery or adventure, as you like to call it, is becoming more and more perplexing as this day-round progresses. Please relax, I have seen nothing yet that should frighten you so. These happenings are odd, yet they have not caused any deaths that I know of."

"How can you say that, Vincen?" Lightning asked. "What about Mystic? Where is he? Is he not dead by now? You say that he was sucked down that tiny hole and into who knows where, but that he may not be dead? I am here struggling with Mystic's wand/staff, which has never, ever to my recollection, done anything until now except lay where it has been laid or stand where it has been stood. Yet, it seems now, that it is showing every characteristic of wanting to do away with me and maybe you and maybe the Cheetah as well. Do you not think these actions deserve a better description than odd?" Lightning said a bit harshly.

"I ah, ah, agree," said Bubba although he was not sure if he was more or less terrified after Lightning's statement.

The Cheetah was no less afraid, but he was settling down a bit. It had taken several lines of calming assurances by Vincen as he carried the cub away over the mountain during that life-altering flight before the cub felt at ease. Vincen noticed and was struck by the cub's way of dealing with the death of his parents. The cub seemed to accept the "takings" better than Vincen would have. The cub was, it seemed, prepared for their departure from the land of the dying. As he cared for the cub, Vincen would quickly come to understand why this was so. As he learned more about the Cheetah and his ways, Vincen's admiration and respect for this cub's parents became a matter of great pride and reflection.

***

Once Vincen had the cub safely back on the ground in the Dwelling Places he asked the cub his name. The cub, still feeling the strain of what had taken place, at last, dropped the small sword from his mouth. After holding the sword tightly in his clenched jaws for so long and being quite dazed, the cub could only stutter,"Buh, buh, buh..." A gray Wolf in attendance who had also been adopted by the Eagle much earlier in life, took an immediate liking to the cub and the Cheetah's mumblings stuck as his name. The Cheetah was affectionately called "Bubba" from that day on, much to the chagrin of the Great Eagle.

***

"Wh, where di did th, the wah, wand/st, staff come from, Vih, Vincen?" Bubba asked as he was becoming noticeably more relaxed. "Cuh, can we tah, take it back?"

Vincen had never known the wand/staff to be anything more than a toy that Mystic had held in his mouth since the time he dragged it in to the Dwelling Places when he was a precocious young Wolf. Mystic had been out exploring when he discovered it. The Wolf and his best friend, Lightning, had been searching the Great Forest on a mission to find a secret treasure as all youngsters do. After the Badger begged Mystic to stop for lunch, they did. They stopped in a clearing neither had ever explored. At the edge, under a tall old maple tree, each sat down unloading their lunch sacks. Well, Mystic's was a sack, but the Badger had brought a rather large lunch pack with him. To tell the truth, the Badger never went anywhere without it and the pack was always full of food. The Wolf and the Badger each ate their fill of food. Mystic ate fruits and plant roots and the Badger ate everything else, including nuts, berries, plants, fruits and his favorite bark kakes, which were never fully appreciated or eaten by the Wolf. After Mystic had finished his food he stood up and began to explore the clearing. Mystic was searching for anything that would be of importance when telling others of this adventure.

Lightning was still actively eating his lunch when a loud voice hollered to him from Mystic's general direction. "Lightning, Lightning! Come help me!" the Wolf called from the bottom of a steep dry riverbed.

The Badger got up quickly and hurried over to Mystic's aid eating his last bark kake as he ran. "Where are you?" exclaimed the Badger?"

"Down here," called Mystic

The burly Badger plodded over to where Mystic's voice had called to him. He spied the Wolf sprawled awkwardly at the bottom of a steep bank of a dry riverbed just on the other side of a short hedgerow. "Why are you down there?" the Badger asked, parting the undergrowth.

"Be careful, Lightning. I got too close to the edge of the bank and stumbled down here. I need you to help me get out. Please find something to pull me up. I hit my head on something hard and I am feeling a little queasy because of it," Mystic explained.

"Sure thing, Mystic, I will find something," the Badger answered.

A large knot was swelling at the back of Mystic's head. It was beginning to ache. He turned his head toward where he had fallen to locate the rock on which his head had so solidly landed. He soon discovered that there were no rocks to be found in this riverbed. "That's strange," he said to himself. "I know I must have hit something hard. What could it have been?"

Mystic clumsily got to his feet and began digging under where his head had landed. His paws had not made two swipes at the dirt before he discovered what he had hit. He couldn't believe his eyes. He had accidentally happened upon a buried treasure! This was just what they had been looking for! He continued digging around the hard object. He soon found that the part he hit was round and had once been shiny. He was excited and dug haphazardly around the object only to find that the round end was connected to an exquisite metal and cherry wood handle about as long as his tail. This handle was not made by any four-legged land walker and, for that matter, neither was the round end. How had it come to this spot? No two-legged land walkers had been in the Great Forest in ages, except for an occasional Talker. It could not have been left by them. They never ventured this deep into the woods.

"Come quick, Lightning! Look what I have found!" Mystic yelled.

"Okay, okay," answered the Badger, 'But I have found nothing to pull you out."

"Never mind about that. I found something I will use to get out of here. Come look!" said the excited Wolf.

The Badger stood at the edge of the bank looking down at Mystic and the object he was holding in his mouth. Lightning asked, "What is that you've found? A big stick?"

"No, it is a buried treasure. I knew we would find one!" Mystic replied.

"Sure looks like a stick to me," Lightning stated, shaking his head.

"Have you ever seen a stick with a round thing like this on the end?" Mystic questioned from the bottom of the riverbed, holding out the clear, ball-like end of the object in the Badger's direction.

"No, I can't say that I have," the Badger replied. "But it still looks like a big stick."

"You must study it closely," Mystic demanded. "This is positively not a stick!"

"Well then, what would you call it?" queried the Badger, "cause from here it looks like a big stick!"

Mystic's head was not hurting anymore. The excitement of the find erased all thoughts and feelings of pain. He scratched and clawed his way up the side of the riverbed using the handle of the treasure as a leverage device to help pull himself up. Once at the top he again showed the "stick" to Lightning. "Now, Lightning, look closely. Does this look like a stick to you?"

"Well, I guess it doesn't after all. If not a stick, then what would you call it, oh Prince of the Great Forest?" the Badger playfully asked.

"Well, I don't know exactly, but I gave it much thought as I made my way up that bank. I have decided to call it a wand/staff," declared Mystic.

"Why not one or the other?" asked Lightning.

"Well, Lightning, you have two names. Why can't this?" Mystic replied. "And furthermore, as Prince of the Great Forest, I will use my wand/staff to appoint you as the Duke of the Great Meadow!" Mystic amusingly added.

"Great, now will you behave so I can finish my lunch?" asked the Badger.

"Why by all means, please do, Lightning, the irregular Badger, Duke of the Great Meadow!" Mystic spent the rest of the Badger's lunch break studying his new-old wand/staff. He was trying to figure out who or what made it and where it came from. The answer would come in time, but not during this day-round. "Come, Duke of the Great Meadow, we must hurry back to the Dwelling Places of your elders or the Great Eagle will deal with us in a most dire way. I believe we have wandered into the South Quarter by mistake. Do you see the top of the Great Mountain just over the trees to the North?"

"I knew we were somewhere we weren't supposed to be!" grumbled Lightning. "My Mother warned me about following you on your adventures."

The big crystal globe was dragging well behind the handle as Mystic led the way back to the Dwelling Places. The round end jostled over every bump and rock in its path. Mystic decided to call the find his wand/staff permanently. No four-legger or sky-traveler seemed to know why it wasn't called one or the other and, when asked, Mystic simply stated that he didn't know either. Maybe it was because of the crystal sphere at the end of it. No one knew and none of his friends really cared. It became Mystic's weapon of choice. The two soon became inseparable. That is, until now.

***

Lightning was still holding Mystic's wand/staff high over his head as the speed in which it circled increased. The round ball end began to glow even brighter as the pulsing, in turn, grew more intense. The Badger looked up in the sky while the wand/staff continued to circle. He noticed that something about where he was standing was eerily familiar. "Vincen, is that not the top of the Great Mountain to the north?"

"Yes, yes, of course it is. Why do you ask?" Vincen answered.

"Oh mercy. Bubba, please come to your senses and walk over to the west side of this clearing. Make your way into the trees and describe to me what you find," the Badger said very convincingly. "Hurry!" added the Badger. The strength was fading from Lightning. How long he could control this wand/staff was any creature's guess.

Sensing the urgency in the Badger's voice, Bubba gathered himself and hurried over to the west side of the clearing. His tail had just disappeared into the trees when he shouted back to the others. "I think I see a big ditch over here. It is quite deep with steep sides. I guess it could have been a river at one time."

Vincen was even more curious now. "Why did you ask him to do that, Lightning?"

"Bubba, come back here quickly. Oh mercy," the Badger said wistfully. Bubba was back in a flash. His speed was absolutely amazing. "This is the very clearing where Mystic and I stopped to eat lunch on the day-round when he found this very wand/staff, that I am holding onto for dear life. He stumbled and fell into that same dry riverbed that Bubba has just re-discovered. I believe if you go to the south side and look under that ancient maple tree, you might find the remains of Mystic's old lunch sack that he never retrieved after he found this wand/staff. I went back to get my pack, noticed that he had left his and, in my haste to return to the Dwelling Places on time, left it where it lay."

This was all very puzzling to Vincen. He paused for an instant before swiftly flying over to the tree that Lightning had mentioned. With his beak close to the ground, Vincen searched the area under the old maple tree. It took about one half of a click until he raised his majestic head victoriously. Gripped loosely in his beak, he held a tattered old lunch sack high for the others to see. "Does this look familiar?" Vincen asked as he grasped the sack with his claws before making his way back to the others.

This short diversion did not take very long, but, by the time Vincen returned, Lightning was struggling tremendously with the wand/staff. The power emanating from it was staggering. It was circling, it was pulsating, it glowed brighter with every revolution. Vincen and Bubba were standing back, watching in awe the display of strength between the Badger and the wand/staff. The Badger was losing his strength as the wand/staff was gaining it. Finally, Lightning could struggle no more. At the top of his voice Lightning took a last valiant stance. The Badger yelled at the top of his voice, "Mystic, where are you? We are here and we have come after you!"

Instantly the pulsing ball on the wand/staff began to shine brilliantly like the brightest mid day-round sun. It was a bright white light that scared everyone, even Vincen. The wand/staff began, now, to violently circle and pulsate, yet Lightning was determined not to let it go. The wand/staff made powerful sweeping circles. The light it emitted was almost blinding in its brilliance. Vincen had never acted scared before, but this, this frightened him, although it was, at the same time, fascinating, very fascinating.

The hole immediately began to open again with a swelling and shaking of the ground that was, quite indisputably, nerve-wracking. The hole loudly opened wide in one huge gulp of earth, not at all like before. The water returned too, only this time there was not bubbling and gurgling, but violent spewing and roaring and thrashing. The water rushed in like it was making up for lost time. Everyone was shaking. They nervously backed quickly away from the opening with the Cheetah leading the way. The three friends' wide-eyed astonishment increased when, just as mysteriously and quickly as it started, the water went dead silent. This whole marvelous and unnerving event could not have lasted more than one click of an Eagle's eye. It was over as soon as it had begun.

Lightning still had a firm grip on the wand/staff and, for all intents and purposes, the wand/staff had settled down considerably. It was now just glowing, leaning toward the opening as if being pulled there.

The Land of Nuorg

The Badger made eye contact with the Eagle and the Eagle with the Cheetah and the Cheetah with the Badger.

"Well, what do we do now?" asked the Badger. "Is this how you remember it Vincen?"

"Yes, Lightning. This is exactly how I remember it, except for the color. It was crystal clear the last time until Mystic stepped into it. Now, it's rather queer. It seems to be thinking, waiting on us to make the first move. I do believe that it is ready," Vincen stated cautiously.

"Excuse me, Vincen", came the Cheetah's voice. "Ready for who, to do what?"

"Why ready for us of course," answered Vincen. "We must each enter that opening in order to find out what has happened to Mystic. It's the only way. You don't see him down there coming for us do you? Hopefully, we will find him unharmed and return with him safely back to the Great Forest."

"You can't be serious?" asked Lightning. "Vincen, what if we don't find him unharmed. What if he is harmed and we end up that way as well? Who will be left to rule the Great Forest? I think I should go alone. I will leave you here to assume Mystic's Rule should I not bring him back. The Cheetah is young. You can groom him for the role of leader just as you groomed Mystic."

Bubba answered, "You are talking out of your mind now, Lightning. I have no ability to rule the Great Forest. I can't even remember to bring food with me when I leave the Dwelling Places. I am fast. That is my gift. I am the fastest land walker to ever run these lands. I have been so since I was born. That is my destiny and the use of my speed is for those wiser than I to direct. I am not, nor ever will I be a Ruler."

"He is correct, Lightning," replied Vincen. "I will go. I will rescue our friend alone. You may rule the Great Forest. You have the means. You are strong and intelligent. You have skills that, if developed, will weigh heavily in your favor."

"I'm sorry Vincen. I can't allow that to happen. You are the Ruler should Mystic not return. I must go after him. As you say, I am strong and intelligent. I will bring him back," the Badger answered.

Vincen rebuffed Lightning's statement, "No, no, no. Can you two not see it? We all must go to be successful. Each of us has gifts. That is true. Each of our gifts is wonderful, glorious and individually unique, but apart from each other they become weak with the passing of time. The Cheetah's speed will one day slow. Lightning, one day your strength, your size, they will decrease as your immense girth and muscles slowly age. My keen vision, too, will fade as will the beating of my wings and the thinking in my brain. Only when each of our gifts is united with the others' will they become invincible. I must add that the key to each of our gifts is Mystic. He is our Ruler. His gentle heart, keen hearing and understanding are what complete our individual gifts. Besides, he is the Prince of the Great Forest. He was chosen, not by us to be so, but by fate to be so. We have no idea why these happenings have been put upon us, but we must believe that we have each been chosen for a common purpose. That purpose will never be fulfilled until we are all together again. This may be just a test to see if our willingness to work together outweighs our individual gifts. Fate must not be tempted by our lack of faith."

With that said, Vincen proudly stepped back up to the edge of the hole. Lightning and Bubba followed in turn. The three stared at the water noticing not one solitary ripple was to be seen. No movement was detected whatsoever. The gentle breeze did not even stir the surface of this water. The water wasn't clear like the first time, but one could still see through it easily enough to imagine that it went on endlessly. The water was turning a beautifully rich shade of purple and green. The green might have made the splendid grass of the Great Meadow want for another color.

The water was so perfect that the three friends were under the distinct impression that it was inviting them to jump in. First, nobody moved, then, Vincen stood up as straight and tall as he could. He folded his wings tightly around his sleek body. Bubba and Lightning knew that the time had now come to start the next phase of their adventure.

"Well you two," stated Vincen very matter of factly, "I do not know where we will end up. I don't know if we all will return, but we are all going in. I know that Cheetahs do not like the water, Bubba. Nevertheless, Lightning, take your ax-pike from Bubba's harness, put it in your belt, hold on to the wand/staff with one paw and grab that Cheetah by the tail if you have to. Do not, under any circumstances, let go of either of them."

Vincen then ordered Lightning to dive into the water before his tail was completely under water. He wasn't sure why he said this, but at the time, it seemed like the correct instructions to give. "Lightning, I will say this one more time, do not release your grip on the wand/staff or the Cheetah!" Vincen took one last look up toward his majestic perch, his eyes caressing the gorgeous serene surroundings of the Great Forest. He flapped his wings once for altitude, then dove down, head first into the calm, colorful water. The water never made a ripple as the Eagle's body sliced through its surface.

Lightning, still feeling the power and determination of Vincen's voice tightened his grip on the wand/staff and grabbed Bubba's tail with his other paw. He dove in exactly as Vincen had ordered. Bubba quickly followed, tail first, crying in pain, because Lightning had taken hold of Bubba's tail in exactly the wrong spot.

Once the last whisker on Bubba's snout had passed through the surface of the water, his cry of pain died away in the gentle breeze. The water lay silently still before it fell away. The hole then closed. It shut itself tight becoming, instantly, as dry as a long dead bone.

8

Mystic thought he was still alive, although he was not sure why. How long had he been in here? However, he assumed that since he was more interested in surviving, time was not a major concern right now. How long he would stay in here, where he was being taken and where he was, were all out of his control. Eventually, he hoped, he would stop sinking, if that was actually what was happening. He was awkwardly confused by the water that was surrounding him, for it seemed to be moving, as a whole, right along with him. The water did not rush by him like a raging river. He was not tossed and thrown about with reckless abandonment. The water did not allow him to rise to the surface as the water in the Black Pond had done on occasion. Undoubtedly, it was not the same kind of water that living things drowned in, for he had never felt any urgency to paddle to the shallows, which was good, because there were no shallows available.

Miraculously, he had continued to breathe in this liquid, and if it was indeed water, then so be it. Mystic took normal breaths at normal intervals with the liquid taking the place of air deep inside him. Mystic felt a bit of relief, since, at any time, he could move where he wished in this unique liquid world. He never panicked. The confines of the liquid reminded him of being inside the hollow log where Vincen had protected him so long ago. However, when looking from the inside out, he saw nothing but a shiny hard surface instead of the dull inside of a tree. This hollow log was also much, much longer. Occasionally, he would walk to the edge of the water and watch the solid mass of brilliantly speckled, glistening rock pass by. He stood up or sat down at his pleasure, although no matter how much he did any of those things, he could never go anywhere besides where the liquid wanted to take him. He could not escape from it. If he did, where would he go? He had never felt the need to struggle since entering the opening. Something about the liquid comforted him, enabling him to stay content and under his own thought processes. Wherever he was headed was not an issue. He had felt that another power had been leading him along throughout this entire journey. He, long ago, decided not to worry about it, instead, he would enjoy it as long as he could. Wherever he was going, he was surely on a direct path there. Then the light began to fade away and the darkness grew.

Mystic saw nothing but darkness for a very long time. Thoughts raced through his mind of his very earliest memories of Sky and Giant up to this very point. "Is this what it is like to be born, or is this what it is like to die?" he wondered. He pondered those thoughts and many more. He wondered again if this was death. "No, this cannot be death," he concluded. His parents had implored him to believe that in death one follows a great light into a new wonderful life somewhere else, somewhere beyond the Great Forest, beyond the edge of all lands. Or one may experience constant tormenting pain as he guessed the killers of his family were dealing with. When he had almost resigned himself to the bleak possibility that he would never see it again, faint light began creeping up on him. Slowly at first, then the light began rushing directly at him. "Hmmm, maybe I am dead," he thought briefly. Just as the light reached the same brightness as the sun had been when he began this day-round, he stopped sinking and started flying. He left the liquid world in a geyser-like plume of liquid. He was thrown a few training beats down into the air, or up into the air. This feat did confuse him somewhat. He floated slightly as his momentum changed direction. Then he proceeded to fall down or up. Whichever it was, he was hoping for a soft landing.

The landing came suddenly with a thud. It was not a hard landing, but it did knock the breath out of him. "No, I'm certainly not dead," he gasped as he attempted to catch his breath, not immediately doing so. He opened his eyes to get his bearings. He discovered he was still moving, albeit sideways. His belly had landed square in the middle of some soft material with a knobby ridge running through it. As his eyes came into focus he saw lush green grass and a well-traveled path of dirt. He also noticed four muscular legs moving in a slow, deliberate fashion as he was being carried along the path as well. Although he was recovering his breath slowly, his mind was working quite well. He slowly came to the realization that he had landed on something or someone. Whatever it was, the addition of his weight had not caused the creature to break stride. It was as if something landed on this thing's back all the time.

"I wonder where I am and what kind of creature I am on?" Mystic exclaimed to himself, never expecting an answer in return.

A belated click later, a merry, but bland voice said, "You, em friend, at least em assume ye are em friend, have landed on em loaded now back. Welcome emto here from wherever ye were. I hope ye stay ye pleasant and short. Em not would want ye hanging around on em backside for many plods of em feet or more. Em should get weary to fall on ye. Much displeasure may ye way come if done. You see em large. Ye are light, but annoying em then as em would struggle to mend ye and be on em legs again."

"Then who are you and where is your dwelling place?" asked Mystic, more than a little confused by this four-legged land walker's way of speaking.

"Who ye ye?" came the voice's reply

"Who ye what?" asked Mystic.

"Who ye ye?" came the reply again.

"Pardon me," said Mystic. "I have no idea what you are saying. You seem to me to be speaking in some kind of flowing riddles, but I will tell you my name, in my speak, in case it might matter to you. I am Mystic, a gray Wolf from the Great Forest. Now who might you be?"

"Em am, em am, and well em don't know who em am. Em really don't have a word," the voice said.

"You don't have a word? Tell me, confusing one, what are you called?" asked an even more confused Mystic.

"Em am called a Donkorse only no word," came the reply. "Em am told em am half donkey and half horse and em don't know which half ye which for em know nil donkey and em know nil horse."

From Mystic's viewpoint, he could not tell either. "Stop moving please. From the moment I landed on your backside you haven't quit walking. Let me get off. I will have a look at you so I can tell you which half is which."

The Donkorse replied, "If ye wish em backside empty."

Suddenly the Donkorse stopped walking and sat down. When he sat down, he sat with a gigantic plop. The plop sent Mystic sprawling off the four-legger's back and rolling off the beaten path. Mystic continued rolling until he found himself tumbling uncontrollably down the steep muddy slope of a deep gully that ran parallel to the path the Donkorse had been following. Finally, the Wolf found himself completely submerged in a very sticky mud hole. He was quite

The Land of Nuorg

perturbed and still could not breathe very well. He managed to stick his head out of the mud high enough to speak to the four-legged creature. "Well, now I feel much better, thank you. Yes, and I can see you so well from down here too," Mystic said loudly and sarcastically from what he correctly assumed was the bottom of the gully. He now raised his head completely out of the deep mud puddle he had just splashed into and shook it madly. Mystic, remaining four-fifths submerged in mud and still not catching full breaths, then added, "Maybe, just maybe I should have asked you to slowly stop walking and remain standing up!"

The Donkorse yelled down the gully at him, shaking his head back and forth in a scolding-like manner. "What do ye think ye ye doing landing on em backside like so y telling em what to do one assumed friend?" the Donkorse asked. He continued, "Assumed friend, ye looked much better be em here."

Mystic seemed a bit surprised and embarrassed by this sudden outburst. He quickly changed the tone of his voice as he struggled mightily to climb out of the gooey hole with the mud clinging to his fur like a second slimy, heavy skin. He dreaded doing any strenuous climbing with his wounded front paw. He had a brief memory flash mentioning this to himself, "My left paw should be throbbing. Was it not the one that Vincen so savagely bit to get my attention away from the well? Yes, it should be hurting, but it is not." He pried his wounded paw out of the mud and studied it. He saw no sign of damage. He licked clean the area where he thought he remembered the wound, only to find no trace of it. Even more strange to Mystic was that he had never felt pain from the wound at anytime when he was bouncing and sliding down the gully. He licked his foreleg completely clean discovering that the wound was gone. It was completely healed. Astonishingly enough, there was no scar to be found either. Furthermore he noticed that the mud tasted quite delicious and helped himself to quite a bit more of it. "Well" he thought, "All of this is a tad unexpected."

For every step he struggled up the slope, he took one-half a step back. His muddy paws were slipping. He could not get a grip to save his life. Mystic had almost forgotten about the Donkorse. He looked up the hill to see him sitting down, getting quite a kick out of watching the mud caked creature trying to climb out of the gully. Mystic, feeling much better now though completely filthy, remembered the Donkorse's questions and replied to him between climbing up and sliding back,

"Well...I just happened to get dropped out of the sky and I...didn't see you. I did not intend...to land on your backside or...anything else's backside. I am very sorry for the trouble...I have caused you. Would you mind...telling me where I am? I've...been traveling in a peculiar fashion...for a while and I've lost...my bearings." Actually, Mystic had been sinking down through the water, but the water threw him up in the air or down through the air and he fell back down or up to the ground in a roundabout sort of way.

"You, em friend, if em can still call ye that, ye climbing to dee top of sweeeet guuully, looking like a mud kaki, beside "The Path To Where I Am Going.""

"Sweet Gulley, humph," aptly named, thought Mystic. "I know that much," said Mystic to the Donkhorse, "but where is this path and where does it lead?"

"This path ye in dee small woods side of dee sweet gully streem and the path, it leads to where I am going," the Donkorse replied. "If you friend must know exactly where it leads, then by surely means, follow it." The Donkorse smiled politely at Mystic, rose to his feet and continued on his way. Suddenly Donkorse grimaced, stopping dead in his tracks.

"Wait...a click...Donkorse," Mystic said, still struggling to get up the muddy slope. "You...just spoke...in my speak, quite...correctly, I might add. Do not...just leave me in this...situation. I have no idea...where your path leads."

"It leads to where I am going," said the Donkorse, thinking to himself that a major mistake had been made. He hurriedly started on his way.

"Please stop...Donkorse!" Mystic pleaded.

"Very good, em will stop." Donkorse did stop and immediately plopped down into a sitting position. This seemed to be the normal way he stopped.

"Thank...you sir," Mystic acknowledged.

"No sir, em Donkorse," replied Donkorse.

Mystic was almost to the top, now talking to himself, "I have got to figure out...what that four-legger is saying...and move on."

Immediately, the Donkorse again got up and left on his way.

"Stop," Mystic cried again.

The Donkorse did and promptly sat down.

"Why were you leaving again, when I...plainly asked you to stop?" questioned Mystic as he finally crawled up and out of the gully looking like a big brown Porcupine. The mud was so sticky that, when he tried to shake it off, it just matted his fur more and more, building many small short spikes all over his body.

"Ye friend politely asked em to move on. Em to go again," said the Donkorse politely.

"I was talking to myself," said Mystic.

"Oh for dee concern, em heard friend say move on, em did," Donkorse replied.

The Wolf closed his eyes, took in a deep breath, slowly let it out and tried to gather his thoughts. He opened his eyes, walked over to the front of the four-legger, looked at the big Donkorse sitting directly in front of him now and smiled. "Fine. Fine, just sit still. I want to talk to you for a little while, if I may," Mystic said calmly, being careful not to say the wrong words to the Donkorse. He had never been more unsure of what to say in his entire life.

"Certainly, friend talk to em ye so fine," said the Donkorse.

"I will assume, that you just said that it would be fine to talk with you, so I will. Please be patient with me and do not get up and walk away," Mystic said very carefully.

Donkorse was ready to stand up and be on his way again when Mystic realized his mistake. "No stop, I am sorry, I did not mean walk away. I meant stay seated, please, please stay seated."

"Please, this or that not both em should stay?" replied Donkorse.

"Yes, yes please stay, please stay. Stay right here," Mystic thought Donkorse got his meaning this time.

The Donkorse was actually a very lovable and kind four-legger, though Mystic could not figure out if he was very intelligent or just the opposite. His vocabulary, his way of speaking, they were giving Mystic crazy fits. Mystic was hoping that this confusing language was not universal in this land.

The Donkorse did not look half Donkey and half Horse. It looked like all of the above. Some might say he looked like a very tall Donkey, but he had no extraordinary, overly tall ears. They were just long, and his tail was not donkeyish. His head did favor a Horse, but it also favored a Donkey somewhat. Mystic just didn't know. Mystic was very impressed with the size and strength of this creature and was pleased that it wasn't an aggressive four-legger. He did know that he had never seen a four-legger like this in the Great Forest.

"Em will stay, till friend say not," said Donkorse nodding his head up and down.

"Good, good," Mystic now had some kind of grasp on the situation, if only for the short time being.

Not too far from where Mystic and Donkorse's conversation was taking place, a pair of small Hawks, perched in a not-so-tall tree, acutely studied the Wolf's interaction with Donkorse. After a bit of conversing among themselves, one casually took wing in the same general direction that Donkorse was following. The other Hawk stayed, curiously keeping up with the goings on of the two large creatures.

Mystic felt he had a captive audience, though he remained very deliberate with his choice of words. "Now, friend Donkorse, where are we? Where have I traveled? Is there a dwelling place near by? Are there more four-leggers like you here? Do you know how I can get back to where I came?" This was a lot of questions for him to ask, but he thought he should give it a try, just in case Donkorse was able to answer them all.

Donkorse answered simply, "Here, here, yea, no, and no."

Mystic should have known better. He flopped down in front of the Donkorse and covered both eyes with his paws, rubbing them hard. Then he used his paws to move his head from side to side and slowly pulled his paws down his snout until they hit the ground in front of his nose.

"My, oh my, oh my. My mistake. Could you please, answer each question one at a time?" he begged.

"Em did not?" asked Donkorse. "Assumed em friend did question em many to one.

Mystic sat up and dropped his head toward the ground, "Never mind, will you take me to the dwelling place, please?"

"Yes te if ye wish, follow em by Path to Where I Am Going," said the Donkorse who was becoming very confused by Mystic's rambling questions.

Mystic gave up. "Fine, I will follow you. Let us be on your way."

Donkorse stood up and began walking slowly, but steadily, toward where he was going.

Mystic tarried a little behind, never letting Donkorse out of his sight. "Do ye travel here much?" asked Donkorse.

Mystic was afraid to answer the question. He closed his eyes and hoped that he was just hearing things. Again Donkorse asked the question, "Friend, do ye travel here much?"

Mystic said nothing. His head was beginning to ache. He finally got enough courage to return an answer, "Yes," he said, and really hoped he had answered the question correctly. He closed his eyes and slightly turned his head in anticipation of another confusing answer.

"Dee good, friend. Em ye long to go," said the Donkorse cheerfully.

Mystic felt relieved and thought to himself, "That went pretty well."

After they had been walking for a while down the well-traveled path, Mystic was still fighting off the urge to try and converse with Donkorse. He had almost cleared the cobwebs of their last conversation out of his mind. He worked on drumming up support, within his own head, about whether to try speaking with the friendly, although a bit confusing, creature again. Mystic was confounded by the beauty of this strange new land. He was longing to ask detailed questions about it to anything who might be able to give answers that he could readily understand. He had tried so hard to communicate with Donkorse and wondered very quietly to himself if all talking creatures here in this world spoke with such a strange sense of composition.

Mystic stayed intrigued by the sweet tasting, very filling mud he encountered in Sweet Gulley. He was confused though by the lack of water but over abundance of mud in the stream bottom. He would have to ask questions about that place before too long. The Wolf was listening carefully for any other creature sounds only to hear nothing. He searched as far as his Wolf eyes could see on both sides of the path seeing no other creature. Was there any other creature around except for himself and the Donkorse? Just as he asked himself that question, he saw a small sky-traveler flying down the path, but still the Wolf had seen no large creatures such as he and the Donkorse.

The question had entered his mind, "Oh why not?" He thought again to himself, "I will strike up another conversation with the hospitable fellow to see what he knows."

Mystic trotted up even with the Donkorse, slowing his gait to walk at his side. He was afraid the large creature might decide to stop suddenly and, if so, he did not want to be crushed for being too close behind the heavy four-legged land walker. "Pardon me Donkorse, may I ask you a few questions?"

The Donkorse continued his steady gait and replied to Mystic, "Em not to stop ye em."

Mystic felt relieved. He was beginning to understand this language he thought. "Why no, there is no need for you to stop. We can converse as we walk, if that is fine with you."

"Ye sure stop not?" answered the Donkorse curiously.

"No," replied Mystic, "we will keep walking."

"This is no bad, em ye behind dee shine passing. Em must ye move," said Donkorse.

"Well, my friend," began Mystic, "Let me ask you this. I am as sure you know nothing of where I came from as I know nothing of where we are. Could you please enlighten me as to my whereabouts, if you should be so kind? I will most graciously answer any question that you may have, if I can."

"Questions, questions, why questions? Ye, ye here friend. Em ye here. Questions, questions," answered Donkorse with his long, but not overly long, ears twitching.

"I understand, dear friend, that I am here, but where is here?" Mystic asked again.

Donkorse slowed a bit showing signs of confusion with the newcomer. He turned his large head, gazed at Mystic and said, "Em is with em walking to others."

Mystic thought again, "Well, that news is somewhat of a relief. I can only suppose that these others; are easier to carry on a conversation with than this fellow." Mystic inquired of Donkorse, "Are the others like you? Are they all Donkorses?"

"No, friend, em ye one be few, dee others ye lots and kinds," Donkorse replied.

"Good, good," said Mystic happily. "Are the others like me, perhaps?"

"Good no, others not talk nil as much ye dee," said the Donkorse, wearily shaking his long face and wanting badly to come to the end of this path.

"Sorry Donkorse. I am very curious about this beautiful land. I wish to ask many more questions of its origin, your ways. I did not mean to bore you with idle chat. Will we soon be with the others?" asked Mystic.

The Donkorse replied, "Nil soon ye em. Friend walk same path ye em many steps."

From this, Mystic gathered the journey to the others had just begun.

***

The small Hawk was making steady progress toward his goal which was the same as Donkorse. The small sky-traveler was presently within sight of the Burg. He could not wait to tell his keeper of the visitor to their land and of the misfortune it had of landing on Donkorse's backside. Could this possibly be the visitor the Keepers had told them about for so long? He certainly looked the part, but after further thought, the Hawk could not imagine any great leader taking the amount of time this visitor had taken, trying to communicate with Donkorse. Was the visitor that wise after all? The Hawk could only give the visitor the benefit of the doubt. The Hawk turned for the Burg, making straight past the caretakers of the drawbridge for the Keeper's ledge. As the young Hawk landed on the ledge, he was just in time to see his Keeper enjoying an after-midday meal of fruit and sweet kaki's with a friend. He excitedly flew to the edge of the modest table. The Hawk announced to the Keeper and friend the news of the visitor, "Excuse me Sirs, if I may, we have the visitor headed this way. It came in right as you said, just south of Sweet Gulley near the Disappearing Well."

The small Hawk took its time to relate the complete story to the Keeper. No detail was omitted up until the time he took flight back to the Burg.

"You have done very well Rakki. Thank you for this interesting news. So, Rakki, you say that our visitor was actually carrying on a conversation with our noble friend Donkorse? That must have been quite amusing. From what you observed, was the visitor able to understand all that Donkorse was saying?"

"Much to my surprise, as well as Karri's, the visitor did quite well with Donkorse's stubborn misuse of the language," said the curious Hawk. "It will be quite a relief for the both of them him when they arrive here."

The Keeper smiled a little smile while he rolled his eyes in wonderment. "Maybe, just maybe, this is the chosen leader. He must pass the tests as spelled out by previous generations. The laws of the tests have been passed down for reasons we do not know, and lest all are passed, we may never know. Your Fathers before us were wise and experienced. The guidelines they have set will be adhered to explicitly. Now, are you sure our visitor was alone?"

"Yes sir, I am sure. I will travel back and ask Karri of any further developments, if you please, sir?" answered Rakki.

"Why of course," said the Keeper, "Please return to Sweet Gulley and keep me posted if anyone else comes through. If our visitor was followed, the followers may be after their friend or they may be after their enemy. We must be very, very careful in dealing with any other visitor."

The small Hawk hopped up on the ledge, turned, bid the Keeper and his silent friend a good farewell and took wing back to the Sweet Gulley. Later, as he passed the Wolf and the Donkorse, he swooped down to take a snip at Donkorse's tail just for fun. He was then swiftly off to the perch at Sweet Gulley.

***

Mystic noticed the small sky-traveler swooping in for the attack. Watching the Donkorse for a reaction, Mystic never got one. The Donkorse never broke stride as the Hawk came in for the kill. Donkorse lifted his tail, as if to swat the small Hawk out of the sky, giving Mystic time to watch the attack in amazement. The small Hawk took a swipe at Donkorse's tail and was gone as if he had made a big mistake. Mystic looked up at Donkorse's face asking, "Is every creature here as aggressive as that small Hawk?" Mystic could only hope not.

Donkorse said nothing; he just kept walking. Later Mystic could make out just a small trace of a smile developing on Donkorse's face. "This creature either knows more than he is letting on or is absolutely the most stubborn creature I have ever met," Mystic said softly to himself.

"Maybe em ye both," replied Donkorse with a wink of his eye.

Mystic suddenly knew that there was more to this than met his eye. He didn't know whether to feel relaxed about the turn of events or nervous. He did know that they had been traveling for some time now because he was getting hungry again. Mystic said nothing as they walked. He did, however, keep closer to Donkorse.

9

As the pair reached the crest of the next hill Mystic saw the end of the path was within his sight. There, directly in front of him, was one of the most inviting dwelling places he had ever seen. This dwelling place was much larger than the Dwelling Places of the Great Forest. It looked, at least to this Wolf, to be much, much more diverse. Who knew how many land walkers, of both the two-legged and four-legged variety dwelled there? It was spread out beautifully beside a medium-sized river that looked, to Mystic, to be as clear as crystal. The water had no color at all, but was breathtaking nevertheless He could hear the water as it moved crisply along, nudging gently against its bank as it flowed making the floating objects, boats he presumed, although he had never seen any this close, bob and dip with each small movement of the current. There was something strange about the way this water was flowing and something familiar about it at the same time. Gazing at the cool flowing water reminded Mystic that he had not had a drink of liquid since he had partaken of the sweet mud back in the gully. He was looking forward to quenching his growing thirst.

The dwelling place was surrounded by two charming stone walls that looked like they were not intended to protect the dwelling place from any attack. One wall was set about a quarter of a training beat inside the outside wall and neither looked very tall from Mystic's point of view. It looked like the walls were designed to lend a quaint charm to the place or maybe to keep the little-leggers in.

At the far right and left edges of the dwelling place were placed some kind of contraptions that looked like smaller gates that could raise and lower on two medium-sized poles set in the ground on either side. These gates divided deep paths that were carved into the ground and past the outside wall. Oh well, Mystic thought, two-leggers were known for having some strange ideas.

There was a long heavily traveled bridge that spanned both walls and the river at its narrowest point along the wide section of the oval that faced the river. The bridge was held in place on only one side of the river and that place was on its dwelling side. The bridge set cradled at the roots of two of the largest trees Mystic had ever seen. One large log stretched between the trunks of these trees and was held in place beneath an enormous root that protruded from the base of each tree like a foreleg grasping each end of the log, like a great bird of prey would grasp a water-livver upon grabbing it from atop the water. These giant roots, upon trapping the log, immediately found their way deeply back into the ground. The bridge rested, fastened securely to this sturdy log. There were thick ropes that ran from the front of the bridge on Mystic's side of the river high up into the trees and over two wooden barrels with poles run through them. The poles were attached with smaller rope and were hanging under some huge center branches of these ancient trees. The ropes traveled back down to the ground, parallel with the trees' massive trunks. They coiled continuing lengths of themselves around two large wheels at the base of each tree with short, stout poles sticking out like petals of a flower. The walkway of the bridge was made from several straight logs, flattened on one side then fitted snugly together. The half logs were tied securely with even more of the smaller-sized rope.

There were a few two-leggers standing around the bridge. These creatures did not seem to be guarding the bridge or the dwelling place as much as they were acting like greeters. From Mystic's point of view they seemed to initiate lively conversations with every two-legger or group of two-leggers that passed on the bridge. There was much traffic crossing the bridge coming out of the dwelling place, as well as traveling back into it. There were small groups of two-leggers and single two-leggers. There were two-leggers sitting in rolling boxes, full of all kinds of things that were being pulled by Horses, Ponies and one or two Donkorses. Mystic was amazed at the size of some of these creatures.

Just beyond the bridge were modest-sized dwellings built in several large circles set within the inside stone wall with the fronts facing outward. The backs of each dwelling opened to a large common area where large numbers of two-leggers were working in a single large garden while young two-leggers played happily together in an assortment of ways. No one dwelling looked any more special than the others, but they all had their own, unique personality that, Mystic assumed, reflected those that dwelled inside. These two-leggers seemed to enjoy decorating and constructing their dwellings more than the four-leggers in Mystic's Dwelling Place, although, Mystic's Dwelling was quite a dwelling to behold, or it used to be anyway, when it housed royalty. Each dwelling had windows facing the outside walls with large window ledges. Very heavy shutters painted to match the color of the dwelling framed each window. The only doors Mystic observed were on what he gathered to be the back of the dwellings. The roofs on each dwelling were made of stone shingles that glistened in the light of what, Mystic assumed, was the last half of sun time for this day-round. Relatively small grassy areas awaited any visitor to the individual dwellings. These were divided by many well-traveled paths lined with more of the shiny stone shingles. These paths glistened with a deep yellowish gloss leading to anywhere one might possibly want to go in this quaint, yet charming place. The grassy areas were all aligned under the outside facing windows. Each grassy area was furnished with inviting benches spaced at short walking distances.

Mystic also noticed that there seemed to be a different use for each of the large circles of dwellings. The traffic in the common areas each suggested different types of activities, whether it be living, trading, growing or socializing. Now, it seemed on further inspection, there was one dwelling that humbly stood out from the rest. It was a much larger dwelling and significant markings were inscribed on it. Mystic made himself a mental note to ask why it was special. On the far side of the walled area appeared to be the socializing circle with several dwellings much larger than the rest. Mystic correctly guessed that these took in visitors. Where the visitors came from? Well, that was yet another question

Donkorse, steadily moving along, was letting the distance grow between Mystic and himself. "This creature has one very ornery way about him," Mystic grumbled.

The Donkorse paused, turned his large head with those long ears in Mystic's direction once again and calmly replied loudly, "Ye em be stop, no? Dee others ye soon be." Donkorse did not wait for a reply and headed off again.

"Fine," Mystic called as he hurriedly trotted up to Donkorse's side again. "I have never seen a dwelling place quite like that in my life, so I was admiring the view. It is far different from the Dwelling Places in the Great Forest. I'm terribly sorry if I detained you."

Donkorse was now at the end of his short string of patience and looked Mystic directly in the eye and said, "You're sorry? All you can do is stand there telling me you are sorry? I have led you down this Path to Where I Am Going for most of my midday, very slowly I might add, trying to ignore your excessive questioning. And all you can say is I'm sorry? Please, are you sure that is the best apology you can muster?"

"Well what would you expect me to say?" asked Mystic. Then Mystic instantly went profoundly quiet. The Wolf's ears came to attention and his eyes grew wide. Irritated, he continued, "Wait a click, you can talk as plainly and clearly as I. Why in this world have you carried on with nothing more than such babble since I was dropped helplessly onto your bony back. To think that I thought you were some kind of new creature with a new language that I would have to, somehow, become fluent with just to find my way out of here. Why, I must add, have you been such a belligerent creature and why have you acted so aloof and ignorant?

"Uh oh", Donkorse's eyes matched Mystic's smaller Wolf eyes in enlarging to the edge of their sockets. He looked at Mystic, swallowed hard, then immediately looked away. His tail dropped and his shoulders sagged. Donkorse said nothing else.

"Ahem?" asked Mystic, demanding a reply with the tone of his voice. Donkorse remained silent and somewhat embarrassed. He shifted his great weight from side to side pondering this most embarrassing turn of events. His eyes searched frantically for a place to rest that was as far away from the Wolf's glare as possible.

"So, have you nothing to say in your defense?" asked the Wolf.

The Donkorse quickly returned to the babbling form of conversation and replied, "Em ye err. Em speak nil ye. Friend speak em Keeper."

He collected himself and took off toward the dwelling place at a considerable hoofed speed. The Donkorse's speed caught Mystic by surprise as he set off running after the deceptively quick four-legger. Mystic did his best to catch this puzzling creature before he arrived at the bridge. He was concerned about the Donkorse's mistake in revealing his true intelligence. He was determined to find some answers to the questions that were flooding into his mind. Mystic shouted between his fast fluid strides, "Please Donkorse, I beg of you. Please tell me what is going on."

Too late! The Donkorse made exceptional time to the bridge and was now stepping onto it. Mystic was unsure of what to do. Would these greeters on the bridge turn violent if they feared for Donkorse's safety? Would they turn into the same crazed two-legged creatures that had slaughtered his family? These questions and more were swirling around in Mystic's confused head.

Donkorse stepped up on the bridge, his heavy hooves clopping steadily toward the dwelling place. He walked to the end of the bridge and disappeared behind the gigantic trees. As Donkorse walked the bridge, he had nodded obligingly to two-leggers and four-leggers he passed in some kind of greeting custom. The two-leggers patted his nose and playfully slapped his flanks with their paws.

Mystic suddenly remembered that his friend Vincen had taught him that two-leggers' paws were called hands and feet. Mystic also soon realized that those two trees were very much larger than he had initially estimated.

Mystic stopped about ten training beats from the edge of the bridge. Then he reluctantly sat down. He raised a paw to his brow to wipe some of the dried mud out of his eyes. Mystic at once remembered what a mess he was and what he must look like, since he had had no time to bathe after the mud incident. The proud Wolf reset his feet under him, immediately putting the most apologetic grin on his face imaginable. He slightly opened his mouth hoping that whoever was watching him would not judge him a threat to their safety. He could think of nothing to do now but wait and wait he did.

Mystic was completely alone again. The gravity of his current situation had been absent from his memory since he stepped into the well. Now, the possible circumstances of his less-than-ideal predicament were becoming quite real. He was, unquestionably alone in a strange land that was not his own. He looked excessively less regal than the Prince of the Great Forest should. The tasty, sticky mud was now frozen in place all over his body. He realized that he was lost mainly because he had disobeyed Vincen's instructions and, secondly, because he had gotten no tangible information from the less-than-forthcoming Donkorse. He became all too aware of the thirst that was begging for quenching along with the hunger that was returning to his stomach. He let out a few deep breaths before he lay down. His bright eyes were dull and sullen. His face sagged as the muscles on his face relaxed. His body language revealed a slight hint of frailty, given his tail could find no reason to wag. Any creature that witnessed the expression that was now on the great Wolf's face would never read it as a threat to anyone. Mystic was tired and he was hungry. He longed for his home and friends.

Mystic could only guess at what the Donkorse was doing or what he might be preparing for the Wolf. High overhead Mystic heard a flapping of wings. He looked to his left just in time to see that small Hawk fly back toward the dwelling place over the bridge. He followed the Hawk until he saw it land on the window ledge of that one large special dwelling. Mystic shrugged his shoulders, swished his tail once and gave in to the sleep that was fast approaching.

10

Vincen was the first one in. He was shocked that the feeling of being in control remained with him. This was not ordinary water. That, he figured, was an understatement of record proportions. He was in liquid, but what kind of liquid? He was breathing this fluid like air and was suffering no consequences of any kind for doing so. He had not been submerged for more than an instant when he looked around to see Lightning coming after him while continuing to grip both the wand/staff and the tail of the young Cheetah. Lightning weighed considerably more than Vincen, so Vincen naturally situated himself neatly out of the Badger's line of descent in fear of being pushed into something he would regret. Furthermore, he certainly did not want the flailing claws of the Cheetah striking him. To Vincen's amazement Lightning never got closer than when they started this journey. There was no out-of-control falling by any of the three friends. Much to Vincen's surprise, even the Cheetah was in control of himself. They each made eye contact and relayed the same look with their eyes: "I'm okay."

"This is odd," Vincen mouthed to no one and everyone.

The Badger released Bubba's tail reluctantly. He watched as the Cheetah stretched out, appeared to lie down and close his eyes. Lightning was not about to release the wand/staff under any circumstances. He would release the Cheetah, but he was not going to release the wand/staff. He looked at Bubba first, then Vincen and joined each of them in non-panicked bewilderment. What was odd at first seemed to be getting odder with each click of the Eagle's eye.

***

Donkorse ambled off the bridge onto the main path that circled the dwellings. He made a stop just inside the base of the huge tree on the right and left a message for the Keeper. The burly guard, who was keeping his post in a hollowed out cavity in one of the humongous roots of the tree, did not act surprised when the large head of the

Donkorse deliberately appeared and stated, "Let him know," Donkorse explained, "The visitor has safely arrived and waits for entry just outside the bridge. He is very disheveled as a result of a comical incident, but he is none the worse for wear. The visitor is tired. I would assume he is also very thirsty and hungry. If the testing is to be administered, make sure he is well nourished 'ere we make an irreversible mistake. I may or may not have opened a door for unwanted questions with my well-published lack of patience. I am returning to Sweet Gulley to resume scouting for any creature that may follow. I will send Rakki or Karri back with any news."

The guard nodded and swiftly made his way out of the post headed to his left on the direct path to the Keeper's house. Donkorse, after removing his head from the guard post, stopped for a quick snack just outside the guard's door. After eating his fill, he gulped a few deep drinks of crystal clear water from a large pail hung from a peg in the tree's root. He nodded as the guard passed by then clamored up on the bridge. He made his way across the bridge heading back to where he had encountered the visitor earlier. There was much to do. If this was the visitor the Keeper had foretold, then he must hurry back to the Disappearing Well in case of any further developments. Donkorse was proud of his position within the Burg. He could not help but feel sorry for the Wolf and what was soon to come his way. Donkorse reminded himself that it was all part of the master plan. Any danger that befell this Wolf, if indeed he was the one, would do so with good reason. Donkorse took in a large breath of air, nodded to the last two-legger on the bridge and, even for his size, gently jumped off the bridge onto The Path to Where I'm Going.

Donkorse slowed as he came to the sleeping Wolf, passing by with barely a sound. "Poor Wolf," Donkorse thought as he passed, "I hope he is the one Keeper spoke of. If not, may mercy be upon him." Donkorse continued walking in silence careful not to wake the slumbering Wolf.

***

The three friends kept traveling or falling or sinking. The three of them remained wide-eyed, curious, yet remarkably in control as their journey continued. Darkness set in on them with no ill effects. They were on a mission, a real adventure to retrieve a very dear friend. Nothing explainable or unexplainable would daunt the determination that welled inside each of them. Vincen conceded to rest. His Eagle eyes closed in deep heavy thought. Lightning did likewise, never releasing his vise-like grip on the wand/staff. Bubba had been resting soundly for some time.

***

Rakki lit on the window ledge again. He forewarned the Keeper about the lack of activity back at Sweet Gulley. The Keeper was not surprised and reminded the small Hawk that all good things require patience. With each passing moment the Keeper was more willing to think that the visitor was the special one and that, if any creature was following to bring him harm, then they would have already fallen through. The Keeper explained to Rakki that if this visitor's friends had been unaware of the disappearance, then more than likely, they would have had to prepare for any search for him. That would take an adequate amount of time. The Keeper politely urged the Hawk to rush back to Sweet Gulley to continue keeping watch. In closing he also asked Karri to make the next trip so that Rakki might get some rest.

The Keeper explained, "Rakki, we will be calling on your speed and vigor soon enough. You must rest now as much as you can. Be off, small one." With that Rakki was flying. He passed the bridge guard on his way to see the Keeper and tilted his wings as a greeting. The guard raised his head and nodded.

The Keeper walked to his large overstuffed chair next to his study table, sat down, bowed his head and clasped his hands under his chin. He looked across the room at his silent guest and softly stated, "It looks as though, my dear friend, that all is coming together. Let us join in good thoughts." The guest nodded in agreement.

Rakki flew until he spied Donkorse ahead on the path. He swooped down and gently landed on the broad, strong back of the four-legger. The Hawk hopped up to a fine resting spot between the well-spaced ears of Donkorse. "Well, what do you think?" the Hawk asked.

"Dear small friend, I am not sure anymore. I do not know this visitor except for our brief conversations and his excessive questioning, yet I fear for the safety of this Wolf if he is not the selected one. I am not sure if he knows why he is here. He certainly did not converse as if he meant to be here. We are doing our small part to protect destiny. I yearn to tell the Wolf of the Keeper's mind, although I know I am forbidden to do so. I almost said too much to the Wolf as he pestered me for answers so. I am afraid I let my guard down and spoke freely to him. I quickly realized my mistake and returned to babbling as I was instructed. This is a wise Wolf; he was most aware of my error. Fortunately for all, I am bred to be stubborn. I would have made my mother and father proud with my belligerence. "

"Who did he say he was?" asked Rakki.

"He told me his name was Mystic. He added that he was the Prince of the Great Forest," replied Donkorse.

"Did he have it?" asked Rakki.

"No, Rakki, he did not," answered Donkorse.

"Rakki was stunned, "Oh my, that could change everything."

"Yes, I know," replied Donkorse, "Yes, I know."

Rakki nipped at one of Donkorse's large ears as he hurriedly took wing to Karri's side back in the tree at Sweet Gulley.

***

Back in the Burg, the bridge guard lifted a paw to scratch at the Keeper's door. The Keeper rose from his chair and walked to the door to greet this next visitor. He opened the door just as the guard rose to stand on his back legs. The large creature rested his front paws almost on the roof of the dwelling.

"Down here, Hugoth," said the Keeper. The guard dropped down to all four legs. He was so big that he was still able to look the Keeper straight in the eyes. The Keeper asked the extra large guard if Donkorse had reported in as planned.

"Yes Keeper, Donkorse is on his way back to Sweet Gulley. I assume you have already heard from Rakki," said the guard.

"Yes, I have. Thank you. Was there anything additional in what Donkorse relayed to you?" asked the Keeper.

"Well, yes sir, he did mention that he might have said a bit too much to the Wolf. He did not let on any more than that. The Wolf is sleeping soundly. Should I wake him?" asked Hugoth.

"No, no, just make sure he has plenty to eat and drink when he awakes," replied the Keeper.

"Yes, sir," said the guard and he was off.

The Keeper returned to his overstuffed chair, sat down, folded his hands under his chin again and nodded once again to his silent guest.

***

Back where Mystic slept, a small crowd was silently gathering. The Keeper was not in attendance, but he made sure that plenty of food and drink was sent for the Wolf with strict instructions not to wake the soundly sleeping visitor. The Wolf would wake soon enough. All creatures of knowledge wished him the best.

***

"Would this ever end?" Bubba thought to himself. The young Cheetah was awake now. He was beginning to look and act a bit uneasy. The Cheetah did not like water very much. He had avoided immersing himself in any kind of water as long as he could remember. Mystic had made it clear to him on several occasions that Cheetahs just don't like to swim. Bubba had never had any reason to doubt that. Then again this did not feel exactly as he thought swimming would. He was totally wet, although it did not feel like the wet he felt in rainstorms. He was neither cold nor fearful. The Cheetah did not feel compelled to escape from this water. "Maybe," he thought, "I will attempt to enjoy swimming when I return to Black Pond." He then tempered his thought with these words, "If I return to Black Pond." Bubba positioned his body as freely as if it were not encased in liquid and cast a glance at the huge Badger, then toward the Eagle. They both appeared just as calm as he considered himself to be. Then it got darker.

Once the light had been extinguished, Bubba's calm demeanor became even more so. The dark reminded him of his childhood. His parents always taught him to be confident when the sun went down. He could see others much better than they could see him. He felt how he used to feel, safe and protected. The dark was Bubba's favorite time. He had never feared darkness. The Cheetah excelled during moon time. The others were often impressed with his uncanny sense of his whereabouts and theirs on such occasions. This was no different than any other moon time except that there was no moon. Bubba totally relaxed and rested. He felt wet feathers lightly brush against his side and turned enough to see that Vincen had backed into him with his Eagle eyes straining to observe any brewing trouble. Vincen was again protecting the young Cheetah. This reminded him of the way his parents had always watched over him at moon time. Bubba was tired. Soon the Cheetah was asleep for the second time.

Lightning continued to clutch the wand/staff in a death grip. He had no desire to let go of the wand/staff until he personally handed it to Mystic. The Badger had no feelings about the liquid one way or another. He was more interested in where they were going than how they were getting there. Lightning's thoughts began to drift back to his Dwelling Place. He had told no one of his intent to begin this adventure. Unlike his three dear friends, Lightning had a large, caring family. No brother, sister, mother, father or cousin had any idea of his whereabouts. He had been too busy collecting food to send any word back to his Dwelling Place. He had not even remembered to tell Bubba to let them know. The Badger was attempting to tell himself that they would not worry about him. He was always staying out late and would often spend many day-rounds out in the Great Forest with his friends. Never did his parents question his motives. He was more than big and strong enough to handle any situation he could get himself into and, well, he was with Mystic and Vincen. That was comforting, but this adventure was not in the Great Forest and he was not with Mystic and Vincen. He was only with Vincen. They were beginning a search for Mystic with hopes of finding him. The Badger was also incorrect about what his parents were thinking. He was grown, but he was still their young one and they did worry for his safety. He was not old enough to be a parent and, when he was, he would understand fully that parents are concerned about their young ones even when they are old ones.

***

Donkorse was steadily making his way back to Sweet Gulley with thoughts of the Wolf's future constantly stirring in his head. Should he be the one, then, the tests would prove that beyond any doubt. Should he not be the one, then, the tests would probably kill the friendly creature and anything that cared to travel with him. Donkorse was stubbornly keeping the faith, trusting that this Wolf would be the special one to protect and lead the dwellers of the First Land into their possibly forthcoming perils.

Donkorse knew that faith and trust were very powerful words. They should never be taken lightly. The Keeper was relatively new to Nuorg. He was constantly making speeches on these two words alone. He would often speak to those who dwelled in the Burg, only to find his teachings sometimes misinterpreted and, even, completely ignored. Donkorse was one of a small group of animals that heard and heeded nearly every word the Keeper spoke. This small group, including Rakki, Karri, along with a few others, traveled about the land telling other creatures who would listen of past events the Keeper spoke of. Now, if there was only a sure way of knowing if Mystic was the correct one or not. Donkorse would have given anything to know that one sure way.

***

Rakki settled on the lookout perch next to Karri. He informed her of the visits with the Keeper and Donkorse. Rakki kept the conversation short and his voice quiet so as not to arouse any suspicion should any other creature come this way. They had been fortunate so far. It was middle evening now, and all of the dwellers of the Burg were settling down within the stone walls getting ready to close the shutters.

"Has any thing come down recently?" he asked his twin.

"No Rakki, not one thing has come through living or not. There has been no activity since the gray Wolf," Karri answered.

"The Keeper has requested that should something happen, you will make the next run to him. He says that we need to stay rested," Rakki added.

"Certainly," replied Karri. "Should the well open again, we will have either very good news to share with him or very bad news. Nevertheless, I will make the next flight as you wish. Now, we must wait."

***

Mystic opened his now refreshed eyes slowly getting accustomed to the light again. Once he got his bearings, he realized he was staring wide-eyed at a banquet feast. Food and baskets galore were laid out within and beyond his reach. "Where had all of this come from?" he asked of no one thing in particular. He looked around and found out that he had asked the question to exactly nothing. There was no creature about from where he rested all the way to the dwelling place and, even there, the activity was dwindling. Without wasting any more clicks, he gave in to the hunger pangs in his stomach. He greedily ate a portion of everything laid out for him. He drank pails of the most enticing water he had ever had the pleasure to taste. This water actually had a taste of its own and was extremely sweet. He remembered the sweet tasting mud in the gully and tried to reason a link between the two. He ate all he could possibly eat without getting over filled. Over-filled Wolves tend to get sluggish and he kept from that. The food was the same food he ate in the Great Forest except that the taste was more pure and crisp. The fruits tasted fruitier, and the nuts more nutty. He did not stop to wonder too much about that. He just ate.

He stuck his nose into the last remaining container and found no food, but legibly written notes on very thin slices of bark. He turned the container of notes over and spread them out the best he could. He had not scrawled legible writings for some time, yet he could still read the writings of others. The Great Eagle had seen to it that reading was learned and remembered by each of his young students. Once he got the notes spread out about him, he took to studying them. The Wolf found that the notes were written in different dialects and, he correctly assumed, that whatever creature had written the notes did not know his preferred dialect. The last note was the correct one. He read it.

The note began,

> *"My good Wolf, please forgive the haphazard scrawling of this content. Study it for its merit. We have been watching your movements. We do not fear you. Likewise, do not fear us. We have been waiting for you. If you are who we are waiting on, then your expertise, wisdom and leadership skills will become increasingly evident with the coming trials. Your success will bear you out. Your failure will do you in. Please come to the Burg once you have partaken of this generously offered food and drink."*

The note was signed, *"Hugoth, Guard of the Forever Trees."*

"What could this Hugoth possibly mean?" Mystic asked himself. The Wolf raised his head, perked up his ears and cast a wary glance toward the bridge. He turned around at least two complete times studying everything within his sight intently and cautiously. He continued, "Who has been watching me and for what reason? I must find who these creatures are to ease my increasingly troubling thoughts." The gray Wolf summoned his nerve and headed directly for the bridge. "This adventure is getting even more complicated with each step I take," Mystic said aloud to himself. He was feeling more confident with a full stomach and a quenched thirst. "To the bridge," he murmured to himself.

***

Vincen was the first to see it. Bubba noticed it next as it brought him out of his secure and protective darkness. Light was rushing in their direction while Lighting noticed a faint glow again in the wand/staff. "Oh Mercy," exclaimed the Badger.

All too quickly they were engulfed in light again. They all felt as if they were traveling at a much faster rate of speed now. Just as suddenly as the light was thrust upon them, they were thrust out of the liquid. High into the air they flew. Vincen did not even have time to open his wings in anticipation of flight. He couldn't have immediately flown anyway because he was soaking wet. Karri nudged her brother. They each arched their head up toward the commotion, round a graceful half circle and then followed the intruder's path of flight down. "We have more visitors, brother," she said.

How high could they have been thrown into the air? The height they had been thrown did not cause nearly as much concern in the three friends' minds as did the distance they would fall. "Oh mercy," said the Badger, when his eyes calculated the distance from where they were to where they were going.

The three landed with a thunderously loud splat, splat, splat exactly in the same mud hole that Mystic had found himself in earlier. Vincen, then Bubba, then Lightning all landed in a pile of bodies. They were all down, but, where were their weapons, food and supplies? In an instant, just like baby ducks following their mother, all of the supplies appeared in the same path behind the three friends.

Karri stared humorously at the activity taking place. "I'll bet they feel that landing for a while," she told Rakki.

"Hush Karri, don't let them hear you. We must remain quiet, observe and report their actions. Do you think they look dangerous?" asked Rakki.

"Sorry dear twin, "They look very dangerous, not to us mind you, though very likely to each other. Lucky for them they landed in the gully I'd say," Karri added between small bursts of quiet laughter.

"Ouch", cried Bubba. "Lightning, you almost crushed my leg and, oh my, here comes everything else! Please excuse me!"

Bubba scrambled for his life off the pile of muddy visitors and watched, in fear of being crushed, as the remainder of their belongings and weaponry tumbled ever so ungracefully downward, only to cause many smaller splats in the muddy confines of their landing zone. It was all there. Mystic's wand/staff landed big end first and stuck, initially, in that position, although, it slowly began to sink. Lightning's ax-pike struck hard into the ground, with a strange sounding thud, taking the silhouette of a tall tree dropped from high above with no leaves or limbs. Bubba's rapier landed sharp end down.

None of the friends asked why Bubba still carried that sword around. They just let it be. They knew the Cheetah's claws, when extended, were amazing weapons in their own right, as well as his unbelievable speed. Vincen, and all other creatures within a short distance were normally very concerned for their own well being whenever the Cheetah felt the urge to practice with the rapier, but they knew it held a place of great significance in the Cheetah's life. Bubba never let the poacher's rapier out of his sight. He had carried it around with him, in one way or another, since the day-round his parents were taken. He had madly swiped it off the ground in his teeth as it lay dangerously close to the poacher's outstretched hand during his dramatic escape. He had it with him at all times as a reminder to himself of the evil in his small world. Whether he would ever encounter the need to use it was of no concern to him.

Vincen always carried his weapons. His razor sharp talons were not weapons as much as they were a necessity, a part of his everyday life. Vincen's most important weapon was the knowledge stored inside his brilliant mind from years and years of study, plus his innate ability to recall almost any of it in an instant. Lightning's ax-pike was something altogether different.

The ax-pike was not a completely odd tool, though it was an odd and overly formidable weapon, if need be, far beyond the stretch of any imagination. It was actually not a weapon at all. The ax-pike was nothing more than a longish oak pole with a crude ax fashioned out of an old rusted part, probably of a two-legger's origination, of something fastened to one end. Lightning found the ax piece one day as he was walking near the border of the Black. One would assume that it was used in some way to grow food or work the land. This piece, once attached to the pole, functioned as a cutting or digging device that over the years had been honed to a very sharp knife-like edge. The ax-pike also had a large round rock tied to the same end with several strips of tree bark. This end came in very handy when the Badger needed to shake nuts or fruits out of the higher reaches of some trees. Still, the friends, especially Bubba, liked to think of every tool as some sort of weapon, whether it be crude and cumbersome or refined and delicate.

The ax-pike took a strong arm to wield and Lightning was extremely strong with enormous forearms. One could barely imagine the terror or havoc that could be wreaked upon an unfortunate creature or structure should the Badger decide to let the weapon speak.

***

Lightning was the youngest of his family. He easily outweighed his parents, cousins, brothers and sisters combined. He was, without a doubt, the largest Badger ever to walk the floors of the Great Forest. He was easily the largest animal in the Great Forrest and outweighed several of the mountain creatures that would occasionally come down during the hottest periods of the mountain year. Suffice it to say, Lightning, the irregular Badger was, by all reasoning and means, a very irregular Badger.

He left his family's Dwelling Place early in his life. He left his family's Dwelling Place and traveled all the way around to the back of it, where his Father had constructed a much, much larger Dwelling Place for his youngest son. After all, Lightning, the irregular Badger was the baby of the family and everyone made sure that he was well taken care of. Lightning was not an orphan in the way that Bubba and Mystic were. As he traveled with the others, he found himself being called brother by the both of them and son by Vincen. The Badger's parents had no qualms with this, as it was all spoken out of love and concern for the large Badger. They also felt completely at ease with his choice of friends and mentor. Their adventures sometimes caused a bit of a stir when the friends returned to the Dwelling Place after rather lengthy sojourns. However, no harm had ever come to any of them yet, and, for most circumstances, all was well within their small world. The Badger's parents also knew a little secret about Lightning. They were curious why no one had ever spoken of it.

***

As Lighting watched in horror, the heavy pack of food that was no longer securely fastened opened and the collected food fell scattered about them. If anyone had bothered to look closely at the Badger, they would have seen quite a look of loss and sorrow on his face. "The food," thought Lightning sorrowfully, as his large shoulders sagged, "What will we do for food?"

11

Vincen was furious. Always conscious of his appearance this majestic eagle now looked more like a wallowing swine. The wonderful feathers that were responsible for Vincen's handsome appearance were matted heavily with the Sweet Gulley mud. His tail and wing feathers were suffering the most from this mud drenching. Vincen struggled to break free of the mud's intense grip and, after a short while, gave up the futile attempt. He was too physically exhausted from the struggle. He fell back, then simply relaxed. He had flapped his wings and clawed his claws so much that, with each further movement, he sank deeper into the muddy mess. The hole was deeper than he was tall and he gave up the battle just as his head began to sink into the unforgiving quagmire. Had Vincen not given up the fight, Lightning and Bubba would have never seen him again. Vincen rested in the mud as motionless as he could and breathed very shallow breaths hoping not to slip completely under.

The Donkorse sat under a tree just to the side of the gulley and silently watched the landing events unfold. On his way back from the Burg he had stopped to sit and rest, a fortunate decision. The bodies and things that fell out of the sky after being thrown out of the well may have landed on his back just as the gray Wolf had done. Donkorse could not have been anymore relieved. After taking one quick look at largest of the group, he was sure that, had that one landed on his back, he would have been flattened like a mud kaki. The trio looked lost as they bobbed up and down in the goo of Sweet Gulley. Donkorse was slightly amused. He did not want to take too much liberty with the developing situation or the participants so he proceeded with his role in the big scheme of things, watching with caution.

Rakki and Karri took wing and glided quietly over from their lookout post. They perched softly on Donkorse's broad shoulders. Karri whispered, "Did they all make it?"

Donkorse answered confidently, "Yes, my tiny friend, they all survived. Just a bit ago, I saw three come down. Now I only see two. Where is the Eagle?"

Rakki replied from experience, "If the Eagle landed in the sweet goo, he is more than likely exhausted from fighting it. I will go check on him for you."

Karri quickly stopped her Brother, "No, you must not interfere. Wait just now. I see the larger one searching for him."

No sooner had Karri's voice drifted away from Donkorse's ears than they all heard the large creature call for the misplaced Eagle. "Vincen, where are you? Answer me if you can. Flap a wing or something. Let me know where you are."

"He must be here, Lightning. I never saw him fly out of this sticky soup. We must be careful where we step," Bubba stated cautiously.

They then heard a rather quiet, but very agitated voice say, "Here I am, you two nutcrackers. You have each missed stepping on me by mere hairs of your tails. Please look down into this muck before you take another step."

The Badger turned his head slightly to the right and looked down into the sweet mud and spotted the irritated Eagle. He hardly looked like an Eagle right now. The Badger and the Cheetah sensed the Eagle's vile frustration. Not even Bubba let out any unwise remark about the Eagle's appearance.

Lightning delicately scooped Vincen out of the quagmire. He easily stepped through the thickest of the mud, then, upon nearing the bank, he placed Vincen safely out of harm's way.

"Vincen," Lightning questioned, "Are you okay? You look solid as a statue. Can you move at all?"

"Frankly speaking Lightning, I have never felt so miserable in my whole life. This gooey mud has frozen me with a bond that is pure stickiness. Every feather on my body is caked in this unrelenting substance. I can't lift a wing away from my body even to save my own life. I beg of you, Lightning, you must find somewhere that I can wash up before we can proceed. I would rather you find that somewhere sooner than later. I feel I haven't very long to exist in this wretched state," Vincen slowly and softly answered.

Lightning had never witnessed Vincen struggling as he was now. The poor Eagle could barely breathe. How could this have happened so fast? The Badger suddenly became exceedingly concerned for

The Land of Nuorg

Vincen's very life. The Eagle was breathing very, very shallowly now. With every breath, the goo seemed to tighten around Vincen's body as it set. The Eagle was exhausted, no doubt, and was bravely facing suffocation if he could not get washed free of the substance very soon.

Bubba rushed back in to the muck visibly concerned about the Eagle's grim state. As he came thrashing into the gulley, he accidentally splashed a considerable amount of the goo on his face. He began licking his lips to remove the debris with slight abandon. He was very pleasantly surprised, as was Mystic before him, with the taste of the goo. The Cheetah found it very satisfying as he licked his snout clean. "Lightning," Bubba asked as he bent his head low to the mud's surface, "Please have a taste of this stuff. I think you will find it very palatable."

"Please, Bubba?" replied the Badger, "Can you not see that we have a crisis brewing here. How can you even think of eating at a time like this?"

"But wait, maybe we can relieve Vincen of some of his struggling," answered Bubba.

A look of astonishment came over the tired Eagle's face and he fought to speak, and did so weakly, "Oh dear ancestors, are they thinking of devouring me like a honey-coated bark kake. Oh mercy, at least that will relieve my suffering, if they make haste," Vincen said as if speaking with an invisible creature.

"Why you are talking as if you have gone mad, Vincen," said a somewhat puzzled and upset Bubba. "As unsavory as it sounds we may have to just lick you clean. I have groomed myself that way for years. Most Cheetahs do. It's not that bad, especially if you are covered in mud such as this," he added taking another swipe at the remaining goo on his snout.

Lightning thought about Bubba's statement for a click and agreed with the Cheetah. He reached down into the hole and pulled a big paw full of mud out of it. With just a short pause to eye the goo a little more closely, the Badger poured some of the goo into his mouth. Immediately his eyes lit up at the surprising taste. "I think you may have something here, Bubba."

Before either the Badger or the Cheetah could begin to work on Vincen, a barely audible last gasp exited from the Eagle's body, the keen eyes glazed over and painlessly rolled back into his head. His body went limp. Lightning panicked. He instantly swept Vincen off the ground and cried, "He's not breathing anymore, Bubba. He's not breathing!"

"That can't be!" answered the startled Cheetah.

"I promise you, dear friend, Vincen is not breathing. He is departed," Lightning cried as tears began to well in his eyes. "This goo or mud or whatever it is killed our beloved Vincen. We have to do something now, whether it be drastic or crazy or insane! We have to exhaust our means to make him start breathing again him now!"

"That situation is turning bad quickly," said a flustered Rakki. "It is not supposed to be like this. This is a dire turn of bad fortune. What do we do?'

"We are not to interfere," replied Karri. "We can't change their fortunes or misfortunes. The tests would be for naught."

"But, the Eagle is dying!" exclaimed Donkorse under his breath. "No one planned on this happening. I will not permit it."

"Please wait," begged Karri. "I feel a peace about this. Call it sister's intuition, but I believe something beneficial is about to happen."

The tears were flowing now in Lightning's eyes as his massive chest heaved with pangs of desperation. Bubba remained stoic, but saddened, as he continued to think of a plan to save the Great Eagle's life. The Cheetah hurriedly backed up, frantically trying to get back on the bank to do something, to think more clearly. In doing so he backed directly into the Badger's ax-pike. He hit the ax-pike so hard that it was knocked from its goo-locked position. The ax-pike gradually began to tilt downward. As it did, Bubba felt the ground below quiver.

"Oh mercy, not again!" he exclaimed to the Cheetah. "Do you feel that, Lightning?" he asked.

"Why yes, I feel something tickling my feet. Is that something to get unnerved about at a moment like this? Isn't there some urgent matter on your mind that should concern you even more?" Lightning asked.

The ax-pike was bending downward faster as the quivering increased. As if called from above, a pool of water began collecting atop the mud hole. As the ax-pike fell past the surface of the mud, a stream of water began to bubble, inching its way up through the sticky gooey mud. Then ever so slowly the stream of water began to sprout like a fountain.

"Stick him in it! Quick, Lightning, stick him in it!" demanded Bubba.

Lightning thrust the stiff body of the Great Eagle into the steady spouting water. The water worked quickly on the thick outside crust of goo that had set on the Eagle's body. Amazingly enough, the water cut through the hardened goo like it was washing away a light coating of dust. Lightning, feeling a bit relieved, began to wash the Eagle like he was cleaning a soiled fruit. He twisted and scrubbed the Eagle's body as the water gently rinsed it clean.

As the Badger worked the Eagle's body under the, now steady stream of water, Bubba struggled back through the muck to the Badger's side. He separately took each of Vincen's wings in his mouth and gently pulled them open. This allowed Lightning to position Vincen's body to flush the remaining hardened goo from under him.

Lightning worked diligently to clean the lifeless bird as the tears continued to roll down his massive face, his great chest heaving uncontrollably. "I hope this is not too little too late," he remarked to Bubba with a gasping voice. He continued washing Vincen's body and was now cleaning the tail feathers.

"I do as well," said a sullen Bubba. "I do as well."

"How did you know that was going to happen?" a disbelieving Rakki asked Karri.

"Remember how long ago the collecting pool was built?" she asked. That big stick, or whatever it is, is so heavy that it broke through the bottom of the collector when it landed, allowing the stream to flow again. The thud that was heard when the stick landed sounded a little like cracking wood to me. I believe, most certainly, that we should repair that before too long.

"Amazing, these coincidences," said Donkorse. "If that water is from the stream, then the Eagle will certainly breathe again even better than before."

"You are correct again," stated a very relieved little Hawk.

Rakki never ceased to be amazed at his sister's intelligence and patient persistence. Karri could always find something good in anything. He imagined that it was because she looked for the positive. But, so far, there still was no movement by the Eagle.

"I am going down there now. We must get them on their way," said Donkorse.

Donkorse rose to his feet, rolled his shoulders, shook the stillness out of his neck and swished his tail. He slowly made his way down to where the three friends had landed and asked of the trio a plain and simple question, "May em help ye?"

12

Mystic had eaten plenty and felt refreshed. Truthfully, he had eaten too much. He scoured the remnants of the food looking for maybe one last bite, correctly deciding against it. After circling the remnants three times, he gallantly trotted off in the direction of the largest bridge he had ever seen. The closer he got, the larger the bridge appeared. "How big is this thing?" he wondered to himself. "And what kind of creature would live in those dwelling places? If they, indeed, are two-leggers, I beg of good fortune that they be not the evil kind."

It had not taken him as long as he thought to make the distance to the bridge. In all fairness to his judgment, it was much closer than he thought. He had made the mistake other travelers that had come this way before him had made. He, as they, confused the distance to the bridge by drastically underestimating its actual size.

"Oh mercy"! Mystic exclaimed when he got to the edge of the walkway.

The Wolf had remembered a considerable amount of activity here before his nap. Now, there was not one solitary individual, be it of the two or four-legged variety, on the bridge. Mystic logically was led to assume that all of the two-leggers and four-leggers were performing some kind of work or eating a meal inside the dwellings. He also could not help but notice that all of the dwellings now had their heavy shutters closed tightly. "I wonder what's behind that," he thought to himself.

Mystic was now at the edge of the bridge finding he had no way to get up on it. The logs that made up the main walkway were thicker than he was tall. The stone fence that had seemed short and easily jumpable was, on further discovery, as tall as some of the middle-sized trees in the Great Forest. Being one of a long line of highly educated and intelligent Wolves, he attributed this mistake in judgment to an incorrect rule of scale. There was, albeit obviously so, no way he could even imagine making an unassisted jump to the walkway. He was even more impressed with the Donkorse's strength and agility now. There had been no smaller entry ramp noted when Donkorse had boarded the bridge. Mystic searched the entire end of the bridge vainly looking for any kind of step only to find none. This was yet another mystery in a long line of mounting mysteries. "What shall I do?" he asked himself. "I guess I could stand here and yell loud enough, make a dastardly disturbance until something came to let me in. Or, I could keep pacing until I found something, or..."

"May I help you?" came a deep voice from high atop the walkway.

Startled, Mystic retreated. He had heard no footsteps on the walkway. This, in itself, was unnerving, given his remarkable sense of hearing. The Wolf swung his head from side to side, up and up higher still, trying to get a glimpse of whatever this voice was coming from.

"Where are you?" Mystic asked.

"I am up here Prince of the Great Forest. We have been expecting you," boomed the loud but pleasant voice.

Mystic answered, "How could you know me? Furthermore, since you do, may I then ask of you mysterious sir, who in this land are you?"

Laughing quietly, the voice answered, "Why certainly, I am Hugoth, Guard of the Forever Trees."

"Well thank you Hugoth, Guard of the Forever Trees, for your kind words. Let me first say thanks for your forthcomings; secondly, for your hospitality; and, thirdly, your gentle tone of voice," Mystic said gratefully. "Forgive me for being more than a little startled at your abrupt announcement of presence to me."

"You are more than welcome Prince," replied Hugoth.

Mystic was not at all accustomed to this level of address. He had always taken his royalty humbly for granted, never wishing it or its practices upon anyone. He was only addressed in this manner, disrespectfully so, when Vincen of the Great Vincen Eagles, Bubba of the Great Plains or Lightning, the Irregular Badger needed to put his pride in check. Feeling a large bit embarrassed. Mystic replied, "Well, Hugoth, your manner of speech seems a bit formal to me, but thank you again. May I be granted the kind favor to see just who and what you are?" asked Mystic, "so that we can continue this conversation face to face?"

The Land of Nuorg

"Yes, yes, of course," Hugoth replied. "How rude of me. Please turn to your left and travel about three of your paces. You will find the entrance ramp most accommodating for a creature of your size."

Mystic squinted his eyes a bit and twisted his head noticeably. He found himself questioning Hugoth's directions. Had he not just come from that very position? There had been no ramp then and Mystic was more than a little leery of its being there now. Obediently, Mystic did as he was told. He steadily followed Hugoth's calming voice with his eyes and blindly stepped directly into the entrance ramp. "Owww!" he exclaimed.

"Is there a problem down there?" asked Hugoth.

Mystic was embarrassed and tried to hide that fact. He grimaced, looked away from the bridge and shook his hurting paw to soothe the stinging pain. "Oh nothing," he said frustrated, "I just stumped my paw. I will be right up."

Mystic hobbled to the entry point of the entrance ramp and gingerly bounded up to the walkway. There, again, his eyes remaining half closed from the pain, he literally bounded head first into something else. This had to be, without a doubt, the largest creature he had ever seen. After colliding with the enormous Hugoth, he was tossed backward onto his hind legs, thus winding up in a remarkably awkward and unstable sitting position. "Oh mercy, excuse me sir," Mystic announced as he ungracefully fell onto his side in a very non-regal heap.

Hugoth was big. He was very big. He was monstrous. This was the largest creature Mystic had ever, ever seen. Hugoth made Lightning, the irregular Badger look normal sized. Mystic struggled to his feet as he studied the creature. He raised his throbbing paw and wiped his snout twice before returning it to the walkway. Again, with his weight firmly balanced on three healthy paws and one that ached, Mystic asked an elementary question, "What kind of creature are you?"

"A big one," Hugoth answered with a hearty laugh.

"That's obvious enough," answered Mystic.

"Please come with me, Mystic, Prince of the Great Forest. We must get you cleaned up." With that Hugoth began to walk the bridge heading for the two very, very, very large Forever Trees.

"How did you know I was coming? What did you mean you were expecting me? How did you know my name? How did you know I was a Prince?" Mystic questioned Hugoth.

"My friend the Donkorse was correct. You never stop asking questions, Prince of the Great Forest," laughed Hugoth. "Follow me Prince, your questions will all be answered in good or bad time."

"You know, Hugoth," Mystic remarked, "You look a lot like a dear friend of mine."

"And who might that be?" asked Hugoth.

"My true and trusted friend, Lightning, the irregular Badger, Duke of the Great Meadow," replied Mystic.

"You don't say?" answered Hugoth as he ambled on down the walkway.

13

"Excuse me?" asked Lightning.

"May em help ye?"

Lightning looked openly dumbfounded at Bubba as if to ask for help in understanding what this four-legged land walker had just said. If all truth be known, neither of them had the slightest clue.

"May em help ye?" the four-legger asked again.

Lighting was at wit's end and was becoming agitated. He was still holding the now clean, but lifeless body of his dear mentor and friend, yet he was now expected to engage in conversation, in gibberish no less, with this complete stranger? The Badger's patience snapped. He roared back while Bubba began growling fiercely at his side, "What are you saying, stranger? Can you not see the two of us have a dear friend, now lifeless, in our midst? What can you possibly be asking us that is more important than our efforts to deal with this loss?"

Snapping at anyone was uncharacteristic of Lightning. Donkorse was taken aback. Still, if the truth be known, he did understand the situation but could not fall out of character. He was, though, a bit miffed by the little cat's attitude. Nevertheless, he collected his thoughts, stood his ground and politely asked again, "May em help ye?"

The Badger could only shake his head in frustration. How was he to deal with this perilous set of foreboding circumstances? Where was Mystic when he needed him? Vincen, his other advisor, was here, but, of course, he was of no use to anything now. All hope for a successful rescue of Mystic that would trigger a joyous celebratory return to The Great Forest was now lying lifeless and drenched in the Badger's strong arms. Yet all was not lost. The limp body cradled lovingly in the Badger's strong paws jerked. The Badger and the Cheetah both looked at the Eagle's body as it jerked once again.

"Stand still Lightning, you are disturbing Vincen's rest or rigormortisness is setting in," stated the young Cheetah, who, obviously, had never had classes in which the correct spelling and pronunciation of that word was taught. "Stop jerking him around!" demanded Bubba.

"I am not jerking him around, Bubba," stated a dazed Badger. "I believe the body is jerking on its own!"

"That can't be happening. You are playing a joke on me of the cruelest kind. Mystic would not like to hear words of this disrespect."

"You don't believe me? Then look for yourself," Lightning said defiantly.

"If it is your wish, then look I will," said Bubba as he pressed his ear next to the Eagle's body.

"Wait a click Lightning, I believe you are on to something. I do think I sense a quaver beneath his feathers. Is he breathing?"

All of a sudden Vincen coughed loudly spewing mud from his beak. He continued coughing as his eyes blinked alertly open just as bright and clear as ever. "This mud does have quite a unique and wonderful taste to it," Vincen sputtered.

"He's back! He's back!" rejoiced Bubba, bouncing around like a younger cub than he was.

Lightning pulled the Eagle tightly to his chest and began sobbing all over again.

"Really now, Bubba, back from where? What are you carrying on so for? Lightning, have a little self-control. You are squeezing me to death. Why did you let me sleep? How long was I out?" The rejuvenated Vincen was asking non-stop questions.

Lightning's sobs turned into laughter. He flexed the strong muscles in his arms and threw the now awakened Eagle high into the air. "Vincen, let me see if you can fly as well as you talk?"

Bubba worked hard to fight back the tears of happiness. Cheetahs don't cry, he reminded himself over and over again.

Vincen took off, flying majestically again far above whatever land they were now in. Bubba and the Badger decided silently together that they would save this story until later, much later. Vincen swooped down and lit on the Badger's shoulder. "I feel more alive now, than I have in ages," he proclaimed. "It's amazing what a little nap can do for you! Now, friends, who do we have here?"

Bubba answered, "We don't know, Vincen. We can't make out what he is trying to say. He is talking a bit gibberishly. He mentioned something about mayhem helpyee, whoever that is."

Watching the scene of the three friends unfold, Donkorse silently enjoyed the spectacle. "Yes, the water in that stream is amazing," he said finally. Then he asked again, "May em help ye?"

Vincen answered, "You sure may. Where are we? Who are you? And have you seen our friend? He is a gray Wolf about 3 times as tall as I am."

"Here. Donkorse. Em see em there yonder soon past ye yes," answered Donkorse.

"That is wonderful news!" exclaimed Vincen to a much surprised and wide-eyed Donkorse.

Bubba was not thinking clearly right about now. He asked Vincen, "Did you understand all that he was saying?"

"Certainly, young Cheetah," Vincen replied as he looked quickly down at Bubba and then back to the humble Donkorse. "Why, he is speaking in the olde language of the Owls, no more, no less. I have no idea how he knows it, but he does, and so do I. I learned it long ago as a third language from the very descendants of the Owls that originated it. "It's quite easy to understand, really it is," continued Vincen.

Donkorse's eyes were as big as saucers for the second time in too short a while, and somewhere, deep inside his large head he was kicking himself. He had been found out. This was not gibberish to the Eagles. "Of course," he thought, "The Owls taught the language to the Eagles who, in turn, modified it into a fourth, fifth and sixth language for scouting missions. Uh-oh!" Donkorse recovered his composure and waited, dumbfounded for the next question.

"So you say Donkorse, shall I speak with you in your language or ours. The choice is yours. What shall it be?" Vincen inquired excitedly.

"Em know ye speak ye em dee ye," replied Donkorse.

"Please," asked the Badger, "For our sake speak in our language."

Vincen obliged and continued with Donkorse. "You say our friend came by a while back, did you? Fine, where is he now?"

"Ye dee be travel em Wolf The Path To Where I Am Going time passed longly ago."

"That is marvelous. Was he healthy and unharmed?"

"Yea yes ye travels well ye em," answered Donkorse.

"Can you take us there as quickly as you took him?" asked Vincen.

"Not em ye travel be back now."

"Oh come now, Donkorse. Surely it can't be that far out of your way. Will you at least point us in the right direction?" begged Vincen.

"Yea, ye The Path to Where I Am Going to follow be em too," Donkorse nodded as he answered Vincen's question.

"We will follow then, The Path to Where I Am Going, friends. At the end of the path we should find Mystic, according to this creature," Vincen stated proudly to the Badger and the Cheetah.

Rakki and Karri flew silently and mostly unnoticed, in closer to hear the conversation. They landed lightly on a branch of a medium-sized sweet gum tree just behind Vincen and the Badger. Donkorse was the only four-legger of the group to spy the two Hawks and blinked an eye as he made eye contact with the small pair.

Rakki whispered softly to Karri, "Now maybe we can hear what is going on."

Karri curtly, yet cautiously said in return, "Why do we not go ahead and land on Donkorse's ears and tell him what to say?"

"Dear Sister, I can't believe you want to get that involved!" Rakki smartly answered.

"I don't, oh nosey one! But, if we get any closer, we might as well," Karri said.

"Shhhh!" Rakki loudly whispered.

Too late! Bubba whirled around and saw the two small Hawks as one quickly was throwing its wing into the beak of the other. He did nothing. In the Great Forest there were always sky-travelers in the trees. These two small ones were no problem. He did not see them as a threat and turned back to the conversation.

Lightning replied to the Donkorse, "Thank you, kind sir. May I ask if he was he in good spirits? We have come to rescue him."

Donkorse answered, "Rescue ye Wolf? Rescue ye Wolf of what?"

Lightning understood this. He replied, "Why, rescue him from danger, of course!"

Donkorse began to tremble and asked, "Danger, where ye know danger?" Donkorse was putting on quite a show now. He hoped to gain a little credibility as a meek humble creature with no knowledge of the danger that could actually be lying in wait for these determined creatures. He looked around and started shuffling his way into the middle of the trio of friends.

"Be there ye danger here round, em know not dee danger."

Vincen calmly said, "Steady, humble one, I am afraid sir that my old friend and your new one, Lightning, the irregular Badger, has prematurely decided there is danger here in this place. Wherever this place may be."

Donkorse was once again surprised. His jaw slackened, his head tilted forward and his mouth fell open as his eyes, once again bulged from their sockets. Rakki and Karri were surprised as well. The Hawks turned to face each other, eyes wide with questions, while silently mouthing the word "Badger" to each other.

"Why he looks just like...," Karri was the one who threw the wing in front of Rakki's moving beak this time.

"Whatever!" Karri said under her breath as she took wing and quickly headed to deliver her report to the Keeper.

14

"Em newer friends," Donkorse said. "Ye older friend, ye Wolf, passed be here not too long been. Dee talk de yes question ye did. Ye ye be a path to dee small woods that leads dee Path To Where I Am Going. Ye older friend followed em, on, on The Path To Where I Am Going ye em left he there. Ye find to friend be dee Burg."

"Excuse me, if you please, sir", Bubba cautiously interrupted. "If the gray Wolf, our older friend, followed you to where you are going then why do you say he is where you were?"

Vincen, somewhat amused, looked at Donkorse and asked, ""Which way should we travel to get to The Path to Where I Am Going?

"Ye would travel dee way be course," answered Donkorse.

"Thank you sir for your help and I hope we see you once again," Vincen replied. Then he looked at Bubba and Lightning. Vincen issued a quick, "Follow me."

He proceeded to lead the group in the direction Donkorse had just come from. Bubba, looking and feeling greatly confused, began to walk the way of the Donkorse until Lighting grabbed him by the tail and begin pulling him in the direction he and Vincen were going. To this day Bubba has no idea what the Donkorse was talking about.

"Well, that went as well as one could expect," Donkorse muttered to himself as he casually walked away from the new arrivals along The Path To Where I Am Going. Donkorse-- as well as Rakki, Karri, Hugoth and a few others--had been given certain instructions by the Keeper in case this scenario had ever come to be. Now it had. There was much work to do. Hopefully, although this was an almost impossible hope, the remainder of the visitor's time spent in this land would now proceed uneventfully. That was the collective wish anyway.

***

The Land of Nuorg

Once past the range of the visitor's eyesight, Donkorse turned down a seldom-used, hidden path that branched off to the right. He followed that path as it wound its way through the thick growth of trees and shrubbery down the gradually sloping terrain to another hidden entrance.

This entrance was to the cave that led under Sweet Gulley. Here the collecting pools were built for Sweet Gulley among other various devices. There were secret rooms and large halls. This cave was a place of much significance if trouble ever developed in this land. Of course, that was almost unthinkable to the dwellers here; still, it was the main reason these four visitors had been called, although they were not yet aware of it. Donkorse quickly passed through the main corridor that led past several smaller shafts that broke off on both sides. These smaller shafts led to places both good and bad. If the visitors ever got this far, he could only wish them the good places, for the bad places were exactly that.

Donkorse emerged from the cave on the far side of Sweet Gulley. From here, he would be able to follow the visitors' movements and relay updated information of their progress back to the Keeper. As he exited the cave, he was met by a steep trail that led to The Path to Where I Was. He climbed down the trail and made a left turn that allowed him to parallel The Path to Where I Am Going. This path was not so well traveled. It would be a much more difficult path from which to follow the visitors, but that was the plan. He quietly and expediently made his way to the meeting place, all the while, staying within eyesight or hearing range of the visitors on the other path. He would soon meet up with Rakki or Karri and receive his next set of instructions from the Keeper.

***

"Badger, you say?" answered Hugoth, "He must then be an enormous Badger, Prince Mystic."

"Hugoth, where am I? Where is this land? It is so beautifully peaceful, yet it remains innocent in so many inviting ways," Mystic asked sincerely. "Who leads the dwellers here?"

"All of your questions will be answered in their own time. I am not permitted to unlock the secrets of where you are. I can tell you only this; you are now in the Land of Nuorg. You have been summoned here for a purpose. There is much for you to do. Should any creatures be following you, they will have much to do also. I hope you all fare well. It is imperative that you survive your stay here. I have said all I can say. Please come with me," Hugoth advised as he continued to lead Mystic along the walkway.

"You must know more than that!" Mystic exclaimed. "What you have shared makes me a bit nervous. Just what should I expect during my stay? Hugoth, you must tell me more, you must," Mystic pleaded.

"Prince, you have been summoned here for a purpose larger than I. Reflect on that fact and do not linger on the details. As I told you, your questions will all be answered in their own time," Hugoth replied.

"Do you know someone who can help me get back to my land, to where I came from?" Mystic asked.

Hugoth replied, "That is certain. I know of someone who can help you. He has a dwelling out in the country. Nobody knows where, but he lives somewhere or everywhere. One of your questions will be answered when you find where he dwells. Let me see what I can do to help you find him."

***

The Keeper heard the light scratching, rose from his chair and walked to the heavy shutters covering his window. He opened them just enough, allowing the small Hawk to enter. Karri hopped inside the window. After she briefed him on all the events that had happened so far, he spoke to her. "So my dear little Karri, the wheels are turning. That is most interesting concerning the Eagle. As you know, that could have easily dealt us a dreadful blow, with very complicated and dire circumstances had it not ended as you say. I am glad you did not interfere. Be away once again, little friend. Inform Rakki that he is to stay with the last group while you go meet up with Donkorse. Keep me informed and get some rest. It is all about to begin. Karri, before you go, one last question. Did either of them have it?"

"No sir, I am sorry to say, none of us have seen it yet."

With those last words haunting his mind, the Keeper, with a tender hand, smoothed the feathers on the Hawk's head and dismissed her. Karri was off.

The Keeper let out a deep breath as he carefully pulled the heavy shutters closed. He returned to his overstuffed chair, sat down then somberly said to his guest, "That was very close to a tragedy. Are you absolutely positive that we still want to go through with it? With this group? Is this a game to be played by destiny's hand or is this luck?"

The shadowed head of the guest closed his eyes, sighing as he did so. He told the Keeper in a very ancient voice, "It must continue." The guest added, "And I hope, I hope that it is destiny's hand."

***

"Well, that was another odd event," Lightning said to Vincen and Bubba. "What do you make of that character?"

"Funny you should ask, Lightning. I will say he acted a bit peculiar but then, when one is attempting to make up an olde studied language on the fly, it can put oneself in a very uncomfortable predicament," added Vincen.

Bubba jumped in, "What did you say? You believe he was making up that gibberish as he spoke?"

Vincen started, "I certainly believe he was struggling to piece it together, yes I do. The four-legger had some of the basic language learned, but his composition was atrocious. It was if he was hiding something from us. I truly believe that creature, Donkorse, was a four-legger of higher intelligence than he led us to believe. He was also doing a poor job of acting. If one had no prior education, he would never know how to begin speaking in the olde Owl language. He would not even know what it was or that it existed. The odds of his just making it up are not stacked in his favor. Somewhere, during that creature's life, he has heard or been taught the elements of the language by someone or something that speaks it. Why he tried to fool an Eagle with it is more than I can gather right now. I can only say this, young friends, I assume that our adventure up to now has been rather mundane. I am now of the mind that it is positively about to begin."

Lightning thought about Donkorse's behavior and concurred with Vincen. "I believe you to be right sir," he added, nodding his massive head in agreement. "There was something strange in his behavior. He was startled twice as I remember: once, when you identified the olde language of the owls and secondly, when you introduced me as a Badger. Oh well, we must be on our way. We should gather our weapons, any food we can salvage and move on. If the adventure is to begin, we need to eat. We must also find containers to carry portions of this water with us...just in case."

"I couldn't agree with you more," said a smiling Bubba. "I will round up the weapons. Lightning, you get the food and water. Vincen, you make the plans for our next move."

"Sounds good to me," answered Vincen.

The Eagle immediately took wing and soared high above the four-leggers, scouting as he could only imagine his ancestors did. Something had happened to him. He was rejuvenated and had absolutely no understanding why that was. He felt young again. He was surprised with the strength in his tired old wings. He thought for a click that he could, maybe, even leave the Cheetah in his wake. No, that was not possible, not even now. Vincen was impressed by this land. From high above, it was magnificent. The rivers and streams he saw were odd. The water flowed as if running the wrong way. From high above the ground, he quickly noticed that the sun never seemed to move. "Well, mysteries do seem to abound here, that much is certain," the Eagle said to himself.

Rakki sat watching from his perch. He admired the Eagle's incredible strength combined with his exceptional speed. This was, without any doubt, one exceedingly special Eagle. Maybe the Keeper does know something more about this small group of creatures than he is telling Rakki thought. He watched the Eagle's flights of fancy for a while then turned his attention back to the others. He wondered when Karri would return and what their next course of action would be. This was becoming interesting. He was beginning to enjoy himself.

"It's not here!" exclaimed Bubba.

"What's not here?" asked the Badger.

"The wand/staff, it's not here!" Bubba repeated. "I have my rapier, we have located your ax-pike, but there is no trace of the wand/staff."

"Really?" asked Lightning.

"Really!" cried Bubba.

Oh no, this could be bad or good, thought Rakki as he heard the commotion. This at least means they had brought something very special. The Cat was sure making a big deal for nothing if it wasn't, indeed, very special. Could it be? Could it be what the Keeper had been telling them about for so long? Could it be the lost "Staff of Hewitt"?"

"Come now, Bubba, it landed with us, did it not?" asked the Badger.

The Land of Nuorg

"I think it did. I scrambled out of its way as it was coming down on top of us. I know it landed in the mud along with the other weapons. It had to."

"Well then, it must be here. Keep looking and keep your head about you. Please don't panic. You know I don't like it when you panic. I can't understand you when you stutter," stated the Badger.

"I'm telling you, it is not here. You know that thing has a mind of its own. It has proven that true already."

Lightning replied, "Dig deep into the mud. Eat it all if you have to. We have to find Mystic's wand/staff!"

"Aha!" thought Rakki, "I must report this, but I can't. I must wait on Karri." Now he was hoping she would show up quickly. This news could be very beneficial.

"Oh mercy," sighed Lightning. "Let me help you look. We will find food on the way. I doubt if we will find another wand/staff."

"Wow, you are a genius, Lightning!" The Cheetahs' attitude was back. He was feeling good.

"Why thank you, Bubba. I suppose you won't mind if I look here then?" Lightning tromped over behind Bubba and jumped on his injured tail. Bubba did not respond.

"Bubba, did you not experience a great pain just now as I stomped on your tail?" Lightning asked.

"No. What did you do that for?" asked Bubba.

"To get you back for that genius remark, I guess. Only you did not jump or yell or anything. Let me have a look at that tail." Lightning grabbed the Cheetah's tail and lifted it high out of the mud. Of course, along with the tail came the entire Cheetah. "Well, look at that. There is not a sign of your bite wound at all. This tail is as good as new. How could that be?"

Bubba did not like dangling above the ground like a sack of bark kakes. "Do you mind, Lightning? You think you could put me down?"

"Sure, if you promise to speak nicely."

"I promise, now put me down," said the Cheetah.

"As you wish."

Lightning let go of the tail, Cheetah and all, dropping the Cheetah headfirst back into the gooey mud. Bubba landed with a large splat while the Badger began another frantic search for the wand/staff. He had already re-collected enough of the original, though now mud covered, food to once again fill his pack. The wand/staff was now his main concern.

When Bubba finally righted himself, he sloshed back to the bank, crawled up onto it and sat down. Shaking his head while licking the sweet goo off his fur, he couldn't help but laugh. The Cheetah closed his eyes and grinned as only a Cheetah can. "There's nothing like staying humble, I always say."

Bubba, after grooming himself thoroughly, checked his tail. Sure enough, there was no sign of the wound. First Vincen, now this, he thought. He did not yet know about Mystic's paw. Even for a young Cheetah, he knew the things that were happening were strange. Yes, this was very strange. Good, but very strange.

Vincen came back. The Great Eagle was enjoying this new land. He swooped to the ground, landing at Bubba's side. "Well Vincen," asked the Cheetah, "What's out there?

My young Cheetah," Vincen answered, "more than you would possibly imagine. This land is magnificent. It compares equally to the Great Forest and more. I lost myself in thought several times as I flew. If it had not been for the recurring thoughts of our original reason for coming here, I could have easily soared the remainder of the day-round. I'll tell you young Cheetah, this land is stunning. Unless there is some underlying evil here--which I saw no hint of--I would have a hard time not remaining here."

Lightning was milling about, still in search of the wand/staff when he heard this remark. He stormed over through the mud to where the other two were chatting and let it be known in no uncertain terms that Vincen was way off course.

"What did you say, Vincen? Did I hear you say that you could easily remain here? Are you out of your mind? We do not live here, Vincen. This is not our land. If I remember correctly, we came here to rescue one of our own and I do not appreciate your forgetfulness of that matter. Am I making myself clear?" demanded the Badger.

Bubba was shocked at Lightning's outburst toward Vincen. He had never seen this before. He cocked his head, cut his eyes at the Badger and then asked "Lightning, are you all right?"

"I most certainly am," Lightning replied. "I would ask that same question to Vincen. He is the one who seems none the worse for wear or care right now! I guess you didn't mention to him that the wand/staff is now missing? Did you?"

The Land of Nuorg

This last bit of news got Vincen's full attention. Bubba immediately noticed a sudden change in the Eagle's personality. It was if the Eagle had been instantly jerked back to reality.

"Excuse me, Lighting, what, what did you say about the wand/staff?" asked Vincen.

"I said it is now missing along with its owner. The two of us have searched in vain for it while you have been up there soaring about without a care of our world. That is what I said in so many words," Lightning fumed without one trace of apology in his voice.

"This can't be. Did it not land right alongside of us?" inquired Vincen.

Bubba interrupted, "Yes, it did. It landed exactly where I did, fortunately for me, a split click later. It just missed me as it struck the mud."

"Then it has to be here," replied the Eagle.

"My thoughts exactly," said a still miffed Badger. "But it is not! Did you see it on your little excursion? We certainly haven't!"

"And you have searched everywhere?" asked Vincen.

"Yes, Vincen, of course we have, to the best of our ability", answered Bubba.

Karri lit softly on the same branch where Rakki watched the three visitors deep in discussion.

"Tell me what is happening, Brother," she asked.

"Karri, I believe that one of these three visitors brought the Staff of Hewitt here with them. The trouble is that it has now disappeared. They are having a lively discussion on that right now," Rakki explained.

"Brother, that is wonderful news. Everything is falling in place just as planned. Quickly, get that message to the Keeper while I go rendezvous with Donkorse. There is much work to be done." Again the little Hawk was off in one direction as her brother set off toward the Burg and the Keeper's window ledge.

"If it landed here, then it has to be here," said Vincen.

"Sir, we have searched and searched. It is not here, I am sorry," stated Lightning.

"We have spent too much time here. We must continue our search for Mystic. The wand/staff seems to be following him. Just maybe, the wand/staff is on its way to Mystic at this very moment. Gather our belongings. We have to find that Wolf," declared Vincen.

"Very well, sir," replied Lightning.

The Badger picked up his pack and his ax-pike as Bubba took one last gulp of the sweet mud. Bubba picked up his rapier and the three friends set off down The Path to Where I Am Going. The Eagle hopped up onto Lightning's shoulders so they could stay in a tight group in case of more trouble.

***

In the bottom of the collecting pool, above the cave where Donkorse had just passed, a leak had formed. Whatever caused the leak had since been removed. Now, steadily, the leak grew a little larger. The bottom layer of hardened Sweet Gulley mud: acted as a buffer between the collected mud and the original stream water. It had been cracked by a concentrated blow from a heavy object. The original stream water had never ceased to flow and now acted to cool the sweet mud directly above it. This was a fortunate stroke of coincidence, for it hadn't been planned this way.

Unfortunately now, the stream water was rising to the top of the collected mud through the crack in the hardened lower layer. At the same time, the heavy mud was seeping down through the crack along with whatever lay in the bottom of the collecting pool. This escaping mud had found its way down through one of the many natural waterfalls that existed in the cave. This randomly selected waterfall was the biggest and most powerful waterfall in the cave. Ever so slowly, the mud began to replace the water. What had once been a beautiful and mesmerizing work of natural art was becoming a tiny, slow-moving mudslide. Then, as oddly as it had begun, a large object passed through the crack in the hardened layer of mud, then through the stream water, then through the waterfall. This medium-sized object dropped into the fall and positioned its form perfectly in place to seal the crack above the waterfall with its ball-like top. The mud stopped freely flowing. Soon it hardened once again above the crack. The hardening mud piled on top of itself, effectively sealing the entire opening in the collecting pool from top to bottom. The mud eventually hardened to its original contours above, allowing the stream water to, once again, take its normal course. The waterfall slowly began flowing again. The water washed the remaining mud off the gleaming object that had found its way down from the collecting pool. The water added a shine to the object, which it hadn't had in a very long time. The object actually seemed to be glowing.

15

Hugoth led Mystic to the end of the walkway. There, at the entrance to the dwelling places, Mystic realized how tall the two "Forever Trees" actually were. These trees were as tall as small mountains. It would take 30 Wolves nose to tail to make a ring around just one of them. Mystic looked between the trees and observed the dwellings. They looked much more ornate when viewed from this closer point of view. The paths were covered in a glittery yellow dust that reflected the light of daytime quite brilliantly.

Hugoth stopped at the base of the right tree and entered, through a tall door with a rounded top, a large, spacious room cut into the center of the tree's trunk. Mystic followed closely. Just before he entered the door, he noticed a pail of water hung on a root with a barrel of oats not far beneath it. The clear, clean water reminded him of how dirty he still must be. He so longed for a dip in a pool to clean his unruly, goo-matted fur.

As Mystic entered, Hugoth must have known what he was thinking. Hugoth guided Mystic through another smaller door that led down a short flight of stairs. At the bottom, a smallish room held a deep pool of clear water. The water was so clear that it appeared to emit its own light. Obviously, it came in through some contraption from the river. A coil of rope hung on the wall next to a large wheel similar to the ones he had seen near the bridge, only much smaller. Hugoth directed the mud-covered Wolf to step in to the water and clean up. "Take your time, Prince Mystic, this may be the last fresh water bath you will have for quite some time."

Hugoth returned to his den and sat down to scribble a note for the Keeper. His desk would have made a large table for most creatures, but because of his size, it was just right for note scribbling. After a few clicks Mystic returned all washed up and shaken out.

"Make yourself welcome, Prince Mystic. This is my dwelling, as you call it. If you are still hungry, eat. If you are thirsty, drink. I have some

The Land of Nuorg

work to catch up on before we continue with your quest to return home," said Hugoth.

"Hugoth, you seem very well informed, though you will answer no questions," Mystic commented. "Can you tell me this? Was I followed?"

"Did you want to be?" Hugoth added while he kept scribbling.

"I don't know, seeing that I don't know if peril or good fortune awaits me. But I was hoping some of my dear friends would at least notice my disappearance and maybe try to find me," Mystic said longingly.

"In time Prince, in good time," answered Hugoth.

Hugoth finished his scribbling and rolled the notations, tied a piece of straw around it and set it in a small box attached to his front door. He, then, returned and sat down across the room from Mystic. "What should we do first, Prince?" asked Hugoth.

"What do you mean?" answered Mystic. I have to find my way back to the Great Forest, of course."

"I thought you wanted to find the one to help you do just that?" asked Hugoth.

"I do. Of course I do," said Mystic.

"Then it shall be, Prince. As I said before, this person may dwell here. Now, what I can't tell you is where or how you will find him. You have the run of Nuorg. No two-legged or four-legged creature nor any winged creature, other than those you know, are permitted to assist you. If they do, you may not be permitted to leave our land. When you find this creature that knows how to get you back to the Great Forest, it will not make itself obviously known to you. As you have probably surmised by now, this will be a trial of your abilities. You may ask questions of the dwellers here, but the answers, to those questions, may or may not be given to you. It's too late for you to decide against it, as you are already here. There could be dangerous decisions made on your part just like there may be incredibly wise decisions made. You will be the judge of that by the outcomes you face. Be careful, not everything good is good and not everything bad is bad. Now, are you ready to begin?"

"Well, you have kind of dampened my excitement," stated Mystic, "but yes, I am ready. How do I get started?"

Hugoth stood up and motioned Mystic to the door. He stepped outside with the Wolf and raised his arms in two directions, left and right. "Find who you are looking for."

After he made that short statement, Hugoth walked back inside his dwelling and closed the door solidly behind him.

Mystic was dumbfounded. "Excuse me Hugoth, Hugoth. What shall I do now?" asked Mystic.

Hugoth slightly opened his door and said once again, "Find who you are looking for." The door was shut again.

Mystic looked around, hoping for some kind of direction. He remembered the note Hugoth left in the door box. He raised himself up on his back legs and looked in the box only to find the note had vanished. "Oh mercy," Mystic muttered. "Oh mercy."

***

Rakki was making good time on his way back to the Burg. Upon approaching the bridge, he noticed Hugoth and the Wolf passing into Hugoth's dwelling. He flew low over the walkway, slowed and lit on the water pail that hung over the barrel of oats. He correctly decided to wait here until Hugoth, as planned, deposited the note to the Keeper regarding his findings, in the door box. He was headed there anyway, so why not take the note as well? That would allow him a little while to catch his breath, so he waited silently on this perch.

His wait was rewarded, as after a comfortable rest, Hugoth lumbered to the door, opened it and without regard placed the aforementioned note in the door box. Hugoth quickly glanced around, then up and noticed the small Hawk on the pail. He nodded a signal to the Hawk as they made eye contact and returned inside. Rakki hopped quietly down to the box, gently picked up the rolled note and took wing toward the Keeper's window ledge. With all of the shutters closed, Rakki knew to be as quiet as possible, since most of the inhabitants of the Burg were sleeping.

The small Hawk traveled from the Forever Trees to the Keeper's window ledge at a steady pace. Not too fast and not slow enough to fall from the sky. He lit on the ledge, carefully setting the note beside him. He moved a little closer to the shutters then scratched on one of them with his sharp beak. After a very short pause, the shutter opened. Rakki picked up the note with his beak and hopped inside the window. He flew over to the well-used wooden gathering table in the middle of the Keeper's large den. He set the note on the table and perched on a stack of thick books across from where the Keeper would be seating himself. Rakki noticed a sleeping figure in the corner of the room and remained silent. The Keeper would ask the questions. He was here to give answers.

***

Karri was so pleased to find that the three new visitors were finally leaving Sweet Gulley. She remained on her perch as they, ever so slowly, made their way onto The Path to Where I Am Going. They ambled a bit in the early going, as they couldn't help but take in some of the marvelous scenery. Even Bubba, as young as he was, felt impressed with the surroundings. As the visitors methodically made their way up the first hill of many to come, Karri looked across Sweet Gulley hunting for Donkorse. She would meet with him before she took another lookout perch to follow Bubba, Vincen and Lightning. After some searching and perch swapping, she spied Donkorse keeping their pace, about one or two leisure beats behind. She rose from her last perch, then carefully made her way to the meeting spot, staying low enough so the Eagle would not spot her. She didn't mind if he did. After all, sky-travelers did fly. She just did not want to interfere with their progress by drawing attention to herself.

She came to the pre-arranged location some time before Donkorse did. She rested and napped for a good while. She would be refreshed when Donkorse arrived.

***

"Did you see this dwelling place that Donkorse was referring to during your flight?" asked Lightning.

"Yes, Lightning, I believe I did," Vincen said from high atop the Badger's shoulder. "I didn't get to observation height, but I did do a bit of scouting down this path. Our destination lies at least 400 pursuit beats away. Sons, I am sorry for my cavalier behavior and the way I said some things back there. I noticed the exact same attitude brimming from Mystic just before he was drawn into the well. He was mesmerized by something. I know you must think that sounds odd. I can't help but think, now, that it was an overwhelming feeling of peace and tranquility, just as I felt while doing my exploring. It did not last long for Mystic, but it did him in. At least it got him here. I had that same feeling as I flew over this land. There is nothing wrong here. I could sense nothing except wonderfully good feelings. I can't explain it and won't try. In order to find our friend we can't let ourselves off guard or we truly won't care if we ever find Mystic or get home to the Great Forest. I'm afraid that would not sit well with destiny. I have an even stronger feeling that we must return. We must."

"You know something else that is odd?" asked Bubba.

"Is this relatively speaking, Bubba?" asked Lightning.

"Well, no. This is just plain odd or maybe just drastically different, or maybe, simply stated, weird," Bubba answered.

"Well go on, let's hear it," replied Lightning.

"Okay," began Bubba. "For one, the shadows are not changing. We have not witnessed any movement of the sun here, if that is a sun. We have been involved in this part of our journey for over 100 clicks and it has not gotten lighter or darker or hotter or cooler. To me, even with my limited education, that is especially odd."

"I believe you are onto something there, Son, albeit, I have no idea what," Vincen replied with a half chuckle.

"I noticed it as well, Bubba," added Lightning. I was not that interested in it, but I noticed it. I gave the benefit of the doubt to this strange land. I have no idea how things work here, so I just let it be. It is odd, granted however, our objective is to find Mystic and return to the Great Forest, regardless, of this land's oddities. Surely, we will find this answer and more, I presume, in good time."

"Well said, my dear Badger. Very well said. I assume then, that we are all in agreement again on our mission here, so let us get to it," stated Vincen.

**

As, the three friends continued traveling The Path to Where I Am Going, Donkorse was reaching his meeting place quicker than originally planned. He was hoping that Karri wasn't there when he arrived. He needed some overdue rest. After all, he had been on his feet for some time now and was steadily approaching exhaustion. In the Burg, he knew, it was time for all creatures to get some rest or sleep.

Donkorse was sure the three new visitors would be stopping soon enough. At least he hoped they would. As he rounded the last tight curve on this seldom-traveled path and dodged another low-hanging branch, he saw the meeting spot. It was a small grassy area with a few sitting stones placed in a half circle facing one large log cut in half lengthwise.

He noticed, unfortunately, that Karri had beaten him to the spot and gotten a head start on resting. He quietly walked in and lay down beside the log. Once his body hit the ground his wait for rest was over. He immediately fell into a much-needed, deep sleep. Karri had not awakened. All things considered, everything was moving pretty much as planned and the Keeper had said to rest when possible. So they did.

***

Rakki remained on his book perch as the Keeper slowly walked over to the gathering table. He carefully untied the straw that held the note and spread it across the table. Hugoth scribbled in such big letters that even a short note took up a lot of space. But this was not a short note. This was as close to a letter as Hugoth had ever written. Since Hugoth had to deliver it so quickly, the hand scribbling was not as easily legible as most of his notes. That was okay. The big creature had not been scribbling long, and he was one of the only four-leggers that had even bothered to give it a try. Donkorse failed miserably at it because he could not fashion a scribbling tool to fit around his hoof, nor did he have the agility in his joints to permit the delicate strokes required. The men, women and children of the Burg found it quite humorous watching these four-leggers as they made repeated attempts learning to write. Even the best work done to date was still scribbling. So, scribbling was now the word used to describe four-legger writing and that was absolutely fine with them. They were happy just to have the opportunity to do so.

The Keeper laid a small weight on each corner of the note as he unrolled it. In order to make out the scribble, he moved a lit candle closer to the edge. His guest was still asleep and he felt no urgent need to wake the old fellow, so he did not open the heavy shutters that blocked the light. "Well, Rakki," he said, "let me read what news Hugoth shares with us. I am sure you have important news as well. Still, I need to find out as much as he knows about our first visitor, the Wolf, before I find out about our newest arrivals."

The Keeper sat down as he began to read the note. Rakki found himself nodding off on more than one occasion. He soon gave up his fight as sleep took over. The Keeper looked up from his reading, took one look at the brave and exhausted little Hawk. Smiling, he returned to his work.

"Hmmm, this is wonderfully interesting," the Keeper said to himself quietly.

"Everything so far has gone as well as can be expected, I think. This Wolf is most certainly the Wolf we have collected so much information on. I trust that he can pass the tests. If he does, I will be well served. I'll let the little Hawk sleep a bit longer while I take a nap. This is good; this is very good."

***

Lightning was tired. "Vincen, may we please rest? I am completely worn out. I am afraid I will lose my bearings. Please, let us rest."

Bubba agreed whole-heartedly. "I would not mind a good rest myself, Sir."

Vincen, not ordinarily one to push too hard, relented. "Fine, Sons, let us rest under the next shady tree that is not on the path. I would rest easier knowing that I could see something else before something else saw me. We will nap and eat soon."

Bubba saw the first inviting spot and called the others' attention to a lovely site just at the top of the next twist in the path. "There'" he said. "Just ahead is the perfect location for us, is it not, Vincen?"

"Yes, I believe it is. If each of you will agree, there it will be," replied Vincen.

Bubba rushed ahead of his two slower friends, claiming the best spot in the small shaded area. Lightning followed suit with the second best spot while Vincen just plopped himself down between them. The shady area welcomed them with a cool bed of tall, soft grass. The Badger doled out food from the pack to each of them. They ate the offerings ravenously, but politely. What none of them had expected, but all relished, was the unique and entirely sweet coating of mud that now completely encased each piece of food served. Once each ate their fill of the distinctively flavored morsels, they fell asleep at their own pace. The sleep was long overdue and very much appreciated.

***

"How can I be expected to find who I am looking for if I don't know who he is or what he is, where he is or if he is even a he at all?" Mystic asked himself. Then he added, "Hugoth was not very much help if the truth be known, at least not as far as my search is concerned."

Mystic pondered this situation before he decided to start off. Where was he to go? He circled the entire dwelling place as questions bounced around in his mind. He found the Burg most interesting as he wandered between the massive stone walls. Every large window on every dwelling had heavy shutters pulled tightly shut. Mystic found this as normal as anything else he had discovered so far. What he had thought odd, he surmised, was interestingly normal here in The Land of Nuorg. At least that much he was sure of. Mystic spent several clicks studying the dwelling places, gardens, paths, benches, nearly everything, but never found anything to help him locate who or what he was looking for. "Maybe I should search out in the country side first. Surely I could come back here should I need more information, although, I doubt if Hugoth or any other dweller here will be any more forthcoming than the Guard of the Forever Trees has been already," Mystic thought. "Oh, what could it hurt?"

Mystic gradually found his way back to the bridge. He returned to Hugoth's dwelling to pay him another visit, finding his enormous entry door solidly closed and bolted. It seemed apparent that Hugoth was tired as well. Indeed he was. Hugoth was sound asleep somewhere within his dwelling. No matter how much noise Mystic made, he knew that Hugoth would be of no help during this visit. The Wolf climbed up on the walkway and turned to study the Burg one more time. Then he began a long, lonely walk in preparation for the second leg of this adventure. He longed for the company of Vincen, Bubba and Lightning. Mystic slowly made his way to the end of the bridge. He quickly sauntered down the ramp turning right at the bottom to head straight to the river's edge for a drink of water. He stalled momentarily. All of a sudden he doubted the wisdom of continuing alone. He turned back to the bridge, but there was no way to climb onto the walkway. The ramp had vanished. The look in Mystic's eyes gave away the astonishment he was feeling. "Okay, that's not completely normal," he thought.

Mystic continued to the river's edge to drink his fill of the unbelievably clear, tasty water. How he would love to take some of this back to the Great Forest with him. The water not only quenched his thirst, but it quenched his hunger as well. He turned away from the river and broke into a trot, heading back to The Path to Where I Am Going"

"Hopefully, I'll find someone to help me... hopefully," Mystic said to himself.

16

"Rakki, Rakki, wake up, wake up little Hawk. There is work to do today," urged the Keeper.

The Keeper reached across the table and nudged the little Hawk. "Come on little one, wake up. It's time to get back to work!"

Rakki slowly acknowledged the Keeper's intention. He woke up, but he needed a bit more prodding to come to his senses. He was more exhausted than he had thought.

"Yes, sir? Are we ready so soon?" asked Rakki, blinking to chase the sleep from his bright round eyes.

"My dear little Hawk, the Burg is awake on this wonderful morning. Can you not see? The shutters are open. The paths are alive with activity. I say you've slept plenty, and as a matter of fact, so have I. I, I mean we both have so much to do and plan for, more sleep will come in due time. Are you ready for your next assignment?" asked the Keeper.

"Of course I am, sir. You know I am. What shall I do?" Rakki responded.

"Here, eat a bit of this sweet kaki as I update you. While you eat I'll share the information that Hugoth has collected for us."

"That will be splendid, sir," replied Rakki.

"Here goes," started the Keeper. "Our dear friend and worthy guard, Hugoth, has shared with us the following information. Wait, why don't you tell me what information you have collected so far in your travels? No, my mistake, you continue eating. I am so excited. I can hardly wait to see what comes to pass this day. Please forgive me for rambling. I will start again."

Rakki had never seen the Keeper so animated. Something must be going very right to make him so giddy. Rakki continued to eat his sweet kaki, watching the Keeper's hand and body motions intently. The Keeper was literally bouncing around his den. Rakki was amused at this sight, though he was becoming excitedly impatient. Rakki said after a short wait, "Quick, go ahead, Keeper, tell me what you have discovered with your reading of the note. How does it relate to the larger plan?"

"It is all coming together, friends," the Keeper stated proudly as he motioned for his, now awake guest and Rakki to move in closer to the note. "Hugoth has now informed us of this much, and I expect you, Rakki, to fill in any holes you can. Let's start with the Wolf. Hugoth has determined that the Wolf is, indeed, Mystic, The Prince of The Great Forest. He came through the Disappearing Well sometime around midday, two days past. Donkorse caught the surprised creature on his back. He conversed with him for quite some time, with Donkorse using that awful mixed-up version of the olde owl languages. He really must stop that, you know. Should an Owl come through Nuorg, it would be most embarrassing if he should accidentally hear that dreadful hodgepodge of wordage."

"According to Donkorse, much to his dismay, the Wolf partially understood the dialects that had been so haphazardly thrown together," the Keeper said. "It is then obvious that Mystic is, as a ruler should be, very well educated in many diverse areas. The Wolf asked several questions, actually too many by Donkorse standards."

"He stated that he did come through the well, which, with parallel thinking, means that he must have recognized some knowledge of the Staff of Hewitt's power. If he did not possess that knowledge, then the Staff, alone, recognized him. How that would happen is a mystery to me. Maybe the impending danger this Wolf faces was conveyed by him to the Staff in some unexplained way. By no means would I think that impossible. Am I moving too fast?" asked the Keeper.

The Keeper's guest finally spoke in a very distinguished learned voice, "No, you are not. How about it, little Hawk, have you got this so far?"

"Yes sir, I do. Please continue, Keeper," Rakki asked reverently.

"Mystic is, quite understandably, at a loss as to why he is here. This, of course, means, given the Wolf's lack of knowing this, that the Staff, not the Wolf's training, led him here. We will find out more on that as time moves on. The Wolf has made statements, be they indiscreet, that there may be creatures following him. By all reports, we now know this to be true, as Rakki will verify shortly. Whether they be friend or enemy is not for us to decide. That will be left to the tests. The tests will start soon. We have a few plans to make, so we must keep Mystic contained within the Burg until all is ready. As you both know, if the Wolf is not the chosen one, he will never leave our land. If those that followed him are not his friends, they will come to very unfortunate, permanent ends. As I am sure you know, we can have no creatures leave here, unless they are worthy. Those that have come before are all good creatures, but none have passed the tests completely and some, such as your group, have decided to educate and teach from here. You, for some reason having to do with your age, old or young, and specific health concerns, cannot return to our homelands. It will soon be a battle of the wisest and the strongest only, if the signs have been interpreted correctly. Dear friends, I hope for my sake that this Wolf can pass the tests."

The guest spoke again, "Your sake? I am sure you mean our sake, Keeper. I think you know that what I have told you is correct. The times are changing. I sensed it myself. That is why I came to you. The fact that this Wolf has paid us a visit, perhaps with the Staff's coaxing, is falling in line with what, I believe, is destiny's matter."

"I agree," said the Keeper, "But, we must be positively positive before we send him back, although, we may never be completely sure."

"Let's hear what the Hawk can add, shall we?" said the visitor.

"By all means. Go ahead Rakki. Tell us about these new visitors," the Keeper asked politely.

"Well sir, they are quite a threesome. There is one Eagle, one Cat and one B...I mean Badger, sir." Rakki began. "The Eagle is called Vincen, the Cat is called Bubba and the Badger is being called Lightning. They are quite a likeable and humorous group. The only mission they are known to have is locating Mystic, rescue him and return him to their dwelling place. There was almost a tragic ending to the Eagle's life before they even got started. Somehow, when they were thrown from the well, they landed in Sweet Gulley. The Eagle was trapped and suffocated."

"Oh my," said the visitor.

Rakki continued, "By some stroke of good fortune or destiny, the placement of their falling tools worked to their advantage, the best that I can make of it. One of the larger tools, somehow, broke through the bottom of the collecting pool, allowing the water to find its way to the top of the Sweet Gulley catchings. The water must have had a mind of its own. It slowly evolved into a water fountain. The B...Badger used the water to clean the Eagle. In doing so, the Eagle was revived."

"Gracious," exclaimed the visitor. "Why did you not tell me of this?"

"No reason to wake you. You were in a deep sleep. I saw no cause to alarm you," stated the Keeper calmly.

"No reason to alarm me? Really!" the visitor said with a little confusion in his voice.

"Rakki, carry on," the Keeper asked.

"Where was I? Oh yes, anyway, the Eagle was revived. His friends began collecting their tools. One was missing, and this is the most important part. They searched frantically for it. I heard much dialogue concerning Mystic's wand/staff. Yes sir, they called the missing tool, Mystic's wand/staff. I was very excited. I watched them until Karri bid me to come and report to you. Is this the Staff, Sir?" Rakki asked anxiously.

"That is a good question. All of the information would lead me to believe it is. Did they find it?" asked the Keeper.

"No Sir, they did not," Rakki replied.

"No "Staff of Hewitt"?" asked the visitor as he began to nervously pace. "If there is no Staff of Hewitt, there is no way the Wolf can return from where he came to do anything. We would be risking a great deal of unwanted exposure to whoever decided to wield the Staff."

"I am not sure about that," said the Keeper. "The staff knows. I don't know how, but somehow it knows. I am not convinced that trouble would come to us if the Staff fell into the wrong hands."

Rakki added, "I am almost sure the Staff is what they searched so diligently for. If it came down with them, then we will find it."

"I hope you are right, little friend," said the visitor, "I hope you are right.

***

Hugoth awoke from his slumber, rolled off of his sleeping pad and stretched a mighty stretch while lumbering onto his four legs. After regaining his balance, the Guard made his way through his den and opened the entry door. It was a glorious morning. He hoped he would make contact with Mystic soon. He must make sure that he has not left the Burg. Hugoth ate a gigantic breakfast of berries and sweet kakis before washing it all down with a huge pail of fresh water. He was plodding down to the river to refill his water pails when he noticed

The Land of Nuorg

something that could, just maybe, be a bit of a problem. He may have trusted the Wolf too much before his last sleep.

Hugoth was casually searching the area under the Forever Trees, when he noticed a set of tracks. The air was always heavy with moisture under the trees causing the ground to remain quite damp. Hugoth could read the tracks in front of his dwelling and know, without a doubt, who had paid him a visit while he slept. It was just like leaving a calling scribble. If a creature left a footprint, Hugoth would know which friend or foe had been searching for him.

In the Burg there was an unspoken rule that allowed no one to wake any other creature from sleep unless absolutely necessary. They were very respectful of each other's habits and, especially, their different sleep schedules.

Hugoth noticed the Wolf's tracks led away from his door and down the common path. He studied them as they made their way back to his door. He saw where the Wolf had tried to sneak a look into his door box. He thought that very wise of the Wolf. He made a note to give the Wolf credit for that bit of ingenuity. All tracks stopped at the bridge. "Oh, no!" Hugoth exclaimed aloud, although there was no one to hear except himself. With the Wolf's tracks stopping at the bridge, that only meant one thing. Mystic had decided to leave the Burg for some searching of his own.

The Guard of The Forever Trees set his water pails down to think a moment. He hung one pail on the peg on the root, while he set the other inside his door. He shook his head, then stretched one more time. He looked around for some clue that would let him know that Mystic was still in the Burg, but there was not one to find. Mystic was gone. Why had he answered the Wolf's questions? He was told not to. Really, he had answered no question directly. Maybe that was the problem. Now what would he tell the Keeper and his guest? Hugoth had been told the Keeper was a wise and patient man, so, he decided to tell him the truth. Everyone in the Burg told the truth, no matter how much trouble it got one into. This was no time for exceptions and Hugoth probably would have never twisted the facts anyway. Hugoth set out quickly for the Keeper's dwelling. This may cause a slight change in plans, but the Keeper must know about this little matter immediately.

Hugoth raced for the Keeper's dwelling like he had bees on his tail. He knew his problem could be worse than that if the Keeper took this news the wrong way. He raced around the common path, passing other Burg dwellers as they set about their morning routines. As he passed, they would wave or throw out a good morning greeting. Hugoth acknowledged each of these with a nod of his huge head. He ran the entire way. He was much too big to run at this pace for long. Hugoth found the energy to race all the way to the Keeper's door. Once there, he banged on the door with a large paw before collapsing with a thump on the Keeper's doorstep. Hugoth was not dead, although he was extremely pooped. He would be fine as soon as someone answered the door.

"Goodness, who could that be at this time?" asked the Keeper. He turned to his company and asked to be excused. He walked to the door and opened it. He managed to step out of the doorway just as Hugoth's enormous head fell onto his floor. "My word, Hugoth, what is the reason for this unexpected visit?"

Hugoth struggled to talk between loud, heavy breaths. "I'm sorry for the intrusion, Sir. I must tell you that the Wolf is gone! He left during my sleep."

"Gone, gone where?" The visitor was now the animated creature demanding to know.

"Please Hugoth, where did his tracks lead? Can you tell me that much?" asked the Keeper, in a surprisingly calm voice.

"I, I don't know, Sir. His tracks ended at the bridge. I assume he has gone to find you, Sir," answered a still-heaving Hugoth.

"To find me? You sent him across the bridge to find me?" asked the puzzled Keeper. "Why did you send him across the bridge when I live within the Burg?"

"Sir, I have no idea why the Wolf left the Burg. I'll tell you this much. he has a very clever mind of his own. He is very determined to see things through, but his patience leaves a bit to be desired." Hugoth collapsed again, breathing heavily.

The Keeper walked to his eating table and picked up a pail of water. He then took the water over to Hugoth and tossed half the water over the guard's head. He set the remainder in front of Hugoth's face while instructing him to drink freely. As it should be very well known by now, he would feel much better once he did.

"Goodness, goodness," said the visitor. "What do we do now?"

"Nothing, I think the tests have already begun. Without our intervention, Mystic will have to be successful at the tests and he must find them on his own. If those new visitors are his friends, all will be fine. They will, together, search for the wand/staff. Of that, I am sure. However, if those new visitors are enemies of the Wolf, we will be called on to change their destiny." The Keeper mentioned this in a matter-of-fact tone. He wasn't overly concerned. He seemed to be feeling pretty confident right now.

17

Vincen was the first of the three to wake up, or so he thought. He awoke to a bright sunny morning. He glanced around to find Lightning still sound asleep. He looked for the Cheetah next. He noticed that Bubba had wandered off a short distance, but remained relatively close to the original campsite. Vincen decided not to wake the sleeping Badger. He decided, instead, to have a chat with Bubba. They had not been able to talk much since the journey began and Vincen needed to check on how the young Cheetah was handling the trip. Bubba was several years younger than the Badger, and countless years younger than Vincen. With fewer years Bubba did not need or want as much sleep. Vincen checked again on Lightning, then curiously strode over to Bubba's side.

The young Cheetah was lying on his back, all legs bent and relaxed above him. The Cheetah had an intense look on his face. If Vincen hadn't known better, he would have guessed Bubba was stalking something upside down. The fur on Bubba's brow and around his eyes was wrinkled, as if he were deep in thought. The Cheetah did not even notice Vincen approaching.

"Good morning, Cheetah," said a very, rested Eagle. "What puts you in such deep thought this fine day-round?"

"Good morning to you, Sir," replied Bubba without taking the time to look in Vincen's direction. "I am studying that," Bubba announced as he pointed with a front paw toward the sky.

"Have you noticed, Vincen, that the sun here, if it is called a sun here, does not move? It does not set in the sky to cause moon time, nor is there even a moon. There is nothing in the sky but that yellow glowing ball. It just sits there. The shadows no not change unless the object causing the shadow is moving. Time, for lack of a better word, is standing still, yet we still tire and need our rest. Vincen", Bubba continued, "We have been here for more than one complete day-round, but the moon time has never arrived. This is certainly a bright sunny morning, but it was also a bright sunny morning when we went to sleep last moon time, if, indeed, it was moon time. I can not believe that we slept for a full day-round. Also, during our time here, we have gotten neither colder nor warmer as I stated earlier. What do you think could be the reasoning behind those interesting bits of information?"

"I think you are a very perceptive young creature," answered Vincen. "In fact, I have never heard you reflect so curiously on any past activity the four of us have ever been involved in. I further believe that you are capable of much more intelligence than we have ever seen out of you. No creature can act as un-intelligent as you do if they were not gifted with enough superior intelligence to do so in the first place".

"Really, Vincen, is that what you think, or are you searching for water-livvers?" Bubba replied with a faint smile forming on his face.

Vincen caught sight of this smile and filed it away. He answered, "Bubba, I think there is more to you than meets the eye, young Cheetah. Anyway, back to your point, I noticed that very same thing as I flew. I was not as concerned about the direction of our travel; I found our destination very quickly. The path is laid out so well that a creature could follow it during a blank moon time if necessary. However, as I am of the same opinion as you, there is never a moon time where we are. By simple deduction, we are not on the same world where the Great Forest exists. My son, I have mixed feelings about this place. I feel we should be here, but, at the same time, I feel we should be very careful if we wish to ever return to the Great Forest. I have come to the conclusion that we will probably experience no bodily harm during our stay that can't be repaired by that wonderful water. We may experience mental anguish on some large or small scale. However, I think we are supposed to grow stronger through it, if our minds aren't already completely inept. The three of us older friends have proven our wits time and time again throughout our past. We are looked up to for that with good reason. You, it's quickly becoming obvious that you are no slouch in the mind power realm, although you have perfected the act of a complete dimwit! The only real danger may not be for us. The real danger may be for those that have remained in the Great Forest. I have an overwhelming urge to complete our business here and return as quickly as we can to our home. I don't know why I feel that way; you may call it old age. I am not completely sure."

"Yes Vincen, I know I am young. Still, the few years spent with my parents were enough to teach me to trust my perceptions. My father was a wise leader, but my mother, my mother was far beyond wise and so radiant to behold. I am so much of both of them, more than I thought any creature knew. Now, I am finding that I haven't concealed certain gifts of mine as well as I once thought I had. Creatures of all kinds would flock to hear my mother speak on any subject from any land. She was quite remarkable. We survived as we did, not by being hasty, but by constantly learning our terrain, added to an abundance of deliberate, forward planning. I, too, have studied our present situation. I am stressed by much of it. I agree with your latest statement. We must return to the Great Forest as soon as we are able. The questions I have about this yellow sky ball can wait for another time. I trust some creature here can share the its mysteries with us."

"Right you are, son. Right you are," Vincen replied as he proudly moved closer to Bubba and joined him in studying the big yellow sky ball.

The silence was soon interrupted by an intimidating low growl. Lightning was stirring from his sleep. "Hello, anybody here?" the Badger groggily asked of anyone who might answer. "Hello."

"Over here, Lightning," called Bubba. "Are you completely up? If not, we shall remain where we sit. A fear of being rolled over and crushed is not worthy of such a beautiful morning. If up you are, we will dash over to join you for our first meal of this day-round."

"By all means, Cheetah, for food I will certainly get up." The Badger deliberately took enough time to fully stretch every muscle comprising his immense body. As he rose, he shook off numerous heavy chunks of dried sweet mud as best he could. "I have a real need to enter a large body of water to rid myself completely of this dried pudding," he stated through cavernous yawning jowls.

"I remember seeing a river close by as I flew over the land yesterday, Lightning. We should be coming upon it soon enough," added Vincen. "Let's eat. It will be a long day-round, I am sure."

The three ate silently as the weight of their predicament settled differently on each one. Well, it may not have settled yet on Lightning's shoulders. He was certainly eating no differently than he did in the Great Forest. With Lightning, eating always took precedent over any other event unfortunate enough to take place at the same time. While Bubba and Vincen ate, they pondered their previous conversation, replaying and rethinking each other's comments again and again. Neither spent too long thinking about the yellow ball in the sky. They were more concerned with their gut feelings about finishing whatever it was they were to do. Only then could they return home to the Great Forest for whatever awaited them there. The three ate for a several reflective clicks until Vincen suggested that they get on with the journey. As far as Bubba and Vincen were concerned, the time where they were was not moving. However, the time in the land they had left behind was ongoing. Maybe it was moving too quickly without them.

***

"Donkorse, Donkorse, I must apologize. I know I shouldn't wake you, but I must. I do so dislike waking sleeping creatures, but it is so important. You must rise now. They are leaving," Karri quietly exclaimed nervously. "We have rested maybe too long. We must get you on your way. Follow them. I will check back with you along this path every once in a while. The Keeper asked me to tell you not to get in a hurry even if the visitors do. You can't draw their attention away from what they need to accomplish. I will follow them in the trees. If I am discovered, that will be no real bother. I will tell them who I am. I will be their guide if needed. But I hardly think they will notice someone as small as I am. You, they would definitely notice! Should something out of the ordinary happen, I will let you know. Then I will fly to the Keeper. He will send me back with any new instructions. We are well rested. Let us sit idle no more. Good day, Donkorse."

"Good scouting, Karri," Donkorse sleepily answered as the talkative little Hawk flew off. "She is correct of course. I'd better get on with my duties," he reminded himself.

Donkorse shook the lingering sleep from his head. He left the meeting spot, silently making his way down the path through the thick undergrowth. His work now consisted of watching the visitors' every move to make sure they were not up to no good. Should they be found out to be enemies of the Wolf's, or enemies of the inhabitants of Nuorg, they would be dealt with swiftly in a most severe way. Those were his instructions for now. He was the perfect candidate for this assignment because of his innate stubborn streak. Descendants of Donkorse, in the times to come, would all share this significant personality trait.

***

"Where could this creature be?" Mystic paused to ask himself. "I remember seeing no dwelling along this entire path as Donkorse and I traveled to his dwelling place. What did I or could I have missed? I hope I did not leave irrationally early. Did I have enough clues to the whereabouts of this two-legger, if that is what it is, to set out on my own? From the looks of things, I obviously did not." Mystic, again disgusted with his lack of patience, shook his head then continued on his way.

Mystic decided to head directly to Sweet Gulley. If he could find no one to help him, he owed it to himself to exhaust all possibilities in finding a way back to the Great Forest. He owed it, not only to himself, but also to his close friends who must, by now, be worried greatly about him. Mystic also remembered the taste of the Sweet Gulley mud. That, alone, was worth a return trip.

***

"Hugoth, when you feel able, go out and fetch me the Eagle. I want to talk to him alone," the Keeper instructed. "Maybe make his disappearance a mystery. Leave a scribbled note and sign my given name to it. I want to confuse them a bit. If I know that Wolf at all, he will search diligently for the others to help in his pursuit of the way home. I want you to make sure that they find each other, minus the Eagle. I want you to first make sure the Wolf knows his friends may have followed him and are searching for him, as he looks for them. If he discovers that the visitors are here, we will know shortly if they are truly his friends. If he discovers only two friends, instead of three, I would venture to guess we will see him work well under pressure. There is no truer test of his heart than his search for the Eagle. Would you like to use this little fellow and his sister?" the Keeper said as he motioned toward Rakki. "They might possibly speed up the process."

"What do you have in mind?" asked the Keeper's visitor slyly. "I think I know what you are up to and I like it!"

"Keeper, if I may, I will quickly eat a fill of your sweet kakis, then be gone", answered Hugoth. "Since you have offered the speed of Rakki and Karri, I will accept it. I ask that Rakki fly immediately to find the Wolf. I would suspect him to be traveling on The Path to Where I Am Going. When he spots the Wolf, ask if he would be so kind as to return directly and tell me where our guest has been located. We will then immediately plot our strategy together."

"Very well, Hugoth. Rakki, please locate the Wolf then return to meet up with Hugoth. You will be responsible for hatching your own plan." Don't forget to include your sister. She may help too. I can know nothing of it. Should the Eagle ever ask me questions pertaining to your plan's details, I won't be able to answer them. If I don't know the details then I won't be lying to the Eagle should he ask me. I never lie and I won't start now," stated the Keeper. "Be off, little Hawk."

Rakki perked up as he strutted to the edge of the gathering table. He spread his wings, then bowed slightly to the Keeper and his guest. The Hawk flew off in a flash. The Keeper had actually asked him to be a part of the planning of Hugoth's mystery. If the small Hawk had ever been happier, no creature in Nuorg knew when it had been. Rakki was honored. Wait until Karri heard this!

***

Vincen, Bubba and Lightning began traveling methodically on their way to the dwelling place. Each studied the surroundings while marveling silently to himself at its unique qualities. They collectively noted several landmarks to help them identify their position should they get separated. Vincen would occasionally point an odd or unique landmark out while giving it a specific name. These names would signify meeting places. The last named meeting place would be the first one they would assemble near in case of an accidental separation. This is how they'd done it in the Great Forest all of their lives and no one could figure why it wouldn't work here as well.

***

Mystic picked up his pace as he began to feel a puzzling sensation deep in his gut. He could not identify the sensation, but, at least it wasn't ominous. It was more of a homesick feeling. The further from the Burg he got, the more the sensation became noticeable. He soon found himself running down the path toward it.

Rakki spotted the Wolf. "Why is he running so?" thought the Hawk. Rakki marked the current location, made a tight half-loop making a quick return to meet Hugoth. Rakki was flying as rapidly as his wings could carry him. He met Hugoth as the Guard of the Forever Trees was jumping off of the bridge walkway. Rakki swooped down and dove onto the lumbering creature.

"What is the hurry, Rakki," asked Hugoth.

"The Wolf is running and making very good time, Hugoth," Rakki replied. We will never catch him together. You must pick up your pace considerably while I fly to Karri for her assistance. We will return the Eagle to you somehow. You can then lead the Eagle to the Keeper as you see fit. Stay on this path, I will return as soon as I can."

"How do you plan on catching the Eagle, Rakki?" asked Hugoth. "He could easily rip you in pieces with only one of his strong talons."

"I hope it does not come to that, Hugoth. Do not worry, I have a plan that may work, but I must enlist the help of my cunning sister. She should be near the second group, so I must quickly go and locate her. Once we have compared facts, we will attempt to secure the Eagle for the Keeper's business." After sharing his immediate plans with Hugoth, Rakki was off.

"Stay the course, little friend!" Hugoth called after the Hawk. He watched Rakki until he was out of sight. Then he said to himself, "Well, I will do exactly as he says, I will increase my pace." Hugoth did just that.

Rakki flew swiftly on his trek to find his sister. He was sure she would help him. This part of the plan should not be that difficult. There were only two paths in this section of Nuorg, "The Path to Where I Am Going" and "The Path to Where I Was." She would be following one of the paths as she trailed the group of three.

Rakki decided to first fly The Path to Where I Am Going. If that did not produce the correct results, he would reverse his path, cross the gully and fly back along the second path. After they met, he would tell her of the Keeper's instructions and his fledgling plan to capture the Eagle. She would, no doubt, think it absurd to even attempt such a daring ploy even though she was quite a free-spirited little Hawk. Rakki was growing confident of their task. Now, if the Eagle would just fall for it.

***

Donkorse was obediently following instructions as he slowly made his way down The Path to Where I Was. Granted, it was more of a chore than he initially thought. No creature used this path anymore unless an unusual meeting was called to discuss some obscure topic of the past.

The Path to Where I Was was used when the history of Nuorg had to be recalled, learned from and dealt with. This was an ancient practice used before the arrival of the Keeper. It had been seldom used since he was appointed. The majority, actually all of Nuorg dwellers two-legged, four-legged and winged--did not worry about the past. In Nuorg, the past was only studied when a lesson needed to be learned. The past was not something to worry and fret about.

The future of things to come got the majority attention in Nuorg. The responsibility of all Nuorg dwellers is this: prepare others not so fortunate for the future. Guard against mistakes of the past. Use every means available to protect the future from itself. The Keeper was well suited to encourage this type of behavior. He had said his own past had taught him more about bad and evil, than should be witnessed in several lifetimes. This is what this Keeper brought to Nuorg. It appeared to be the greatest of his many talents, even though no inhabitant had witnessed many of his other self-described talents. He firmly believed and taught a master plan for all creatures of all lands near and far. Free will, of course was something he did not teach.

Nuorg had thrived under the current leadership and that was good for all. The dwellers were each chosen in their own individual way. If one forced his or her way into Nuorg or came in under false pretenses being cast out of this land was to be regretted for all their years to come. It was absolutely crucial that only those of impeccable character find a way into this land. Mystic had stumbled upon only one way in. There were other ways in, not many, but there were most definitely other ways.

***

Donkorse was finding his way under an extremely low-hanging branch that stretched completely across the path prompting him into a few very uncomfortable contortions. The sizable fellow pushed and tugged, scrunched and swelled, crawled and slid until he finally scrapped his way under the annoying branch to the other side.

He was met by high-pitched laughter coming from the small bodies of Karri and Rakki. They had been marvelously entertained by Donkorse's unpleasant predicament. They wished him no harm, but still, the two were finding it very difficult to speak. They were barely able to keep their balance on their perch. When Donkorse eventually appeared, looking completely tired, frustrated and disgusted, they both tried valiantly to gather their composure as they flew from the perch to land on Donkorse's scratched and dusty back.

"Excuse me, Donkorse, I left a most delectable piece of sweet kaki on the other side of that branch. Would you mind, too terribly much if I asked you to go back and get it for me? I am so hungry," Karri asked in the saddest, kindest and sweetest voice she could muster.

Rakki heard this and laughed so hard he fell off Donkorse's back.

"I can only guess that you are somehow making light of my attempt to squeeze under that dreadfully low-hanging branch, are you not?" asked Donkorse.

"I'm sorry, friend, but had you watched it as we did, you would have to agree that it was quite entertaining," answered Karri between small, petite guffaws that were not contained very well.

Rakki regained his balance and popped up beside his sister. "Donkorse, in all seriousness, we have come to you with a change in plans from the Keeper. We have been given instructions to separate the Eagle from his group and return him to the Keeper's dwelling."

"What?" asked the shocked Donkorse. "Why in Nuorg would that be proposed? Is the Eagle not the most important member of those three? Would that not spell doom for the overall plan?"

"Things have happened that are not exactly according to the plan, so the plan has been amended," stated Rakki.

"Like what, for instance?" asked Donkorse.

"Well, the major change is the Wolf left the Burg. He asked Hugoth several questions and, as he was instructed, Hugoth never gave one complete answer. That reasoning spurred the Wolf into leaving the Burg to find his own answers. Remember, this is one highly motivated creature," answered Rakki.

"How does that involve the Eagle?" Donkorse then queried.

"That I don't know. I was instructed to enlist Karri and yourself to separate the Eagle and return him to the Keeper's dwelling. I have no intention of getting inside the Keeper's head to understand why," said Rakki knowing Donkorse was a bit confused with the idea.

"I have an idea as to why the Keeper wants to see the Eagle," Karri injected. "The Eagle is the Wolf's adviser, as Hugoth is ours. What better way to discover the true intelligence and leadership skills of the Wolf than to subject him to the disappearance and subsequent search for his beloved mentor. This will be a great challenge to overcome for the Wolf and his two remaining friends. They must locate the Staff of Hewitt, survive the taking of their tools and then find their friend.

Should these challenges be completed successfully, they would continue on to the planned tests."

"I don't know how you do it. Karri, but you have, I believe, correctly interpreted the Keeper's intentions," said Rakki with admiration in his voice.

"I agree with your brother, Karri. I am constantly amazed at your intuition as well," replied Donkorse. "Now, if I may ask, how do I fit in to this plan you have concocted to separate the Eagle?"

***

Mystic began to tire. "What was I thinking?" he asked himself over and over. "Why did I take off so hastily from the Burg? There was no reason for that impulsive behavior. What kind of leader am I?"

To say that Mystic had begun to doubt himself would be correct. However, there was some longing that was guiding most of his thinking of late. The Guard of the Forever Trees did not, exactly, prohibit his leaving, nor did he bid Mystic to stay. In later writings, some may attribute this behavior to "the call of the wild." Mystic thought it odd that The Prince of The Great Forest could not find his own answers to his own questions. He could not have known that this was one of the most important reasons he needed the Land of Nuorg.

Mystic had never been beyond the help of his friends. He had never been beyond the aid of any dweller in the Great Forest. Cooperation or the lack of it was how a land fares well or poorly. If every creature worked together for the common good of the land, how could it fail?

The words spoken to him throughout his life were playing heavily on his mind at this moment. He had no one to share thoughts with. He had no one to talk to. And he had no one to talk to him about anything. He was totally alone. Why was this bad? Why was this good? Every creature deserves the time to be alone and ponder such mysteries, but in Mystic's way of thinking now was not that time.

He was beginning to crave conversations with his friends--be it one of his closest three or any of the many other creatures he came into contact with on a day-round to day-round basis. Did Vincen, Bubba and Lightning follow him to this land or not? Did they sacrifice their comfort and safety to seek him out? Had they felt great concern for him or had they merely decided to wait for his eventual return? Mystic was doubting probable things. He was losing self-respect and his great but humble self-esteem was waning.

The Wolf, as all creatures eventually do, was feeling alone. But, was alone not a good thing? Indeed, it is not a bad way to be when others don't depend on you. But Mystic was depended upon by hundreds of Great Forest dwellers. Now was not the time for him to want to be or have to be alone. He must return to his friends and the Great Forest in that order.

What of his wand/staff? Why had he neglected to bring it with him on that fateful morning? How long ago was that now? He thought deeply and sincerely. He argued with the sky over his current situation. How could he have let so many down or had he let them down? Mystic had absolutely no idea what lay in store for him, absolutely no idea.

***

"May we rest?" asked the Badger. "How much further have we to go?"

"Yes Lightning, we should rest and find water," said the Eagle.

The three quickly settled under the next shady tree they encountered. They all sat down comfortably in the cool shade as the Badger opened the pack of food.

"Obviously, I have underestimated the distance we must travel. Several factors are not familiar to me, the yellow sky ball being only one. Time is not standing still, but it seems to have no real bearing on existence here. Let us rest well," Vincen said, "I must have some time now to ponder our situation."

"Gladly," answered Bubba. "But first, Vincen, may I scout ahead, over the next rise? I will return to you as quickly as possible."

"Yes, young Cheetah, please scout ahead. I see you are much to young to need the rest that Lightning and I demand. Please scout quickly as we need to begin moving again shortly."

"Yes sir, I will do the best I can. I will not expose all of my speed in case some creature may be watching, but I will use about half of it. I will return." Bubba took a quick look around to lock in his bearings, nodded to both the Badger and the Eagle and was gone.

"I wish so for his youthfulness and speed, Lightning. I wish that nothing happens while he is away," noted Vincen. "Please Lightning, toss me a fruit, will you?"

"Certainly," replied Lightning. "Vincen, I have one question, which in turn, leads to several more that have been nagging at my mind since this whole adventure began. Why, first of all? Why Mystic? Why us? Have you considered, Sir, the consequences to the Great Forest if none of us returns? Why would this situation present itself, and why are these particular players, including you and me, involved?"

"You have been doing much thinking, Lightning. Yes, I have thought about and considered every situation you have mentioned. I have but one answer. I don't know. I have determinedly tried to figure everything out, only to find myself circling back to one basic, elementary answer. Mystic, my friend, is the reason for this. He was brought here to fulfill some task I know nothing about. I am sure I observed him behaving strangely at the well, although strange may not be the best word given the current circumstances. However, he seemed to be under a power that was not all together his. He was in a daze, as if he were seeing into the future. I did not understand it then and I cannot explain it now. I have to believe that it has much do with destiny and the future of the Great Forest. Other than Mystic's role as Prince of the Great Forest, I can justify no further answers.

"Very well then, let us eat. We will save the Cheetah some food, then rest." Lightning lay back on the soft thick grass that covered the ground as far as one could see, even under the shade trees, and stared at the yellow ball in the sky. He said to himself, "I wish someone could explain that to me!"

Vincen left the Badger alone to ponder as he flew up to look out from a high branch in the tree. He was thinking that maybe he could watch the Cheetah's progress. Vincen soon discovered that Bubba was out of sight. He fought the urge to leave the tree and follow the Cheetah. They had found out long before that if you told someone you would stay put, then the best thing was to do exactly that.

***

Bubba needed this. He had not run this fast in several day-rounds. He longed for the thrill of a good run. His muscles, shortly before, had been aching from lack of use as he talked Vincen into letting him run. No more. Bubba was now feeling better with each long stride of his strong legs. This Cheetah was born to run. His head hardly made any movement as he gracefully covered ground at a breakneck speed. He used his tail as a counter balance, which enabled him to make turns that would have other creatures rolling across the ground, wholly out of control. His eyes stayed clearly focused as he traveled the path scouting for Mystic.

When he was younger, Bubba would race Vincen around the Great Forest. He was so fast that he was constantly outrunning Vincen wherever they went. There was no question concerning his speed. The talk of the lands around and in the Great Forest was that the young Cheetah would someday be able to outrun the future. If this was going to happen anywhere, it might happen here in the Land of Nuorg. Bubba was blazingly fast. He had promised not to show off his true speed, so he was struggling to keep it under wraps.

As he sped down the path, the Cheetah was noticed by more than one creature. From a distance Rakki and Karri witnessed the Cheetah's speed and were visibly impressed by it. They would later talk of the Cat's speed when informing the Keeper of how their plan progressed. They would have no idea how much they had underestimated it.

Bubba had raced his way over hills and around the twisting turns of Sweet Gulley. The gully had, at last, twisted its way clear of the path. Bubba was now running the path as it headed straight between two big hills or small mountains. He had just cleared the foot of the biggest hill on his right when he burst over a small rise into a wide-open meadow. He slowed to a trot as he scouted along each side of the path for Mystic. He slowed down until he was walking at an average four-legger pace. He was hoping for just a slight glimpse of a Wolf's shape somewhere on the horizon. Bubba, at that moment, noticed yet another quirk of this land. The horizon did not have an end to it. He had not noticed this while they were among the trees, but now it was obvious. The Cheetah marked another oddity down for this strange landscape.

***

Mystic was getting tired. He longed for the youthful endurance of Bubba. The more Mystic thought about it, the more he realized a Wolf is simply not designed for sustained running. He was walking now. He needed water. His tongue was hanging out of his mouth as he panted to cool himself down, his paws damp from sweat. He thought he should be nearing the turn in the path where Sweet Gulley meets The Path To Where I Am Going. If he remembered correctly it was on the other side of the Twin Mounts as Donkorse called them. He could make out the profiles of the hills in the distance. He was almost sure he could make them in 10 clicks or less. At least he would try. He had slowed enough to rest a bit and was now ready to make another attempt at long-distance running. He gradually increased his pace until he felt comfortable in a faster lope. This would be fast enough he decided.

***

Rakki and Karri were flying low as they circled far in front of the second group's position. They were intending, for anyone watching, for it to seem that they were flying from the Burg and not from behind the trio's position. Donkorse was making his way across Sweet Gulley to approach the trio from behind. He would begin his role in this yet-to-be hatched plan after receiving a signal from Karri.

Karri and Rakki were approaching the resting place of what was now only two members of the original three. How would the plan be changed to adjust for this new scenario? Neither Karri nor Rakki, seemed worried about the slight deviation in numbers. The decrease from three to two members may might make the plan easier to implement. Or it could trigger an assault on the two by a very perturbed, very large and powerful Badger who would, no doubt, be angered by the abduction of his remaining friend.

***

Bubba stood watching a tiny cloud of dust appear in the distance ahead of him.

"Could this be Donkorse coming back for them? No," he thought, Donkorse was headed the other way when he left them last and the swift Cat was pretty confident that Donkorse could not move this fast. "Well then, what could it be?"

Bubba moved to the side of the path, crouched down and waited. He would not be hasty in retreat from something he could not identify. He never ran off too soon. Because of his speed he knew it was almost never too late for him to take off. Nothing but trouble had ever come close to catching him before. Bubba waited anxiously.

***

Karri and Rakki flew by Vincen and Lightning's resting place without even noticing the two situated beneath the tree. They were searching along the path so intently they bypassed anything that sat any distance from the path. The Hawks came upon Donkorse quickly thereafter, surprising themselves greatly. "We spotted the cat. Where are the other two?" Rakki asked of Donkorse. "Have you passed up their position?"

"I imagine they are ahead of me," said Donkorse. "I have passed nothing since I began traveling this path. I believe they are just ahead of me."

Rakki replied, "We have flown this entire length of path without seeing them. We did fly over the Cat as he was making good time toward the Burg."

"Did you search beside the path?" Donkorse asked. "They may be resting as I should be very soon."

"No," replied Karri dejectedly. "We did not bother to check on either side of the path. I'm sorry. That would be my mistake. We will fly back and fly lower. We should be able to spot them if we do. Remember, Donkorse, you keep making your way in their direction. When you hear three of my calls, assume your role. We must be off."

"Yes, Karri, I understand. If you don't hurry, I will be too in need of rest to help you. I must warn you, I am fading fast," Donkorse said.

The Hawks promised Donkorse they would hurry.

***

Bubba squinted his eyes as the tiny cloud of dust became a larger. He brought his tail around and laid it above his eyes to block out the glare from the yellow ball in the sky. He was stunned when the cloud of dust dissolved enough to give away the creature causing it.

"Eeeaahhhh!" Bubba cried as he burst, full speed, toward the emerging creature.

Mystic was taken aback by the sudden jolt he felt in his side. Before he could fully recover, he was hit again and again. The creature was attacking him. His eyes were so clouded by the dust; he could not identify the crazed creature. For an instant his eyes cleared as a yellow gold flash struck him again. He suddenly realized his good fortune.

"Is that you, Bubba? Is that really you?" exclaimed Mystic.

"Yes, you old dog, it is me. I have found you!" Bubba said.

"Where did you come from?"

"The Great Forest of course," replied Bubba.

"No, I mean where have you been? Did you come alone?" Mystic asked excitedly.

"No, Vincen and Lightning are here. We came to rescue you."

"Rescue me?" Mystic asked.

"Yes and take you back to the Great Forest," answered Bubba enthusiastically.

"Well, where are the others?"

"Come, I will lead you to them. They are resting. I requested to run ahead and scout. I am really glad I did. Vincen and Lightning are not too far behind me. Let's go!"

"Yes," replied Mystic. "Let's go."

"Mystic, you are a welcome sight for my eyes. We have been so concerned for your well-being," continued Bubba.

"Fine, let us go. We can talk when we are all together. There is so much to discuss."

With Bubba leading the way, the two reunited friends were off.

***

"There is the B...Badger," Rakki whispered to Karri as they flew closer to the path this time.

"Let's light near him. I know the Eagle won't be far away."

"As you say, brother," answered Karri.

The two Hawks landed mere steps from the sleeping Badger. As they silently crept closer, they studied his massive body. "I don't know about you Karri, but he sure looks like a B......

Vincen was on the two small Hawks in a flash. His wings remained spread in an alarming fashion, dwarfing the two smaller sky-travelers. Vincen terrified them with his menacing look. Vincen did not take lightly to uninvited and unannounced guests. The two startled Hawks cowered beneath the Great Eagle's outstretched wings.

"What do you want, you little sneaks?" demanded Vincen. "How dare you spy on us"?

"Excuse us, Vincen, we meant you no harm," said a scared Rakki.

"If you mean us no harm, why have you flown by us once scouting only to turn and come at us from the rear? Surely you know that either of us could tear you both to shreds! Are you out of your minds?" stated a very unhappy and alarmingly irritated Eagle.

"Well Sir, we apologize for our manners. We did not want to wake this creature. You must surely know that we are intelligent enough not to threaten two creatures of your size," said Karri as she struggled for calming words.

"Whether I know or not is no concern of yours," Vincen commanded in a very threatening tone. "You came in without warning and easily could have gotten yourselves killed by an ill-placed move of this creature's paw. That is not a show of intelligence where we come from. What do you need of us?"

"Well Sir," began Rakki, "Donkorse is in terrible need of your help. He is back down the path injured or sick, we cannot determine which. He asked for you, so we came to you. You know we have kept up with your movements since you arrived. If we wished you harm, it could have come to you at any time. Please, Vincen, come with us. Donkorse needs you."

"I can't wait any longer Rakki," said Karri, "I must go back to inform Donkorse of the Eagle's unwillingness to lend his help. Do what you can, Brother, I must go!" Karri immediately left looking very hurt.

"See?" asked Rakki, "My sister can do nothing for Donkorse alone! Nothing! Now, either help us or fly back up to your perch and watch for the Cat to come back."

"How do you know the whereabouts of the Cheetah?" asked Vincen.

"We passed him as we circled the area looking for you. We saw him without you while following the path this way. He was making very good time heading for the Burg," explained Rakki. "I, like my sister, have wasted enough time trying to persuade you to help. If you will not come, then fine. You stay. I, at least, will be with a friend who needs me. Your friends are healthy and need you not right now. Donkorse needs us all. Please come."

"Okay young Hawklet, but be warned that you have not made me want to help you," Vincen huffed. "Let me awake the Badger to inform him of my plans and, may I add, he won't be happy with them."

Vincen woke Lightning. He explained his intentions to the groggy Badger. He then told him, as the large creature struggled to become fully awake, to carry on toward the Burg when Bubba returned. He assured the Badger that he would absolutely catch up with them. He returned to Rakki begrudgingly. Together they flew off to meet with the ailing Donkorse.

As they flew back to Donkorse, Rakki and Karri separately regretted the false stories they had told the Great Eagle. They could only wait to see if he would forgive them for what they were about to do.

On her own, Karri let out three loud, high-pitched cries. Donkorse heard them, laid himself down on the ground and waited. He had never completely deceived anyone before. Now he felt terrible about it. He rolled his eyes back into his head in disgust.

***

Hugoth began to regret leaving the Burg. This assignment was meant for smaller, much swifter creatures. How he had gotten into this bit of work was still a little confusing to him. He was, now after his hurried travel, a tired, weary creature. He stepped off the path to rest. This was a good move. He would be needed soon enough.

18

Donkorse was lying on the side of the path in the shade with his legs stretched out into the moist grass adjacent to Sweet Gulley. He hardly looked the part of an ailing creature in dire need of immediate assistance. Karri was mortified when she saw his positioning.

"What are you doing, you tree limb?" she called angrily. "You don't look like you have a care in this land, much less like that of a dying creature!"

Never even raising his head, Donkorse admitted, "Karri, I can't do it. I cannot deceive the Eagle. It goes against everything this land is. We either tell him the truth, or I want no part of it. We can leave the Keeper's note as planned, but I will not be a part of any deception."

Karri's head fell to her chest. As she let out a long breath she replied to Donkorse, "I understand completely, Donkorse. What has become of us? I am sorry for my demeanor as well as my impulsive agreement with this farfetched plan. I agree with you. I am of the opinion that we tell the Eagle the truth. If that doesn't get him to the Keeper, then we did our best and did not deceive him. The Eagle must decide what is in the best interest of his land. All we have been trained to do is facilitate their survival. I will not take part in the deception of these brave creatures."

As Karri finished her statement, Rakki and Vincen landed beside her. "I told Vincen the truth," Rakki stated.

"Vincen, we are so sorry for the attempted birdnapping. We were instructed to take you to the Keeper. We were caught up with excitement and rational, honest thinking escaped us. Please forgive us," pleaded Karri.

"I forgive you, little friend," Vincen replied. "I assume by now you are all in agreement that we have no ill will against Mystic. We came to rescue him from a plight we knew nothing about. We still must take him back with us, but I am willing to give your Keeper a little of our time. I have gathered that in order for my friends to prove whatever

The Land of Nuorg

they must prove to your folk, I cannot be with them. That is fine with me. I know they will be under your constant surveillance should anything go wrong. I trust nothing will happen to them. Should anything bad come their way, I will deal with the Keeper myself. Now, if we must go, let us get to it. I could use a rest. I could also use a good meal."

As the three sky-travelers prepared to leave Donkorse, Vincen added, "Donkorse, please continue to safeguard those two friends of mine. I wouldn't want to hear that something happened to them without you knowing."

"Sir, I will watch them like a Hawk!" Donkorse answered as he winked one of his large eyes at Rakki and Karri.

"Thank you, I will rest easy knowing that," said Vincen.

"Let us go quickly," said Rakki. "This note will turn to mush if I don't take it out of my claw soon!"

The three winged creatures rose into the sky. They returned from where they had met with Vincen. They quietly set down to place the note clumsily scribbled by Rakki under the Badger's nose. They circled away from The Path to Where I Am Going in hopes of avoiding Bubba or Mystic heading their way. Vincen was once again overwhelmed with the beauty of this strange, inviting land.

***

Mystic and Bubba made good time back to the shade tree. They found Lightning asleep again just where Vincen had left him. They also found a rolled up piece of thin tree skin. "Now there is a sight that only a Mother could love," Mystic whispered to Bubba as he looked on the Badger. "I've also seen one of these before," he added as he picked up the note. Mystic carefully unrolled the current, though badly worn and badly scribbled note. He read it aloud to Bubba. They were still waiting for the Badger to awaken. The note read:

Dear visitors,

We have taken Vincen. He will remain safely with us until you bring to us the "Staff of Hewitt." You have as much time as it will take to do so. Vincen will not be harmed. Please be careful, watch your tools and complete this task. Your friend Mystic is on his way to meet you. He will not know of Vincen's absence until you inform him of such. Do not try to rescue Vincen. No harm will come to him as long as you succeed with your task.

Sincerely,

Charlie, The Keeper of Nuorg

"What does that mean?" asked Bubba.

"It means that our dear hosts have a more puzzling riddle for us to solve than I first imagined," said Mystic. "I came out here to meet with the three of you to find who I was looking for. I was told the Keeper was the one who could help us get home. With Vincen's absence, along with this note, I am not sure we can leave yet."

"But, what of this Staff of Hewitt nonsense?" Bubba inquired.

"That, I can't answer. Let's wake this big fellow, shall we?"

Bubba nudged Lightning with his head. He swatted his tail against his snout. The Badger would not budge. Mystic began to shake the large creature by pushing on his shoulders.

Ever so slowly, Lightning came around. His eyes opened and he found himself staring into the pale eyes of a dust-covered Wolf. He closed them again immediately.

"Aaahhh, Bubba, Bubba come quickly. I am dreaming," roared the Badger. "I saw Mystic. He looked terrible. He looked like death. He had no color to his face. He must be in serious trouble. Come quickly!"

"What?" answered Bubba.

"I saw Mystic," cried the Badger. "I saw him and he looked dead. He looked, he looked..."

"Like this?" Mystic asked as he stood in front of the Badger.

"Yes, he looked just like you! Aaahhhh!"

"Settle down Lightning, it is me. Mystic, Prince of the Great Forest at your service." Mystic bowed.

"Aaaahhh!" bellowed Lightning as he jumped to his feet and tackled the long lost Wolf. "I should squeeze the breath right out of you, you toad. Where have you been? Why are you here? Vincen, Vincen, it's Mystic, he's back!"

Mystic was solidly pinned to the ground and could not utter a word in response to the Badger's questions.

The Land of Nuorg

Bubba quickly reprimanded the Badger. "Lightning, I believe you are going to suffocate our long lost friend him unless you get off of him quickly!"

"Sorry," replied Lightning as he scrambled off of the welcomed Wolf. "Where have you been, Mystic?"

"That, my friend, is as long a story as yours would be, should I ask you the same question. Let us be happy for the reunion while we make plans to find Vincen," Mystic said.

"Vincen, where is Vincen?" asked the bewildered Badger.

Bubba stepped closer to Lightning and handed him the note. "Here, read it for yourself."

As Lightning read the note, Mystic stepped back onto the path. He looked up and down for any sign of Vincen. He quickly came to the realization that he would never locate Vincen by tracking him. He undoubtedly had flown wherever he was now, so no amount of tracking would locate him.

"What is this?" demanded the Badger.

Bubba gritted his teeth, furrowed his brow and then turned to Mystic. "Well Prince of the Great Forest, it's just us again. What do we do?"

"We must first solve this Staff of Hewitt mystery. What exactly are they talking about? Secondly, Lightning, is there any food remaining? I must eat in order to think," said Mystic.

Under normal circumstances this would be a much more joyous reunion with Mystic. However, the four were now only three. Vincen was missing. They could not go home without him. After all, he was the one that had led the journey in pursuit of the Wolf.

While Mystic ate enthusiastically, Bubba and Lightning argued over who was at fault for Vincen's disappearance. The battle waged back and forth with blame equally cast and equally shared. Their conclusion was no conclusion. There had been no scuffle associated with Vincen's disappearance because Lightning stated numerous times that he would have heard any such ruckus. Bubba countered that he and Mystic had scuffled with him when they tried to rouse him from sleep to no immediate avail. Finally they got tired of arguing about it. They each skulked back to take a seat on the ground next to Mystic.

"Well, just like old times, huh?" asked Mystic laughing.

Not a word was spoken in return.

"May I ask a question?" Not waiting for an answer, Mystic continued, "Why do you have your weapons with you?"

Bubba was the first to speak, "Why do you think? We were on a rescue mission. Who knows what kind of trouble we could have encountered here."

"Oh very well, at least you did not bother to bring my wand/staff," replied Mystic.

An "oh mercy" look suddenly came to the faces of the Cheetah and the Badger. They each puffed out their jowls and rolled their eyes away from Mystic.

"Oh no, tell me you didn't. That thing was behaving very oddly before I left and I made deliberate attempts to leave it before I set out on this journey. Please tell me you didn't bring it," pleaded Mystic.

"It was his idea," stated Bubba, pointing an accusing paw in Lightning's general direction.

"I believe young lizard, that it was Vincen's idea," replied Lightning. "I just told you what he told me! My job was to collect the food. If I do say so myself, I performed that task quite well too, thank you."

"You made me go get it, remember? As I was leaving the fortress, you yelled, Don't forget the wand/staff," came Bubba's retort. "At least I tried to do as I was told. At least, I didn't lose Vincen!"

Lightning let a low and thunderous growl escape from his mouth. "Listen, I told you it was Vincen's idea!"

Mystic was still laughing at the two of them. "How it got here is behind us now. All I want to know is, where is it now? I don't see it lying around here."

Lightning and Bubba put their front paws up to cover their eyes and began to rock slowly back and forth at the same time.

"Oh no," stated Mystic. "You went through all of the trouble to bring it, then you lost it? Oh mercy!"

"Well," Bubba explained, "I said I tried to bring it. Tried is the key word here. Mystic, I looked all over your dwelling for that thing of yours. It was not there, anywhere. Lightning got angry with me for not bringing it, even though I couldn't find it."

"Wait a click, what do you mean you couldn't find it?" inquired Mystic. "I left it just outside my front door. It was leaning on the box when I last saw it."

"I saw it there too when I passed by to check things out," Lightning added.

The Land of Nuorg

"Why did you go by my dwelling? It's way out of your way as you travel to the fort, is it not?" Mystic asked, somewhat confused.

"I went by your dwelling because you were acting as odd as I believe you thought your wand/staff was acting." Lightning continued, "Anyway, don't worry, we did not bring it."

"What do you mean you did not bring it?" replied Mystic.

"Lightning's correct, Mystic. We did not bring it. It brought itself and us!"

"What?" Mystic asked.

"It sure did. It brought itself. I did not retrieve it from your dwelling. Lighting did not retrieve it from there either. How it came to the clearing, neither of us knows. Not only that, it practically killed us until Lighting got a death grip on the blooming thing," Bubba stated, quite animatedly.

Suddenly Mystic was struck with a "why didn't I think of that before" look on his face. "Oh mercy, my wand/staff, what if it is this Staff of Hewitt every creature in this land is so preoccupied with? What if you two lost exactly what the note is requesting us to bring to get Vincen back?"

The other two immediately quit rocking, lowered their paws, slowly turned their blank faces to Mystic, while simultaneously mouthing to each other two words, "Oh mercy!"

19

As Vincen was being led back to the Burg by Rakki and Karri, he got a glimpse of the lands that existed on the other side of Sweet Gulley. It was more of the same, unbelievably spectacular landscapes that stretched for endless pursuit beats to the far reaches of his vision. The Burg was directly ahead. Approaching it from the backside made no difference in one's first impression. It would be a wonderful place to dwell.

The high walls that bordered each side of the river formed a perfect oval around the neatly kept dwelling places, suggesting adequate protection from any intruders. Vincen admired the huge scale. He asked no questions. He would admire the view and direct all questions to the Keeper, whoever that was, soon enough. As the three sky-travelers flew over the Burg's river, Vincen noticed how clear and deep the water was. He was surprised that the river flowed past the front of the outside wall, leaving no way for the water to be reached from the city, as it was completely surrounded by stone walls.

The sky-travelers flew completely around the Burg to satisfy Vincen's obvious curiosity with the place. Neither Rakki nor Karri uttered a word. Sooner than Vincen wished, they began a descent into the Burg. They flew directly down the main path that was occupied with different creatures going this way and that. Rakki led the way as they slowed near the largest of the dwellings. Rakki, Karri and Vincen lit on the sill of a large open window. Rakki hopped inside the window while Karri requested Vincen to remain outside until he was formally introduced.

Vincen noticed that no matter how casual the small Hawks had been with him, the respect for whoever, or whatever, lived in this dwelling was great. Karri followed Rakki through the window.

"We will call for you shortly," she said.

Rakki and Karri flew from the window and gently landed on the gathering table. The Keeper was not in at the moment and neither was his dwelling guest. Rakki did not mind this. He was not altogether comfortable with the Keeper's guest. He had never seen him completely out of the shadows.

Karri hopped over to a fine crystal glass that sat on the gathering table. She pecked it with her beak. As she did, a clear bell-like sound emanated through the dwelling. "Where do you think he is?" Karri asked.

"I don't know, Sister. Did we get here ahead of schedule?" replied Rakki.

Vincen was mesmerized watching the traffic below the sill. No one seemed bothered by his being there. It was almost like they were accustomed to seeing him. Did they, too, know him? He could not help but doubt that.

Rakki and Karri were nibbling on a partially eaten sweet kaki when the door opened.

"Ah, just as I hoped, hello there my small friends. Where is the Eagle? Were you able to bring him back with you?" asked the Keeper as he entered the door with his guest in tow.

"Sir, we must apologize first," said Rakki. "My first plan was built around deceiving the Eagle. I am truly sorry for that mistake. My Sister and I, along with Donkorse, could not see it through in its first edition. We changed our thinking completely when challenged initially by the Eagle. He could have easily punished us for our lack of manners, but that is another story. Sir, the Eagle is outside the window on the sill. Would you like to meet him now?"

"Yes, I certainly would. Thank you for your honesty. That was very good of you to confess your shortcoming. Make sure I thank Donkorse as well the next time I see him," answered the Keeper as he positioned his visitor on a nearby chair and put his outer wrap in a nearby room.

"We will, Sir," said Rakki as he flew to the window. He hopped out on the ledge and told Vincen, "The Keeper would like to see you now. Sir."

"Very well, thank you, dear little Hawk."

Rakki led Vincen through the window as they glided onto the gathering table. Vincen was much larger than the two Hawks, so having to fly over and land on the large table felt a little awkward. The air movement caused by his immense wings played havoc with everything in the room that was not firmly held in position by its own weight. When Vincen landed on the table the two small Hawks were each blown back to the edge of the table as were some notes, quills and light dishes. He looked around the spacious room and felt a little ill at ease. Was that the Keeper in the corner?

The shadows did not allow Vincen to see this creature at all. He was able to detect a small reflection in the eyes, but that was it.

Vincen saw a wooden chair with a tall back next to the table and took the liberty of perching on the back of it. Soon enough, a two-legger came through a side door. As he entered the room, Vincen closely watched him glance around at the suddenly untidy mess of the room and was awed by his seeming normality. "Who is this?" he thought. "Surely this is not the Keeper."

The two Hawks backed away from the edge of the table, then perched themselves on the same stack of books Rakki had used not too long ago. Karri then spoke up, favoring a wing in Vincen's direction, "Keeper, may I introduce you to Vincen, the Great Eagle of the Great Forest."

The smiling Keeper strode politely over to meet Vincen while extending his hand to welcome the Great Eagle. "At last Vincen, It is a pleasure to make your acquaintance. I have heard so much about you for such a long time."

This took Vincen by surprise, "Excuse me?"

"I said I have heard so much about you," replied the Keeper.

"No, after that," answered Vincen. "For such a long time? How is that so?"

"That will become obvious very soon, Vincen," stated the Keeper. "Let me welcome you to the Land of Nuorg."

"Very well, it is a pleasure to meet the Keeper of this wonderful land. You have some very loyal dwellers here," said Vincen.

"Please call me Charlie. My proper name is Sir Charles Craton Hewitt the Third. I am of the original Hewitts from Blacktonburg."

"From Blacktonburg? Why, that is the land that lies on the outer fringe of the Great Forest," said Vincen. "Your family was decimated during the Terrible Years, scattered here and yon if I remember correctly."

"Yes, Vincen you are correct. I am all that is left."

"As I believe am I of my family, but how, how did you arrive here?" queried Vincen.

"I have nothing for you but answers. They will all come in..."

Vincen finished this statement for Charlie, "Time. Well, it seems this will be a long stay given all of the questions I have for you." Vincen was becoming aware of a feeling coming from the shadows that had been absent from him for too long. He was not sure what it was and continued, "By the way, Vincen is not my given name. It is my last name. My given first name is..."

A strong voice sounded from the corner shadows to finish this sentence for the Eagle, "Fantahngheo..."

Vincen and the little Hawks were wide eyed. All eyes instantly jerked to the corner of the room, intently trying to focus on the guest in the shadows as the powerful voice continued, "meaning faithful, loyal and wise caregiver."

Vincen was astonished. A euphoric feeling came rushing up from his talons so fast that his head almost exploded. "Who is there?" Vincen asked, visibly shaken.

Out of the corner and out of the shadow swooped another Great Eagle. The large Eagle landed softly on Charlie's outstretched arm. This Eagle could easily have been Vincen's slightly smaller twin Brother except for a slightly graying plumage. Vincen's heart stopped briefly and he struggled for balance while he tried to catch his breath.

Charlie had a radiant smile on his face as he witnessed Vincen's reaction to this surprise. "May I re-introduce to you, Vincen, Mystic Vincen of the Great Eagles of Blacktonburg. He is believed to be your Grandfather."

Rakki felt a rush of emotion and fainted. He landed with a barely audible thud on the gathering table. Karri's eyes welled with tears at this emotional moment.

"Grandfather?" Vincen whispered as he fought back euphoric feelings of emotion that completely engulfed him. "How, how can this be? The Terrible Years, all of the stories, how can it really be you? Are the others here also?"

"There will be time for those answers later", the elder Eagle reassured Vincen. "Let me see you, Son. His head clicked up and down Vincen's entire stature. Yes, you have the color just like my side of the family, but you are so much, so much bigger. Your wingspan easily makes two of mine. Your mother's side of the family was given size, but still not as much as you exhibit. Your parents would be proud as I am proud of you, Vincen. You have matured into a remarkable Eagle. Now, Charlie has much to say to you. You must listen closely to all he says. When the Wolf Mystic--I can't believe you named a Wolf after me, but that's another story--gets here, we will have much for him to hear too. Well Charlie, he's all yours. Should I be needed, wake me. I am old and it is time for my nap."

Charlie spoke first to the seriously dumbfounded large Eagle, "Okay Vincen, you first. What is your first question?"

***

Mystic plopped down to the ground, crossed his front legs then shook his head in minor disbelief. "You did lose it, didn't you? You lost my wand/staff. You lost a wand/staff that may, very well, be the same Staff of Hewitt that is required to be in our possession when we return to the Burg to get Vincen. I can't believe this."

"Excuse me, Mystic, but your wand/staff did try to kill us," exclaimed Lightning."

"It sure did," added Bubba.

"Oh please, it tried to kill you? Is that not stretching it a bit you think?" asked Mystic.

"Well, it was certainly acting pretty strangely if that was not on its mind," answered the Badger. "I wrestled with it for a few clicks before it pulled us into the hole. Then I fought with it all the way down the well. It certainly has a stout determination to find you, Oh Great Prince! Maybe it wants to kill you!"

"I doubt that it does Lightning," Mystic answered reassuringly.

"It almost knocked me into the hole as it came shooting across the ground and would have if Lightning had not sat on it," added Bubba.

"Sat on it?" asked Mystic.

"The thing was acting crazy, I tell you. It came from behind a tree, bolted directly for the hole, then Lightning jumped on it, trapping it with his leg. He raised it above his head as it..." Bubba continued, "Circled like a wind storm in bigger and bigger and bigger circles. The ground shook and rumbled and the well water churned and roared, then stopped."

"Quiet down, Bubba, you are mixing things up. Anyway, it basically pulled Bubba, Vincen and myself into the purple and green water, through some kind of tunnel and then unceremoniously threw us into the air. We are here, are we not?" asked Lightning.

"Was it glowing?" asked Mystic.

"I'll say it was, almost blinded us!" replied Bubba. "We were hurled into a liquid tree trunk of water. Then in due course, we were tossed way up out of the water with all of our weapons falling wildly, scattering all about us, only to land in a sticky, but tasty, mud hole."

"And then our food began spilling all around us. Then," Lightning went on, "Vincen got stuck in the gooey mud and died. Then..."

"Wait, Vincen what?" asked a stunned Mystic.

Bubba excitedly answered, "Yes, Vincen got stuck and died, and then I backed over Lightning's ax-pike which was also stuck in the mud. I guess I knocked it over because it began to fall down. As it fell, water began bubbling up through the mud from somewhere. Then the water began to shoot out of the mud like a geyser. Lightning started washing the goo off Vincen's body in the shower of clear water and, accidentally but fortunately, got some water down Vincen's throat."

Lightning took over because Bubba was out of breath. "The water must have revived Vincen, 'cause, like we said, he was dead, dead, really dead, not breathing or moving dead. He absolutely was. We were awfully upset. We were crying like little cubs."

Bubba interjected, "Lightning, you were crying like a little cub, not me."

"Oh well," the Badger continued, "Vincen unexpectedly coughed and woke up and we lost the wand/staff. That's about it."

"Whoa," said an exhausted Wolf. Mystic raised his paws to his eyes and rubbed the side of his head in slow little circles. "Well, that's a pretty encompassing story there. Do you remember where you were exactly? We have got to find my wand/staff. We must first go back to Sweet Gulley and search the mud hole again."

"Search in it again?" asked Bubba. "I'm not even clean from my last dip there!"

"You are young. You will be okay", said Mystic. "Oh, by the way, did you have any wounds on your body when you fell into the well?"

"Yes," answered Bubba, "Why do you ask?"

"Vincen nipped me pretty good at the well. It brought a substantial stream of blood. However, once the water touched it, the wound was healed with no sign of a scar."

"Me too, only it was where I bit my tail," Bubba muttered.

"You did that again?" remarked Mystic. "Mercy, when, when will you learn? Let's get moving. We need to find Donkorse. Maybe he can help us find the wand/staff."

"Or maybe I can."

Mystic, Bubba and Lightning were so caught up in their lively conversation that they failed to hear or see Hugoth as he lumbered into their midst.

"Who is that?" the Badger asked Mystic.

"Friends, let me introduce you to Hugoth, Guard of the Forever Trees in the Burg," Mystic proclaimed. "Did you hear enough to know of our predicament, Hugoth? Oh, how rude of me. This is Lightning, the irregular Badger, and this is Bubba."

"I remember you mentioning Lightning, but you did not tell me about this little Cat," said Hugoth chuckling as he looked at Bubba. And this, yes, this must be your friend you say looks a bit like me. I have to agree with you, that he does, that he does."

If Lightning, the irregular Badger, was enormous then there were no words in the Great Forest to aptly describe Hugoth's size. He was, at least, a head taller than the Badger and he could have easily weighed twice as much. Hugoth was very, very big.

"Yes, Prince Mystic, I heard enough to know that you need to be on your way now to Sweet Gulley. Let us go. I will lead you there. I know a short cut."

Bubba rolled his eyes at Lightning as he chuckled, saying, "Prince Mystic?"

The two friends began to chuckle even more as they headed down the path behind Mystic and Hugoth.

Donkorse came over the hill just in time to see Hugoth leading Mystic and his two four-legged friends up one of the small mountains away from the path. They were now heading away from Sweet Gulley. Donkorse said a few short words of protection for the visitors. The tests or trials had begun. The Eagle was safely with the Keeper, he correctly assumed.

"I know my job," Donkorse said to whatever was listening. "And Hugoth knows his. I shall now follow the parade from a safe distance."

Donkorse hurried to catch up. He would follow from a distance just far enough back to know what was going on, but far enough back to not be noticed.

20

"Vincen, are you all right?" asked Charlie of the Eagle who looked to have had one too many blows to the head.

"Yes. Yes, I am I think. It's just that I am completely, totally overwhelmed. Is there no way you could have allowed me to gradually discover this somewhat shocking secret?" Vincen answered.

"No," answered the elder Eagle. "None that I could think of. Please, Ghee, make yourself at home. You have way too much to learn in the short amount of time you have left here."

"Sir, what did you say?" Vincen asked quietly.

"I will let Charlie begin. I will fill in any blank spots. Go ahead, Charlie, start as far back as you wish. If I doze off, bear with me. I will come back around."

"No, please Sir," Charlie begged, "I would like to hear all you have to say about our land. I am sure you are a much more learned historian than myself".

"Very well, I will do my best," said the elder eagle as he began the story. "Vincen, you and your friends have found your way to the Land of Nuorg. Our land is populated by creatures of both the two- and four-legged variety. Every individual has a specific task to perform related to our job of keeping watch over the world from which you have come. Our job in Nuorg is to protect those inhabitants of your world from evil of all types. We negotiate with the dwellers of your earth to keep us informed as to what is happening there. A few of our inhabitants have earned protector status, enabling them to travel back and forth between our worlds. Our protectors are called many things in many places. You have, on occasion, known them in your land without ever knowing them at all. Sometimes, actually more often than not, their appearances go completely unnoticed by those of your world."

"Your friend Mystic is, we believe, a very important creature," the elder Eagle continued. "By his good fortune and possibly yours, he came into the possession of the Staff of Hewitt. The staff was evidently summoned from here somehow and was on its way back with Mystic chosen as its host. We are not completely sure how that happened. The staff will enable Mystic as well as his companions to travel between your land and here. The Disappearing Well is not the only pathway to Nuorg, as this is not the only Burg in Nuorg. There is information in the staff that will lead you to the location of other windows here and there.

"When the staff was lost, which has never happened before this incident, it was incorrectly assumed by most to be gone forever, along with its information. This information is known only to a few, and fortunately none of them are of the remaining Hewitts. The staff can never be wielded in all of its power by any creature it does not wish itself upon. If this had not been so, the power-mongering Hewitts would have destroyed your world and ours as we know it. This staff is not ordinary. This staff is a direct link to the knowledge we acquire here and contains extraordinary power to control a myriad of things in your world and here. The staff, now missing, proved itself to be extremely useful, almost too perfect in its function. This staff fashioned by the original creator of Nuorg was stolen and abused by several greed-driven creatures, all of which have long since disappeared...we hope.

"The Staff of Hewitt, as it came to be known, was, in its innocent state wielded only by uniquely gifted individuals. The founding member of the Hewitt clan was deemed to be the first wielder of the staff several ages ago. The staff was obviously named The Staff of Hewitt simply to identify it and tie it to the original clan to whom it was bestowed."

"The Hewitt clan's world of that day benefited greatly in their early years from the power contained within the staff. Their problems started when the clan began to take its magnitude for granted. The clan accrued wealth and land of obscene proportions through very unscrupulous methods. Their problem grew from greed. The more riches they got, the more riches they wanted. The staff was passed around often. Soon, it was used for many purposes other than the original intent."

"A dispute broke out among the family that split them into factions, one-half of good intentions and one-half of the opposite. The original Hewitt clan, rest their souls, died out given the later heirs' possession of the Staff. The factions battled bitterly for control of the Staff. One nameless individual succeeded in removing the Staff from under the very noses of those so driven to misuse it. He separated himself far

The Land of Nuorg

from the Hewitt clan, including each and every faction thereof. In the end, he was tracked down, forced to relinquish the Staff and was subsequently presumed dead. Very much alive, he managed under very mysterious circumstances to regain the staff and escaped once again. This time, he was hunted down by the bad factions of the clan. While he did not survive, the staff did. He had hidden it well."

"The good Hewitts had no further interest in the Staff, as everything with them was going quite nicely. They had no idea how evil the bad side had become. Separation from the staff, combined with the unsatisfied greed in their wanton lives, drove the bad Hewitts to uncontrollable lust for more power. They correctly decided that controlling the staff was the only way their goals would be met. This time fell just before the era known as the Terrible Years. For many years thereafter, the Hewitts searched relentlessly for the Staff over mountains and through valleys. When the search depleted the able-bodied Hewitts, those that remained hired the lowest of creatures to help them. After tremendous agonizing and long efforts, a small remnant of these creatures recovered the Staff. It was returned to the Hewitts. And the Terrible Years began."

"During the reign of the Terrible Years, jealousy among the evil divisions grew. Amid the infighting, the Staff was again stolen by an anonymous hero. He disappeared, taking the Staff with him. This creature was viciously pursued by the Hewitts, but never found. Gradually, without the Staff, the Terrible Years tapered to an end. The Staff was never seen again until Mystic discovered it."

Responding to all he had heard, Vincen said, "That is a lot of information Sir. Still there is much room for questioning within it. Now, please tell me of the geography of this place and where it really is."

"Wait", interrupted Charlie. "Is there not more to the Staff's history than you have described? Who now knows how the power is brought forth?"

"Of course, Charlie, maybe I can delve into that later," the Great Eagle continued, "Mystic has asked another pertinent question that I will answer first."

"Very well, as you wish. I am sure you have only piqued Vincen's interest," replied Charlie.

Mystic, the Great Eagle, continued, "Vincen, Nuorg is inside your world. Your ground is our ground. It will be until this orb is no more. Our land parallels your land. Your horizon falls; ours rises. Your waters run down hill; ours run up hill. If you scribe a circle on a tablet, then scribe another circle within the first, you would have our location. Your sun rises; we have no sun. Our light emanates from the yellow ball you see in our sky. It does not set; it does not rise. It is a constant reminder of the evil in your world. It keeps us alert."

"The yellow ball burns without ceasing. If one were to touch it, it would burn them beyond recognition. The yellow ball is fueled by evil. When an evil is cast out of Nuorg, it is locked away inside the burning flame that is that yellow ball. The goodness of your world and ours surrounds the evil in that ball. The evil can't escape unless the good allows it. With the yellow ball as constant reminder of evil's power, the good will never, voluntarily, let it escape. On your world, light is chased by darkness and darkness by light. There is never one that wins against the other. It is the same with good and evil. They are at war and are constantly in pursuit of one other. We have a clear view of the bad in our world. You do not have that option. When one leaves here, his eyes are open and attentive to the slightest hint of evil, as your eyes will be, until the instant you take good for granted. Then the cycle will begin once again. Evil resides dormant in the darkest part of every creature."

"What about the water?" Vincen asked.

"Oh yes," replied the Eagle. "That water comes from our river, The Hopen River. The water is pure hope. It runs throughout our land and is just under the surface of yours. It is another gift we have here in Nuorg. It overwhelms people. The Hopen River can provide water for everyone, though it is not as easy to keep fresh as other water. Our river's water will spoil quickly if left unused. The river will never run dry. It has always been there for us. It was crafted that way. You drank of it. What did you feel?"

"I am not familiar with that you speak of," replied a confused Vincen.

"Vincen," the elder Eagle continued, "You, Grandson, departed. You quit living. You left us. That huge friend of yours did not give up on you. He saved your life by forcing the river's water in you."

"I do remember feeling somewhat revived. I felt young again. I was stronger than I have been since my youth," Vincen said as the feeling came back. "However, once I began to worry about our situation and all of the other problems, I felt myself aging again. Does the water have a permanent effect?"

Yes, it does. To get the most out of it though you have to constantly drink from it. The only problem we have encountered is, you can't let it become stagnant. Sometimes it is hard to get the taste again," Vincen said. "Every inhabitant of Nuorg drinks water from the river every day. It's habit forming. We couldn't live without it. It is the best tasting water we know of."

"Well that explains the taste of the mud in Sweet Gulley," Vincen recalled.

"Yes, you are correct. Even the worst of our worlds--the mud, the bad fruit, everything--can benefit from our river's water."

"Vincen, your world once was as pure as Nuorg. Everything changed and your land became tarnished as more and more inhabitants lost sight of what our river is made of, hope," said the elder Eagle.

He continued, "We are doing the best we can, but there are only so many of us. Not enough of those inhabiting your world believe we can do them any good. The protectors are taken for granted. We are there to help. There is a swelling of the yellow ball. We are most concerned about that at present. Bad times are soon coming for your lands. The evil is abundant there. There seem to be a few surviving members, or imposters, of the Hewitt family that know too much of the Staff of Hewitt. Their information is formidable though incomplete. Should they regain possession of the staff allowing them access to this land, the evil we hold imprisoned in the yellow ball could be released. That would be detrimental to the existence of, not only Nuorg, but your land as well. We would, more than likely, survive in darkness until the evil was recaptured and once again imprisoned. It has happened before."

"The Terrible Years?" asked Vincen

"Exactly," answered Mystic the Eagle. "The Terrible Years, yes, those years were very problematic for us. It is hard to realize that one creature was ultimately responsible for that entire episode, besides the Hewitts. Really, it was quite a ridiculous turn of events. Solving those kinds of problems exhausts our energy as we try to recover the ground lost, but it can be done."

Vincen asked, "So, where does Mystic, or for that matter myself, fit into this plan of yours?"

"I am glad you asked. I will elaborate more on your roles in a moment," Mystic answered. "We are talking about a problem several times worse than the terrible years. Those purveyors of no good are in your world now and they are scheming as we meet. To keep them under control, they must be brought here immediately to be imprisoned. Unfortunately, this time, there are several creatures involved".

"When I go back to explain this, what will keep me or any member of our traveling party from being labeled as a crazy fool?" asked Vincen.

"Do I look like a crazy fool to you, Ghee? Besides, you are not required to explain the land of Nuorg to anyone. Your job is to convince two and four-leggers of what we tell you," stated Vincen's grandfather.

"No sir, you don't and I think I can see your point?" Vincen answered.

"Then will you do as I have said? What is protecting your world worth to you, Ghee? Is it worth the ridicule? Is it worth being labeled? It certainly was to me," Mystic of the Vincen Eagles continued.

"I see, Sir. Thank you," uttered the humbled Eagle.

The wise Eagle, a bit weary, began speaking again, "Your friends are about to go through some rough times. They should come out fine, but their lives will be changed forever. If they come to retrieve you, we will tell you more. I must get some rest now. Charlie can entertain you in my absence. It could be a long wait."

***

Hugoth was leading the way through the mountains, hiking over the roughest terrain the three friends had ever traveled. The Guard of the Forever Trees was making his way handily through the rough stuff as the others struggled behind him. Lightning dropped his ax-pike on one of the steepest sections of the trail and Hugoth forbade him to go after it. Hugoth also knew that Donkorse would find it soon enough.

Bubba also slipped on a loose section of trail and lost his rapier as he tumbled down the trail. Hugoth also forbade him to scramble after his rapier. Later, Donkorse successfully collected both tools and turned back for the Burg.

"I am so glad they lost these so early," Donkorse said as he carefully descended the steep trail, all the while wondering how in any world that Badger's weapon came into existence. It was big and it was heavy!

The Land of Nuorg

Hugoth was beginning to tire. He stopped the group on a small, flat area between two steep sections of this rarely used trail. Lightning dropped to the ground in a pile, as Mystic and Bubba chose to settle down a little less dramatically. They were all thirsty. The Guard was too preoccupied to notice the exhausted look on the visitors' faces as he listened intently for the sound of falling water. He had passed this way before and he was sure he remembered a water source nearby. After a quick pause, Hugoth smiled and left the three others lying on the ground. He had detected the faint sound of falling water after a short walk through the thick brush.

His memory had not failed him, for soon he located the source of the pleasant sound. A small waterfall, hidden in a crack of the mountainside, was gurgling into a natural catch basin worn into the rock. It took him a while to drink his fill before he called the rest of his party over. Hugoth drank the basin dry and it was filling up when Mystic arrived.

"Is this the same water that flows in the river near the Burg?" asked Mystic noticing the cloudy colorations in this water.

"No, it is not. This water will not taste the same to you if you have already swallowed water from the river. This water is raw water. It has not been purified yet," Hugoth answered.

"Whatever do you mean and are you sure this is a shortcut back to the Gulley?" Mystic inquired.

It was now time for Hugoth to begin answering questions. "The second question I will answer first. Yes, this could be considered a shortcut. Now, for the water, this water flows to Nuorg from your world. All of the impurities of your world are cleaned from the water as it passes under our land toward our river. The taste you will notice in this water, Mystic, is caused as pure water washes over the bad things that are allowed to happen in the world where you live. The water becomes dirty. The water soaks into your land and runs here for purification. The more a creature drinks, of this unclean water, the more it causes that creature to forget how good the pure water actually is. Before you know it, this water tastes normal and the pure water is only a small trace of a memory."

"Really," the Wolf answered. "Is this water dangerous to us?"

"Yes, in some ways it is if you drink too much. Another thing you must know is that the taste of this water is habit forming. If you don't drink enough of the water from our river, this water will be the only water you will wish to drink."

Mystic was too thirsty to argue. He bent down and took a swallow of the water in the basin. He quickly jerked his head away from the basin and tried to wipe the water's disgusting taste from his tongue. "Hugoth, that water tastes awful; it's dreadfully sour!"

Bubba followed by the Badger came to join Mystic and Hugoth. "Hey, were you ever going to tell us about this water. Our tongues are as dry as yours!" Bubba said.

"He's right," added the Badger. "I could drink a complete pond dry. Quickly Bubba, I'm drying up."

Mystic gladly backed off from the basin. He was anxious to see if either of his friends noticed the same sour taste of the water. He had no way of knowing yet.

"Wow," exclaimed Bubba, "I don't know if that water tastes good enough to drink or not. He desperately tried to shake it out of his mouth.

"Let me in," demanded Lightning. "It can't be that bad!"

The Badger took a drink of the water and tried hard to swallow it. Instead, he spit the foul fluid out. "My, are you sure we can drink that?"

Mystic was surprised. "Does it taste that odd to both of you?" he asked.

Bubba was the first to answer. "The water we used to wash the mud off of Vincen was wonderful. It tasted so much sweeter than this. This tastes worse than branch water. What is it?"

"You drank water from the river?" inquired Mystic.

"No, it was water from the stream that bubbled up through the mud in Sweet Gulley," said the Badger.

"Well, that is still closer to our river water than this we have just drank," Hugoth interjected. "The Sweet Gulley stream water has almost purified, but it still lacks a little processing. If you have tasted the water from the gully, you should have an even stronger desire to drink yourselves full of the water from the river."

Hugoth was thinking that his first task had instantly gotten much easier. This job might not be too bad after all.

***

"Vincen," Charlie asked, "Do you have any other questions for me now?"

The Land of Nuorg

"Yes I do, Charlie. How did my Grandfather come to be here? How long ago did he arrive?"

Charlie had just sat down and was beginning to get comfortable in his overstuffed chair, "Wait, I will find out." Charlie rose from his chair and walked over to a well-used bookcase. He searched each row of over a hundred books and picked up the next to the last one. "I should have started looking from this end," he said with a grin. "Let's see, Mystic, Mystic, Mystic, Vincen. Yes, here it is. I know you do not keep time as we do here, but nevertheless I will try to pinpoint the date for you. It is scribbled here, yes, that would be right in the timeline corresponding to the ending of the Terrible Years. Um, okay Vincen, your Grandfather arrived here when you were four complete day-round records, or years, old," Charlie said to all.

"My, that was sometime ago. Has this been planned the whole time?" questioned Vincen.

"No Vincen, it wasn't. That's free will's role in all of this. Several things you did during your lifetime led to this occurrence of events. Mystic, the Wolf, was brought here to prepare him to lead inhabitants of The Great Forest and the lands beyond in the event of a potential return of the Terrible Years. We hoped if we got him here, we could prepare him first hand. The fact that he did not bring the Staff of Hewitt complicated matters. However, the fact that your whole little group came will work out to the benefit of all concerned," Charlie explained.

"How did the well open without the Staff?" asked Vincen.

"I can tell you this, Great Eagle, stranger things have happened. The staff may have returned on its own, pulling you in with it," Charlie answered. Then he turned his attention to Karri.

"Karri, would you please find Donkorse, ask him of Hugoth's position and get a report from him? Your brother seems to remain in a surprised stupor."

"Yes, Sir, I would be more than happy to. I will hurry!" Karri flew off immediately.

Vincen closed his eyes and spoke aloud, "Four, that was over one hundred and more years, as you say, ago. Does he know the fate of the other Great Eagles of our family? Am I allowed to know this?"

Charlie walked back to his chair and sat down. "No you are not Vincen. I'm sorry."

21

Hugoth smiled as he led his small group away from the water basin. This was better than he anticipated. Each of the four visitors had drunk water from the river and were, arguably, better for it. Of the three with him, each had a seed of knowledge on which to build. The tests of the truths were soon to be administered. Although he wouldn't be within their grasps, he would know the location of each test. He would not be far from them in case of an accident.

The first test would be the easiest for two of them. Mystic and Bubba had dealt with the first of the four subjects early in life. Lightning had been spared. He would be the question mark. How he dealt with the first subject would tell much about the big-hearted creature and his ability to proceed with the subjects to follow. Hopefully, he had learned enough from his friends' experiences to deal with it properly.

Hugoth led the group to an opening in the side of the mountain. It looked and smelled like a cave, but it wasn't a cave as much as it could become a nightmare. Hugoth instructed Mystic, Bubba and the Badger to follow him inside.

"To each of you," Hugoth began, "I bid you welcome to the "Halls of Truth." In here you will begin the first leg of your journey back to the Great Forest. It could easily be a long journey. It is a journey that you may not want to take. If you have any reservations, please tell me now. Once you begin, I will not be able to help you until you can take no more and completely give up. Once you give up, your journey is over. You will stay with us in Nuorg for the rest of your days and no harm should ever come to you. If you decide to press on to the end, you will be rewarded accordingly. May you each succeed and find yourselves wiser and stronger when you reach your goal."

When Hugoth had finished talking, he and the opening disappeared. Darkness was all that remained.

"What was that all about?" demanded Bubba.

The Land of Nuorg

"Where did our fellow Hugoth get off to? I have a few more questions to ask of him," added Lightning.

"I believe we have seen the last of Hugoth for a while," replied Mystic. "Is seems to me that his job was to lead us here, then turn us over to ourselves and whatever we find ourselves to be. It's up to us to find our way out of this place and whatever it may lead us into next. Our weapons are gone. We were supposed to lose them. We were not going to be allowed in this cave with them anyway. Answer me this, friends, if you will. Have you seen one creature of any type in this land carrying a weapon? Why, they even call our weapons tools. They don't have a use for weapons here. We polluted this land when we came in with ours."

"But Mystic," Lightning asked, "Why are they so concerned about your wand/staff? It seems strange to me that they would not consider that a weapon."

Mystic answered, "Think about it, Lightning; is the wand/staff actually a weapon? No, as long as it has been in my possession it has not been considered a weapon. I have never used it as such, nor could I imagine what kind of damage it could inflict. What could it possibly do? It has no blades or knives. It is too fragile to beat anything with."

"I'll tell you what it can do," said Bubba, "It might very well kill you! It certainly acted as if it could right before it pulled us in the well."

"It did not pull you into the well," said the Badger. "I did. I grabbed your tail and in you came."

"Well maybe not, but it still had quite a bit to do with us being here."

Mystic paced around the entry chamber of the cave as he thought about why they might be here. There was no light in the cave. It was pitch dark, yet not one of the three friends panicked. There was no cause for it. The chamber was carved out of rock. It had smooth walls that glistened until Hugoth shut out the light. Mystic walked completely around the chamber and found no obvious exit.

"This must be another odd phenomenon of this land," said Mystic. "For I see no way out of here. Hugoth welcomed us to the Halls of Truth. Well, how do we get out? How do we continue our journey home? Any suggestions?"

"I think, obviously, that truth has something to do with it," answered the Badger.

"We are always truthful, are we not?" asked Bubba.

"One would suppose so," replied Mystic.

***

Vincen was thinking of hundreds of questions to ask Charlie. He paced around the large gathering table non-stop, his razor sharp talons leaving noticeable marks with each step on the surface of the table. Charlie watched him and knew the Eagle felt a loss for his friends. Vincen assumed the same body position as he always did when he found himself in deep thought. Charlie looked closely, and like many before him, imagined the Eagle with hands folded behind his back.

"Come now, Vincen, what causes you to fret so strenuously?" Charlie asked.

"If you must know, Charlie, my head is filling with questions faster than I can work them from my beak. May I ask you a few more?" Vincen inquired.

"By all means, go right ahead." Charlie rose again from his chair to close the heavy shutters at the window.

"Why the shutters?" asked Vincen.

"That is an easy one," Charlie chuckled. "In order to rest, we must block out the fire from the yellow ball. Some of us get weary from the presence of the evil in that dreadful thing. One can only take so much. We find that, in order to keep balance in our lives and stay alert to our duties, we have to shut ourselves off from those things that can dilute our mission. We use dimmed light within our dwellings to rest and regain our strength. When we close off the outside we can concentrate more on the tasks assigned to us. Vincen, we exist in an almost perfect little world here, yet we need the quiet times inside. Now think of your world. Do you ever take the time to completely shut out the noise and listen to what is inside your head? Have you ever taken the time to grow closer to those around you without the worries of the lands beyond clouding your thoughts? If you haven't, you must try it. I don't know how you could continue to survive up there if you don't."

"Charlie, I haven't really thought about it like that. I live splendidly. I care for others as I would like them to care for me. I was taught by the wisest creatures and I do not dwell on many worrisome details. I am old now and not too busy to notice and appreciate the small wonders of the Great Forest. Would that not set well here? What more would one expect?"

The Land of Nuorg

Charlie crossed his arms on his chest as he leaned way back in his chair looking at Mystic, the Eagle. The Eagle was not quite asleep, so he responded to Vincen's question. "Much, much more. Vincen, do you remember the taste of the water in Sweet Gulley?"

"Yes, I was asleep, but when I awoke there was a wonderfully sweet taste in my mouth. I attributed it to the mud that was caked all over me. Is that wrong?" Vincen answered.

"Vincen, you were no more. You had breathed your last breath. You had suffocated and died. Your friends were devastated. You should have heard the story Karri told me about how your friends worked to save you. You did breathe again, but it was only because of your friends' willingness to sacrifice their time to come to your aid. You had lost hope in your struggle to be free of the gooey mud. You gave up. The hope your friends had that you would come back to them awakened you. The water was merely a way for the hope to get inside of you."

"Yes, I see that," Vincen answered a bit fidgety.

"Well, the original creator of this land made it clear to all Nuorgians that hope is a very important force to keep evil at bay. You were given a second chance because of the love your friends demonstrated for you. They held you under the water until you breathed again. If you had not ingested some of this water, you would not be here any longer. Hope would not have reached inside you because you had closed your mind so tightly against any possible chance of escape. Do you not wish to drink more, knowing what you do about it?

"I would be lying if I said otherwise," Vincen said.

"You are a wise Eagle, Vincen," Charlie interjected. "Your Grandfather was correct about you. When he left you, followed by your Parents, then your Sister, there was no one remaining to tell you what you needed to know about hope, although you have demonstrated a wealth of mercy."

"What about the Owls" Mystic asked. "Are they not the wisest creatures of the Great Forest? They made odd references to what you have explained on occasion."

"I am sure they are wise and I am sure they did mention hope," replied Charlie. "However, just because a creature knows about the existence of hope and can speak of it, that does not mean that the creature actually knows the basics of how to use it. The Owls may be wise in the ways of the Great Forest, but they may have taken hope for granted, thus relying too heavily on their intelligence. That can be a dangerous combination."

"I think I understand what you are saying."

"Vincen, you and your friends are fortunate. You three have unwittingly ridden The Wolf's adventure here and benefited greatly by it. Great things lie ahead for your friends and yourself, especially under Mystic's leadership. I can also tell you that you would be even more surprised to know all about that little Cheetah's history."

"Really? The Cheetah?"

"Yes, the Cheetah," answered Charlie. "Now, what is your next question?"

"The Cheetah?" Vincen asked again, dumbfounded. "Well, if you promise to tell me more of that story, I will ask my next question."

"Go ahead."

"Why does your water run up hill?"

"Good question and one I can answer," replied Charlie. "Our water is completely purified by seeping through our porous ground. Your water is heavy with the impurities of your world. It is heavily laden and runs here for purification. Once it is filtered, it runs directly into the Hopen River. It is there where the cycle begins again. It runs up our hills and into wells located at the top. These wells route the water to your world as rain, mountain streams and the like.

"On the surface, it all seems so simple", said Vincen.

"We must rest now, Vincen. I will answer more of your questions later," Charlie stated as sleep began to woo him.

Vincen could not sleep. He had three friends somewhere out in this odd land that he longed to be with. "Do be careful," he whispered to them.

***

Mystic, Bubba and Lightning paced quietly around in a circle. No words were spoken as they each pondered the meaning of this hall. Lightning was the first to stop pacing. Bubba followed soon after when he fell after being bounced off the Badger's side. He was knocked to the ground and remained there, resting. Mystic eventually succumbed to the monotony of circling. He joined the two others on the chamber floor.

"What now?" asked Lightning.

"The truth, I imagine," answered Mystic. "What more could be asked of us here?"

"Is it the truth that we supposedly hide from each other or is it a deeper truth?" Bubba wanted to know.

"What does that mean?" asked the Badger.

Bubba continued, "I mean do I need to tell you everything about my early life, about the persecution my family faced for being different, about being thrown out of our own home or what my family really did during their lives? If so that could take many day rounds and moon times. Is it not the deeper truth that we need to know while we sit here? Do you two have something I need to know?"

"What do you mean, deeper truths?" asked Lightning.

"Mystic, would you like to answer him?" asked Bubba.

"I'm sorry Bubba, but I would like to know also. What do you mean?"

"So you are telling me, the youngest, by many day keeping records, that you have never heard of the deeper truths?"

Bubba was having difficulty believing this.

"I guess the answer would be yes," answered the Badger.

"Very well then, listen. I will explain them to you." Bubba began speaking from a wealth of knowledge that far eclipsed his young age. "The deeper truths I am talking about concern the beyond. What happens after the life in the Great Forest is over for each of us? There is so much more. It is called the 'beyond' in my family."

"Cheetahs were never concerned with dying or being taken, as we called it. We lived our entire lives roaming from dwelling place to dwelling place telling others of the beyond. The Cheetahs believe that when you were taken, you left the land of the dying and crossed over to beyond living. I even think that this land we are in may be a similar place, although I have never been taught of its existence. My kind were hunted down and killed for no other reason than that of telling creatures about hope in the beyond. Most creatures were set in their ways; they wanted no changes brought to their lands. We felt called to go out and tell of this way of thinking. My kind did that with a type of zeal unfamiliar to most creatures," Bubba.

"As I said, we were hunted down by poachers working for those who misunderstood our intentions or absolutely did not care about anything except taking us. Our skins were sold to the buyer with the most money and highest dislike for our kind. Our skins hid some of the richest creatures in our world from themselves. It was a hard life, but a life that we never gave up. It would have been easy to stay in one place and forget about spreading our ideals. We did it because we believe so strongly in that beyond where there are no more takings, no more wars and no more evil."

"The Great Forest is but one of many dwelling places," Bubba continued. "Dwellers of each place hope and think they will never see the Terrible Years again. But I tell you this: you can never let your guard down, for evil is alive on our world. It was never truly defeated. There is just too much of it left hiding in too many creatures. It patiently sits waiting to boil. When it does, events resembling the Terrible Years happen. You must have hope that it will one day be defeated and believe in something. For us it is the beyond. The dirt of this life will wear you down. The beyond cannot promise you a trouble-free life in the Great Forest or anywhere else, but it can and does give you something to look forward too once those places are gone. Am I making any sense to you at all?"

"I have heard what you are saying," said Mystic, a tinge of pain rising from deep within. "Unlike you, I never really knew my family at all. All I've known is Vincen and he is certainly no Wolf. My family was slaughtered! My Uncle came back to me with the news of their deaths and died at my side when I was a mere pup. I cannot understand this hope or the beyond you talk about, knowing what I know. I can't forgive the two-leggers that wiped out the gray Wolves of the Great Forest! They deserve to die with the evil in their lives! Furthermore, they should never have the promise of a beyond!"

"Mystic, I have never heard you like this," Lightning said as he sat stunned at the Wolf's outburst.

"That's because I try not to think about it, Lightning. What would you know? You live in the same dwelling as your parents. They are both still alive and you play with your brothers and sisters every day-round as you have done your entire life. You know nothing of my extent of sadness and loss. You live an ideal life."

"Try being the so called Prince of The Great Forest for a few day-rounds," Mystic continued as tears flowed down his snout. "I have no training; I have no sense to rule. I have spent my life searching and running from responsibility. I thought my wand/staff would cure all of that. I believed that wand/staff could make me a proper ruler. Did it? Of course not! I heard the laughing every time I showed up with it. Do I look like a ruler to you?"

Lightning was hurt. He had never known Mystic to talk this way. All of these feelings had been kept deep inside the Wolf for so long.

"Wait a click here, my life is not perfect!" Lightning protested. "Where are you going with this? When I asked my mother long ago to be irregular, do you think I had any idea how irregular I would actually turn out? Mystic, I am a freak, an oddity. I do not live in the same dwelling as my family. I had to move out when I was a cub because I was too big to fit through their doors. I could not play with my siblings because I might accidentally hurt them. Sure, I still live behind them and they care for me very much, but my size has made me a sideshow wherever I go. Creatures are afraid of me except for you two. How would you feel if you knew that everywhere you went creatures would do the best they could to avoid you? No one talks with me; they change to the other side of the path if they see me coming. I hear all of the jokes about my size and the names I am called and I laugh along with the ones telling the jokes. But to me, their jokes aren't funny. I am hurt that you would speak of me as you just did. You are feeling sorry for yourself and have no idea how hard my life is. You should never make that kind of judgment until you have walked in my path."

"Wow, this is good," exclaimed Bubba, "Do you each feel better now?"

The cave was getting less dark. The three were beginning to make out each other's shapes. Mystic and Lightning were wondering where the light was coming from. Bubba knew.

"So, tell me what else you are feeling," Bubba continued. "Mystic, you have to be able to forgive the two-leggers that did you so much harm. I feel that all of them did not intend to commit all of the carnage. I heard my Parents tell stories of that fateful day. Like I said, we traveled to a lot of dwelling places. There was a story about one two-legger that was run out of town after the slaughter for igniting the anger. Several two-leggers were able to hand down stories about what had actually happened after they awoke from the violent trance that consumed so many on that day. It was said that the two-legger that instigated the slaughter was never welcomed in or around there again. Later, they said, he was fatally wounded in a grisly accident No one shed a tear for him. The rest of the two-leggers in that dwelling place hired a Talker to beg the Wolves for forgiveness, but no Wolf was ever encountered in that Talker's later travels."

"Do you know why no Wolves were ever encountered?" Mystic asked. "Because I was the only one left! I was it. Poor little Mystic. The timber Wolves are no family of mine, probably not even true Wolves! They are useless and slovenly. They only came into the Great Forest because they were weak and had no leader. Now, I am supposed to be their leader and I end up doing all of the work I want them to do! I have no patience with them at all. How do you know that what you have said is the truth anyway?" asked the perturbed Wolf.

"I told you before, we traveled much, listened much and learned even more," answered the Cheetah.

"Well I would like to hear that from those two-leggers," declared Mystic, "If I could keep from tearing them apart".

"Who knows, maybe one day you will," answered Bubba.

More light began to fill the chamber. The tear-soaked snouts of the Badger and the Wolf sparkled in the growing illumination. They began wiping the tears off of their snouts and eyes with their paws.

"I could be persuaded to talk with one of the two-leggers if what you say is actually true," Mystic said reflectively.

Bubba looked back at Mystic, "It is true, Mystic."

More light filled the chamber.

"I am so sorry that I hurt you Lightning. I was way past my manners. I should have thought of your feelings more than my own," apologized Mystic.

More light crept in as Mystic squinted his eyes as they tried to adjust to the brightness in the chamber.

"All is forgotten," the Badger replied.

The three continued to talk and shout. They continued to question. They continued to open up. Eventually, the light became as bright as the late sun time in the Great Forest.

"Mystic," said Bubba, "I have seen many rulers in my short life and you have every talent imaginable to be one of the greatest."

The light completely filled the chamber and all of the nearby nooks and crevices.

The three friends sat in a circle absorbing the warm bright light. "Well," said Mystic, "Now what?"

At the opposite side of the room from where they had entered, a large hole was growing silently in the wall. "Well, I assume we should

The Land of Nuorg

continue through there," Bubba stated as he pointed toward the opening.

Mystic and Lightning looked at the growing opening, then at each other, simultaneously nodded and together answered, "We assume so!"

Led by Mystic, all three of them raced to the opening. They shot through and immediately found themselves falling. The solid ground had stopped at the opening, but they had not. They failed to look before exiting the hall. Now they were falling fast and falling far. Remarkably, they each made eye contact as Lightning quite loudly exclaimed, "Oh meeeercyyy."

***

Karri made quick time of finding Hugoth. She spotted him as he crossed the clearing leading from the foot of the small mountain to The Path to Where I Am Going. He needed to follow the path back to the cave entrance that Donkorse had used earlier that led under Sweet Gulley. Karri sounded a loud call that got Hugoth's attention. He looked up as she came diving in. She landed on his tree trunk-like neck then hopped down to the ground in front of Hugoth. Hugoth needed a short rest, and he respectfully stood in the presence of this female Hawk.

"Oh please, Hugoth, be seated. You look tired," Karri said.

"Thank you, Karri," replied Hugoth. "You can tell the Keeper that the first test is under way. Our visitors may complete this test quicker than we expected. I must get to the Gulley Cave before they do. They may need me."

"I won't keep you long. Did you know, Hugoth, that the Keeper's dwelling guest was the Eagle's Grandfather? That gave me quite a shock. Do you think he will be assigned to them?"

Hugoth thought about what she said for a minute, then replied, "Yes, I knew the Eagle was related in some way, but I had no idea it was such a close relationship. As for your second question, no, I don't think so. He may be a little too closely related. It would be hard for him to not get caught up in personal feelings and emotions. I don't think the Keeper would make that decision. Anyway, doesn't he have a Burg of his own?"

Karri nodded her head in agreement, "Yes Hugoth, you are correct. The assignment may still be open. Is there any other news that I should share with those back at the dwelling?"

"No, not at this time. Tell them all is proceeding as we had hoped. Did you pass over Donkorse?"

"Yes I did. He was grumbling about those tools. They must have been awkward to carry. They were not strapped to his back. He had the little knife in his mouth and the big stick, looked to be, fastened to his neck. It kept popping him if he tried to walk too fast. I may take the knife back for him. I am sure he won't mind."

"That would be kind of you, Karri. I think he would be grateful if you even asked. I must be on my way. If you will excuse me?"

"Certainly Hugoth, keep up the good work! I will go find Donkorse. Rakki will be out to see you next. I must rest."

Karri raced off. She was determined to locate Donkorse before he became too frustrated with those tools. It would be an easy chore for her to carry that little knife for Donkorse. Then, he would not need to struggle so with the big stick. She was not at all sure what that tool was used for.

Hugoth made straight away for the entrance to the cave. It was not a short walk for him. He feared it would take a longer period of time than he actually had. For this reason, he began to amble a bit faster than normal. It was quite a sight to see, the Guard of The Forever Trees moving fast enough to officially call it a trot. It is a shame, but no creature in the entire Land of Nuorg witnessed this rarely seen feat. Hugoth would always know and, more than likely, would never tell anyway.

***

Vincen could not sleep. He paced the room then moved to the window. He silently lit on the windowsill and pushed open a shutter. He looked out at the sleeping Burg; all shutters on all dwellings were tightly closed. The dwellers were resting comfortably, as they did every day-round in the Burg. His eyes drifted to the Forever Trees. The size of the trees had him longing for his favorite perch back in the Great Forest. The Great Eagle was not comfortable knowing that his students were somewhere out in the unknown land with no clue as to why or what they would be doing that was required of them. He then directed his attention to the yellow ball in the sky. It seemed to be heaving like some legger's chest while in a deep sleep. He wondered why such an incredible land was constantly monitoring, as Charlie had earlier stated, the evil inside that thing. He remembered Charlie saying, "Bad can only escape when good allows it" or something like that. Well, Vincen was sure he would chase that statement around in his thoughts for a while.

***

"There he is!" shouted Karri. "Donkorse, Donkorse, please stop."

The little Hawk tucked her wings and dove straight down at Donkorse. She pulled up just in time to land face first in Donkorse's thick mane. "That was a bit less than graceful," she said as she struggled to free herself of the long, coarse hair.

"Welcome," Donkorse greeted her as he dropped the rapier out of his teeth and exercised his gums. "That feels good. I think I've lost all feeling in my mouth. Any news of late happenings?" he asked.

"Yes, everything is going according to plan. I am here to lighten your load," she cheerfully exclaimed.

"Good, you take that big stick and I will continue on with this little tool," Donkorse directed jokingly. "I know that brother of yours would certainly give it a try."

"Ah yes, I'm sure he would," she answered, "but I won't. I will take that little knife for you if you wish. Of course, you could keep it and continue struggling with both tools all the way back to the Burg, if you like. I will update the Keeper of your progress."

"Wait, not so fast, here Karri, please take it. Little Hawk, you are so quick to call my bluff. I was about to lose my patience with both of these tools. You arrived at the perfect time. You would do me a tremendous favor if you would take this little thing back to the Keeper for me. I will have a much better trip if I am able to breathe."

"Certainly I will. We will expect you soon," Karri answered. She hopped over to the rapier. She clasped her talons around the blade then lifted off. She continued swiftly on her way.

***

Mystic, Lightning and Bubba suddenly stopped falling. They had stopped just short of the rock floor below and were now slowly being lowered to the ground. They each landed with no damaging effect from the fall. They were all puzzled with their gradual stop; well, at least two of them were. Bubba wasn't. The young Cheetah continued to impress the two older creatures with his grasp of what was going on around them. Mystic decided then and there that whatever the young Cheetah was talking about, he was determined to find out more about it.

"More strangeness, I gather," mused the Badger.

"Bubba, an explanation please?" Mystic asked.

"It is not time for us to be taken. That fall was just for show," Bubba replied. "Think about it. We are here, together for a purpose we know nothing about. We don't know why, how or what. Something went to great trouble to see that we have gotten this far. I will not start doubting that now, nor should you."

The three landed softly on a thin ledge of rock that would, eventually they presumed, lead to somewhere else. They were correct, of course. Every path leads somewhere, so where did this one lead? They followed the ledge as it spiraled even deeper under the mountain. Eventually the three stopped where the path split into three separate paths. Mystic was the first to ponder which direction should be taken. Should they continue to follow the ledge as it ventured on to the right? Should they take the path in the middle or the one on the left? The path to the right led them, Mystic assumed from his first impression, on a very clear and wide trail that spread out in front of them like a welcome rug. This trail would be the easiest of the three to follow, but they noticed that it got very dark very quickly. Another question: would it take them where they wanted to go? They had climbed up the side of the mountain to access the cave. Now one would naturally think they should head down to reach The Path to Where I Am Going which would lead back to the Burg and back to Vincen.

There was one small problem with the path to the left. Although it was better illuminated, it was narrow and did not at first glance offer a comfortable or easy journey back. The path was steep, but it did seem to grow brighter the farther back it went. Mystic took a few steps down it and noticed how rocky it soon became. Mystic carefully stepped back to join the others who were busy forming their own opinions of which way to go.

The third path was nothing special, a gradual easy slope straight through the mountain. It could be traversed with the least difficulty.

"Well?" asked Mystic. "Which way shall it be?"

Lightning intently stared up toward the wide and clear path. "That way looks the easiest to me," he said, "Although I am not convinced that it is the correct way to go at all. If we follow this path to the right, I am almost completely sure that it is the wrong way."

"Why do you say that?" asked Mystic. "How about the middle one?"

"For obvious reasons, of course. The middle path, I would never choose the middle one," answered the Badger. "It is entirely too easy and inviting. What would it prove? Nothing, that's what it would prove. It would prove only that we are searching the simplest way out. I don't think we should start using that method after we have come this far by besting difficulty."

Mystic looked around. He was obviously in a quandary. The Wolf shook his head, to clear a few cobwebs, slowly acknowledged Lightning's reply and agreed. "Yes, Lightning, I do believe you are correct. This one path looks more accommodating to our party; however, I do not have a good feeling about it. The middle path, I agree, looks too easy. Not only does it lead us back to where we were, it also requires no thinking, no work and lastly no desire. This other narrow path is the one we should follow. It won't be as easy. Still, we will be heading in the correct direction. Bubba, do you have any observations one way or the other?"

"The easiest path is not always the safest or the wisest choice," Bubba replied. If my family had always chosen the wide-open roads to follow, we would have been wiped out before we had the chance to escape. We would have grown no stronger by doing no work. I say we take the narrow path. It may be more difficult, yet I believe the rewards are greater in the end."

"Let us begin," said the Badger.

"Very well," said Mystic, "Follow me."

The three set off on their choice of paths. They carefully walked in single file while staying close behind each other. They may have decided on the correct path to follow, but, it was most certainly not the easiest.

No sooner had they started than the first problem became readily apparent. The footing was terrible. Rocks slid or crumbled out from under them with each step. This path became narrower than any of the three could have possibly imagined. Not only did it narrow, it narrowed even more ahead of them as the rock ledge became the longest, thinnest, weakest-looking bridge over the deepest, darkest chasm any of the three had ever observed. The next test had begun.

"Oh mercy." The Badger was the first to speak up. "Are we absolutely sure that we took the correct path? From where I stood, I did not see this particularly narrow stretch. Is it too late to try the other way?"

"Lightning, come now. We are all here. We are all going to be okay. Our journey will be better once we cross this bridge," said Bubba. "It is much too easy to take the other path. If you did what would you learn about yourself?"

"Well, we all three might actually make it to the end of the other paths for starters! Each one of my paws is wider than what I see to be a bridge up ahead," answered Lightning. After getting strong-armed looks from the others, he retracted his stance. "Okay, so be it. Let's go."

Mystic was far too concerned about crossing the bridge to worry about how impassable it seemed. Carefully, they inched their way across the narrow span. Lightning felt he was walking on a crumbling rope. He had been correct with his earlier assessment. Each, of his paws was much wider than the widest part of the narrow bridge. Bubba scampered lithely across the bridge, casually running to and fro. His agility and his lighter weight were factors to his advantage over his friends. Mystic was somewhere between the other two. He, by no means, was comfortable, but at least his feet were fitting nicely as they walked. All was going relatively well until they approached the midway point of the bridge. Without warning Bubba ran smack into a solid barrier that knocked him back. He landed precariously, straddling the walkway on both sides. They had all stopped. Their precarious journey was now abruptly halted. Immediately in front of Mystic's nose another solid barrier appeared between him and Bubba. The same could be said of Lightning. There was nothing they could do but stop. It was too late to reconsider. Impenetrable walls of shimmering rock now separated them.

"This can't be happening!" Mystic shouted, his growing frustration becoming apparent. "Is this more of the beyond thing?" he yelled at Bubba.

Before Mystic could release another word from his mouth, he let out a howling yelp that fell somewhere between intense pain and even more intense fright. When he turned around to get a closer look at the wall, a two-legger with a grain sickle held high over his head eyed him in bewildered hatred. The sickle began to swing in a powerful downward arc aimed right between Mystic's ears. Mystic ducked just in time to avoid the sickle almost upending him from the narrow footing beneath. The implement swung completely around the two-legger's head and came back for a second strike.

Meanwhile, Bubba was dealing with his own problem. A net had been cast down on him from above, trapping him in his already dangerous position. Where did it come from? Bubba went wild with fright. The rarely used claws on his paws extended as he began slashing violently at the entrapment. He thrashed his head with little concern for his own good as the poachers approached.

The roars of the Cheetah and the howling of the Wolf were suddenly drowned out by a fit of riotous, hideous laughter emanating from the rock walls. Lightning's roar did its share to add to the intensity of the nerve-shattering, mind-numbing explosion of sound.

Mystic snapped fiercely at the two-legger as the blade swung down on its second attempt to rob him of life. This time the blade missed by half the margin of the first swing. The blade was swinging yet again, the eyes of the two-legger burning a hole right through Mystic. Mystic lunged at the arms swinging the blade with his jaws spread wide apart in anticipation of sinking his teeth to the hilt in at least one of them. With perfect timing, his gaping jaws made contact with salty flesh. His canines sank deep into the two-legger's arm. Without a sound, the attacker pulled the mangled arm back. The menacing blade fell harmlessly to the deep chasm's floor, far below the bridge where the three adventurers were trapped as the injured two-legger drifted into the darkness. Flakes of numerous stalks of grain clouded the air. Out of the corner of Mystic's eye, he saw a dark gray blur flash pass by. Before he could get a direct look at the flash, another rushed by, then another. Blood dripped savagely from his jaws, his eyes raged as he plotted his next move. Mystic readied to pounce as, with the next gray flash, came the shadow of an animal almost as large as Mystic. The flash came to an abrupt halt at Mystic's side. Another large shadow stopped at his other side. A second two-legger floated swiftly away shrieking into the chaff-clouded air, chased by hundreds of flashes of dark gray shadows, his limp leg grotesquely torn in half, dangling behind. As Mystic stood watching, a two-legger on horseback raced directly at him from the front. The two large shadows on both sides of Mystic stood their ground as the horse and rider stopped. Mystic felt a blow from behind as a dark shadow trampled over him. His body was wracked heavily to one side as the club fell solidly on his flank. Mystic was surprised that he had not been knocked to the ground by this last blow; it had connected so directly with his body. He noticed that the two shadows were not advancing or retreating. They were turning into three-dimensional figures on each side of him. As the club made contact with Mystic, the figures never swayed. Mystic yelped with pain as he glared straight at the two-legger astride the Horse. He was doing his best to make eye contact, but the two-legger was not looking at him.

The two-legger was, instead, staring at the fully materialized, adult Wolves on Mystic's flanks as tears poured down his rough, wind-weathered and sun-colored cheeks. The two-legger kept mouthing words over and over to the Wolves. He had no idea that the Wolves could actually understand him. The two-legger repeated the same two words again and again: "I'm sorry. I'm sorry."

***

Bubba fought the net with determined vengeance. This would be no repeat of the last time he had been trapped by a poacher's net. His bared teeth ripped savagely at any poacher part that came near him. The Cheetah had clawed so ferociously at the net that it was now in shreds falling away on both sides of the terrified Cheetah. Bubba sought out the poacher with a renewed vigor. The poacher backed up to the edge of the bridge and began struggling for balance. Bubba menacingly circled the poacher, growling low and angry, never taking an eye off of his target. He sought to push the poacher completely off and into the bottomless chasm. Like vapors out of the shadows, a second poacher rushed to the aid of the first. The second was followed by a third and the third by a fourth and so on, until poachers completely surrounded Bubba as he continued to circle his prey. Each poacher wore a coat of Cheetah fur. The furs were draped around the necks of the poachers. Each fur was still attached to a head with eyes that peered helplessly into Bubba's innermost being.

Bubba felt completely ill at ease as the poachers with their furs closed around him. The eyes in the heads of the furs began to twitch in pain as Bubba looked on. From beneath each fur, legs and paws quickly materialized. The furs were coming to life. Each poacher instantly felt the wrath of their neckwear as the Cheetahs, now fully developed, began to tear the poachers apart. Mystic's dazed eyes drifted toward the commotion from his side of the barrier and he was horrified by the violence he saw. The poachers began screaming in pain as the Cheetahs ripped their flesh to pieces. They began suicidal leaps off the bridge two at a time, taking a Cheetah with each of them. Bubba closed his eyes tightly and turned his head away from the horrible scene. As with Mystic, Bubba sensed a warm figure on each side of him as if they were protecting the young Cheetah.

***

Lightning covered his ears with his two massive front paws, but the laughter continued unabated. This laughter was louder and more insulting than any the Badger had ever heard in his entire life. He was in no danger for his life, yet he agonized over the sincere callousness the laughter betrayed. This laughter was not caused for comic relief. This laughter was mean and selfish. The laughter was meant to punish Lightning for being an oddity.

How cruel the world was to a creature that was different. Lightning could have easily taken the life of many creatures that had used him for the purpose of enjoying themselves, but he didn't. He could have grown into an inhospitable and vicious brute, an ogre, but he didn't. Lightning rose on his hind legs and circled in small steps, as the noise of laughter grew louder and more piercing. Covering his ears had made no difference, so he removed his front paws and dropped back to all four legs, bouncing uncontrollably and hysterically while torrential rivers of tears streamed from his sad eyes. His chest heaving with anxiety, heart racing, he anxiously paced the narrow confines of the bridge, terrified, as the laughter chased him one way and then the next.

***

Mystic was ready to leap upon the Horse's rider and take him to the ground until something astounding happened. The two Wolves on each side of him took a few steps ahead. As they turned to face him he lowered his head toward the ground, preparing to leap at the rider.

"Mystic, look at me son, look at me!" the largest of the two Wolves demanded.

Mystic raised his head toward the voice and was awestruck. The largest Wolf was a magnificent creature. The second Wolf had a glimmer in her eyes that was hypnotizing. Mystic was looking eye-to-eye with his father and mother.

"Is this a dream, mother?" Mystic asked.

"No, Mystic, this is not a dream; you are experiencing your worst fear," said the smaller Wolf.

"You must overcome this fear to move on with your life, son. You can't hold on to fear and hate, Mystic; you must let them go. You must," said Giant.

"Mystic," Sky whispered, "We are okay now. What happened to us is the past. Do not dwell on it. You have much to live for. Please, you have made us so proud. Please, please let us go."

"Son, you are the Prince of the Great Forest. No creature can take that from you and you are here in The Land of Nuorg to learn and grow. Listen to Bubba as he tells you of the beyond; we are there. We were never able to tell you how much we believe in the beyond. It is the reason for all we were and all we attained. We are very proud of your young friends. Do as they wish. Believe what the Cheetah tells you and we will be together once again. Do not rush it though. You have great decisions to make," stated Giant.

"Good bye, Mystic. We love you still, Son. Until we see each other again," whispered Sky.

Sky and Giant approached Mystic, nuzzled him and vanished. Along with the two Great Wolves went all of Mystic's fears and regrets. The wall halting his progress was removed.

***

"Bubba," said one of the figures, "Is this how you wished it had been? Did you enjoy the taking of the poachers?"

"No, no it was horrible. I did not wish that horrendous death upon any creature. What happened to me? Why did it have to happen that way? Why did I kill them?" asked Bubba.

"Bubanche, you experienced the horror because that is the revenge inside you that has never escaped. That is what could happen to any creature if you wish it to be. You could take others the way we have been taken, violently. You have the ability to rip flesh off bones if you so desire. Instead Bubanche, you must rely solely on your gifts of speed and knowledge. Just now, you decided to project an attitude of invincibility. You thought creatures would admire you for your projected self rather than for your true inner self. Use your gifts, Bubanche. Use your gifts wisely. It is not impossible to think that one day you may have to take another creature. You must exhaust your gifts first," said the larger of the two radiant figures.

"Father," Bubanche asked. "Is that you?"

"Yes, son, in a way it is me as well as it is you," the figure replied.

"Mother? You also?" Bubanche added tenderly.

"Yes, Son. We are both here."

"How? How is it possible? Have I passed on? Have I been taken? It is so real," Bubanche answered.

Bubanche," said Kotay, "You have been given a special group of friends. There is no limitation on your possibilities. Stick with them in all they do. Be the rational one. Be the thinker. Teach them of the beyond and more. They will listen and heed your words as you did ours."

"Father," asked Bubanche, "Does being taken hurt terribly? Do you miss our time together? Do you miss me?"

"That is not for you to consider, Son. The taking does not hurt. The pain one experiences before being taken is real and begins when you are born. Moving from your land of the dying to the beyond is a relief from that pain but should not be taken lightly," answered Shuko.

"No, Bubanche, we will never forget our time together. It is and will forever be a part of our substance. We do not miss you because we have never left you and you have never left us. You are a part of us and we will never leave you. How could we do so? We know you will return to us when you are taken. Then you will know of what we speak. Do not rush through your life. We will be here for you when the time comes. Do not dwell on our departure from your land. You are watched and we are fine." Kotay finished Shuko's answer to Bubanche, they each rubbed necks silently. Kotay followed Shuko as they walked from the bridge and were gone.

Bubanche called to them as they left the sight of his misty eyes. "Remember I love you so much!"

Kotay and Shuko heard Bubanche's last words and smiled to each other as they continued back to forever.

Bubanche looked up for Mystic and found that the wall keeping him from crossing the bridge was gone as well.

***

"Leave me alone!" pleaded Lightning. "Please let me be! Don't make me hurt you."

Mystic and Bubba heard the cries of their friend. They tried rushing to his side to comfort him but, were blocked by the rock wall. Each of them desperately scratched on the immoveable rock with their claws in a futile attempt to remove it.

"Lightning, what is it? What do you hear?" begged Mystic. He and Bubba were beside themselves with grief for the large Badger.

"This horrible laughter, where is it coming from?" he shouted, begging for an answer.

Mystic and Bubba did not have to talk to each other to know what had just taken place in their lives. How would Lightning be affected? He had no family here to comfort him. His family was, more than likely, concerned about his prolonged absence from the Dwelling Place. How could they help him here? They reluctantly backed away from the wall and the useless clawing. Again, they cautiously approached the barrier, placed their paws and ears to the wall and cried tears for their friend. This would have to do. They knew of no other immediate remedy. They kept close to the wall as Lightning worked his way through this turmoil. This lasted for over 26 clicks. Neither Bubba nor Mystic released their grip. This was a true test of their friendship. They were always there for each other.

After many tears were shed and much yelling was completed, even so much as to make one Badger's throat very sore, Lightning came back. His fears were not as easily dealt with as the others because his were not so apparent or distinct. The Badger's fears were of non-acceptance. These are the most complex fears to conquer and the hardest to fight. It takes a very strong creature to even admit such fears, and this Badger was a very strong creature.

Eventually, Lightning's wall came crumbling down. Mystic and Bubba rushed to his side, hugged him the best they could and cried together for a very long time. Pieces of Lightning's wall fell far down into the chasm for many day-rounds to come. Small parts are still falling.

The three friends were drained of emotion. They carefully crossed the second half of the bridge without talking. They were too busy rethinking their experiences. They were also, once more, exhausted to their respective limits.

22

The Burg was awakening again. Charlie came walking through the gathering room, a two-legger with a mission. Mystic, the Eagle, sat perched on a chair back watching and waiting for Vincen to enter the world of the non-sleeping. Karri had flown in during the night, safely delivering the rapier and was perched, asleep next to Vincen. Rakki was hopping around on the floor nibbling at sweet kaki crumbs and bits.

"Looks like a great day to me, Sir Mystic," Charlie clearly stated. "Where is Donkorse, he should be here by now. I am glad to see our newest guest getting some rest. Rakki, for your sake, would you please eat fresh kakis instead of those stale crumbs?"

"Certainly Sir, but it seems that Vincen ate most of those you put out during the night. Do you have more, by chance?" Rakki gleefully inquired.

"Yes, yes Rakki, I have plenty. Let me get some out for you," Charlie said as he opened the cupboard and removed a tin of sweet kakis.

Charlie returned and placed the tin on the table. He removed the lid and placed several of the sweet pastries on a large pewter platter in the middle. A wonderfully sweet aroma rose from the platter. The aroma wafted into every corner of the now tidy room. Vincen and Karri began to fidget as the aroma passed them as they slept. It did not take long before all breathing creatures in this room were awake and feasting on a quickly disappearing platter of sweet kakis.

Charlie had a few kakis as he retrieved a large pewter water pitcher out of the cooling box. Charlie took his time and carefully filled several small bowls with fresh water and filled one large goblet for himself. He pulled one of the high back chairs to the table and began the day.

"Let us have a moment of contemplation for our visitor's travels," Charlie said as he pulled himself closer to the table.

"There now, another day has officially begun," Charlie continued. "Rakki, you should have eaten your fill by now. Please rush off and locate Hugoth. Bring us back a report as quickly as possible. Oh yes, if you see Donkorse, take a nip at his tail and tell him we are patiently awaiting his return to us!" Charlie added with a smile in his voice.

"Yes Sir," Rakki replied and off he flew.

Vincen was beginning to feel very relaxed around Charlie and his Grandfather. He was gobbling his food as if he had not eaten for some time. "Charlie, I presume that you are a talker; are there any other talkers here in Nuorg?"

"No Vincen, I am the last Talker in this Burg. All of the others have moved on. As I told you earlier, there are several Burgs throughout Nuorg. A Talker once lived in each Burg. Now, I travel to them or they travel to me when needed. Talkers are rare. In the years to come, sadly, Talkers will become fewer and fewer. It is a lost art and a gift that two-leggers shy away from if they recognize it at all. Each Burg used to think it mandatory to employ at least one Talker. Now, sadly that is not the case."

My family, the Hewitts, consisted of many educated Talkers. We, in turn branched off by marriage into the Mountes of Hewitt. Actually, the only talker left in your land is a distant relative of mine who is called Frederick. He has lost much of his skill and desire after the terrible tragedy with the Great Wolves. Should you return to the Great Forest, I implore of you to seek him out. Give him refuge in the Great Forest and in the coming years he will be of great service to you."

"I see," said Vincen. He was trying, hopelessly, to place Charlie's last bit of information in line with what his Grandfather had told him previously about the Hewitt clan. Instead of pursuing that kind of questioning with Charlie, Vincen made a mental note to ask his Grandfather about it later.

"Please, excuse me if I sound disrespectful, but I cannot continue to act as if I have no worries about the future of the Great Forest," said Vincen. "You Charlie, as well as all of your friends here, have spoken on numerous occasions, about the future of The Great Forest, the future of our lands. What is it that you know and we don't? Are we in danger in the Great Forest?"

"Vincen, why do you need to know?" asked Mystic, the Eagle. "To know one's future is not an option for you. We cannot tell you what is to come, for we don't know the details. And if we did we could still-not relay it to you."

"Vincen, we are not to interfere with your steps," said Karri. "Believe me, it is a very difficult job for us to watch and not get involved. Your walk is for your legs; your flight is meant for your wings. We can interact with you, as you can interact with others of your land when needed, but we can't make your decisions or do your work. We also can't tell you the path for your life or your friends' lives. That decision lies within you and them. We can only advise you of what may come."

Charlie spoke next. "Vincen, Mystic is a special case. As you know, his family was stolen from him. This happened before he was old enough to make his decisions. He was summoned here to make a decision regarding his role in the legacy of the Great Forest."

"What decision?" asked Vincen, "Bubba's family was taken during his early life as well. Was he old enough to make his decisions? What about me? Was I?"

"One question at a time," replied Charlie.

"Fantahngheo," interrupted his Grandfather. "The decision we speak of is the decision to either accept the challenges ahead of you or dismiss them. This decision has a tremendous impact on many creatures' lives. Whether the challenge is accepted or not helps the protectors to ward off the spread of evil. Once a creature accepts the challenges, we are permitted to become advisers instead of gatherers."

"The Wolf was denied the opportunity to accept the challenge he faces now when his family was removed from your world," said Charlie. "The Cheetah was not denied that same opportunity. It was never intended for him. Also, the Cheetah was older when you rescued him. The Cheetah was raised in a family that believed in and worked steadfastly together, teaching the premise of the challenges life will surely bring to the cub. The Wolf, meanwhile, was too young to be accountable for knowing of these opportunities or what to make of them. He is of an age now when it is harder to make the decision to accept his responsibility. It may be easier for him to live his life as he does rather than risk his life and position to accept the challenge."

"The decision is based on simple faith," continued Charlie. "You either have the confidence to believe in yourself or you don't. As a creature ages, he becomes more and more set in his ways. These ways are hard to re-direct. The optimum time to make one's decision is in one's early to middle lifetime. Creatures offered the challenges can make decisions well up into their waning years. It is just easier to make the decision when one is younger, accept the challenge and grow into a life guided by one's own responsibilities to others than to try to make up for so much lost ground late in life. Now..."

"Wait," said Vincen, "You just stated that Mystic was too young to make the decision, yet you say it is best to make the decision in one's earlier life. I don't understand."

"Yes, that is a wonderful point," answered Mystic, the Eagle. "The Wolf was too young to make any decisions in his life. His parents left him to you for that very reason. They knew he would never survive alone. You were his decision maker; unfortunately, your parents and I also left you and your sister too early in life. You are here to make a similar decision as well. How do you feel about making it?"

"I feel that I already have made it," replied Vincen. "The great Owls taught me of a challenge that would one day come to a selected group. I have lived knowing that a group would one day be selected for that challenge. I had no idea that I would be one of that group."

"Do the Great Owls know the challenge is soon to be issued?" asked Karri.

Vincen turned to the spirited little Hawk, "I would assume that they do, yes."

"Did they tell you they did or did they just lead you to believe that they did?" She asked.

The little Hawk was getting on Vincen's nerves somewhat. Charlie leaned back in his high-backed chair, shook his head and chuckled at her determination. Vincen's Grandfather nodded his head in agreement with Karri.

"I don't know exactly!" Vincen replied.

"There you have it!" Karri continued. "Vincen, so many times creatures are led to think that in your world. The truth is, just because you know of the challenge, does not make you worthy of accepting it. The Owls are intellectual giants. They know many things. Did you ever stop them and ask them if they would accept the challenge, or did you just learn it as you did numbers and history?"

"No, I never questioned them on it."

Karri jumped back into the discussion, "You just told me that, indeed, they did tell you about the challenge. They also taught you how to keep time, read your land and estimate distances. Can any of those things bring you closer to the challenge if you don't know what it is? No, they can't. If you return to the Great Forest, you must give them the answers you will have by then. But, while you are here..."

"Vincen," Charlie said he tried to slow the conversation, "We know what you are going through. We have all been where you are. We had to make the decision ourselves. Remember your Grandfather spoke about being set in your ways. Well, you are. Take a while and study what we have said and what you have discovered since you arrived here. Think about the incident in Sweet Gulley and the way you felt after you swallowed the water from the river. Think about this place and what I have told you about it. We will welcome your decision whenever you make it. I hope Karri did not press too hard. She is a very lively little thing."

"I will ponder what I have," said Vincen. "There is so much I was unaware of. I have taken your words to heart. I must ask this, is my group the group that will be issued the challenge? And what is this challenge?" asked Mystic.

"All in good time, Vincen," replied Charlie.

***

Donkorse was entering the Burg, big stick in tow, as Rakki dove in nipping at his tail. "Hey, watch that, little Hawk!" he called.

"They are waiting on you, Donkorse, in the Keeper's gathering room. They said hurry! I will return as soon as I have spoken with Hugoth!" Rakki exclaimed as he floated just above Donkorse's nose.

"Thank you, Rakki!" Donkorse answered as he continued on his way.

***

Hugoth made it to the cave entrance with time to spare. There had been no signals from the three friends far above on the mountain, so he rightly assumed that they were progressing as planned. If they had taken the wrong path from the Halls of Truth they would have been here long ago. Hugoth felt confident that he would have heard their voices coming from one of the many side tunnels.

He discovered a fresh pool of tasty Sweet Gulley mud underneath a recently self-repaired, small crack in the cave's ceiling. He lapped up most of the mud, then stopped inside the main chamber to rest. As he rested, he noticed the small crack above his head led off down a small side tunnel. As he studied the crack, he noticed a dim, barely visible glow peeking out of the side tunnel's entrance. He would check this out later; now he would rest.

Donkorse lightly knocked on the Keeper's door with his front hoof. When the sound of approaching footsteps ceased, the door was opened by the Keeper. He graciously invited Donkorse in. Donkorse lowered his head to keep from bumping against the top of the doorframe. With a flick of his head, he loosened the strap securing the Badger's tool to his chest. The tool fell to the ground with a loud bang. He continued to nudge the ax-pike ahead of him as he made his way toward the gathering table. Vincen's eyes could not hide his startled reaction to seeing this rather large animal enter the room like he was a two-legger.

"Donkorse is allowed inside?" Vincen asked.

"Why not?" replied Donkorse.

"I, I'm not sure," answered Vincen.

"We treat all creatures the same here, Vincen. No one is any better or worse than another. You are not like me, but I allowed you to stay, did I not?" said Charlie.

"Well, I'm a sky-traveler, or a bird if you will."

"Does that make you more welcome than I?" asked Donkorse.

"No. I guess not", replied Vincen.

"Let us move on, shall we?" stated Charlie.

"Please forgive my manners, Donkorse. As is well known by now, old ways are hard to change. I have never been a witness to this kind of equality. Even in the Great Forest, there is some separation between creatures."

"There should not be any," said Donkorse. "Maybe you will learn a greater appreciation of acceptance while you are here."

"I believe I already have," answered a much humbled Eagle, as Vincen's Grandfather and Charlie quietly nodded their approval for Vincen's benefit.

Vincen was blinded by Donkorse's acceptance in the room. Once he regained his composure, he focused his attention on Lightning's ax-pike positioned on the floor. "Oh mercy, has danger befallen my dear friend? Is he in good health? Why do you have his ax-pike? Be it not by his bidding that he is retained here." Vincen drifted into the olde style of speaking again.

"Hold there, Grandson," interjected Mystic, the Eagle. "There is no cause for alarm. Please do not resort to speaking in the olde style. All is well."

"Vincen," Charlie explained, "Tools of this type are not permitted within Nuorg. There is no reason to endanger one of the protectors with an impulsive display of sometimes misguided training by visitors to our land. These tools are needed in your world, but not here. We will take this and the sword. Karri, we do have the little sword, don't we?"

"Yes Sir, I brought it with me on my last trip in," she answered.

"Very good," Charlie continued, "We will take these tools to our craftsmen for repair and safe-keeping. They will be returned upon your departure."

"Donkorse," Charlie said, "Welcome back. You have performed your tasks admirably. Your help has been and is greatly appreciated. Thank you. Did Hugoth get the tests started?"

"Yes Sir, when I left, he was leading them to the Hall of Truth without their tools. There, he was to leave them, then proceed to the cave under Sweet Gulley," said Donkorse.

"Perfect. Rakki should meet up with him soon. We can enjoy the day until we hear from him. Mystic, take Vincen soaring. You two need to get re-acquainted," said Charlie.

"I agree," said the older Eagle. "Vincen, come with me."

"Yes Grandfather, it will be my pleasure," Vincen answered.

"Karri, do as you wish. Please come back when your brother does. Donkorse, get some food and rest." Charlie dismissed the group as he led them to the door. "I have much work to do. I also will take these tools with me to the craftsman. We will meet again this evening."

***

"Does anyone have any clue where we are headed now?" asked the Wolf.

"How long were we stopped on the bridge?" asked Lightning.

"For most of a complete sun time, I think," answered Bubba.

The path looks to split again ahead," noted Mystic. "I know we are protected to some extent no matter which path we choose."

"Yes, we are protected, but the path we choose will have a great impact on the rest of our lives," Bubba stated cautiously.

"What more could be asked of us? We have so far dealt truthfully with our innermost feelings. We have conquered fears that we didn't realize we had. What else could be waiting for us to overcome?" Lightning inquired.

"Lightning, I don't know the answer to that," replied Bubba. "I do know that we can't stop here. Let's continue."

"I agree," said Mystic. "Let's move on. Hopefully, we will find some food. Remember, we must find my wand/staff before we can gain Vincen back."

"I really do not think we will be held to that," Bubba added.

"Whatever, we will do our best to find it," Lightning promised.

Mystic led the others down the path as it meandered around hundreds of rocks and crevices. The path remained very narrow as they followed it deeper down inside the mountain. The three walked carefully in single file until they came to a level section of the path. They fought with the idea of taking a short nap before deciding against it, instead the three pressed on. Before too long, the path opened wide ahead of them. In the distance they saw several lights along a long wall to their right. To their left waited more solid rock. In the middle, there was a large, flat void. As they came closer to the lights, it became evident that each light originated within its own portal.

"There must be a thousand options here," Mystic remarked.

"Each of these portals leads to a light, but how do we know which portal leads to the light that will save us from this darkness and confusion? Will every portal lead us out? I think not. It is time for a rest. We cannot rush up to the first lit portal and throw ourselves through it with reckless abandon," Bubba stated very clearly.

"This is not meant to humor you both," said Lightning, "but is this not the way we have lived our lives to this point? Have we not rushed head first into everything we have ever done in the Great Forest? We rush in and deal with the consequences later. That is all we have ever known. My size causes me to never underestimate myself. I feel I can muscle my way out of about any situation."

"I feel the same because of my speed," said Bubba. "I know nothing in our world can outrun me. Even over long distances I can outpace the fastest Eagle. I have never experienced being slow, that is until now. My speed has no value here."

"I must admit that even my hearing and sense of smell have been cancelled out here," said Mystic, at a loss. "My knowledge is of no use either. I am struggling to make sense of this hunt on which we have

The Land of Nuorg

embarked. Vincen would fare no better than we are. He could not fly in here for any distance and, even though his eyesight is awe inspiring, it doesn't enable him to see around corners or into the future."

They plopped themselves on the floor below the solid rock wall that faced the wall containing the lit portals and waited for a sign of some kind. Their backs rested against the cool slab of rock that rose high from the floor forming the wall. Each adventurer was hungry, thirsty and tired. The moisture within the cavern that collected on the rock wall dripped sparingly onto the friends' backs, but, the trickling droplets were not enough to hint at quenching their thirsts. As time slowly passed, the amount of light within the cavern dwindled. There was not as much light as before. Once they recognized the dwindling number of lit portals, they incorrectly guessed that their initial estimate of portals was wrong. It was not wrong. There had been, in the beginning of this portion of the trip, hundreds of lit portals. As they continued to wait, the conversation wandered while the number of lights continued decreasing.

"Am I seeing things?" Lightning questioned the others. "Were there, or were there not more lights to be seen when we arrived at this stop?"

"I don't know, Lightning. My eyes have been closed most of the time," replied Bubba.

Mystic raised his head to get a good view of the lights and, he too, came to the same conclusion as the Badger. "Bubba, open your eyes now. We may have a problem. The lights are going out. The longer we wait here doing nothing, the more lights disappear. Would you think that normal?"

Bubba opened his eyes while he stretched his legs. He glanced over at the wall, not surprised at the accuracy of his friends' assessments. There were not as many lit portals. Bubba stood up. He looked over at Mystic and Lightning before curiously trotting over to the wall of portals. He scanned the vast wall from floor to ceiling with thought-provoking thoroughness, his brain speeding to come up with an appropriate reasoning or answers.

"What is he doing, Lightning?" Mystic quietly whispered.

"I have no idea, Mystic, absolutely no idea," said Lightning.

"Well, let's watch him closely. I would never forgive myself if something happened to him."

"I agree with you completely."

Bubba paced back and forth in front of the wall, not knowing exactly why. His mind was racing back and forth to the time spent with his parents. There had to be some clue to solving this oddity using the knowledge gained from his early teachings. He thought back on the many studies Shuko had conducted under the shade trees as they traveled from dwelling place to dwelling place teaching other creatures about the beyond. Bubba stopped. Without changing the expression on his face, the young Cheetah returned to the other two. He unhurriedly sat down next to his friends and rested.

"Well, do you have the answer," asked Mystic.

"Yes, I do," replied Bubba.

"Do you think you could share it with us?" asked Lightning.

"Why? The answer is making itself more than obvious as we sit here," Bubba replied.

"What are you saying?" the Badger asked again.

"Don't you get it?" Bubba relented. "We will know in time which portal to use. If time wishes us to sit here until we grow old, the portal to follow will never be plainly seen by us until then. We are tired. We knew that we needed to rest and so did whatever is leading us through here. We could have rushed into every lit portal available to us and still not found the correct one. By doing so, we would have completely exhausted our minds and bodies. We would have been wasted for our mission. However, the longer we sit here the fewer options we have to deal with and the more rested we become. The answer to this test is patience, P...A...T...I...E...N...C...E. The portal to follow will be revealed when time sees fit. Whether we need more rest, more time to think or just more time to wait for guidance, we don't know. Our next action is to wait patiently for the signal to proceed. I suggest you do as I say and rest," Bubba concluded.

"It's that easy?" asked Lightning.

"Yes it is," Bubba answered, "Yes it is."

"Okay, I'll do it. I will rest. When I awake, if the portal is not yet clear, I will rest again and again and again," Mystic whispered as he nodded off into a much welcomed and deserved sleep.

The three tired friends slept like they had not slept in many moon times. The dwellers in the Burg, meanwhile, opened and closed their shutters three times.

**

The Land of Nuorg

Vincen had a long, eye-opening flight with his Grandfather throughout the Land of Nuorg. They visited other Burgs and met with a few four-legged creatures regarding two-legged talkers. During this time Vincen asked hundreds of questions as his Grandfather answered most and did not answer others. They slept as Eagles, perched in tall shady trees as they felt the need. Vincen was schooled in the ways of the protectors and scouted by some to be one. This was a life-changing experience for Vincen. He came to appreciate the promise of the challenge, whatever it was. For the remainder of the flight home it was hard for him to contain his composure.

***

Life in the Burg carried on as usual. Rakki came back with good news from Hugoth. The meeting at the Keeper's house was informative, but uneventful. Karri and Rakki flew their normal routes and teased Donkorse at every opportunity.

***

Lightning stirred first. This was an event in itself. The Badger was never the first one to awaken. He rubbed the slumber from his eyes and nudged the others awake. As he did, he glanced over at the wall that was once full of glowing portals. Only one portal remained lit.

"Wake up, you two. It is time! It is time!"

Mystic was the next one roused from sleep. He immediately sprang to his feet and studied the lit portal. Bubba followed Mystic. The three of them were well rested and in high spirits.

"Take a look over there!" exclaimed Lightning.

"I will be," Mystic calmly said as he looked toward the only lit portal on the entire wall.

Bubba added, "Do you see what we are seeing? The lit portal is the very first portal we would have come to and probably the last one we would have explored. I knew this would happen. It does so often. When one allows himself to wait, the answer, more often than not, becomes obvious."

Bubba led the charge to the portal. He arrived way before the others. He had run full speed, leaving the others breathing his dust. Mystic arrived next followed by an elated lumbering Badger.

"Lead the way, Bubba!" shouted Mystic.

"You want me to lead?" Bubba asked hesitantly.

"Yes, go!" exclaimed Mystic.

"Wait just a click," Lightning announced. "I am sensing food in there. You better move fast, Bubba, or I will trample you!"

Bubba stepped inside the opening. The Cheetah could not believe what he was seeing. He wanted desperately for more eyes to see everything there was to see inside this portal. "Get in here quick; you won't believe this!"

Mystic and Lightning stepped in to join Bubba. As the Cheetah had said, they could not believe the sights inside the room. To the left was a crystal clear pool deep enough to swim in. Without hesitating, Mystic dove straight in and swallowed water until his dry throat could take no more.

To the right was an assortment of fruits, plants, vegetables and nuts that could easily feed a fully inhabited dwelling place. The Badger dove into the food as Mystic had the water. Bubba was caught in the middle. He hesitated: water or food, water or food? His stomach won, as he made a mad dash for the food.

The ceiling was transparent. The wonderfully blue sky was visible far above their heads. The ground was lush green grass, perfect for resting rough paws, now accustomed to hard rock floors. Mystic crawled out of the pool then sprawled down on the grass eating any food he could fit into his ravenous mouth.

Bubba ate a few mouthfuls of food before he found a tree to stretch out on. He stretched his claws, his paws, his back, his neck and even his tail. Once completely and properly stretched, he jumped into the pool much to the enjoyment of the other two pairs of eyes.

Lightning continued eating. Then, after much prodding, jumped into the pool causing such a splash that Bubba was thrown completely out of the basin. No worries, the Cheetah's landing was cushioned by the soft green grass.

This merriment lasted longer than anyone would have thought. The three travelers wanted for nothing. Something or someone had supplied their needs and more. Their patience had been well rewarded and then some. Someone had to end the frivolity. It was unexpectedly Lightning.

"We have work yet to do. We must get to it!" he exclaimed.

Feeling better than they ever had before, even in the Great Forest, they again set out on their quest to find the wand/staff, retrieve Vincen and return home to the Great Forest. Lightning revealed a well-hidden gift for leadership as he led the others through the long portal. The lush grass eventually turned, once again, to rock and the food began to wane. The diving pool's bubbling noise faded behind them as they trekked steadily on their way.

The path became straight and was easily manageable. Bubba had expected this to happen eventually. From the look of the path and the surroundings, the hardest section of this part of the journey was over. They continued walking down the narrow path in single file. The path turned down for several pursuit beats before it began sloping back up. The light had been lost somewhere behind them. As the path began to rise, a warm glow was visible ahead. The glow appeared to breathe. As they neared the pulsating light, Mystic picked up a distant sound of water falling. This excited them.

Their pace picked up. Before they knew it, they were running as fast as the Badger could run in these confines which was surprisingly fast. The light grew closer and the sound of water grew louder. Sooner than later, they each felt mist on their snouts. Suddenly, Lightning slid to an abrupt stop. The other two piled into his back knocking them to the ground. The Badger did not budge even a little.

"Why did you do that?" asked Bubba scrambling back onto all four legs.

"Yes, why?" Mystic concurred as he slowly gathered himself off the ground.

"Look up there and see for yourself," Lightning told them as he pointed his huge arm to the top of the rushing water falling in front of them.

"Is that it?" asked Mystic.

"It must be it! Let's get closer," Bubba eagerly shouted to Mystic.

Bubba led Mystic while Mystic led Lightning into the next chamber. This was the largest and most stunning room they had yet to see. The Forever Trees could easily fit on either side of the waterfall with room to spare. If the glowing object of their undivided attention was, truly, it, then it had gone through quite a change. As they approached the waterfall, the object looked more and more like what they were searching for. At the base of the towering waterfall they all stood mesmerized by the powerful beauty of the falling water.

"How do we get up there?" asked Lightning.

Bubba quickly scanned the area around the waterfall. "Look," he shouted, "Over there!"

The Cheetah pointed to a set of stairs cut into the side of the chamber wall. He immediately raced over to the stairs and began climbing them at a breakneck speed. The Cheetah easily cleared 14 or 15 steps with each excited bound. Mystic and Lightning chased after the Cheetah as fast as their slower legs would carry them. The stairs were plentiful. Bubba reached the top even before the others had gotten a good start. His sleek and agile body was built for quick movements. The Cheetah took advantage of this as he quickly ascended the far-reaching flight of stairs.

When Bubba reached the viewing platform at the top of the stairs, he immediately identified the object in question. "This is it, Mystic! This is your wand/staff. It looks brilliant!"

It was, indeed, Mystic's wand/staff. But, Bubba had never seen the wand/staff in this pristine condition emitting this amount of glorious light.

Mystic and Lightning clamored up the final stairs and joined Bubba as he stared at, what was now, a magnificent work of art. What had been, for years, a dusty, dim makeshift weapon was now an object worth admiring. The wooden handle glistened as mist from the falling water collected on its deep reddish-brown skin. The globe on the end of the staff was clear enough to see through. There was a golden collar that encircled the base of the crystal globe with inscriptions unseen before. The inscriptions were not familiar to Mystic or the others, but in the middle of many other letters, one large and ornately carved letter stood out. That letter was, of course, an "H".

"Is that the same wand/staff that you carried around in your mouth all that time?" asked Lightning as he stood at Mystic's side studying the object.

"I think so," answered a stunned Mystic. "I have never seen my wand/staff glowing as this one does. Can you reach it, Lightning?"

"Possibly," he replied. "And, just to let you know, I have seen it glowing, though not like it is now."

Lightning moved past the waterfall's curtain of mist and eased closer to the attention grabbing wand/staff. He carefully raised himself to his tallest standing position, which easily let him tower over Bubba and Mystic. The Badger was, then, easily able to get a firm grip on the now glorious handle.

"I hope it doesn't try to eat me this time!" he said, only a little bit jokingly.

Lightning tugged gently on the handle as he tried to work it free from its position lodged between a small rock ledge and the bottom side of a yellowish, crystallized formation. After a bit of gentle, but firm, tugging by Lightning, the glowing wand/staff fell free into his strong paw. He immediately and reverently handed the wand/staff to the still-amazed, gray Wolf. Mystic received the recently lost treasure with a great degree of reverence. Bubba stood slightly behind the exchange and watched in awe. The three friends closed in on the wand/staff. They quietly began voicing comments concerning the wand/staff.

Ever so silently, from just inside a tunnel leading away from this chamber, a hulking figure watched the reclaiming of the staff with guarded expectations. He closed his eyes, took a deep, well-earned, stress relieving breath then slipped into the chamber behind the waterfall. He proceeded around the fall to the meeting spot of the three friends. He stepped up behind Mystic and found that the three visitors were too busy admiring the wand/staff to notice him.

"Well, is that it?" he asked.

All talking stopped as Mystic whirled around to confront the additional visitor.

"Hugoth!" Mystic exclaimed to the large figure as he struggled to hold the newly found wand/staff. "How long have you been standing there? Did you know this wand/staff was here before we discovered it? And, if so, why were we not told of it?"

"For some time and no. The answer to your last question is more difficult, Prince Mystic," Hugoth replied dryly as his eyes became focused on the brilliantly radiant wand/staff.

"Prince Mystic," Bubba repeated with a just a trace of sarcasm as he turned to meet Lightning's eyes swinging to meet his own. "That's kind of formal, isn't it?"

"Never mind him. Hugoth, please tell me how much you actually know about this staff and all of the other events that have taken place in our lives inside this mountain recently," Mystic begged.

"Let's begin our journey to the Burg and maybe, just maybe, I will answer a few of your questions," replied Hugoth.

"You mean all of the tests are over?" the Badger asked with hope filling his voice

"Not completely, but all of the tests in here are over," Hugoth answered. "Correct answers have saved you three much turmoil and dangerous pitfalls. There is still the most important test of all waiting for you back at the Burg. Let's not waste our time together fretting about the last test. With the way you have handled the previous trials, the last one, although he most important, will not cause you much grief if handled properly. Please, follow me. We should make our way to the Burg soon."

Hugoth turned to lead the three friends out of the small side tunnel and into the main cave. As they followed Hugoth, Mystic carried his wand/staff more carefully and respectfully than ever. Bubba and Lightning, tried to make sense of Hugoth's tidbit of information concerning the last test. Bubba convinced the Badger with almost complete certainty that no harm would come to them. They wasted no time making their exit from the side tunnel into the main corridor of the cave. All four-leggers thoroughly enjoyed navigating the cool climate of the main cave and begrudgingly made their way out and up the tight, twisting trail to The Path to Where I Am Going.

"Are we now headed to the Burg?" Mystic asked with as much excitement as he could possibly summon from his body.

"Yes, Mystic, we are. You three have fared quite admirably, much better than we initially suspected. It is now on to the Burg, the Keeper and, last, but not least, to your friend, the Eagle."

"Mystic," Hugoth continued, "You will be welcomed most joyously in the Burg upon your arrival. I will not dwell on the reasons why right now as they are of no consequence in getting there."

Mystic began to think uncomfortable thoughts. "What had he done that was so worthy of a joyous welcoming? He had done nothing spectacular except show up. What could it be? He certainly wanted no unmerited attention.

23

Mystic, the Eagle, had long desired the Great Forest's return to glory. The Terrible Years had been so horrible. The four-leggers had been so ravaged and betrayed by the onslaught of misguided and evil two-leggers that he doubted if any of them would ever trust humans again. "Isn't that usually the case," he said over and over to those that cared to listen when he was among the dwellers of the Wolves' world. The story he told went like this.

The times of man began innocently enough as lands after lands were discovered, established and populated. It was such a wonderful idea in the beginning. All lands would work with other lands to survive and prosper. Trading of goods was to be the common link that would bind them together. Farmers would trade with merchants. Merchants would trade with manufacturers and so on. Unfortunately, the wealth accumulated by a few over a shorter period of time than ever deemed possible, drove divisive wedges between neighboring lands.

Trade turned into a game won by those that had and lost by those that had not. Good was nurtured as an equalizer by the intelligent men, while evil was cultivated by the jealous and ignorant. These factors and many more too numerous and varied to mention contributed to the length of The Times of Disenchantment that preceded the Terrible Years.

Charles Craton Hewitt III was an old man when he left the Wolves' world. He had lived his life struggling to make other men understand the answer to the troubles of the times. The Talkers knew it, the animals knew it, but the common man, whether noble or not, would not grasp it. The answer to the problems of The Times of Disenchantment was the same as the answer to the problems of The Terrible Years. Charles and hundreds of other Talkers would speak of the answer, only to have the answer fall on hearing, but uncaring ears. The answer, which was the demise of evil, was ignored. It challenged rationalization in the eyes of the intelligent lands. The demise of evil was shunned by the lands that had not. They wrongly assumed that no great and compassionate creature could be a leader. They believed someone who wasn't greedy and strong-handed would allow these lands to wilt away into barren remnants. This way of thinking brought more self-inflicted damage to these lands than Charles and the other Talkers could imagine.

Charles was born after The Times of Disenchantment when all seemed to be right in the rapidly changing world around him. The Terrible Years came stampeding by as he reached the later stages of his life in the Wolves' world. The Times of Disenchantment had faded in the memories of those who had survived them. Known to some and not to all, was the truth that allowed The Terrible Years to overcome them. The men of the Wolves' world had become complacent. They had withdrawn to their immediate concerns, whether it be life's stability, family, fortunes or not, even individual beliefs and theories of what the demise of evil actually was. No land felt a compelling call to go through the extra work and effort required to move beyond complacency into the next level of life. However, complacency soon failed. Selfish survival was the next level down from complacency, followed by bare existence, and then fatal gullibility.

Fatal gullibility doomed the lands to The Terrible Years. Evil was rampant, the demise of such all but forgotten. Any man willing to promise any kind of prosperity, be it false or evilly attained, was followed. These men feasted on the rotting minds of the gullible. These men quickly became great leaders to mindless flocks of followers. The more power and followers these leaders attained, the more evil and outrageous they grew. The remaining Talkers recruited their own followers. These were the strong-willed creatures that were different from man. These were creatures that man had cast aside because they were different. These creatures were the animals, creatures pure of heart with a yearning for survival and no lust for greed...

***

Hugoth, Mystic, Bubba and Lightning made straightway for the Burg. Time passed hurriedly by. Great anticipation for their reunion with Vincen increased as the distance to the Burg decreased. As they came to the split where Sweet Gulley and The Path to Where I Am

The Land of Nuorg

Going went their separate ways, Lightning's stomach growled noticeably and ferociously.

"Would it be asking too much to stop quickly and partake of a filling of Sweet Gulley mud?" the Badger asked.

"Of course," answered Hugoth, "Jump in! I see it doing us no harm. Let us partake of this territorial delicacy. I would be more than happy to, again, share it with you."

Hugoth continued to lead the group as they broke off the path heading for Sweet Gulley and the delicious mud. It was a short break in traveling and, to each creature's stomach, well worth the trouble.

"If we ever leave this land," the Badger began, "This is truly one of the most flavorful treats I will regret not having in the Great Forest. How is this made possible, Hugoth?"

"The trees that line this gulley are sweet gums, sugar maples, all manner of fruit trees, along with honeysuckle, blackberry, raspberry vines and more. It makes no sense to those who visit our land. It does not make much sense to those of us who dwell here. It just happened and we accept it. I have a hunch that it relates directly to the purity of this land. Raw gully mud is not fit to eat. This is not mud; it just looks and acts like mud. You would be surprised how normal this kind of phenomenon is here. All of our work here is not as exquisite as that staff Mystic found. The beauty of Nuorg can be in even the plainest of objects, if we bother to look with a pup-like attention to the obvious."

"Take me, for example," Hugoth continued, "I am a big, overgrown, furry creature. I do not have a handsome coat like my friend Bubba. I am not one of the most majestic creatures ever created as your friend Vincen, but I have a purpose. Because of that, I am unique no matter how I look on the outside. It's the same with the Sweet Gulley mud. If we only looked at it as gulley mud, think of the wonderful treat we would have missed."

"I understand," the Badger responded. "I am much like you, Hugoth. I am big, strong, caring, yet creatures shy away from me or run from me before they try to know who or what I am. It is very disturbing at times. I haven't dealt with it well in the past. However, I think now my behavior will change. I have learned much in this land of yours."

Mystic and Bubba listened intently as the two gigantic creatures carried on their conversation.

"Mystic," asked Bubba, "Do you hear what Hugoth is saying?"

"I think so. I am not sure. I am more concerned about Vincen's well-being right now."

I do not believe what I am hearing!" exclaimed Bubba. "How in this world can you still be worried about Vincen? What could happen to him here? You are the most hardheaded creature I know. Have you not paid attention to anything since we have been here? You amaze me sometimes, Mystic!"

"Now be more understanding, Bubba. Mystic can deal with his own mind in his own time. You are wise past your years and see logic well, but you were raised on it. You cannot pound it into someone's head. You, young friend, have planted the seed. Give it some time. Let it germinate. Some things are not meant to be rushed," said Hugoth.

"You are correct. I'm sorry for my impatience. It's much easier to be patient without the thinking," the Cheetah answered.

Lightning rose to his feet saying, "Let's get going. We can't keep the Burg waiting."

Mystic was next on his feet. With determination set in his face, he picked his wand/staff from the ground and trotted off ahead of the group. The others looked at each other, watched as Mystic headed down the path, collected themselves and soon followed.

***

As Charlie excitedly paced around and around his dwelling, Rakki and Karri were feeling the same excitement as the Keeper. They felt the urge to check on the progress of Hugoth and his band of travelers. They were young and impatient. The two Hawks waited until they could stand it no more. After begging the permission of Charlie, they quickly prepared to depart the window ledge.

"Just a moment, you two," Charlie said as they assembled at the window. "As you leave the Burg, please fly by Hugoth's den. Donkorse should be there, bored to fits. Tell him I said to raise the bridge."

"Raise the bridge?" asked a stunned Karri. "I thought everything was well with these new visitors?"

"It is, young one, it is. Just tell Donkorse to raise it. All will be well. This is part of my final test for the Wolf. This is the test that he must pass," answered Charlie.

"As you say, sir," responded Rakki.

In an instant the two were off. They flew straight to the bridge station and gave the Keeper's instructions to Donkorse who was almost as stunned as Karri had been.

"Are you absolutely sure he said raise it? Furthermore, are you sure that we are supposed to follow this kind of a directive?" questioned Donkorse.

"Yes," Karri replied, shrugging her wings. "We both heard him say it. That is exactly what he instructed us to tell you."

"You are very sure. Rakki, this is what you heard also? Very well then," Donkorse answered as he began to make his way over to the cranking wheel. "Rakki, is she sure about this?"

"Yes she is. The Keeper told us to tell you to raise the bridge. He said it was the final test for the Wolf, whatever that means."

Donkorse shook a rigor from his shoulders and nodded his head, "Very well then. I guess I will raise it, but I know someone who will not appreciate it."

The Hawks immediately left Donkorse to do his work and flew out from the Forever Trees and down The Path to Where I'm Going. The Hawks raced to meet up with Hugoth and the visitors. They correctly figured that Hugoth's group's first sighting of the Burg, with no way in, would be a very interesting one to say the least.

Charlie was right. Donkorse had taken up temporary residence in Hugoth's dwelling and was functioning quite well as the temporary guard of the bridge. Of course, there was never any real threat to the Burg or reason to guard the bridge, but it did keep Hugoth entertained and it certainly kept him busy.

Donkorse lifted one hoof off the ground and placed it on the closest of many wooden arms that protruded from the side of the giant raising wheel. Once the first hoof was solidly set in place, he lifted the other and placed in directly next to the first. Donkorse then shifted all of his weight to his front hoofs and pushed down on the wooden arm with all of his strength. The wheel turned smoothly, but not effortlessly. Donkorse was surprised how well the wheel worked, since it was hardly ever used. Nevertheless, he stayed at his task as the enormous bridge began to pivot on its axle and lift high into the gap between the two Forever Trees.

As the bridge slowly lifted, a crowd of Burg dwellers assembled. They also wondered why drawing the bridge was required. Those that came assembled immediately to take up pre-assigned positions. They quietly and methodically began to operate several other smaller wheels that were located under the bridge and accessible only as it began to lift. These smaller wheels operated basic machinery that helped several gates reroute the flow of the river. The water was now rushing into the space that existed between the stone walls surrounding the Burg. Once the bridge was raised to its highest resting point, the river would be completely rerouted around the Burg. There would be no way into the Burg and no way out of the Burg until the bridge was again lowered.

***

Vincen and his Grandfather arrived back at Charlie's dwelling from the backside of the Burg. They flew in just as Rakki and Karri were passing along Charlie's instructions to Donkorse. Once at Charlie's, they were welcomed inside as their host offered up a spread of food that would rival anything Vincen had ever had the pleasure of seeing. The gathering table was loaded with every type of food eaten within and around the Burg. The Eagles eagerly perched on the backs of two chairs located near the table and began to partake of the feast. Charlie quietly walked over to the window and, under the watchful eye of the elder Eagle, closed the shutters tightly then latched them as a wide, satisfying grin formed on his face.

Vincen seemed undaunted by the Keeper's actions. He was so busy choosing which type of food to taste next that he failed to notice the extra few precautions Charlie had taken when closing the window shutters this time. The elder Eagle did notice. He noticed every single move.

Charlie stepped back from the window as he put his hands into his large side pockets. He made two tight fists, took a deep breath, closed his eyes, exhaled slowly then turned his attention to his guests. "So Vincen, I assume you and your Grandfather have made the rounds, have you?"

Vincen, being polite, but rather busy, turned to Charlie as he swallowed the latest tasty morsel of food with a very noticeable and large gulp. He then answered the question. "Yes we have, Sir. May I say that I am still in absolute awe of this magnificent land of yours? I could have made my home in any of several spots we visited. The magnificent trees growing in grounds down past the mountains on the edge of the river are breathtaking. If it wasn't for the gentle nudging from my Grandfather, I would still remain there hypnotized by their beauty."

"Yes, Charlie," The Great Eagle insisted, "Vincen would do well here. It is a shame that he must follow the others back when they go."

"You know as well as I do Mystic, that everything is going as planned and we have no right or option to change anything at this point. We must wait and be patient in doing so."

"Yes Charlie, I know. There is not much time left, but I know that Vincen would, or will, be a great asset to those of us here," stated The Great Eagle.

"He is needed in other ways now. Do not become selfish this late in your life, dear friend," Charlie added.

Vincen was not paying too much attention to the banter of the old friends, but he did make mental notes of a few catch phrases. He was intrigued by the fact that he might be of use to someone or something in this land at some future time. He made the note and decided not to dwell on it. He missed the Great Forest and he was beginning to miss his friends. He wondered as he returned to the feast where they could be and just what sort of mischief they were into now?

24

Hugoth continued to lead the party back to the Burg. Mystic followed with the wand/staff. Shortly behind him came Lightning and Bubba. Rakki and Karri flew in with a rush, landing on Hugoth's back. Karri quickly hopped up onto Hugoth's head then leaned over and whispered something in his ear.

"It's what?" Hugoth exclaimed so loudly that Karri staggered a bit, digging her talons tightly into the thick fur on the giant neck to keep from falling off. "Why was that done?" he demanded.

Rakki clamored close to his sister. "Well, that did not go over very well," he whispered.

Hugoth rose up on his hind legs, sending the pair of Hawks scrambling. He turned his body left then right searching for the two as they clung tightly to his fur to keep from being thrown off.

"Where did you go, Karri? I must have a word with you in private! Come with me."

With that Hugoth stormed off towards the thick trees near the edge of the path with the two wide-eyed Hawks in tow.

Mystic, joined at once by his stunned companions, turned and looked on as Hugoth stomped into the trees with the Hawks clinging to his back.

"What was that all about?" asked Lightning.

"I have no idea", answered Mystic. "How about you, Bubba?"

The Cheetah just shook his head side to side and followed the commotion.

"Look at this", Mystic wondered out loud. "My wand/staff is vibrating."

"Not only that", added Bubba, "Look at the globe. The color and intensity of the glow is changing drastically. It looks to be panting".

Mystic held the wand/staff up higher to get a better view. The sky flashed and the wand/staff was nearly ripped from his grip. "Whoa! Grab it Lightning," He yelled.

Lightning remembered this happening before. He jumped to Mystic's side. Together, the two of them secured the wand/staff, jerking it back to the ground.

"Oh mercy", muttered Lightning. "Please, not again!"

Bubba's mind was frantically trying to reason with this unexpected turn.

Hugoth continued to barrel through the trees until he assumed he was out of hearing distance of the three visitors.

"Now Karri, tell me everything you know about that little secret you just told me", Hugoth demanded.

"I am sorry, Hugoth. That is what has happened. I don't know why. Do you think I was elated to hear it?" Karri snapped back.

"But why? These three passed the tests! What else could be wanted from them? Why block their entrance to the Burg? It could very easily turn mighty dangerous out here," said Hugoth.

Rakki picked his way back to the path to keep an eye on the visitors. Suddenly, a flash of crooked, stringy light reached out of the sky, followed by several more flashes in the general direction of Mystic and his friends. The flashes of light were attempting to locate something. Rakki with terror pulsing through his veins rushed back to separate the pair of quarreling creatures.

"That's enough! I think we had better get back to the visitors and fast!" stated the Hawk, visibly shaken.

"What's wrong now?" asked Karri.

"The yellow ball is seeking them out," replied her brother.

"NO!" Hugoth bellowed.

He raced through the trees back to the path, knocking aside anything and everything in his way. Karri and Rakki were directly behind him as he charged, his heavy body rumbling across the forest floor. Hugoth shot from the trees, his body directly aimed at Mystic and Lightning as they struggled with the wand/staff. Other blasts of light landed amid the group. It singed fur and feathers. Hugoth leaped over Bubba as he flew toward the two creatures with his front paws stretched out, posed to clamp his claws viselike on the staff. His brawny paws joined with Lightning's and Mystic's as they secured the pulsating staff on the ground. Again, another series of strikes peppered the ground all around them. In an instant Hugoth wrested the staff from the two smaller creatures, tucked it into his chest, doubled back and charged once again into the trees with storms of light flashes attacking them from one central source.

"Follow me! NOW!" Hugoth roared.

Without pausing to fear or question, all remaining creatures--the Wolf, the Badger, the Cheetah and the two small Hawks--took chase as the Guard of the Forever Trees hastily blazed a new trail off the path and through the trees. The group plowed deeply into the forest. Hugoth never slowed until the staff stopped pulsating and the light from the yellow ball faded far behind them. Hugoth knew where he was headed, but he had not traveled off the path in a long, long time. He made as directly as he could back to the mountain. Maybe, once they reached the caves they could stop, regroup and make some sense of this latest twist. On they went, prodded by fear of stopping, deeper and deeper through the trees. Hugoth and his party reached an ancient outcropping of rock. This was a sign from the mountain. Now they must find an entrance inside. The rocks became larger as they neared the mountain face. Finally, they could go no further. Hugoth halted, turned to those following and pressed his mammoth body against the cool rock wall. The staff had returned to normal and he let it slide to the ground out of the death grip he had held for too long.

Lightning immediately pounced on the staff as he had earlier in this journey. He covered it completely with his tired mass. He labored to speak as his words were interspersed with heavy breaths, "I have seen…what this thing can do…when left alone. I will not…will not allow it to travel on its own…again."

"Thank-you…Lightning," Hugoth replied through his own heavy breaths. "I must rest…before we find the entrance…to this side of the mountain. We must remain in hiding…for the time being."

"What just happened?" Bubba asked.

"I am afraid what we knew was coming is arriving sooner than we had planned," Karri mentioned to all. "I have only heard tales of what we just witnessed."

"That was close," added Rakki. "We must not let the staff out of our sight until we have the pattern."

Mystic let out a baffled sigh. "What pattern?"

"The pattern of containment," whispered Hugoth.

"Is that a magic spell or something?" inquired Bubba.

"Uh-huh," Rakki answered. "It is a pattern made up solely of Protectors and your staff. It is used to contain the evil inside the yellow ball. Usually, it is recounted in stories from the past that evil will grow when it mixes with its own kind. The actions of the yellow ball are precursors. Evil in your world is soon to run rampant. That evil is beckoning the yellow ball. The evil from your world wants to free the evil in the yellow ball, thus rendering our land useless in a battle above. This evil would rush to the aid of that evil to combine in an evil power strong enough to extinguish every good thing that has come to be so far. Hope would be lost here and in your world. Well, who knows what would become of it? We can only deal with the evil of your world when we know its point of origin. That is precisely what you were supposed to let us know once you got back to your world. Now, I'm afraid, it may be too late."

"So," Bubba surmised, "The staff is the key. It escaped down here to avoid being captured by those perpetrators up there. Had it been captured, whoever obtained it would then be able to open all of the access windows to Nuorg, if they could find them. That is where I lose the continuity. How would they locate all of the entrances?"

Hugoth pulled himself away from the cool rock slab, bent down to Lightning and asked for the staff. Lightning obliged. Hugoth took the staff from the Badger and walked over to Mystic. "Here, Prince Mystic, let us see if you are the one for the job. Take this staff from me and knock the handle on that rock below your feet two times. Turn the staff over and quickly twist that little knob on the end."

"What?" Mystic replied.

"Just do it," Hugoth said sternly.

Every eye was firmly fixed on Mystic as he pondered what was about to happen. Lightning and Bubba quietly took a few steps back. Rakki and Karri jumped to the safety of Hugoth's shoulders. Hugoth backed away from the Wolf as well. "I must admit each of you is acting in a way that is beginning to frighten me," Mystic declared.

Without waiting any longer, Mystic lightly tapped the staff's handle on the rock, flipped it over, fumbled for the small knob and twisted it to no avail. Nothing happened. Rakki and Karri let out a heavy sigh. They cast their heads toward the ground dejectedly.

"I said knock it on the rock, Mystic! Don't tap it on the rock, then quickly flip it over and turn the knob. Get a grip!" Hugoth stated none too politely.

Mystic was taken aback with this altered attitude of Hugoth's. He snapped to, readying himself for another try. This time Mystic defiantly held the staff and brought it down forcefully two times on the rock. Everyone heard a slight crack. Mystic flipped the staff in mid-air, caught it between his paws and, with the same motion, grabbed the knob and twisted with his mouth for all he was worth. Suddenly, the knob and the staff separated. Mystic held the two pieces away from him not knowing exactly what he should do now. He looked to Hugoth for instruction.

Hugoth was surprised that the two pieces separated so easily and was more impressed that Mystic had actually succeeded in doing so. "Well, Great Wolf, I see now that all of our diligence has paid off. You, indeed, are the one to accept the challenge. My congratulations to you. You truly must be the Prince of the Great Forest and more. Now, if you please, would you turn the staff right side up and shake it."

Rakki and Karri perked their heads up proudly.

"Go ahead, Mystic, turn the staff over," Lightning told him.

Mystic did as he was asked. As he did, everyone heard something inside the handle begin sliding out. A tightly rolled manuscript slid out, landing on the ground at Mystic's feet.

"There is your continuity, Bubba," Rakki exclaimed as he hopped down for a closer look.

"Don't touch it, Rakki. Mystic must unroll it," Karri blurted out.

Hugoth walked up to Mystic and gave him a fitting embrace as he smiled at the Wolf. He pulled Mystic to his side and pointed at the rolled-up manuscript. "There Prince, there is the challenge."

Mystic was speechless. All of this was happening faster than he could comprehend. Bubba and Lightning cautiously approached the manuscript as if it were alive. Given their previous experiences with the staff, who was to blame them?

"It looks harmless enough," observed Bubba. "What would happen if Lightning or I unrolled it?"

"That's easy enough to answer," boasted Rakki. "You would, more than likely, abruptly stop breathing followed by your skin breaking out in hives. That would, at some point in the very near future, lead to convulsions and, eventually, your death."

"Really?" Bubba asked.

"I am afraid he is right, but you may not really expire that quickly," chimed in Karri. "It would not make a pretty sight when we are already in the midst of a slight disaster."

"What does that mean?" Lightning inquired of the little Hawk.

Hugoth's celebratory demeanor changed instantly. He was immediately sullen and wary again. He asked, "Mystic, please place the manuscripts back into the staff and seal the handle once again. It will cause you no ill affects, I assure you. We must now do some planning. We are not out of this bind by any means. We have escaped for now, but we may have to expose our whereabouts again to make it to the Burg. There may be an alternate way, if I can remember it. Still there is no guarantee of our safety until you are instructed how to use the staff properly and we construct the pattern. If we can make our way into this mountain, we can use the caves to work our way closer to the Burg. I don't want to alarm anyone, but no creature in the Burg knows where we are or why we are where we are. The shutters are all tightly closed and no one has seen the dancing of the yellow ball. When they awake, all will seem normal because we have, for the time being, ducked in here, escaping its pull. They will be expecting us at the normal time."

25

The Burg was beginning to stir. The inhabitants had had a good rest and were ready for another day. Charlie was up and unusually chipper. Mystic, the Eagle, was feeling even more alive than in the past several years. Donkorse busied himself around the guardhouse waiting for Rakki or Karri to bring the word to lower the bridge and drain the moat. That message would not be coming any time soon. He became bored with waiting. He decided to proceed to the Keeper's dwelling and ask for the order first hand. As Donkorse made his way to Charlie's, he kept an eye open for one of the two messengers. They were always swooping in and among the dwellings at every opportunity to ambush Donkorse. This was a game that had been played since they were fresh from the egg. Donkorse thought to himself that their absence was more than strange.

Charlie stepped up on a stool, threw open the shutters, placed his goblet of drink on the windowsill waiting for word from the Hawks. He spied Donkorse making his way down the lane. He hollered down a welcome greeting. Donkorse looked up to the window and nodded. Charlie hopped off his stool then crossed the gathering room. He quickly opened his door to wait for Donkorse's arrival. Donkorse soon stuck his large head in the door and was granted entry.

"What's on your mind this morning, Donkorse? You look flustered. Is there something wrong?" asked Charlie.

"I certainly hope not," answered Donkorse. "Have you seen either of the two Hawks? I haven't had one sighting of either of them today. That doesn't set well with me. Did the plans go awry?"

"Well I can only assume so," Charlie replied. "I also find their absence a bit unsettling, now that you mention it. I have food on the table and water in the goblets, yet I have no Hawks waiting on my sill. What do you make of it?"

"It does not bode well with me, I assure you", answered Donkorse.

Charlie turned to the Eagles. "Mystic, may I ask a favor of you, Sir?
"As you wish. What shall it be?"

"Will you two fly The Path to Where I Am Going for me? I want to be sure that our group is still headed in our direction."

"We will leave at once." The Eagles took wing and flew out the door.

Charlie nodded confidently to Donkorse, "This won't take long. Let's eat, shall we?"

The Eagles made quick work of their assignment. Mystic, the Eagle, was bothered because he saw nothing of the group. They returned along the path and lit high on the East Mountain. They scanned the land as far as they could see. They neither saw nor heard anything. Next they made their way to Sweet Gulley a second time, perched in a tall sweet gum tree and again saw nor heard nothing. This was bothersome. The pair of Great Eagles had been searching for nearly 80 clicks and nothing even remotely crossed their path. Once more they took wing and headed back to Charlie's dwelling. Landing on the windowsill, they made their way to the gathering table. Donkorse and Charlie had been pacing all morning and had just sat down for a bite of lunch. As the Eagles lit on the back of a chair, their expressions did nothing to lighten the solemn mood that had taken over the room.

Charlie broke the silence, "Well?"

Mystic the Eagle, answered, "Nothing. I saw nor heard nothing. I encountered not one creature all morning. There was no trace of our group. No flyer or walker was seen. Something is wrong. Creatures don't just vanish in Nuorg!"

"What do we do now?" asked Donkorse.

"We wait", Charlie answered. Hugoth will bring them in."

***

The mountain was giving only small hints of opening, as members of the group poked and prodded their way along the rocky base. As they did, they used every means possible to avoid the yellow ball. At last, Bubba discovered an opening that only he and the Hawks could fit through. He motioned for the others. They hurriedly rushed to his location.

Bubba calmly stated to Hugoth, "I think I can squeeze through this crack in the rock. If I can fit then so can the Hawks. Once we are in Hugoth, where do we go? What do we look for?"

Hugoth was at a loss for words. "Just look for something familiar."

"Familiar? How would I know if something looked familiar?" asked Bubba.

"The three of you spent a long time in this mountain not too long ago, remember?"

"That was in this mountain?"

"Yes, this is the East Mountain. We use the other mountain for something altogether different."

"Well, I don't even want to know about that one!" replied Bubba. "Wish us luck!"

Bubba lithely slid through the opening followed by Karri. Rakki waited until Karri was safely through the crevice and entered. Bubba made his way back to the opening and made one last remark, "We will find a larger opening and come back for you. Stay put!"

With time to waste Mystic inquired about the Pattern of Containment. "How many Protectors does it take to construct the pattern, Hugoth?"

"It takes seven, Mystic. It takes seven."

"How many protectors are left in the Burg?"

"Six."

"Six? There are only six in the entire Burg?" Mystic was incredulous.

"No, Mystic. There are only six left in the entire Land of Nuorg! Aren't you glad you asked?"

"How about that creature I was supposed to find? Isn't he out in the land somewhere?"

"It is assumed that he is, but he may have gone up. We don't know for sure."

Mystic just shook his head, "What are we going to do?"

"I have no idea, Mystic, I have no idea," Hugoth replied.

***

Bubba pulled away from the slit in the rock wanting for somewhere to go. Rakki and Karri were of no real use. The small room was too cramped for them to take wing and it was too dark for them to see. Bubba stood on all fours sniffing the air in the cave. He hoped to smell his way into a larger room and, hopefully, a larger entrance. Bubba paced around taking readings on the air quality. He was able to discern the smallest of differences in moisture, freshness and breathe-ability. He paced around to different areas, sniffed the air, then tasted it. Rakki and Karri continued to watch the Cheetah pace as they peered into the dark.

"A-ha, this way, little friends!" Bubba called to the Hawks. "Unless I am dead wrong, we should head this way."

"What have we got to lose?" Rakki asked Karri. "Shall we?"

"Why, yes we shall, Brother," she replied.

Bubba led the way as the trio wound their way through tight, twisty tunnels. A few clicks turned into many while Bubba followed his nose. After what seemed like forever they came to what they hoped was a large cavern. They inspected each wall by feel until they had searched around in a complete circle. They found no exits to the outside, but they did locate the spot where the original tunnel led out of the cavern. After a brief rest Bubba tested the air again, hoping for a scent of direction. He discovered nothing special, then confidently led them on as the tunnel turned to the right then back to the left. Just as they were beginning to wear down, the tunnel split. One shaft led down a steep incline and the other led up a slippery slope.

Bubba turned to Rakki. "Would you please fly up that shaft and see if it will do us any good? Please be careful. Try not to bump into anything".

"Sure, I'll be right back." Rakki flew off.

"Should I check out the other shaft?" asked Karri.

"No, If Rakki finds nothing, it will be our only option. Let's wait on Rakki before we proceed," Bubba replied.

Rakki came flying back down the shaft. "I have found an exit, but it is very small. I don't think we can use it. It's too dangerous. I am afraid we will have to use it only as our last option."

"I agree. Thank you, Rakki. Let's proceed down the other shaft."

Bubba took one step in the second shaft. It was the wrong step and his only step. He instantly fell to the slick floor and began a speedy slide to wherever the slope was leading. The Hawks without hesitation took flight after the Cheetah. They each gently grabbed a flailing paw with their razor sharp talons and flapped their wings wildly trying to slow the Cheetah's descent. At first no decrease in speed was noticed. However, after several desperate tugs they were able to slow the Cat to a more controllable speed. Bubba did not try to fight the slide. Instead, he opted to ride it out. Without warning, the slippery slope abruptly stopped. He continued to sail through space on the same trajectory as his slide with the much smaller Hawks hanging on for dear life

"Wait, what is that?" he thought as he fell a medium distance before ending with a familiar plop.

The Hawks let go of Bubba's paws and hovered slightly above the Cheetah.

"Are you okay?" Karri asked.

"Yes I think so. I know I have recently been in a predicament like this before." Bubba acknowledged her question as he began to lick the sweet gooey mud off his snout.

He landed in a dimly lit area of Sweet Gulley that was hidden beneath low hanging limbs of very shady trees. Behind the trees was a recess in the side of the mountain. Bubba looked straight up and saw the hole in the side of the mountain from which he had been ejected. When he looked above to his right he saw an entrance to the mountain big enough for Hugoth to easily fit through. Rakki and Karri proceeded to perch on a small ledge just above the Cheetah awaiting the instructions they both knew would be forthcoming.

"Karri, fly to my left; Rakki, to my right. Fly low and keep in the shade. One of you should encounter our companions. I am not going anywhere. Bring them back. We will enter the mountain here."

The Hawks took off as Bubba continued to remove the mud from his fur. Waiting here would not be that difficult.

The Hawks flew blazingly fast and low. Karri's flight path was less overgrown than Rakki's which allowed her to cover ground much faster. All were surprised when she quickly rounded a corner of the mountain nearly hitting the Badger right between his eyes. "Whoa there," she exclaimed. She did not take time for greetings or chit-chat or mention anything about the caves, but very deliberately spat out the directions. "Follow me, Hugoth. Stay close to the mountain. There are a lot of openings between here and the entrance to the mountain. If you lose sight of me, keep the mountain on your right. The opening is not that far away," She said as she immediately reversed her course and without another word or explanation of any kind headed for her Brother.

Rakki had flown far enough. He realized he was going in the wrong direction and would soon run out of the thick, leafy cover that was concealing his whereabouts to whatever unfriendly force was out there. He wasted no more time and turned back to Bubba's location. "Maybe we will get out of this," he thought to himself.

26

Bubba was beginning to struggle in the goo and found himself frantically clawing for solid ground. He was wearing himself out trying to stay afloat. A bank to crawl out on was not to be found. This inlet of Sweet Gulley was bordered by sheer faces of rock. The entrance was out of his reach. He was doing his best to wait patiently for his larger friends. Hugoth and Lightning might be able to reach the entrance and drag themselves in. He and Mystic would have to be pulled up into the Mountain. Bubba gave up his fight to break out of the goo. Instead he rested and partook of a little more sweet tasty mud. He did not allow himself to dwell on the fact that Cheetahs don't swim.

The wait was uneventful and time seemed to drag by for Bubba as the remaining party made their way to where they had been told they would find him. Rakki was the first to arrive. He landed on a thin ledge near where he had left Bubba. However, Bubba was noticeably absent. Rakki suspiciously eyed the inlet's smooth surface to no avail. He reasoned that the Cat had ventured in Karri's direction to meet up with the others. Upon further notice, he spied no way out for that land walker. Where had he gone? Rakki pondered this development with growing dread.

***

Bubba had been resting very comfortably in the mud bath. He was experiencing no real worries or concerns. He decided that he was not sinking. He quit struggling. He closed his eyes, relaxed and calmly waited for the group to return to him. Maybe he should have been more aware.

Out of nowhere he heard a light plop in the mud surrounding him. He was startled. As the sound died away, he settled down once again. Gradually, he began to feel he was being watched. At the same time a large loop of rope was inching its way around him. His eyes darted around looking for the source of his uneasiness. He was slowly backing his way to the face of the rock. He figured there he could see trouble before it saw him. He was wrong. The Cheetah was hair-widths away from the safety of the rock when he was catapulted up towards the door to the mountain. Something had yanked the rope so hard that it jerked the Cheetah completely out of the sticky mud. Bubba tried too late to fight free as the noose tightened around him. The rope drew taut. The Cheetah was pulled upward. In an instant, before he could call for help, Bubba was tightly bound, then, carried inside the mountain in pitch darkness.

"Who are you?" a strange voice whispered in his ear.

***

Rakki had flown back to the spot where he had left the cat. He paused briefly to verify his surroundings and soon became anxious. Bubba was nowhere to be found. This was not supposed to happen. This was very troubling. He incorrectly reasoned that Bubba had proceeded in exploring the area or sank out of sight in the goo. Either way and with no other obvious option available to him, he quickly took flight to meet his sister. Fortunately, they met shortly after he took wing. Rakki steadied his wings to arch a path directly beside her then asked, "Have you seen the Cat heading this way?"

"No, but I did find the others. They are making good time and should be here very soon. Why?"

"He is not where we left him. There is no way out of Sweet Gulley from his vantage point, as far as I could tell. I fear he may have been swallowed by the mud."

"We must tell the others to hurry!"

The two messengers doubled back and met the trio huffing and puffing around the very next turn of the mountain. "I am afraid you must quicken your pace," Karri began.

Rakki ended the news, "Something has happened to Bubba. I am afraid he is gone."

"Gone? Gone where?" asked Hugoth.

"I don't know," answered Rakki. "That is what we must hurry to find out. Follow me. We are almost there."

***

"Who are you?" replied the wary Cheetah.

"That is not important. Why are you here and how did you find this entrance?" the strange voice inquired.

Bubba responded, "There are several other powerful creatures who know of this entrance. They are coming to meet me and will be crossing it very shortly. Why have you bound me? Again, I want to know, who are you? Are you two-legged or four? I have a right to know of my poacher."

"Poacher?" the voice snickered.

***

Hugoth was leading the other four at a rapid pace. The trail came to an abrupt dead end as an insurmountable rock wall rudely jutted out in front of them and thick undergrowth blocked their left. "Well, Rakki, where to now?"

"It's just on the other side of this rock wall. You must press your way through this undergrowth. Be careful as you do. Sweet Gulley is just beyond. If you struggle too much, you know what will happen. I believe it is quite deep there."

"Sweet Gulley?" asked Mystic.

"Yes", explained Rakki. "Sweet Gulley stretches far through this land. This may be an origination point. It is tucked under this dense over-growth as well as being protected and hidden by the mountain."

"Here I go, follow me," Lightning responded. The Badger bowled his way through the thicket. He had not gone 30 steps when he plummeted into the deep end of Sweet Gulley. "I found it. It's quite deep. He lightly paddled out of the way as Hugoth landed beside him with a huge plop! Lightning looked up as Mystic was about to step off. "Hold on tightly to your staff, Mystic".

Mystic did as he was told. He put the staff in a death grip then followed the first two down into the gooey mud.

Hugoth stood on his back legs as he settled into the mud. Lightning was right. The mud was deep. With Hugoth standing, the mud was level with his chest. Lightning stood as well struggling to keep his head above the surface. Mystic was holding the staff in his mouth and kicking his back legs to stay on top of the muck. Hugoth reached out, grabbed the Wolf and held him above the surface as they looked to Karri or Rakki for direction.

"From here to where?" asked Hugoth.

"Follow me." Rakki flew over to the narrow ledge where he had perched previously to guide them in.

The three made their way under the entrance. They were relieved to discover the mud became much shallower as they approached the face of the rock. Hugoth was able to let Mystic down. The Wolf stood on his hind legs and had but a little trouble maneuvering. Fear pecked at their confidence as thoughts returned to the Cheetah.

Mystic was the first to mention his smaller friend, "Could Bubba be somewhere under this mud? There is no way for him to stand up in this." Mystic began gently probing the bottom by stepping around lightly with his hind paws. I suggest you two do the same. Please be careful. Either of you could crush the life from him without even slowing your step!"

The two larger creatures began to probe as Mystic had. Around and around they went without one hint of anything but rock below their feet. "I'm sorry, Mystic," said Hugoth. "But we must get you, Lightning and that staff to the Burg. Hopefully, Bubba will show up. The undercurrent may have pulled him to safety."

"Or maybe not," replied Lighting despondently.

"I'm sorry," said Hugoth. "Mystic, It is partly your call, but you well know that we must move on".

"Bubba is wiser than we ever gave him credit to be. I have no ominous feelings about him now. Deep inside myself, I believe he is all right."

Lightning reluctantly added, "I agree. We must move on. Rakki, where is this entrance you three found?"

"It is right up there." With that Rakki motioned up the wall with his wing to where Karri was perched at the doorstep to the mountain.

"Oh mercy," Lightning said as he looked up the rock wall to the entrance.

Hugoth trudged his way over directly beneath the entrance. He reached for Rakki's perch grabbing a solid chunk of it. He very nimbly, to the amazement of all, scaled the wall. He pulled himself gracefully from ledge to ledge. He aimed his progress to the edge of the opening, heaved his great weight upward and fastened his claws inside the opening. He then pulled his entire body through the opening as his rear legs scratched for traction at the smooth rock surface. He hauled himself through the opening and rolled inside. He quickly hopped onto his four legs and returned to the opening's edge.

The Land of Nuorg

"Well, who's next?"

***

"I assure you I am no poacher." The voice continued, "I should ask you, are you some vicious creature yourself? Tell me something of yourself and the powerful others that are following you. I have been here for countless years and have seen no creature except for you. How did you come to this land and how did you find my dwelling?"

"Excuse me?" begged Bubba. "You have been here for years and have never seen any creature? How can I believe that? There are dwelling places throughout this land. There is one Burg no more than one day-round of travel from here. There are creatures of the air and the ground. There are four-leggers like us and there are many two-leggers as well."

"Four-leggers like us? You do mean you and your others, don't you. I am certainly no four-legger."

"You must be a four-legger. How else would you be able to communicate with me?" asked Bubba. He was now more than a little curious.

"Where I came from I was called a Talker. There were at one time very many of us scattered about. Our numbers dwindled drastically during many different struggles. I am afraid I was the only one left, although I did hope for so long that I would make contact with others of my kind."

***

"Come on, Mystic," Hugoth called down from the entrance, "You will have to be the next one. Lightning will be the last in. Let him hold the staff for you."

"I am sorry, but my legs will not work as yours just have. Is there no other way?" Mystic asked.

Lightning was quick to decide for the Wolf. "Rakki, you are stronger than your Sister. Come, fetch this staff and fly it to the entrance. I know a way to get Mystic up there. Hugoth, ready yourself to catch this Wolf."

Mystic looked unsure of his friend's last words. It was too late. Rakki snatched the staff lightly before Lightning grabbed Mystic's front legs. The Badger lifted the visibly shaken Wolf completely out of the mud. As he did so, he released one paw from Mystic's front legs and clasped the Wolf's back legs with it, as he began to swing the Wolf in a circle. The Badger swung Mystic around three times and launched him towards the entrance. "Here he comes," Lightning warned those above.

"I would never have thought of that," Karri added as she and Rakki watched in amazement.

Rakki whispered to Karri, "Don't ever let me get on that Badger's wrong side!"

Hugoth caught on to the plan instantly. "Send him up!"

Mystic went flying through the air as Lightning released his grip. He felt like a sack of food tossed up on a shelf. He looked longingly at the entrance to the mountain as he passed it before his path of flight sent him arcing back down toward the waiting Hugoth. Hugoth reached out and caught a dazed Mystic around his chest in a vise-like grip that took the breath out of the Wolf for an instant. He then whirled his body around, depositing the Wolf on the cool rock floor.

"That was the most fun I've had in a long time, Lightning. Shall I throw him back to you so we can do it again?" Hugoth let out a big overdue laugh.

Mystic heard this exchange, slumped to the floor and began shaking his head.

Lightning used the same procedure as Hugoth to easily scale the rock face. The Badger was more adept at this skill than he had ever thought possible.

Mystic stood up, shook out the queasiness and stepped to the lip of the entrance in time to see Lightning quickly scaling his way up the rock. Mystic had never seen this happen before and gained a new respect for the large creature's agility.

"Wow, you made that look easy," he told the confident Badger.

Lightning climbed into the mountain as Hugoth had. He hopped up on his paws very proud of his accomplishment. "I could start to enjoy that!" he said. "Now, Hugoth, where do we go from here?"

"I don't know, but we'd best be going somewhere."

Rakki placed the staff in front of Mystic and felt quite relieved with doing so. "I believe you can carry that again now, Prince."

Mystic willingly obliged, picked up the staff and fell in line behind Hugoth who was hurriedly leading them through the cavernous mountain. The five of them were feeling better about their chances now. No one seemed to be too outwardly bothered anymore about Bubba, for somehow they knew he was going to be okay.

***

"What did you say?" Bubba asked, baffled. "You are a Talker? You are a two-legger? You must take this cover from my eyes, leave me bound if you must, but please let me see to whom I am speaking."

"So be it. What have I got to lose?" The two-legger cautiously lifted the cape from Bubba's eyes, holding the cape and his hands up where Bubba could see them. A dim light was now coming from some small object burning at his side. "See, I am a two-legger. Now little intruder, I want an immediate answer to three questions before I ask anymore of my questions or answer anymore of yours. Otherwise I will cover your eyes again and leave you here to, to whatever. First, who are you? Second, where are you from? And third, how do you know about Talkers?"

Bubba felt relieved, for this two-legger had not yet tried to take him. After his experiences recently, he had decided to think differently about their kind until they gave him reason to loathe them again.

"I, Sir, am Bubanche, a Cheetah. I am the sole surviving member of the Great Plains Cheetahs. Our kind was decimated several years ago by two-legged poachers, not unlike yourself."

"As to your second question, I am not from this Land of Nuorg. I now dwell in the Great Forest at the edge of the Black. Our world exists on the other side of this world's ground."

"Your third answer is this. I have only heard of Talkers from my friends in the Great Forest. Before I came to the Great Forest, Talkers came and went with much frequency. After the Terrible Years, so I have heard, the Talkers became afraid of the Great Forest. That is all I know. I have never encountered one until now."

"You don't say." The two-legger was cautious of the intruder's answers. However, they sounded much like his own answers had he been asked those exact questions.

Bubba's head instinctively twitched as he heard a faint muffled sound coming toward him. The two-legger, who was not so skilled of hearing, noticed the twitch. He quickly threw the cape back over Bubba's eyes, grabbed him and backed into a recess in the wall.

"For your sake, Bubanche, your friends had better be well behaved!" he exclaimed in a hushed tone.

At the last minute he blew his candle out.

Hugoth heard the rustling ahead of him and stopped in his tracks. "Did anyone hear that noise? It sounded like scurrying feet."

"Yes, I heard it", Mystic replied quietly. "What do you think it is?"

"We don't have time to wait for it to expose itself to us. We must proceed with it or without it. Lightning, come up here with me. I doubt that anything in here could be as formidable as the two of us."

Lightning rushed from the end of the line and stood to Hugoth's left. They began walking slowly, but deliberately. The two Hawks perched on the shoulders of the two huge creatures. Karri on Lighting's right and Rakki on Hugoth's left. Mystic closed in tightly behind with the staff pressed against Lightning's back. The tightly packed group moved cautiously forward. A dim light came into view before it was quickly extinguished. The Hawks, but not their transporters, noticed one figure pulling another quickly to the side.

"Be careful here," Rakki quietly told Hugoth. "Whatever put out that light is directly ahead to the left. There seems to be some kind of opening in the wall there."

Without warning a voice came out of the wall. "Know before you take another step toward me that I have your companion. He is in mortal danger if you do not stop where you are."

A light returned to the darkness and a figure stepped out of the wall exactly where Rakki had noticed the movement. The two-legged figure held a bound creature over its head as if to bash it to bits on the rock floor.

"Bubba?" Mystic growled angrily at seeing a real two-legger. He poked his head out in front of the wall of fur made up by Hugoth and Lightning holding his staff behind him. "Is it you?"

The figure spoke next, "Yes, if Bubanche the Cheetah, is Bubba, then I hold him aloft here. Who might you be?"

Hugoth and the Hawks noticed something familiar about that voice, but could not quite identify it.

"I am Hugoth, Guard of the Forever Trees of Nuorg. These are my Messenger Hawks Rakki and Karri, direct descendants of the famed Red Warrior Hawks of Olde. These other creatures are not from this land, but they come from the lands above as does that Cheetah you are holding so threateningly. Might I add that we would readily sacrifice the one you hold to gain our passage back to our Burg. Our immediate task is larger than either of you. You would not put up much of a fight with me, Sir."

Mystic and Lightning immediately turned to each other, quite surprised with Hugoth's statement concerning Bubba. They, too, noticed that Rakki and Karri's eyes gleamed with stony defiance not seen before. Their posture was now similar to some of the Great Eagles, only smaller. Hugoth's fur bristled as his stature became taller and more bold than ever before. This was a side of the Nuorgians these travelers have never seen before.

Karri was next in line to speak. "Sir, you are obviously a Talker. From where do come? Why have we not spied you before? We fly this land constantly and have never laid our eyes on you. How long have you been in our land and why have you deliberately remained hidden away?"

Rakki added, "How, Sir, did you gain access to this land. The windows will not open for just any creature. You either gained entry falsely by doing away with a protector or you were summoned here as were these creatures. Which was it? If you have in some way harmed a protector, you will be cast into the yellow ball for the eternity of our watch, along with thousands of other evils."

At Hugoth's cue, Lightning joined him as they slowly approached the two-legger. The Hawks tensed for attack as they kept a watchful eye on the two-legger's every breath. These little sky-travelers had become quite formidable in their own right.

All at once Bubba began shaking his head. He threw the cape off and begged for a calm resolution to this stalemate. "Hugoth, this two-legger means me no harm. He could have taken me at any time over the past many clicks. Please do no harm to him."

"I will not make any promises until he puts you down, unbinds you and releases you to us," Hugoth stated with a voice that sent shivers down the spines of all those present.

"As you ask I shall do." The two-legger laid Bubba on the floor and unknotted the ropes that bound him. "There you go, Bubanche. Go to your companions."

Bubba jumped up and hurried toward his group then unexpectedly stopped halfway between the group and the two-legger. He tilted his head a bit then turned back to the two-legger.

"Wait a click here." Bubba walked back to the two-legger and sat down in front of him. With the determined group behind him he felt able to chat with the two-legger at his own pace, at least as long as Hugoth would let him. "Now ,Sir, let me ask three questions of you. Who are you? Where are you from? And how did you get here?"

The rest of Bubba's group moved closer to him. Still posed to strike the two-legger, they gathered around and protected the Cheetah as he spoke.

Hugoth added, "I also want to know who you are. I want to know it now. Several questions have been asked of you and you have failed to answer any of them. I suggest that you answer these questions in a very direct manner in the very shortest period of time. That time starts now."

"Very well. If you can't afford me much time, I can't give you many answers. That's all I can say. The answers to those three simple questions may be rather lengthy at best. I will answer the questions in order until you call my time. Before I begin with the first answer, let me say this. I am almost joyful at your presence. It has been so long since I talked with anything, two-legged or four, had it been another time I may have actually been joyful. I am Frederick Mounte, descendent of the Hewitt-Mountes."

"Excuse me, Sir. Let me have one quick click here." Bubba then turned, motioned for his group to follow then huddled them up. "Uh, was I hearing strange ramblings or did the two-legger just say he was descended from the Hewitt-Mountes, a la the confounding Staff of Hewitt?"

"I believe that is what I heard as well", chimed Lightning, still not visibly thrilled to be in the two-legger's company.

Mystic, Hugoth and the Hawks were all ears. Mystic continued to hide the staff.

"Okay." Bubba walked back to the Talker. "You may proceed, Sir. Pardon the interruption."

"Absolutely," continued Frederick. "As I was saying, I am descended from the Hewitt-Mountes. I find it hard to believe that this Cheetah is from the Great Forest. It is further beyond my comprehending to believe that he," as he points to Lightning, "is of the Great Forest either. My family lived in the lands surrounding the Great Forest before it was the Great Forest. We were the last and most skilled of the Talkers. My family was large and we had our problems during the struggles of our land, especially during The Terrible Years..."

"Excuse me again, Sir." Bubba turned around away again and gathered his group. "Is this two-legger for real?"

"How would he have known this if he's not?" replied Mystic, still not overly convinced that he could trust any two-legger.

Bubba again returned to the Talker. "Okay, back again, continue, please."

"Very well, but my time will run out if you keep interrupting me." The Talker continued his story. "During our struggles and The Terrible Years, my family members were captured by every vile creature imaginable. We were prized possessions for our enemies. Our unique abilities to communicate with those like you brought upon us many dreadful hardships. When we refused to cooperate, we were killed. When we outlived our usefulness, we were killed. Those of us who escaped were chased all over our world. In my family there were nine of us. I have no doubt that I am the last.

I escaped here by accident. My last mission as a Talker left me with a bad taste in my mouth for other two-leggers. I was duped and, in being so, was responsible for the loss of a great many lives. I was badly hurt during the mission and crawled away to safety. When I awoke I was inside this cave. All that I had came with me -- my clothes, my cape and one sack in which I carried my necessities. I have been here for many of my years, but I don't feel I have aged any at all. As a matter of fact I feel younger now than before I came. I have lived on the sour water in this cave and the marvelous mud outside in your gully.

I have hidden from what I feared was out there. I had dreams of being chased here. I have kept myself hidden away for fear of being discovered. I had no idea that there were logical creatures here."

"Here," came a voice from behind the two huge furry creatures. Mystic stepped to the front and held the staff out to the Talker. "Do you have any idea what this is?"

Frederick paled as if he had seen the dead. He cowered back a step, "How did you survive? I thought they killed every last one of your kind?"

"What are you talking about, Sir?" asked Mystic. "Do you recognize this staff or not?"

"No, I do not." Frederick replied. "But I recognize you. Yes, I recognize you from long ago".

Mystic looked around at his companions a bit confused. He didn't know what to say now, so he said nothing.

Frederick was stunned, but he continued, "You are Giant of the Great Gray Wolves." He hurried to Mystic and knelt down to look him directly in the eye. "I met with you and your packsters on a very fateful day many years ago. You were the last creature I spoke with before that vile little man nearly killed me. I have not long ago stopped wishing that he had. He, you and the destruction of your pack are most of the reasons I am here."

Mystic was startled by this misidentification. "I am very sorry, Sir, but I am not Giant. I am his only surviving son. I am Mystic, Prince of the Great Forest. I was never told the full story of the killing. The details were never made known to me. Maybe you could help me fill in the blanks someday, if we make it back to our land."

"I can see it now. Why, you are the spitting image of your father, only much, much larger. He was a great leader. I trusted him the moment I laid eyes on him. They don't come any better. It is such a relief and a joy to meet you. I so wished you were he so I could apologize. It was such an awful day." Tears began to flow from Frederick's eyes as he confronted the agonizing past.

"I appreciate and accept your apology on my family's behalf. It is of no use to dwell on it any longer. Free yourself from any guilt. It has been made right," Mystic assured the Talker. "It has been made right."

Lightning felt badly, but interrupted anyway, "So, Sir, you say you know nothing of this staff, even though you say you are descended from the Hewitt clan?"

"That is correct. The staff must be considerably older than I. I heard rumors of it, but I never saw it or knew of any family member who possessed it. I feel you will need to find a true Hewitt if you must locate the two-legger who has knowledge of it," Frederick stated, shaking his head. "I am afraid that won't be a pleasant task. The only Hewitts I can recall were not very nice people. They were a very honorable family until they got a bit too full of themselves. The good ones separated and married well, thus the two-part names. The bad ones got worse. As history extended, so did their legacy. It was not a legacy of good. They instigated the Terrible Years and were sorry to see the destruction and death end. I do not have time to tell you of all of the atrocities that family either paid to have done or performed themselves. My concern about the staff is two-fold. One, how did you come to possess it? And two, are you sure you are not with them?"

"I can assure you I am not one of them. I came upon it completely by accident as my friend here can attest," Mystic deferred to Lightning.

"And who might you be?" Frederick asked the Badger.

"I am Lightning, the Irregular Badger of the Great Forest, Duke of the Great Meadow," he answered with a wink to Mystic and Bubba.

Frederick shook his head as if he misunderstood. "The irregular what?" he asked.

"Lightning the Irregular Badger, Sir."

"But you ar…" Frederick was cut off.

"I am very happy that we are all reminiscing and getting well acquainted with each other, but we have to be leaving now. I strongly suggest, Frederick, that you come with us," Hugoth more or less demanded.

"As you wish, Hugoth. I am wary, but I will come with you," Frederick said, though not completely convinced it was a good idea.

"Good, let us be going," Hugoth once again was leading the growing parade. "Karri, go back and ride with Frederick. Keep an eye on him."

So off went Hugoth and Rakki, Mystic, Bubba, Frederick and Karri. Covering the rear was Lightning, the Irregular Badger.

27

As they headed down the cavern, Hugoth summoned Frederick to join him. The Talker caught up to Hugoth quickly.

Hugoth asked him, "I hate to bother you, but do you know a way out of here?"

Frederick smiled and replied, "Yes, as a matter of fact I do."

"Lead on," suggested Hugoth and lead on Frederick did.

***

"Enough of this!" Charlie blurted out. "Where are they? We have had three meals today. We are finishing up our late evening refreshments. This can't be tolerated. We must go find them."

"You know we can't, Charlie," Donkorse reasoned. "The shutters are closed and we are staying put--period, end of conversation. Sometime after we open the shutters tomorrow we will once again search for them, but not now."

"Donkorse is right, Charlie. We can't do a thing tonight," the elder Eagle shrugged his wings then trudged to his perch in the corner of the room.

Vincen wasn't nearly as easily convinced. He demanded to know the reasoning behind what he considered foolishness. "Will someone please tell me what is with these confounded shutters? Why are they shut? Why, why are they shut?"

Vincen beat his wings violently as he raised himself off of his perch, scattering light moveable objects throughout the cavernous room. He raced toward the closed opening and slammed into the shutters with his full force. He slid helplessly to the floor and cried himself to sleep, never leaving the spot where he landed.

Charlie and the others watched helplessly. Vincen had to learn self-control. This was not the worst that things would get for him. He still had much to learn.

***

The Land of Nuorg

As Frederick led the tour under the mountain, he paused many times to explain small details of the caverns. Hugoth was sure that Frederick was a wealth of knowledge with regards to this cave system. Should Nuorg ever need to regroup, this would be the place and Frederick would be the one to plan the sanctuary.

After much walking and lecturing, the group approached a series of forks. Based on answers given to him by Hugoth, Rakki and Karri, Frederick picked the fork that would provide the best option.

Bubba had not spoken in a while, so he was overdue. "Are we under the same mountain where we took the tests? If we are, then can we make it to the wall of portals? I have a suspicion I want to try there. I believe it might lead us back to the Burg."

"Yes," answered Karri, "This is the same mountain, but it is a big mountain. These shafts could go on forever."

Frederick listened intently to the dialogue between the Hawk and the Cheetah. He came to a conclusion very quickly.

"I know of where you speak. Let's take the right fork coming up and we will double back to head deeper under the mountain. It should take us a fair amount of time. Here we go. This path is steep so watch your step."

They traveled down for several clicks before coming upon a large room with numerous openings. The group rested briefly as Frederick stepped into and out of the openings to get his bearings. "Here we go. We are just about there."

No sooner had the last member of the party passed through the opening than the first member stepped into the hall containing the wall of portals. They were all lit.

"Here you go, Bubba. I am passing the lead over to you now. I have never needed to explore this far down," Frederick said as the leaders changed.

Bubba quickly explained his theory. "Every port now is lit. I assume that somehow light from the yellow ball is eking its way into every crack and crevice in this mountain. If we could follow the shaft behind each portal, we would eventually find a way out. However, it may be too small for even the smallest of us to fit through.

By the same measure, we can assume that the portal we correctly chose does not make it all the way to the outside of the mountain because its light never goes out. It leads to a source of light that is not dependant on the yellow ball. We thought that light emitted from the staff. We were wrong. That light emitted from the river. The water from the Hopen River radiates light because of its purity. You can think of it like this. Picture a young cub's eyes. Do they not sparkle? Picture the stars at night above the Great Meadow? They sparkle. Both are examples of hope. The cub's eyes, until they experience loss or tragedy know only hope. The stars have not experienced the pain of our world. They only know hope. We gaze at those stars during our moon-time and wish for our utmost dreams to come true and we hope. Face it, hope shines bright even when all else seems to fail. We chose the correct port then and we will choose the same one now. Frederick, please extinguish your candle and follow me."

The others were very impressed with the Cheetah. They would follow him until all hope was lost.

The group entered the first portal and quickly passed the gardens and watering pool that had fed the three previously. Nothing stopped them from eating their fill now except a need to move on. They came upon the staircase at the waterfall. Instead of climbing the stairs they wound around behind it. They noticed several puddles of shining water leading them onward. Each puddle was caused by a tiny hole in the rock that allowed the water to drip into the shaft forming a perfect mirror of the river running above it. This was the path to the Burg.

Hugoth knew this location and its distance to the Burg. He had never been down this deep under the Mountain. He decided it would probably be a good thing to know. They followed the shaft for more than 150 clicks. The shaft soon split into two distinct smaller shafts. One contained many more puddles than the other. The shaft to the left looked like it didn't get wet nearly as much as the shaft on the right. The right shaft appeared to stay wet continuously.

"I know where we are," Rakki exclaimed. "We are directly under the first end of the Burg. This shaft on our left follows the same path as the moat. If I can fly through the shaft on the right, I can pinpoint the precise location across from the Keeper's window."

"So can I," Karri agreed. "We will be right back."

The Hawks flew as fast as the shaft allowed. Each Hawk counted the beats of their wings while they swooped and dodged obstacles above and below them. They stopped at the very same time.

"That was quite enjoyable," Rakki mentioned. "Are we now where I think we are?"

"I am certain of it, brother. We are now directly under and across from the Keeper's windowsill. Since we've come this far so quickly-let's continue on. We might as well fly the entire border of the Burg. I think it would be good exercise for us. Our wings have not gotten too much use as of late. It shouldn't take long. We will scout as we go. Pay close attention to the formations in this shaft. Who knows? It may prove useful one day."

The Hawks flew off. They slowed their pace somewhat, studying each nook and cranny of the shaft as they went. Up ahead the shaft narrowed just before a cavernous room with, what looked like, large trees growing through it. Rakki lit first.

"We must be beneath the first Forever Tree. Hugoth's Guard Dwelling is above us. Look how these roots have formed around the rock. I am wondering if every root is solid and healthy. If just one is hollowed out from old age, we may be able to make our way through it. What do you think?" Rakki glanced at his sister for approval.

"Maybe for another time", she replied. "Remember this. We will come back and inspect these in more detail. Now we must navigate our way through these roots, those of the second tree and continue scouting. The others may be concerned if we don't hurry."

Off again, the Hawks tested maneuvering skills not used very often. They chased each other beyond the very old root system, bouncing off the last slick skinned growth for fun, then headed back into the tunnel which, they presumed, led to the second end of the Burg. The shaft melded with the other where the river continued past the end of the Burg. It swept gracefully off to the right and continued on. One day the Hawks would fly the entire route, mapping the magnificent passageway as they flew.

Karri was the first to make a very sharp u-turn and head back down the second shaft. She had not flown very far when a third shaft appeared. She slowed for a closer look. With no warning, Rakki did not slow soon enough. He knocked his poor sister to the ground.

"What did you pause for?" he asked, landing in front of her. "You could have been hurt!"

"Look there," she said, pointing to the third shaft. "Where does that one go?"

"It's a good question which we don't have time to answer?" Rakki flatly stated. "We'll come back."

Again they were off, this time with no stops. They did, however, locate two more passages, another to the left and one on the right. Mental notes of each were detailed then stored away. The remaining distance to the starting point was covered quickly. There were no oddities in the passage to dodge, so the Hawks flew faster than anticipated. They came upon the remainder of the group resting in the fork just as planned, steadily gazing in the original direction, watching for them to return. Karri landed on Hugoth from behind.

"Who are you watching for?" she asked with a chuckle.

"Why, there you are. We were beginning to worry. Bubba and I were about to set off after you. I see you made it all the way around?"

"Yes we did, with only a few surprises. There are three other shafts leading from these two. We could have explored them. Instead we came back to report to you. One day we may all get to map them. Anyway, we located the spot across from the Keeper's window by counting our wing beats from this end. We are positive that we located it accurately."

Rakki continued for his sister. "We also located the roots of the Forever Trees in case that might be of some use. I wanted to spend more time there searching for a means of access into the tree, but time was not on my side."

"Really, the roots are that noticeable?" Hugoth asked.

"By all means. I am sure you should familiarize yourself with them since you know those trees so well", Rakki noted.

"Yes I should. Let's be on our way. I want you to put us directly under the guard house."

Karri took the lead, playfully darting back and forth through the shaft. The group followed her without incident. Soon enough she flew into a spacious chamber with a very tall ceiling. Tangles of gigantic roots and smaller roots wove a canopy of plant growth that covered a majority of the granite slab ceiling. Several growths of various ivies and oddly blooming, but dull flowers clung tightly to the smaller roots. The roots of each Forever Tree reached from deep below the solid rock floor up and through the canopy far overhead. Given that the room was dark except for several glimmering damp puddles on the floor, it gave off a well worn look of subdued majesty. All present were awe struck by the grandeur and warmth this particular chamber exuded. The little Hawk lit on a comfortable spot halfway up one of the taproots. Rakki alit politely at her side. Before speaking, they quietly observed as each of the others took in the wonders of this room. Once the members of the group composed themselves, Rakki nodded to her prompting her to speak.

"Here it is!" she announced, "give or take a few of your steps in either direction, you are directly under your guard house."

The glow of the water illuminated the shimmering walls providing enough light to discover, sadly, absolutely no connection to the Burg above. After a thorough search along the perimeter base of the walls led by Hugoth, the group proceeded back to the central root system of the Forever Trees. If the living entanglement of roots did not present an entrance to the Burg, they agreed among themselves to keep looking. Even if these roots did not present an obvious entry to the Burg above, each legger was equally impressed with the magnificent structure.

"This may take a while," Hugoth told the group. "Mystic, I want you to open that staff again. Unroll the manuscripts. Then you and Frederick here see what you can make of them. Maybe they will provide some clue to where we are. I have to believe that some creature has been here before us. Rakki, Karri, you rest for the time being. Lightning, Bubba, come help me investigate these roots. Look for anything out of the ordinary. Bubba, if you will, climb up on the tallest ones and listen to the roof. You may hear Donkorse stomping around up there. Remember, the trees have a large hollow inside each of them. We need to find a way to access either of them."

All creatures quickly jumped to their tasks. Bubba raced up the larger root trunks, then, carefully worked his way between the canopy of plant life and the rock ceiling. What he found really did not surprise him. The actual chamber ceiling was far above his head and the roots continued their noble climb, towering high over the top of the canopy. His search would turn up nothing useful, but he clearly knew he had never seen trees this big and may never again. Lightning began rummaging under and around the thick tangle of roots looking for even the slightest of clues to a way out of this cavern. Rakki and Karri napped. Mystic returned to the perimeter walls, diligently searching for a well-lit nook to unroll the manuscripts. Frederick did his part to help Mystic. They, for the most part, all worked without speaking.

"Mystic, over here. I believe this shelf may work for you." spoke Frederick.

"Where are you?" Mystic asked.

"Come toward my voice about 20 paces and slip into the crevice on your right. There is a small room here with a rock ledge right in the middle. I don't think you will find a better spot."

"Why did we not notice this room the first time around? This flat rock will certainly be of help. And, since it is our only option, it will have to do," replied Mystic as he stepped through the crack then made his way to the Talker's side. "Let me see if I can open this again."

Mystic securely held the large end of the staff then slammed the small end on the floor twice. The impact with the floor caused quite a bang that echoed through the tunnel for a nerve-shattering instant. The clamor startled everyone, but they were soon back to work.

"That was quite loud was it not?" Mystic asked as he flipped the staff over and swiftly twisted the small knob. This time he gently slid the manuscripts out of the handle and shook the staff one time for good measure.

"What else were you expecting," Frederick asked. "A ring?"

Mystic glanced at The Talker quickly. "What?"

"Oh, never mind," Frederick replied.

Mystic laid the staff on the floor and placed one rear paw squarely on the bulky part of the handle. Frederick thought this odd and quipped, "Why must you hold it down?"

Mystic turned to Frederick and replied, "This staff has been known to run off on its own. No creature in here wants that to happen again, I assure you."

Mystic delicately tried in vain to untie the fine string that so tightly bound the manuscripts. His paws were not made for this, so he asked Frederick to assist him. Before Mystic could withdraw the statement, Frederick touched the string with his finger. Another, much louder bang preceded Frederick as he shot through the entry passage and slammed hard onto the floor skidding to a halt outside in the larger room. Mystic rushed out after him. Frederick used his sore arms to raise his bruised head and looked at Mystic through dazed eyes. This explosive noise was loud enough to get everyone's undivided attention. It even woke the Hawks who had been sleeping so soundly.

Mystic, holding the tight manuscript roll above his head, exclaimed to those listening with a bit of a laugh, "I cannot untie the string binding these manuscripts." Mystic looked across at the fallen, dazed and confused Frederick and added, "Obviously, neither can he!"

The Land of Nuorg

Frederick slowly shook his head and lay it back dawn on the hard floor. Hugoth and Lightning both raised their left arms and scratched their heads in exactly the same spot at exactly the same time. From high above the ado, Bubba peered over the edge of the canopy. Rakki closed his eyes once again. Karri groggily asked, "Mystic, can you not just slide it off?"

Mystic's ears perked up a bit. He had not thought of this. It was obvious that he did not practice untying tightly rolled sets of manuscripts every day-round of his life. Mystic placed one paw gently on the string and successfully slid the roll from its capture.

"I got it, thank you," Mystic declared to all before returning to his new map room.

Mystic rolled out the manuscripts on the shelf ledge. He counted the corners. There were more manuscripts here than he thought. He counted 44 individual sheets of parchment thinner than a blade of grass. Frederick gradually found his strength to stagger back to Mystic's aide.

"Sorry about that. I'm glad you're back."

"Glad to be back. Did you know that would happen?" Frederick asked.

"Well, I didn't know it would happen quite like that, not to a Hewitt descendent. Anyway, there are 44 pages here. What should I look for?"

Frederick stepped safely back from the manuscripts. "See if they are sorted in some particular way. Look for an index. Are there any maps? Oh, just tell me what you find on each page. I will help as best I can." Frederick then opened his sack and withdrew a writing tool and a roll of his own parchment. "I will list each page you describe to me. Then we will study them together."

"Page one," began Mystic. He carefully lifted each page, scanned it, gave a brief description to Frederick and stacked them to the side. After sorting through the first 10 sheets he stopped.

"Here is a map!" he exclaimed.

As he looked over the map he recognized several landmarks. He was sure he saw the outline of the Great Forrest. He carefully studied the bottom left corner. At once he noticed a "P4" in small, but bold, black letters. "This is interesting," he thought to himself. He quickly described it to Frederick as he jotted down the remarks. Mystic continued to study the map then placed it face down atop the stack of pages. As he did this, he noticed something on the back of the page. He picked the page up and placed it front of him. On the back of the map was another map. He flipped the map back and forth as he pored over every detail.

"Look at this," he whispered.

On the back of page 11 was a map of Nuorg! Unfortunately the light was not bright enough to make out each and every detail. Mystic laid the map on the stack again. The next page had writing that Mystic could not make out. Page 12 was more of the same. Page 22 was another map. In the top left corner was a "P3" in the same print as the "P4". On the back of this page was a map drawn in the same fashion as the earlier one. Page 23 was similar to page 12. Page after page was turned and described to Frederick. Page 33 was another map with a "P2" in the right center of the page. Page 34 was similar to 12 and 23. Page 44 was another map drawn the same way with a mirrored map on the back.

Frederick stopped taking notes and looked up at Mystic. "There is one page missing. What we have here are four complete journals. Each, of course, details a different location. What is missing is the page that ties all of the others together. There has to be another page in that staff somewhere. If you would, check it again."

Mystic obliged. He took the staff from beneath his paw and shook it several more times. Nothing came out. He hit the ground with it two more times. Still nothing came out. He gazed at Frederick with a "now what" look in his eyes.

Frederick quickly flipped through his notes. His mind was sorting through notes while calculations whizzed through his head. Suddenly he looked at Mystic and explained, "I have every indication to believe that not only this staff, but this whole world we are in here is based on some modification of four. There are 44 pages of manuscripts divided into four books describing four separate lands. Each book contains 11 pages. The map pages actually use the front and back resulting in not 11 pages, but 12. You were instructed to hit the staff on the ground two times to dislodge the end sealing the manuscripts chamber. I would assume that the two times directly relates to the two pieces you end up with—the knob and the remainder of the staff. Now, the handle of the staff is taller than the pages, so I would further assume that there is second chamber within the handle. Actually I believe there are three separate chambers. Obviously the globe on the end is the fourth

The Land of Nuorg

chamber. You have opened the first of three with two significant hits. One hit, more than likely, will open nothing. If you will please, knock the staff on the ground four times. Let us see what happens."

Mystic followed most of that speech. The Wolf hit the floor with his staff four times. A crack developed as the upper handle slid away from the bottom. Mystic was surprised. He tried pulling the pieces farther apart with no success. He then began to turn the bottom. It turned four times then stopped. He tugged on both ends. Still nothing budged. He then turned the staff up and shook it again. Instantly another roll of manuscripts fell onto the shelf.

***

Bubba jumped from root to root listening carefully for some sound from above. Suddenly he froze with his ear pressed firmly to the rock ceiling. Unless his ears were deceiving him, he was hearing some muffled sounds. He discovered the sounds were coming from the root he was on instead of the ceiling. He pressed his ear instead to the root on which he was standing.

"Hugoth, Hugoth come at once. I hear something!"

***

Charlie had not slept the entire shuttered night. He waited patiently as the time slowly arrived to safely open the shutters. He nudged Donkorse awake. "Donkorse, go now and lower the bridge. I will pack our supplies. We will be leaving soon. I will wake the Eagles. I am sure they will accompany us. Don't stop to eat. Hurry!"

Donkorse waited as Charlie opened the door and he scrambled out and down the lane to the Forever Trees. Once he arrived, he unlatched the door with his nose and clip-clopped into the Guard's quarters. As he prepared for the lowering of the Bridge he kept forgetting the proper order of procedure. He was making a lot of noise with too many excess hoof beats.

"What is it, Bubba?" Hugoth asked.

"If you can, climb up here and listen for yourself. Something is up there. I know I hear something."

Hugoth scurried up the root as easily as a much smaller four-legger could. This large creature was full of surprises. Hugoth pressed his ear to the smooth wood, patiently waiting for a sound. There it was! He heard it too. "I heard it, Bubba! It sounds like Donkorse is terrorizing my den. We have to make some noise. He has to know we are down here. Lightning, throw me a loose rock if you can find one. If not pull one out of the wall!"

Lightning did as he was told. The Badger reached down and plucked a rock off the floor that was too big for any but he and Hugoth to lift. "Catch"!

The enormous boulder sailed past Bubba's head, just barely missing him, and landed in Hugoth's outstretched arms. "This should work fine."

At the very moment Hugoth started to bang on the root, Donkorse succeeded with the last step in lowering the bridge. He quickly stepped outside to the cranking wheel and began lowering the bridge with all of the loud stomping and creaking one could possibly ask for.

Down below Hugoth felt the rumbling as the gate began to lower. This sound, he knew, would overpower any sound he could make. He slumped back on the root in a helpless mood.

"It's no use. The Bridge is being lowered. No creature up there will hear us until the bridge is completely down." A mighty sound of rushing water emanated from the rock ceiling. "Don't be alarmed, they are draining the moat. We will wait".

***

Mystic and Frederick continued their task oblivious to the commotion the others were causing. The Wolf carefully placed both pieces of the staff under his paws as Frederick kept watch. Mystic removed the new manuscripts from their binding as he had done the others. He looked on as Frederick readied his notes. He flexed his paws and separated the pages. Page one contained the largest letters so far. Beneath a heading were four individual titles.

Page two was a diagram of the staff with what looked to be instructions. If they were instructions, the light was too dim to read them.

Page three was a picture drawn of what looked to be a two-legger holding the staff aloft with a thick line of light connecting it to a ball floating in the sky. On one side of the two-legger were two eyes belonging to a creature almost as tall as the two-legger. Mystic searched the edges of the page not wanting to overlook any detail. At the very edge was a thin barely legible line drawn in an arc from just below one corner to the top of the page and then down below the other corner. This line appeared on all four edges. Mystic turned the page over. There was nothing on the back.

"Mystic", asked Frederick, "Please describe to me in detail the diagram. We need to find the third chamber."

After much describing and note taking, Frederick was still at a loss to explain the third chamber. It was not on the drawing that Mystic could see. Frederick continued poring over his notes.

Mystic was tired. He sat on the floor, then, rolled the ball end of the staff closer to him. As he studied it, he lightly tapped the globe eight times for no other reason than it was there. The globe dislodged from the staff and rolled onto the floor as a surprised Wolf swallowed hard and tilted his noble head sheepishly, glaring at the movement cautiously. "Uh oh," he thought. The globe started rolling slowly and deliberately with an unmistakable etching sound which drowned out the silence. All activity in the cavernous room ceased as all eyes and ears were drawn to the annoying noise. Soon, the globe was halfway across the map room headed on a pre-calculated path. Frederick noticed the intent. He quickly scrambled well out of the way, plastering himself to the slick rock wall watching in horrified amazement as the sphere continued to track him. The globe rolled directly toward Frederick teasing him before instantly changing course when it almost touched him. The remaining five creatures caught sight of the globe as it cautiously rolled through the crevice, onto the main floor and into their midst on a mission of its own. The globe cautiously rolled to a stop out in the main floor halfway between the two groups. Mystic and Frederick could not squeeze out of the room fast enough. Their two bodies were wedged tightly in the crevice. Finally, Mystic extruded himself out between Frederick's knees. The two-legger literally fell out of the room after the Wolf escaped. Mystic and Frederick rejoined the group as all seven of the creatures took notice with wide bulging eyes and dropped jaws when the eerie, hair-raising, rolling sound ceased. Each creature gingerly took a few deliberate steps back.

"What is that doing?" asked Lightning, never taking his eyes off the meandering globe.

Before Mystic could answer, the globe steadied itself before it burst into a blinding light brighter than the sun had ever shone over the Great Meadow. The Yellow Ball in Nuorg was no match for the brilliance the globe displayed. The light was so bright that none of the group could look directly at it or stay on their feet. Creatures tumbled and eyes were closed tightly. When that didn't block out the light, paws, hands and wings covered them up. Still the attempt was useless. The emitted light penetrated deep inside each observer, diligently searching for something. They had no idea what. After almost a click, the light faded back into the globe. None was worse for wear, but it did take a while to get their sight back entirely. The light had penetrated into the rock walls and tree roots leaving a bright glow on everything it had illuminated. Inside the chamber, it was daylight. Frederick quickly got his bearings, stood up and hurried to the ledge where the manuscripts lay.

"Mystic, Mystic come here immediately. No, no, no, first fetch that interesting little globe of yours and then come over here. I don't trust that thing."

Mystic did as he was told. He gathered the globe holding it in his mouth as he hurried over to Frederick. "Gibberish, and more gibberish?"

Frederick looked at Mystic, "Take the globe out of your mouth! I can't understand a word you are saying,"

Mystic immediately set the globe next to the manuscripts, "Sorry about that. How can I help you?'

"Look at these pages now!" he exclaimed. "Every word is now clear as can be. Every detail has been enhanced. There are lines here we didn't even see before. There are entire letters here where there used to be only fragments. Please go through them again. I'll get my notes."

Quite a crowd now peered into the map room. Everyone was suddenly interested in what Mystic and Frederick were finding.

"All of that came out of the staff," Bubba said to all. He had returned from the canopy immediately upon regaining his senses.

"Yes, my friend. This is all we have so far. I am thinking there may be something else yet to be found," remarked Frederick.

"I see what you are saying, Frederick. Some creature can surely interpret this for us now." Mystic was drawn to the picture another time. He picked it up to study it once more.

Bubba chimed in again, "Hey what's on the back?"

"There is nothing on the back. I have already checked," Mystic answered, surprised that the Cheetah was now at his side.

"You'd better check again!" said Bubba.

Mystic turned the picture over. This turned out to be the front page. There were now four pages in this second set. Another picture was drawn in more detail with smaller pictures forming some kind of time line. There was a four-legger in the center surrounded by seven others, both of two legs and four. The centered creature was holding the staff backwards, pointing it at the circle in the sky. The staff was connected to the circle by a tapered cone. Each smaller picture showed an evolving progression of creatures forming a very distinct pattern. Above the drawing, in big letters, was a title that Mystic could not interpret.

"Can any of you make out these words," asked Frederick.

Karri spoke up from behind, "Maybe I can. If I can't, we will let Rakki try. He has a way with this kind of thing." She had been awakened by the globe's explosion of light. "Let me in there." She gazed at the writings only to recognize a few letters. "Rakki," she called, "You give it a look".

Rakki flew in, landing near his sister. "Yes, I recognize that style. It's of the Eagles. Let's see, the first word is plouti, I believe that would translate to pattern, the second long word is fautanstomera meaning to hold. I believe that is a drawing of the "Pattern of Containment".

"How many other words do you recognize?" asked Mystic.

"Oh, bits and pieces of quite a few. Let's see, show me another page, please."

Mystic held up page two of the second manuscripts.

"Please, Rakki, just tell us what it says. Don't worry about teaching us this language," Karri told him sternly.

"Whatever," Rakki continued. "This page explains what we have just experienced. The globe tested each of us for pure intentions and we all passed."

"How do you know that?" Bubba asked.

"Well Bubba, if we had not passed we would now be locked inside the globe. The globe holds evil until it is cast into the yellow ball. It seems the wielder of this staff has quite a responsibility." He then hopped down onto the pages and began studying further.

"No, cried Frederick, don't touch the manuscript!" Frederick ducked away, as if at any moment Rakki would be splattered all over the onlookers. Frederick slowly raised up, his eyes wide with horrible anticipation.

"It's okay. We can all touch the staff, the parchments, anything. We have been purified. It is perfectly harmless...to us."

Hugoth could not squeeze his head into the room, but his voice made it in easily. He interrupted the history lesson, "We must get to the Burg. If the yellow ball is still dancing, every creature there will be in trouble when the shutters open."

Rakki was intently staring at one paragraph of section four of the first manuscripts. "Mystic, pack the staff just as you found it. Do not omit one stage of the procedure. When you complete that let me know. I have something to show all of you."

Mystic, with Frederick's help reassembled the staff in a few short clicks. Rakki patiently waited. The others waited very impatiently. Finally Mystic announced, "We are ready. What have you to show us, little Hawk?"

"If you please, walk this way." Rakki strutted out of the map room, took wing and glided over to the root system. He sized up the tangled mess, looking this way and that. He nodded his head, as if in agreement with himself. Hugoth, would you and Lightning come over here."

The large creatures ambled over to the Hawk. Rakki then gave some instructions, "Would each of you step behind that largest root there. Now, to your right is a middle-sized root trunk and behind you is a large root trunk. Would you please push each of those toward the back of this area?

Hugoth and Lightning exchanged curious glances and did as they were told. Oddly enough, it did not take a lot of power, but push they did. As they pushed the trunks apart an opening in the largest trunk, the same one Bubba had heard the sounds through, swung open. Rakki hopped in and shot straight up inside the root. Shortly he came back down.

"What are you waiting for? The Burg awaits!" He shot back up the hollowed-out root followed closely by Karri.

28

Rakki and Karri burst through an opening high in the first Forever Tree and together, breathed a big sigh of relief. They were excited to move out into the fresh, bright air.

Karri saw him first. She swooped down in the shadows and tagged Donkorse on his ear. "Where have you been?" she asked.

Donkorse swung his head around just as Rakki was making a dive on his neck. The little Hawk and the large Donkorse met face to face. Rakki flattened out on Donkorse's long snout then slowly slid to the ground. Rakki raised his head mumbling, "It is so good to see you again, Donkorse." Then he lay down to rest.

Hugoth stepped into the hollowed root. He looked straight up, way, way up. He stepped back out into the cavern. "Well, we land-walkers are still out of luck. There is nothing in there but slick sides all the way to the Forever Tree's leafy canopy."

Mystic stepped in next. He glanced around and stepped back out. "Well, I know I can't climb out. If Hugoth can't, I know I can't. Where did those Hawks fly off to?"

***

Karri inquired about the Keeper. "He should be headed this direction shortly." He was to meet me at the gate. You can see it is not quite down yet. See if you can catch him," Donkorse replied, very happy to see the Hawks again.

Donkorse turned his attention to Rakki who was coming to at the edge of the lane. "Welcome back," Donkorse said as he jostled the little Hawk with his nose. "Wake up. Wake up. Where are the other four?"

"Well there has been a change, Donkorse. We picked up an additional two-legger. He has been in the lower levels of East Mountain for, he says, years."

"Really?"

"Yes, that's what he said. We did not believe him at first, but he passed the test as did we others."

"What test?"

"I'll tell you later. It will be long story. We must return to the Guard House and bring them up."

"From where?"

"Please quit asking questions of me right now. There will be time for that. Let's go get them first."

"As you wish," conceded Donkorse.

Karri spotted Charlie heading down the lane in her direction. She swooped down to greet him. She was very excited. "Keeper, come quickly. We must bring them up." She did not mince words.

Charlie had no time to ask whether they had fared well or why the delay. He broke into a trot as he followed her. Charlie would reunite with the Eagles after their return from the scouting mission, flying the Paths.

Rakki soared high up into the first tree with Karri on his tail feathers. The two banked sharply and dove back down the tree trunk to the floor of the root. They angled their wings and rose out of the opening onto Hugoth's shoulders. "Donkorse is expecting you," said Rakki.

"Charlie is on his way too. I did not see the Eagles," added Karri.

Bubba had something on his mind and pleaded with the others to listen before speaking. "I have concerns that are unresolved. My main concern is the attitude of the yellow ball. We have been hidden away. The staff also has been hidden with us. What will happen when the staff is exposed? Will the yellow ball not start dancing once again? What then?"

Bubba continued, "Now, this may be a touchy subject, but here goes. Who can we trust up there? I haven't met any of them except Donkorse, I know nothing of this Keeper. He may be perfectly fine, but I don't know. How many others are up there? I personally think the staff should stay here. I do know this for a fact. We all passed a test that we knew nothing about. Who up there would be able to pass the same test? Does anyone know? I had doubts about Frederick until he passed the same test we did. Now I doubt him no longer."

Mystic spoke next, "I have doubts too. Until I understand more about this staff and how to control it, I feel very uneasy about exposing it to the yellow ball. Send the others down. Frederick and I will stay and take notes of the translations. You are welcome to stay down here with us if you like. The Burg is a very friendly place. You should like it. Our stay may be long or short. Vincen should have a say in it as well. If you decide to stay here with us, I will still need you to go into the Burg for provisions."

"I agree with most all you have said," Hugoth said. "I must admit I am a little angry by the distrust displayed toward us by the Keeper, but then you don't know him. I was hesitant about Frederick as well; now my conscience is clear. Mystic, you are right. You must stay here. I will send the Eagles, if I can get out."

Lightning simply added, "Bubba and I will get the provisions."

Frederick spoke next, "I appreciate your taking me in. I too doubted each of you until the purity test. I must say, together you form a very determined group. After much consideration on the subject, I believe no one outside the seven of us should know of the staff's disassembly or of anything that is contained within. Every action has a purpose and I believe the seven of us are together for something other than getting back to the Burg. For all practical purposes we are back now. Rakki, Karri how do you stand on the secrecy issue?"

"I agree completely", Karri stated plainly. "No one, not even the Keeper or that ancient Eagle should know. I don't even know where he came from. We have been through too much to lose it all now."

Rakki was a bit nervous, "I told Donkorse that we passed a test, but I did not go into details".

"Good, it could have been any test. Don't say anything further," Frederick suggested.

"I won't," he replied.

"Now, about our dilemma," Hugoth said. "Did either of you Hawks see any way for us larger creatures to get up that tube?"

"I think I saw an alcove about halfway below ground level," Rakki mentioned. "I'll be back shortly." He left Hugoth's shoulders to have a closer look at the tube."

Rakki flew up and down many times studying what he thought to be a blemish in the tube. "There it is," he exclaimed to himself. He pecked at the fine outline of a small box. A slender handle folded out of the wall. Rakki wrapped his talons around it, pushing it down. It moved easily. The handle folded all the way down. At the bottom of the handle, a panel popped up and out from the wall. A rope uncoiled from behind the panel dropping to the floor in front of Hugoth. Rakki perched on the bottom of the opening and peeked inside. He saw a large pool of water and a set of stairs leading up to something. He flew back down to tell of his findings.

"You did find a room and it had a what?" asked an astonished Hugoth.

"Yes, I did. I discovered a room containing a small pool of water at the base of some stairs that led up to somewhere," repeated Rakki.

"Why that's the counterbalance room for the bridge. There is a room just like it in the second tree," explained Hugoth. "Was this rope attached to anything?"

"No, I don't think so."

"Okay, try something for me if you will. I want you to go back up to that room, attach the end of this rope to the cranking wheel, if you find one. Now this is a hunch, but there should be a peg near the bottom of the wheel on the wall. You need to pull the peg toward you. If it moves out smoothly, pull it all the way out until it stops. When you have finished, come back down here."

Rakki was back quickly to everyone's delight, "All done, Sir. Have you been in that room before? I had my doubts, but I found everything just as you mentioned. The rope is now attached firmly to the wheel and the peg you spoke about slid out all the way quite smoothly."

"That is wonderful news, my friend! Okay, if the machines in this trunk work like those in the other... stand back." Hugoth tugged on the rope. The rope began moving upward, sliding smoothly between Hugoth's gigantic paws. At the same time, a loud creaking noise began and grew steadily louder as more rope passed by Hugoth.

"Where is that coming from?" asked Lightning.

Soon Lightning's question was answered. A heavy thud was heard that shook the floor. Directly behind Hugoth, a tall section of one of the largest root trunks swung open. In the opening was a gigantic wash bucket full of water. Hugoth smiled as he patted down the strong timbers that formed this container. He then felt his way around the lower edge of the bucket. With a satisfying sparkle in his eyes and a convincing grunt, he pulled a wooden plug out of the side near the bucket's bottom. As he laid the plug close by, he smiled watching the clear water rushing out across the floor.

As the remaining water drained out, Hugoth climbed over the rim and positioned himself in the center of the damp wooden floor. "Going up," he proudly said to anyone who cared to listen.

The Land of Nuorg

Bubba and Lightning hopped in the vehicle for the ride up, excited to get out of the darkening cavern. Karri immediately perched on Lightning's shoulder, while Hugoth began to pull on the strong rope. With each stout pull, the large bucket lifted its occupants higher and higher through the hollow in the tree. After much rope pulling, the bucket full of passengers made it safely to the guardhouse level. The Hawk, the first one out, flew around the room. Bubba deftly leaped out, clearing the tall side of the bucket with room to spare. He perched near the outside door to watch as Lightning fumbled clumsily with the slick side in an attempt to make his way out. Finally, Lightning grabbed the top edge with his front paws and sank his rear claws into the old wood, scratching his way out. At the top, he lunged onto the floor, much to Bubba's amusement. Hugoth made the trip next. Something was happening that was changing this jovial giant's light-hearted attitude. Now in a big hurry with a bad attitude developing, the large Guard jumped completely out of the bucket. He politely, although abruptly, pushed past the other two, who were again amazed by this creature's surprising agility, before heading straight out the door.

Donkorse could not keep up with Rakki, but he did finally make it to the Guard House. He stood outside the door, eating from his bucket. Suddenly he was startled by Hugoth storming through the front door leading a party of five. "Good day, Donkorse".

"Good day, yourself, Guard of the Forever Trees. Where have you been?"

"One day my friend, one day I will tell you, one restful day. But, today is NOT that day!" Hugoth began to pace, his eyes revealing hints of a fire raging within. "Where is the Keeper? I am sure you remember Lightning and Bubba?" He nodded in their direction.

Donkorse tried to figure Hugoth's mood. The front limbs of the Guard were swollen. Inside each, the extremely large muscles stretched thick fur to its limits as his paws were flexed in and out of tightly clenched fists. Hugoth's neck resembled a large tree trunk now more than ever. Through the beast's veins, blood was beginning to boil.

"Yes I do. It's wonderful to see you again. Was your journey pleasant?" asked Donkorse.

"Not exactly," replied Lightning, "Not exactly."

Charlie arrived just as Lightning came out the door. He watched as Bubba followed closely behind. His eyes went straight to Hugoth, while sarcasm flooded from his mouth. "Hello Hugoth, a great adventure, I presume? You sir, have some explaining to do."

Hugoth bristled. He stood up to his full height, towering over those around him. He then viciously thrust his monstrous head down toward Charlie. He nearly roared in anger, "Yes sir, I do. I will explain it to YOU IN THREE LITTLE WORDS. Dancing. Yellow. BALL!"

Charlie was not visibly frightened by Hugoth's words. However, his intimidating tone added to his intense actions clearly bothered the Keeper. Taken aback, he meekly muttered, "No, it can't be. Why? When did it happen?"

"Yes, it CAN be and it DID! I can only guess that it happened the day before yesterday. We were walking along The Path to Where I Am Going. Karri entered our parade and lit on my shoulder. She whispered into my ear that some CRAZY person, and I mean YOU, decided to close the gate and flood the moat. May I ask you why that was ordered? That was absolute nonsense. The tests had been passed. I was leading our guests back and YOU issued the order to draw the GATE! You, my dear Keeper, have the explaining to do. If you will be so kind as to follow me so we can talk in private, I do not wish to quarrel with you in front of these visitors. They have been through much more than I. Now, are you coming or am I going to forcibly carry you? It is your choice." He turned his menacing head to the others as his eyes still blazed. He stated very distinctly so none would misunderstand. "Donkorse, if you see either of those Eagles before I do, hold them here. I don't care if it is by force. You hold them here! If Bubba and Lightning are still here, have them take the Eagles directly to Mystic, again by force if need be"."

Charlie was terrified after this performance. Hugoth was always a no-nonsense creature, but this, this had reached another level, a level he was not comfortable with in the least. Understandably so, Charlie was speechless and shaking uncontrollably.

Hugoth again turned back to the Keeper, raising one of his massive front legs as if to merely swat the Keeper out of existence. He grimaced, "Well, shall I carry you?"

"No, of course not, no, no, I'm coming," replied Charlie. "I'm coming."

"You'd better! Rakki, Karri take care of the visitors. Get them everything they need. Tell Mystic I will come see him before too long.

Lightning, you work the bucket." Hugoth was still irritated. It was not difficult to tell that much.

Hugoth stormed off toward Charlie's dwelling with the Keeper reluctantly struggling to keep pace. Hugoth did not say another word during the trip.

Very disturbed from Hugoth's angry demeanor, Bubba humbly asked Donkorse, "Has anything like that ever happened with you present before?"

"Not since I can remember," replied Donkorse. "Hugoth has most of the responsibility around here. He is in charge or takes charge of everything. We all depend on his unerring leadership, plus Charlie is relatively new here. I guess Hugoth is about to remind him of that!"

"Come now, Hugoth will take care of his situation. Let's get provisions for all. It looks to be shaping up as a long day," Rakki suggested.

"Why did Hugoth mention either Eagle? Am I missing something?" asked Lightning.

"I picked up on that too," quipped the Cheetah.

***

Mystic and Frederick sat quietly with their thoughts. Frederick was rehashing his notes, while Mystic practiced dismantling the staff. "I have had this amazing relic since I was big enough to carry it. I never, ever imagined the power it is capable of. I can't help but wonder, why me? Why did I get chosen to be… the one?"

"Ah, for reasons beyond your control I'm sure," answered Frederick. "I have to tell you Mystic, your father was an amazing creature. I never saw your mother. She did not make the trip all the way to the meeting place. Your father was, beyond any doubt, the biggest Wolf I had ever seen until I laid eyes on you. He was so trusting. Intelligence shone brightly in his eyes, along with a great compassion for all living creatures. You could clearly see his gracious, giving soul laid bare before you. It was as if he were inviting you to be a part of him. Your eyes are exact copies of his. Obviously, you have nobility, honor and a great role to play in our future."

Mystic laid out the first manuscript again. The drawing of the two-legger with the staff was worth another look. He quickly opened the second compartment and unrolled those three pages, pulling the drawing out.

"I would normally not believe this, but here everything seems possible, so, as we sit here, this drawing is getting clearer and clearer and clearer. All of the details are becoming extraordinarily vibrant. The colors are so lifelike. Here Frederick, look at these eyes, do those eyes belong to who I think they belong to?"

Frederick stared at the picture, then quickly made up his mind. The answer was clear. "If you are thinking a Wolf, then yes. But they are not just any Wolf's eyes. That is you, Mystic. Those are your eyes. If it's not you, then I am not a two-legger. When was this picture drawn?"

"What creature knows? It is hundreds of complete day-rounds old. Maybe, ten hundred..."

While Frederick studied the drawing, it continued to evolve. Even the lightest etching within the details came to life, especially the eyes. "Mystic, again, these eyes are definitely the eyes of a great gray Wolf. The eyes are like your Father's, but they are not your father's eyes. They are your eyes. It is obvious to me that you are not descended from the Wolf in this picture. You are the Wolf in this picture! Funny thing is, this two-legger holding the staff is wearing the same clothes that I am wearing right now. Explain that one, if you will."

Mystic stared deeper into the drawing. "Yes, It does seem to be as you say. I wish I could explain it. I wish I could explain anything right now. When Vincen gets here, he can translate the complete manuscripts for us. In the meantime I'll put everything back."

Mystic was getting very skilled at the staff's disassembly / reassembly procedure. He could now comfortably perform the complete process without thinking about it. The staff was becoming part of him.

***

Without bothering to unlatch the handle, Hugoth burst through Charlie's door sending splinters from the door and frame flying throughout the room. Getting madder by the moment, he stomped across the meeting room to the hearth. With each step, his heavy back legs pounded the pads of his paws across the floor shaking the dwelling to the foundation. He swatted a heavy stack of firewood out of his way sending split logs tumbling through the air. He angrily sat down, his heavy mass taking up most of the hearth. But he was too mad to stay seated. He got up and began pacing, rather stomping, around the room. Every heavy step caused the room to vibrate. Charlie quietly stepped over the threshold following the angry four-legger into the dwelling. Hugoth turned. As the silhouetted figure entered through the ruined doorframe, he snorted in disgust. Charlie looked the damage over, deciding to forget about bolting what was left of the door. It continued to hang precariously within the shattered frame for the length of the meeting.

"Charlie, Keeper, whatever you want to be called, what were you thinking? I have a mind to rip your measly arms off your scrawny little body. That bridge is never, NEVER lowered while inhabitants of the Burg are outside the wall! I am asking this question out of a decreasing respect for you. Whose idea was it? If it was yours, you have until the end of this conversation to be expelled from here! You need to remember that I AM TRULY THE ONE IN CHARGE HERE!"

Hugoth did not relent. "You are in this dwelling because I allowed you to be here! It was much too small for me to inhabit. It was vacant when you arrived, so I let you move in. Now, your two-legged ego has convinced you that you should be afforded the same courtesies and respect as the original dweller. Let me tell you once more, YOU DO NOT! Where that absurd thinking came from needs to be torn from your shoulders! I, from this moment on, will no longer allow you any say-so in any decision-making here in this Burg. What was I thinking? You and your incredible story! I gave you a chance. You have wasted it! We have catered to your arrogance long enough. I am the Keeper here!"

Charlie was pacing as well, making sure to stay out of Hugoth's way. He had to deflect this blame. He had to quickly think of some excuse that might throw Hugoth off this current course, "Hugoth, you are not thinking rationally. It was not my idea to draw the bridge. Mystic, the Eagle, thought it would be a good way to protect the Burg since you were away. He was very sure about the decision. His pedigree is very honorable. I am just a pawn in his play, Hugoth. I would never willfully disobey your wishes."

"What? Are you serious? Do you think I am going to believe that? Charlie, do you know this Eagle? I said NO ONE gives the order to draw the bridge but me! Why would a guest suddenly have that authority? Where is he now? Where was he while we were missing?"

"He was out flying the paths scouting for me." Charlie waved both arms to distract Hugoth's attention. He continued, "Vincen was with him. He should now be on his way back, if they are coming back. We were to meet at the Forever Trees."

Charlie slowly backed himself toward what was left of the door. He groped blindly for something hidden close to the door, hoping it was still near by. Once a finger grazed its smooth surface, Charlie carefully picked it up and hid it from his guest within his long jacket.

"What?" cried Hugoth. "Follow me if you can. Never you mind." Hugoth roughly grabbed the Keeper and threw him onto his back. "I am not going to bother telling you to hold on, but if you fall off I will probably turn around, find your tiny neck and crush it, which might be the best move I could make!"

"What is wrong, Hugoth? Why have you suddenly begun to doubt me? You are raving like a crazed maniac."

"Everything is wrong, everything," Hugoth yelled as he galloped down the lane toward the Forever Trees with Charlie holding on with a death grip to thick tufts of fur.

***

Donkorse was standing watch as Lightning, Bubba and the two Hawks brought packs of fresh food and buckets of water back to the Guard House. As they chatted about their haul, Vincen called down from the sky. He landed in the middle of the group giving wing hugs to all creatures great and small. The look on his face was triumphant. Another Eagle, although a slightly smaller version, landed outside of the group. This Eagle nervously scanned the gathered crowd before he strutted in beside Vincen.

"Why, I think I'm seeing double," remarked Lightning.

"An old friend of the family," Vincen introduced the honorable, but agitated Eagle to his friends. "This is my Grandfather, Mystic, of the Great Eagles. I named Mystic the Wolf after this fine Eagle.

"Good to meet you, I'm sure," said the elder Eagle coldly. "Where is the staff? Where is Charlie? Where is Hugoth? It's getting late and I want to see the staff and Charlie together immediately, absolutely before any shutters are closed. Is it not what we've been waiting for?"

"Slow down a little, Grandfather, we have some catching up to do," Vincen fired back.

Mystic, the Eagle was becoming increasingly agitated. "You can catch up on your own time in your own land. We have a mission here.

The Land of Nuorg

I've waited long enough. Let me see the staff. I need to authenticate it, if indeed you do have it."

"Watch your temper, sir, in good time," Donkorse interjected. The elder Eagle gave Donkorse a look that would have terrified smaller creatures. It just made Donkorse mad. "Fine, put him in the bucket head first. By all means, let's get him down there!"

"That's more like it, you stubborn mule!" Mystic the Eagle said bitterly.

"Mule, what's a mule?" asked Donkorse. The others blankly shrugged their shoulders.

Lightning, Bubba, Rakki, Karri, Vincen, Mystic the Eagle and finally Donkorse piled into the bucket for the trip down. Bubba made eye contact with Vincen's Grandfather. He did not like what he saw. Bubba, like his mother, could see into creatures' hearts. Though it may be temporary, this creature's heart was difficult to understand.

As soon as the heavily laden bucket landed at the bottom, all the creatures climbed hastily out of the bucket. Vincen rushed straight to Mystic. He tried to hug him with his wings the best he could. It was sad, heartwarming and comical, all at the same time. Mystic the Eagle strutted directly into this emotional display. Again, he immediately demanded to see the staff. Vincen was hurt that his grandfather was being so rude. He did not bother stopping to meet Mystic or acknowledge him other than glaring sternly into his eyes.

"I want to see the staff now!" the elder Eagle demanded.

***

Hugoth made it to the Forever Trees with Charlie still clinging to his back. He rushed through the door and down the stairs to the bucket. But the bucket was not there. Hugoth stuck his head in the tube roaring for someone to send the bucket up. Donkorse heard the order, quickly sending the bucket up with Lightning doing the work. Hugoth, with Charlie still in tow, jumped in the bucket as soon as it was close enough.

"Down, get this thing down now!" Hugoth roared.

Mystic the Eagle, was very agitated now. "Show me the staff! Where is it?" He flapped his wings, screaming, "Get me the staff". He was flying around the cavernous room before the gathered crowd realized what was going on. He circled the crowd with maddening flaps of his wings, clicking his ancient head up and down. His piercing eyes searched every crack in the cavern. At last he spied it. "There it is!"

The elder Eagle swooped upon the staff like it was a water-livver flopping on the surface of a pond. He grabbed it with both claws. He rose, then adjusted his aim directly at Mystic. The crowd was pushing in every direction hoping to escape being battered with the big end of the staff. The crazed Eagle adjusted his angle of descent shooting straight at Mystic's heart. At the very last instant, he suddenly spread his wings, thrust the staff in front of him and hurled it into Mystic's open mouth. Mystic instinctively caught the staff as if he had been practicing for this moment all along.

Hugoth, Charlie and Lightning finally made it down. They plunged headfirst into the turmoil that was developing. All creatures backed away, giving plenty of room when Hugoth rushed into the middle of the fray. Charlie was barely hanging on to his back.

The Eagle swooped down at Mystic again and again, screaming the same scream over and over.

WHERE IS THE STAFF?" demanded an extremely defiant Charlie from no creature in particular as Hugoth skidded to a stop in the middle of the cavernous chamber. The Keeper's eyes scanned the ceiling for the mad Eagle. With a practiced move, Charlie deftly reached into his jacket, felt for the item he had carefully hidden away, placed his hand around its sculptured handle and pulled out the long slim metal stick. It flashed high above his head before plunging down, propelled by every ounce of strength the small two-legger could muster. It also happened much faster than the shocked eyes of those watching could comprehend. Hugoth arched his massive back, lurching forward only to stop and cry out as only a four-legger of his size could. The Cheetah's newly refurbished rapier pierced an opening in the tough hide before burying its length deeply into the Guard's front shoulder. The attacker then twisted the hilt of the rapier and grunted before yanking the weapon out of the crippled shoulder. Again, the rapier was held high above Charlie's head. "Bring me the staff or the next stab wound will be between his eyes," yelled Charlie.

The Eagle swooped again, still screaming, deadly talons wide open, positioned for a direct attack. Those talons barely missed the Charlie's head as he cowardly ducked. Charlie, unaware of the Eagle's next direction of attack, had readjusted his free arm causing his entire body to fall away, off axis of a fatal strike. Charlie wrapped his arm as far around Hugoth's muscled neck as he could reach, readying his aim to take the rapier deep into Hugoth's skull. This time Mystic understood the scream. "Roll the Globe, ROLL THE GLOBE!"

"Give me the STAFF!" Charlie's eyes were wide with rage.

Mystic quickly tapped on the globe eight times. The globe popped off onto the floor. He gave it a quick kick for good measure. Charlie raised the rapier to the highest point of a deadly arc one more time. This time, he assured himself, the blade would inflict a potentially deadly blow to the wounded Guard, "GIVE ME THE STAFF!"

"PLEASE, no more, here it is, Here is what you asked for," Mystic barked as he tossed the staff up in the air toward the Keeper.

Charlie's crazed eyes widened with glee as he caught sight of the staff tumbling through the air toward him. He was now totally consumed with greed for the power and wealth that would soon be his. Being ecstatic with himself for defeating these ridiculously naïve animals, he was taking no chances with the rapier. He continued to swing it down. He hoped for a kill this time. Hugoth roared. Miraculously, he managed to swing his head away from the direct path of the rapier just as Charlie let go to reach for the wonderful, promising, gleaming staff. The rapier came down in celebration. Instead of a stab wound between the eyes, the thin blade bounced off the thick skull. It did not miss completely. The rapier struck Hugoth again in the shoulder, coming to rest very close to important, life-maintaining organs. Hugoth let out another intense cry of pain.

All eyes were now watching in horrified amazement at the scene before them. Hugoth had crumbled to the floor in a growing puddle of his own blood. The rapier was still embedded in the second stab wound. Charlie gazed rapturously but confused as the partial staff came down into his waiting arms. At that very moment, every creature in the room witnessed a blinding flash of lingering light, brighter than any could describe. A tortured wail rose in the middle of the room before the light was extinguished. The beating hearts went silent momentarily as those that remained waited to view the result of the staff's judgment. The light's brilliance slowly dissipated leaving a vibrant, living glow to eventually fade from the walls, ceiling and floor. Lighting, Bubba, Rakki, Karri and Donkorse were accounted for. Mystic, Frederick and Vincen were present. Hugoth was still in the middle of the room, but he was lying motionless on his wide belly. Out of the high ceiling the elder Eagle screamed triumphantly. He dove to softly light on Hugoth's wounded shoulders. Between Hugoth's body and the somber crowd, two objects were laying on the floor. One was a glistening staff, fully assembled. Beside it lay a shining rapier. Charlie the Keeper was gone, gone forever.

29

In the many days that followed, the Burg underwent several changes. All of Charlie's belongings were removed from the Keeper's dwelling and the place was given a thorough cleaning. No one knew whether a new dweller would be interested in occupying the old place, once everything settled down. Mystic the Eagle tutored all interested in the Olde Eagle language. Frederick took meticulous notes. After classes Frederick and the two Mystics deciphered and translated all the manuscripts contained in the staff into modern day language.

Every secret and pattern was diagramed and described. There were two patterns constructed and implemented before the journey home. The Pattern of Containment was built using seven protectors. Leggers were deemed protector status if they remained after the light explosion generated by the globe. This pattern was used to stop the yellow ball from searching out the staff and wielder. It was the most challenging of the two. The protectors experienced some precarious moments as they learned the pattern on the fly; still, eventually, it was successful. The second pattern used was the Pattern of Purging that emptied the globe of all captured evil. This pattern was simple to construct, but the staff bearer took quite a beating as the globe violently expelled the evil it imprisoned.

The day-rounds leading up to the return to the Great Forest were passing leisurely in and around the Burg. However, the almost dreaded, day-round for departure did eventually come. When it did, no creature felt that it was yet the perfect time for the visitors to return home, but they had tasks waiting for them in the Great Forest. In the last meeting of the visit, the old Eagle perched on top of one of the high-backed chairs with his back to the hearth in the large gathering room of the Keeper's dwelling. Mystic the Wolf sat to the left wing side of the old Eagle. Lightning sat left of Vincen with his newly returned ax-pike at his side. Bubba sat left of Lightning with his still glowing rapier at his side, although it had been wiped clean of Hugoth's blood. Vincen was perched to the left of Bubba on another high-backed chair. Donkorse, Rakki and Karri were positioned side-by-side next to Mystic the Eagle's right wing. Frederick sat enthusiastically recording the dialogue among stacks and stacks of previously taken notes spread out from one end of the gathering table to the other. He was enjoying the experience using a new feather writing implement, a token from Mystic the Eagle's tail. Mystic the Eagle began the meeting with a cordial greeting then nodded to Mystic the Wolf.

On cue, Mystic the Wolf began to speak. "Friends, we travelers are returning soon to our home in the Great Forest. Frederick has decided to come with us as he wants to learn more about the staff. His diligent work with quill and parchment have become invaluable to our future endeavors. He will be my assistant as we attempt to properly decipher and wield the staff's power. Of course Lightning, The Irregular Badger and Duke of the Great Meadow, and Bubba, Swiftest and Wisest of the Great Plain's Cheetahs will return with us as well. Vincen, Sir, the choice is up to you whether you return with us or not. I cannot help but envy your reunion with such an integral member of your great lineage. You can learn so much from him here. However, as you and every creature here know, you are needed during our impending adventures in our land."

Mystic the Wolf turned directly to Mystic the Eagle before he continued. "I would like to say again--even if I seem quite redundant as I do so--Sir, please know, beyond any hint of doubt, that we are eternally at your service."

The Great Eagle nodded his majestic head at the heart-felt words of thanks. "I appreciate that very much and will expect much in the times to come."

Bubba asked, "Elder Mystic, how did you know about Charlie?"

"My dear Cheetah, the original Hewitts were not from Blacktonburg. The original Hewitts were from Graylington on the Bahley River. I knew Charles Craton Hewitt the Third. The man died long ago of old age. This Charlie was an imposter. We may never know who he actually was. He may have been a true Hewitt and, from his misconstrued intentions, I believe he was. But he was not Charles Craton Hewitt the Third. Charles Craton Hewitt would never have allowed himself to be called Charlie by any creature. Also, even though he had the ability to do so, he would never have conversed with a four-legger. He spoke with Eagles on occasion, but that was it. He was a good Hewitt, though extremely eccentric. We played along with this two-legger's charade until the last possible moment as I felt we must. Hugoth became suspicious of this imposter's intentions and sent the dear little Hawks in search of me several shuttered nights ago. I hurriedly came at once."

"Excuse the interruption, Sir," a deep voice called from a back hallway. Everyone turned as a slow-moving Hugoth approached. "Let me add, that the imposter became overly obsessed with the reclamation of the staff."

The crowd broke into celebratory cheers for the Guard of the Forever Trees. Hugoth limped gingerly into the room, his wounds still aching and wrapped in clean cloth. He had stubbornly refused the water treatment that had worked so well on Vincen and Bubba. Hugoth, instead, opted for a more traditional way of dealing with his wounds. He reasoned it would only make him stronger and more likely to realize suffering on many different levels.

"Thank you, Hugoth," the elder Eagle announced over the vocal crowd. "My friends, Hugoth recognized the imposter early on, but until the time was right, our dear Guard went along with my ploy. We knew something was soon to come. When the signs were obvious, we decided to act. We have no idea how he learned of Nuorg or the staff. There is, unfortunately, an unknown window to enter here. We were not able to find out where it was or any information of how it came to be. The circumstances led to a rather unceremonious end for that two-legger. However, that unknown window must be found and closed."

"As is commonly known among the ancients, the good-hearted Hewitts changed their names to track their good ancestors and as a constant reminder of their not-so-good ancestors," the elder Eagle continued. "This man had no knowledge of that long-standing practice. Frederick Mounte-Hewitt over there is a fine example of that practice. The remaining true Hewitts are going to be difficult to track. I wish you luck. They are bad seeds. I am sure they are after the staff in every fashion they can imagine. Obtaining the staff would wreak more havoc in their possession than it can do good for The Prince of the Great Forest. One of those treacherous two-leggers will locate it again. When they do, they will come after it. I have sources telling me that time will come very soon. We can also thank the departed Charlie for some of the unexpected, but helpful, bits of information. From the first instant you step back into the Great Forest, beware of everything, every creature, every happening, every gust of the wind or sound on the breeze."

"That settles it for me, grandfather," said Vincen. "I'm returning with Mystic and my friends."

"Very well, Ghee, I am proud of you," continued the elder Eagle. "As you have learned there are, at least, four windows and one lost, stolen entrance that lead here. These windows are located in your world. You have maps showing generally where those lands are, but you don't have a key map showing exact locations. Such a map does exist. I heard tell of it long ago. Its whereabouts, I have to believe, are revealed somewhere in the manuscripts. It needs to be found. Frederick, that will be one of your tasks, probably the most time-consuming one, as you pore over the translations of the manuscripts in search of it. I can be of help to you should you need me. You know the way back."

"Don't be discouraged friends, even though the tasks ahead of you seem exceedingly daunting. It will take many complete day-keeping records, every breath of energy and massive amounts of intelligence gathering. You will need help and must enlist the assistance of those you can trust."

Should you require the use of Hugoth, Donkorse, Rakki, Karri or any other inhabitant of our land you may, at any time, come and retrieve them. You know they can and will do whatever you need. My only stipulation is that you only borrow two at a time."

Mystic the Wolf glanced at the four creatures sitting across from him. They each acknowledged this statement with a definitive nod of the head.

"Mystic, if we are going, we need to be about it soon," suggested Lightning. "The Burg is about to close the shutters."

"Very well, let us go now. Now, how do we get back to the Great Forest?" Mystic questioned.

"Oh yes, I forgot to mention that small tidbit of information," replied the elder Eagle. Come, we will travel with you to the well."

Along The Path to Where I Am Going the creatures shared farewells. Karri shed small tears of sadness. Rakki assured her they would be reunited many times to come.

Time flew by as the Burg residents journeyed back to where their adventure had started. It did not matter much to any of them. The sky-travelers would be back at the Burg in a fraction of the time spent on

The Land of Nuorg

the path so far, well before the shutter closing. Even though it would take Donkorse and a recovering Hugoth much longer, they didn't mind. They would arrive with plenty of time to rest before the next day began.

The aroma of Sweet Gulley was especially strong this day-round. Each traveler filled a small souvenir sack full of the gooey treat. Ample amount of sweet kakis filled packs on their backs. One or two goblets of water were included also. The water was not for drinking; it had another use.

"Well," asked the Wolf, standing with the staff beneath him amid the group of adventurers, "What do I do now?"

"If I remember correctly," Frederick stated, "you should tell it in the Olde Eagle language to open the window and the rest will take care of itself."

"Gather close," Mystic the Eagle instructed as he stepped back. "You must be close to travel together. Let me add that if you are in the company of others you don't want with you, then you must separate from them."

Gather they did. Mystic the gray Wolf's group had no idea that everything capable of breathing within 16 steps could be carried with the staff, if need be.

Mystic glanced longingly again at the remaining Nuorgians--the old Eagle, the two small Hawks, the Donkorse, then last but not least the gigantic Hugoth. These intelligent creatures had taken their positions out of range of the staff. They had heard many stories earlier and knew of its range and power.

As Hugoth stood there watching and smiling as only he could, with Rakki and Karri perched on his shoulders, he fired a parting shot at Lightning. "Oh Lightning, I meant to tell you. You are not a Badger!"

Lightning jerked his head around to Hugoth. "What did you say?"

Mystic held the staff firmly. "Staff of Hewitt, otah petir Pah fiyg. Take us back."

Suddenly a burst of purple and green light was cast around them. The ground did not shake, but the power in the staff was felt by all. Instead of being lifted high into the air, the four friends begin to spin. Faster and faster until they were almost drilling a hole in the ground they were standing on. The liquid again formed around them, enveloping them, before speeding them on their way. They progressed deeper and deeper through the stream until darkness befell them. Deeper and deeper into the pitch darkness... Deeper and deeper...

until a tiny glimmer of light was noticed. Out of nowhere, the sun came glaring down on them. Then, at last, the spinning stopped and all grew quiet. The light from the staff extinguished itself once again. The brightly colored cocoon of liquid fell away then dissipated. The small group arrived back in the small clearing in the South Quarter of the Great Forest. No ideas crossed their mind of how long or short a time they had been away.

Vincen, the first to have the courage to look up, broke the news to the others, "I think it worked. We are back. This is just as we left it."

Mystic looked around at his friends as they collected themselves. He suddenly felt quite somber. Reality hit him square in the head with questions, for he now recognized that not only were they home but the staff was home as well. Questions abounded. Who is to come looking for it? What are they willing to do to get it?

It will now be their duty to train themselves to be more than just friends and adventurers. They must now train and study to become investigators, fighters, leaders. They, the five of them, must assemble an army in the Great Forest and beyond the borders they now know. They must protect the staff at every risk. It must never fall into hands of those not pure of heart. What will they do? Nobody knows for sure. But, they must train, they must study and if they have to...they must learn to fight.

As the seriousness of the moment was realized by the five companions, on the mountain beyond the tree line just outside the forest a two-legger on a black Horse with flaring nostrils looked back down into the clearing one final time. He held tightly to a large black sack. Whatever is in the sack is very much alive and is not pleased to be a captive. With a gleam of victory in his eye, the two-legger threw the sack over the Horse's saddle, tied it to the horn, pulled his dark grey cape from around his smooth face, viciously dug his spurs deep into the stallions side and laughed. His steed immediately broke into an angry run. The laughter became louder and louder until the very blades of grass shook under his galloping steed. They too were on an adventure, an adventure to find something that was once pure and powerful until it was stolen. At the end of the terrible wars, it was stolen again. He could not wait to tell his leader this great news. He could hear himself now, "Yes sir, the Great Staff of Hewitt has been found."

There it was again, that laugh. That screeching, awful, revengeful laugh.

Vincen, eager to stretch his wings, flew up to his perch on the highest branch of the oldest oak tree in the forest. He solemnly reflected on all that had happened in the last day-rounds. As he surveyed this Great Forest of his, he watched in the distance as a Horse and rider stole away on the mountain's ridge. He sensed a perplexing feeling. He believed something very important had just happened. Whether it was good or bad could not yet be determined.

Glossary

Kaki--(ka' ke), A sweet confection of Nuorg, eaten separately or with meals. Made with generous amounts of Sweet Gulley goo.

Two-legger --(too' leg gar), The animals' word for a human being, male or female.

Four-legger--(4 ' leg gar), The animals' word for all creatures that travel on four legs.

(Bird)let -- (byrd' let) Any bird older than a hatchling and younger than a tweenst.

Bark kake--(kak) Small muffin-like snacks of the Great Forest made from any favorite ingredient. When dry these delicacies resemble tree bark in look and texture, thus the name.

Water-livver--Any of a number of creatures who live their entire life below the water's surface. A high source of protein when eaten by leggers.

Secret sharer--One of a group of elders in a pack burdened by experience and wisdom.

Sky-traveler--A winged creature that does not depend on its feet for anything other than standing.

Droopers--Fruits roughly the size of an apple, that taste like an apple and, when ripe, cause the tree limb to droop.

Packster--A member of any pack of four-leggers.

Watcher--A sentinel or guard

About the Author

Chris McCollum lives with his wife of 23 years, Jeanne Coffman McCollum, and their 2 teenaged children, Christopher and Madilynn, in Franklin, Tennessee. A longtime fan of J.R.R. Tolkien, C.S. Lewis, Clive Cussler, McCartney/Lennon and many more varied wordsmiths, he has spent the better part of his life crafting words into some form or another whether it be short stories, bedtime stories, anecdotes, poems or songs. Fortunately for him, his parents allowed lots of room for creativity in his early years. Originally from West Tennessee, He has made his home in Franklin, Tennessee for the last 31 years.

Please visit the website: www.landofnuorg.com

LaVergne, TN USA
16 February 2010
173190LV00001B/94/P